INSIDE MAN

INSIDE MAN

JEFF ABBOTT

GRAND CENTRAL
PUBLISHING

NEW YORK   BOSTON

Grand Central Publishing
Hachette Book Group
237 Park Avenue
New York, NY 10017

www.HachetteBookGroup.com

Printed in the United States of America

RRD-C

First Edition: July 2014
10 9 8 7 6 5 4 3 2 1

Grand Central Publishing is a division of Hachette Book Group, Inc.
The Grand Central Publishing name and logo is a trademark of Hachette Book Group, Inc.

The Hachette Speakers Bureau provides a wide range of authors for speaking events. To find out more, go to www.hachettespeakersbureau.com or call (866) 376-6591.

The publisher is not responsible for websites (or their content) that are not owned by the publisher.

Library of Congress Cataloging-in-Publication Data

Abbott, Jeff.
Inside man / Jeff Abbott.
pages cm
ISBN 978-1-4555-2845-5 (hardback) -- ISBN 978-1-4555-2846-2 (ebook) -- ISBN 978-1-61969-714-0 (audio download) 1. Murder--Investigation--Fiction. 2. Dysfunctional families--Fiction. 3. Organized crime--Fiction. I. Title.
PS3601.B366I58 2014
813'.6--dc23
2013048121

For Leslie, Charles, and William, always

O

THE CAR TUMBLED off the cliff, hurtling toward the distant blue shimmer of the water.

The first, instinctive reaction is to draw in, brace yourself for the impact. Brace for, never mind *survive,* the impact.

Next was the peculiar itch in my daredevil's brain, figuring gravity's pull at 9.8 meters per second squared, thinking, We have five seconds before we hit.

In the second of those seconds I felt the gun's cool barrel press hard against my temple, realized my passenger was aiming right at my head in case the crash or the water didn't end me.

That is attention to detail. That is commitment.

Three: The water rushed toward us. I moved forward, reaching, the cool steel barrel staying on me, my fingers along the floorboard groping for my one chance.

The sky, the water, my last breath, everything blue.

Four: The gun fired.

I

Four Weeks Earlier

You're something, aren't you, Sam?"

"I'm just a guy who owns a bar." Someone had left an abandoned checkers board on the bar and I moved the fresh glass of beer I'd just poured for Steve around the game. The guys who'd left it might be back tomorrow to finish it. Stormy's was that kind of place.

"But you used to be *something*," Steve said. A little insistent.

"A bar owner is being something." Why is there no one-word term in American English for being a bar owner? "Publican" sounds too English and formal. "Barkeep" isn't enough. I glanced through the windows. A young couple sat on the outside couch, a dog at their feet, and I could tell from the angle of their beer bottles as they sipped that they were nearly done. The covered patio of the bar was otherwise deserted, a slow Sunday night headed toward empty. I had to close at midnight and that was twenty minutes away.

"But you used to be *something*." And I couldn't miss the prying hint in Steve's voice.

"We all used to be something," I said. "You too, Steve."

Steve smiled. "The way you move. The way you eyed that jerk who bothered that young woman in here last night. You didn't even have to raise a fist, threaten to call the cops. Or even boot him. Just the look you gave him stopped him cold."

I shrugged. "Looks are cheap."

"The way you study every person who comes in here, Sam. One glance of assessment. That's from a habit of being in tough situations."

"I just don't want trouble and it's better to see it coming than be surprised."

"So the something you were," he said. "I think if you were ex-military or an ex-cop, you'd claim it right away. But you don't."

I shrugged again. Bartenders are supposed to listen more than they talk anyway. I wiped the bar. Every night was too slow. My other bars around the world were mostly high-end joints but Stormy's wasn't, it was a certified dive. It had been open for years, sliding through an assortment of owners until it came into my possession. The other nearby bars in Coconut Grove were a bit higher-end than Stormy's. Scarred bar, couches under a crooked TV, games such as checkers and Connect Four on the little tables. No fancy drinks: beer, wine, and your basic hard liquor. If I told people I owned a bar in Miami they'd automatically assume I lorded over some über-trendy nightclub in South Beach, women pouring out of limos in tiny skirts and huge heels. Many of my customers walked to Stormy's from the surrounding neighborhoods in Coconut Grove. We were not a tourist draw.

And tonight Stormy's wasn't exactly drawing the locals. It was just me and the couple on the patio and Steve and two older guys watching a West Coast basketball game on the corner TV; they'd already finished a pitcher. Miami wasn't playing, so there wasn't a crowd.

"So. Since you won't claim what you used to be, maybe you can't." Steve kept playing Sherlock. He could play all day. I don't talk about my past, not my real past, and for sure not to a guy who drinks too much. Even if he was my best friend in Miami.

"You mean like I was in jail?" I said. I didn't smile. I had been in a prison once, but not the kind he thought. A CIA prison is a different proposition.

Steve laughed. "No. Maybe you were working in something you can't talk about."

"Maybe you're just underestimating the skills involved in running a bar." I didn't have a manager in place at Stormy's, which was why I'd spent two weeks in Miami. Maybe I could offer Steve a job. But that would mean being honest with him about the quiet work I did now, what I'd done in my previous life, and asking him to stay silent. I wasn't sure he could keep my secrets.

I would wonder, later, if it would have all been different if I had trusted him. He might not have taken the job that changed everything for us both.

"I know what I see," Steve said, suddenly serious. "You know how to handle yourself, Sam. I could use some help."

"Help how?"

"Well, you know I work in freelance security." I'd first met Steve when I was fifteen years old. He'd worked a security detail attached to my parents' team of relief workers in central Africa. He'd saved my family's lives during a chaotic evacuation from a war-torn nation, pulling my parents and my brother and me from a wrecked vehicle. He'd gotten us to an airport to board the final military evacuation flight before the rebels bombed the runways. I could remember his face, looking at me through the broken window of the car, saying, *Come on, Sam, you're okay, let's go.* He'd stayed in steady touch with my parents over the years: sending us Christmas cards from Africa and Southeast Asia and the Middle East, a pen and pencil set for my high school graduation, flowers and a thoughtful note when my brother, Danny, a relief worker in Afghanistan, was kidnapped and executed.

But that had been contact with my parents, not me. I'd barely known him, and when his cards arrived I'd think, Oh, yeah, Steve. The guy who saved us, how is he? He was a wanderer in his work and so I hadn't seen him since that violent night in Africa. When I'd come to Miami two weeks ago to address the nagging problems of this bar, he'd showed up and claimed a barstool the next day. I first assumed my parents had sent him to watch over me; after years of estrangement they'd decided to take an interest in my life. He didn't say. But he'd inherited his parents' house in Coconut Grove and was already a semi-regular at Stormy's. He said he hadn't done security work overseas in a while. He seemed happy to guard the bar against any potential danger by occupying a seat and helping me fill the bar's nearly empty cash register.

But he saw something of himself in me right now: the guy who went into dangerous situations. It was unnerving that he could read my past in my movements, my attitude, like there was a sign on my skin. I thought I had mellowed more.

Part of me just wanted to tell him to forget it, that he was entirely wrong, and hope he'd let it drop. But spies, by nature, are curious people. We want to know things. Even when we're no longer spies in the conventional sense. I was twenty-six and had spent three years with a secret division in the CIA. I guess it showed. Or Steve knew more about me than he was willing to admit.

"You're wrong about me, but what is the job?"

He smiled as though he could recognize my little white lie. "I could use an inside man." I shrugged like I didn't know what the term meant and went to the guys watching the basketball game to see if they wanted a last beer, which was an unusual level of service here at Stormy's. But I wanted Steve to change the subject. Inside man, I thought. To be a spy again. The basketball fans wanted nothing more, so I returned to the bar and resumed tidying.

Steve lowered his voice. "So. I'm meeting a friend here tonight. A woman."

I frowned. If I were trying to impress a woman Stormy's was not my choice of venue, and I owned the place. "Uh, you know I'm closing in a few minutes?"

"I just need to talk to her for a bit. You don't have to serve us. It'd be a big favor. You'll be here anyway." That was true. I lived in an apartment above the bar; every one of my bars around the world, they all had living quarters above them. There was a reason for that, and it was the reason I didn't think I could offer my talkative friend a job. But Steve was here every night when I shut down the bar, and we'd hung out and chatted after I turned off the neon Open sign.

"I should charge you rent," I said, joking. The couple on the patio left; the two guys watching basketball departed. I left Steve for a moment to collect their tips and their empties. I dumped the glasses and slid the money into the cash register.

"I could pay you, Sam."

"What, your tab? I thought you had a friend coming…"

"No, dummy. To help me with this security job I got."

"Thanks for the offer," I said. "But like I said, I'm not anything. Just a bartender."

Steve studied me. He was in his mid-forties, burr haircut going silver, a man who had once been handsome and still could be but there had been too much beer and too many fights. He looked worn and beaten down. "You sure? I still think I'm right about you."

"My brother always told me to stay on my guard. I think that's what you see."

"You know how sorry I am about Danny."

"I know."

The thing was—I don't think I'd talked to another guy as much as I had to Steve since Danny died. Most hours that the bar was open, I was there, and Steve was there, drinking sodas during the day, tapping at his laptop, or reading or watching the TV. My closest friend from my days in the hidden Special Projects branch at the CIA was a guy named August Holdwine, and August and I no longer talked much. And as far as my friends from my Harvard days went, to them I was a mystery. I graduated, went to work for a London consulting firm that was secretly a CIA front, and had ended up owning bars. I had fallen out of the drawn lines for what was acceptable success. And I wasn't on social media, posting pictures of my child, recording what I'd eaten for lunch, or talking about my favorite football team.

But every day for the two weeks I'd struggled with getting the bar on its feet again, Steve had been here. So we'd spent those past fourteen days and nights talking for hours, everything from basketball to women to books to movies. I hadn't had a friend in a while. I hadn't had the time for one. And he was someone who had once helped my family during a dark hour. I owed him. Maybe I should listen to his offer, help him. I felt torn.

"When's your friend coming?"

He glanced at his watch. "Any minute now."

Then the woman walked in. Even in the dim light you could see she was striking. Long dark hair, a curvy figure.

She glanced around the room and I saw it in her eyes: she was scared to death.

I knew fear. I'd seen it in the stares of people facing CIA interrogation in Europe, in the eyes of a woman who thought she was going to lose the child she loved as her own, in my own face when I'd lost my family. This woman quenched the fear when her gaze met mine. She was trying to be brave.

She was my age, mid-twenties, and I thought, She's not really Steve's friend. This is about his problematic job.

She smiled when she saw Steve and her expression shifted to a look of polite surprise. Like she couldn't believe she was here. It was close to midnight and we were in a cheap bar. Who meets at a bar so close to closing?

"Hello," she said, shaking his hand. "Let's sit over on the couches, where we can talk." Her voice shook a little at first, but she steadied it.

She clearly wanted privacy. But Steve, ever gregarious, said, "This is my good buddy Sam. He owns this dump. I just keep it in business."

The woman offered her hand and I shook it. She had a confident grip. She didn't tell me her name, though, and I couldn't tell if she simply forgot to or she didn't want me to know. Steve didn't introduce her.

"Hello," I said. "What may I get you to drink? We're about to close but you're welcome to stay and talk."

"I don't want to inconvenience you."

"Sam lives above the bar; he can't be inconvenienced," Steve said. "This is a very private place. Like you asked for."

She glanced at Steve's empty beer. "All right. That's kind of you, Sam." And her lovely eyes met mine. "May I please have a club soda? With lime?" And her voice was low, and slightly loping in how she spoke, and heating you while you stood there.

"Of course. I'll bring it to you." I muted the post-basketball game analysis that was playing so they could hear each other more easily.

The woman gave me a grateful smile. "Thank you, Sam; you're kind." That molten voice, like warmed honey.

They headed for the couches and I got her a club soda. I wished our bar glasses were better crystal. I saw her glance at the vintage Miami Dolphins posters, worn signs from local breweries, a framed photo of the bar's original owner—a famously irascible woman named Stormy who had died a few years back—and Ernest Hemingway from the 1950s. A message blackboard where anyone could write a morsel of wisdom. This evening it announced, in blue chalk: TONIGHT'S SPECIAL: BUY TWO DRINKS, PAY FOR THEM BOTH. I hoped she'd think the bar was retro cool instead of outdated lame.

I brought her the club soda, with the nicest-looking lime slice in the whole bar. Steve shut up—nothing could get Steve to hush normally—when I set down the drinks. I wondered what kind of job he'd needed help with—he hadn't seemed at all busy the past two weeks. I left them and they resumed talking in low voices, too low for me to hear.

She was afraid. Why?

I turned off the Open sign, locked the door, retreated back to the bar. I wiped the already-spotless counter, working around the checkerboard, and did a quick inventory. Steve's problems were Steve's: I loved owning these bars and if I wanted to keep on owning them I'd have to make each one profitable, including this loser. I was short on wine and beer. I'd have to reorder, eating up the scant profits. Beer is the least profitable alcohol you sell in a bar but is the most popular choice. Maybe Stormy's needed some signature drinks, hard-liquor treats that would generate a much higher profit margin, bring in some new business. I could add food; the Stormy's kitchen was unused. I'd have to invest in new equipment, hire a staff.

Yet I dragged my feet on these decisions. And then I'd have to decide if I was going to go home next weekend, to New Orleans, and see my son, Daniel. The weekend would be the busiest time, and the bar couldn't easily afford me gone. And given that the bar had its own secrets in the apartment above it, I needed a manager I could trust entirely. I could maybe recruit one of the managers from my other bars: Gigi from Las Vegas, Kenneth from London, Ariane from Brussels…The Europeans might particularly enjoy a stay in Miami. I wondered what paperwork I'd have to fill out to get them a work visa.

I saw Steve lean back suddenly away from his friend. They'd become huddled, her talking so softly that I couldn't even hear the murmur of that honey river of a voice of hers.

I glanced at the clock. Ten past midnight.

"No one can know," she said. "No one."

I heard him say, "They already do. I got a surprise in the mail." And then I didn't hear the next few words as he brought his beer glass close to his mouth. Then I heard him say: "How did anyone know you hired me?"

She said, clearly, "Maybe someone's following me? Ever since the ten million…" Then she glanced at me, as if realizing that she might have spoken too loud.

And then Steve's voice dropped back down again.

Ten million? Not my business; I'd said no. I opened up a laptop I kept under the bar for the extra-slow times like this. Keyed it on. Typed in a website and then there was a video feed of my son, Daniel, asleep in his crib. His sleep was so deep that for a moment I got worried, and nearly called Leonie, his nanny (of sorts—she used to be a forger and I saved her from her life of crime, long story). She'd set up the feed for me, the traveling dad who had to be away too often.

Then he stirred, that magical breath of life, and I watched my baby sleep.

This is why I can't help you with your security job, whatever it is, Steve, I thought. I need to stay out of that world.

"I'll check it now," I heard Steve say. "Sam?" I closed the laptop.

"You all want something else?" I asked. The woman still sat on the couch.

"I'm going to go get her car and bring it around, then I'm going to follow her home on my motorcycle." Steve only lived a few blocks away, in a nice lush corner of Coconut Grove, near the landmark Plymouth Congregational Church. When he didn't walk to Stormy's, he rode his motorcycle. "Will you stay in here with her, please?"

"Sure. Is everything okay?"

He watched out the windows for a moment, staring out at the dark, rainy night. "Just keep an eye on her." He turned to go.

"Steve? Seriously, is there a problem?" I raised my voice.

He cracked a smile. "Just keeping her safe. You sure you didn't used to be somebody?"

"Just a bartender," I said automatically. Three words to haunt me in the days to come.

He paused, as though wishing I'd finally given him another answer. He headed out the door. Most of the parking for the bars in this part of Coconut Grove is either valet (with several restaurants sharing the service) or individual paid lots of banks or other early closing businesses scattered through the neighborhood. The closest parking for Stormy's was a paid lot three blocks away.

I walked over to her table. "What's the problem?"

"Steve said you wouldn't be nosy."

"You're afraid and now he's worried."

She glanced up at me. "You're a lot younger than Steve is."

"So?"

"I don't think you can help me." She got up and looked out the window, but didn't stand close to it.

"Are you his client who needs an inside man?"

She didn't answer me. "It's not what you'd call a nice bar, but I like it," she said. "I like that you have left that checkers game untouched. That's some customer service, there." She tried out a smile. It was lovely.

I shrugged. "Every game should be finished until there's a winner."

"I agree completely." She watched for him at the window. Steve's motorcycle was parked out front, under the awning, and he'd left his jacket and his helmet on the barstool. I moved them down to his table and I could hear his bike's keys jingle in the jacket pocket.

I joined her at the window. A block down was another bar, with no one sitting outside. A moderate rain had started, chasing the Sunday-night drinkers inside. Traffic had thinned, a light mist coming with midnight. The street was empty. "I'll be fine waiting for him."

"He asked me to stay with you," I said.

"That's my car," she said. I wondered why on earth he would have insisted that he bring her car around rather than just walk her to it if he were concerned for her safety. Steve was Steve. It was an older Jaguar, in mint condition. I saw Steve at the wheel, turning onto the street from the prepaid lot, three blocks from us.

He pulled up in front of Stormy's. He stepped out onto the brick sidewalk. He started to walk along the car, checking the fenders and the wheel wells, I realized, for a tracking device.

Then from the opposite direction, from the road Steve took to his house, a heavy SUV roared down the street, slowed when it reached Steve. He turned to look at them.

I heard a single shot, muffled.

Steve fell. The SUV roared past us.

The woman screamed.

2

I RAN ONTO the bar's front patio. I could see Steve, eyes open, the top of his head obliterated, lying next to the Jaguar. I touched his throat for a pulse. Gone.

The SUV had roared away. I didn't have its license. I wasn't even sure of its model. The back of my brain took over. I ran back inside, grabbed Steve's jacket and helmet.

"What are you doing?" she screamed.

"Lock the door! Call the police!" I yelled.

Then I ran to Steve's vintage bike. Pulled on the windbreaker, fastened the helmet. Found the keys in the jacket pocket, started the ignition. I wheeled in the direction the SUV had gone.

I leaned down into the bike, revving through red lights on the vacant streets, roaring past the entrance to The Barnacle State Park, where boats had delivered supplies to Coconut Grove's first residents. I headed toward Cocowalk, the large shopping district, full of chain restaurants and stores. I glanced down the side streets as I raced through the intersections. I zoomed through another light, a car honking at me. Then I saw the SUV; it had already turned to my left and I veered across the scant traffic. It was three blocks ahead of me.

The SUV was driving through the old Bahamian neighborhood of Coconut Grove, where the houses were smaller and often colorfully painted.

The driver took a hard right and accelerated. He had a gun, at the least, and I had nothing. So I wasn't exactly about to ride up close. But I could hear the engine and I stopped at the intersection, watching them accelerate fast down 32nd, headed toward the US-1 highway. That was how I tried to refer to it. Every major road in Miami seems to have three names, which had caused me endless confusion when I arrived.

I took off after them, hanging back. The license plates were smeared with mud. I could maybe get close enough to read it, but a fever—that deadly burning that wouldn't let me walk away from trouble—began to ride my brain hard. They'd killed my friend, the one friend I had in this town. Did I just let them walk away? Steve hadn't left our family in our moment of need; he didn't abandon us and call for help, he stayed with us, made sure the job was done. I could get their license plate and then what? Go back to the bar and call the police? What if the car was stolen and dumped? They were *here*, I was *here*, the fever told me: stay with them. Here's the reality after a hit: you want to run and you want to blend in. You have to vanish, twice, first from notice that you killed someone and then into the crowd. They hadn't accomplished stage one yet.

I followed.

They pulled onto the entrance ramp for Highway 1, heading toward downtown Miami, and I followed. If they recognized this motorcycle as the one parked outside the bar, then they'd know I was chasing them. Hopefully they didn't see, with the rain and the head start they'd had, that I was following them.

So I let myself get a little closer. I wasn't armed. They were two cars ahead of me and I could hear my own hard breathing over the rush of the late-night traffic.

We zoomed onto I-95 North, went past the towers of downtown. Miami is a city of light, and through the rain the skyline glowed. I thought they might veer off toward the dazzle of Miami Beach, but they stayed on the highway. I risked getting ahead of them; glancing over I could see a driver and a passenger. I slowed and they revved ahead of me and I let a few cars get between us.

I wondered, Are they leaving town? How far are they going to go?

We entered North Miami, them four cars ahead of me. On one side was the town itself, on the left was an array of businesses and warehouses. The SUV was in the left lane and suddenly it boomed across all the lanes and took the exit.

No choice. I followed them. A noble citizen honked at me and I wondered if the sound carried above the rain, which had begun to ease. At the bottom of the ramp they caught the green light just as it changed and veered hard to the left, under the highway, toward the warehouses and complexes.

I stopped at the yellow light. Counted. The light turned red. I watched their taillights turn out of sight, and then I ran the light. I got to the highway's opposite frontage road and saw them heading south. In a matter of seconds they turned into one of the business complexes. I followed, at a distance.

They'd just killed a man. They were either waiting here to be paid if this was a hired job, or to celebrate, or hide. Or to ambush me. They stopped at a building two blocks ahead of me, fire-escape stairs running up its side, a For Lease sign prominent on the front. I suppose the smartest thing for me to do was to watch them go into the building, surveil them, see who arrived there next or when they left.

But I wasn't set up to spy on them. Later I would think about why I did what I did, and the reasons for it would shine like stars coming awake in a sky without clouds. But I wasn't calm, cool, collected. I was...vengeance. I was a fury, with a motorcycle instead of black wings. Not my finest moment.

Two guys got out of the SUV. One skinny, one heavy, the skinny one on the driver's side. Guns in hand. Talking. Not noticing me.

Then I realized I *was* armed. No turning back.

So I roared Steve's bike—my weapon—straight at the skinny one. Normally I would have attacked the bigger guy first, but the skinny dude was the driver and therefore had the keys. I didn't want the other one escaping into a locked building if this was home base. The skinny guy turned at the approach of the motorcycle and fired at me and I felt the bullet ricochet off Steve's motorcycle helmet.

Then I slammed into him. Hard. He went down, the tires skidded across his groin, chest, and head. I lost control of the bike and I hit the wire fence that lined the lot. My leg got trapped and I squirmed free. The heavy guy was running, down the gap between the buildings.

I grabbed for the driver's pistol. I steadied my aim, my right arm and leg hot with pain, Steve's windbreaker in tatters.

"Freeze!" I yelled. He rounded a corner. I followed, running as best I could. I waited at the alley's bend, risked a glance, saw the heavy guy running, trying to find a place to hide in the maze of warehouses and office buildings, probably just long enough to phone for help.

I stayed low. Trying to keep my breathing silent. Moved through the labyrinth, listening to his footsteps. The driver's gun was a Beretta 92FS and I made myself check the clip. It was fresh, just two shots fired, one in the chamber, twelve in the clip.

"You're not a cop, who the hell are you?" the voice rang out. From my left.

I didn't answer. I don't believe you have to answer every question, every e-mail, every phone call. I like to keep my own counsel.

"You don't know what you're messing with!" the guy yelled.

"Tell me," I said.

"Tell her it's for her own good." Then the distant thunder rumbled and his words went indistinct.

I stopped and listened. I'd seen but not registered in the few moments he'd stood in the pool of security lights that he was wearing a dark suit and cowboy boots. Bad choice, but one presumed he didn't anticipate being chased on foot. And those thick heels were loud on concrete.

I could hear him, heading back into the maze of buildings in the complex. Then his boots against metal.

A fire escape.

I turned a corner and then I saw him, two buildings ahead. He ran up the four-story fire escape. I waited until he reached the roof and vanished. I followed, much more quietly.

All the advantage was his. I'd seen that he had a gun. If he were bright he'd wait and see if I climbed to the roof and then shoot me. So I got off the fire escape, silently, finding a sliver of ledge. My hobby in happier days had been parkour, the extreme running sport where you vault walls and jump over spaces and ignore heights. But the building's ledge wasn't made for walking, it was decorative, and if he decided to risk a glance down he could simply fire straight down into my head. Two feet out onto the ledge I questioned my decision: I should have smashed through a window, except that would have telegraphed where I was and what I was doing. I had no guarantee that from the top floor I could reach the roof—the door might be locked, there might be people inside—and in that time he could retreat onto a neighboring building or back down the fire escape.

So the ledge. I just had to hope he was too freaked-out—Steve's killing had not gone quite the way it was supposed to go.

I moved faster. If I fell I'd be dead and with Steve at some heavenly bar and he'd probably say, *What the hell were you thinking?*

What was I thinking? The flame in my brain raged, the need to stop them, to not let them get away with cold-blooded murder. For a moment I saw my brother Danny's face, shaky on a handheld camera, kneeling before his executioner. I couldn't think about him. Then Steve's face, looking at me through a broken car window in a long-ago African night, the distant sounds of shelling a fierce echo. I shoved all the thoughts away.

I rounded the corner of the building. He wouldn't expect me from this side. I wanted to be behind him.

At the same moment, I heard the rising approach of sirens. Someone had heard the earlier shots. And here I was, stuck on the side of the building.

I raised my head past the parapet and risked a glance onto the roof. I could see the heavy guy standing by the fire escape, peering along the complex's alleys, trying to see me in the shadows.

In one move, I pulled myself up. I hurried toward him. He spun toward me and I fired, aiming at his leg. I missed; he jumped back; and in his surprise and fear he lost his balance against the roof's edge.

He fell. He plummeted toward the alleyway. Twice I heard sharp clangs, him hitting the metal of the fire escape. When I reached the edge and looked down, he lay broken on the asphalt. Dead.

I ran. But not down the fire escape, because the approaching sirens told me I had less than thirty seconds and no way could I clear the steps before the police arrived. So I ran to the opposite edge of the roof and jumped. Grabbed hold of a sign jutting out from the building, swung, and jumped again, landed on the lower roof of the neighboring building, hit, rolled onto my back to spread the force of the impact, ran at higher speed, jumped, landed on the next building, which had a lower roofline. Normally when I do this kind of parkour run, I've walked the route, studied it to plan my jumps and runs. Here I ran fast and unsure of what came next. I was lucky the buildings were close together, their loading bays all facing the same road. I heard the sirens hold position and I figured the body had been found. At the edge of the next building was the frontage road, and I ran out of room. I went quietly down that building's fire escape and walked away. I tucked Steve's motorcycle helmet under my arm.

I walked into the night, into the rain.

The heavy guy was dead. The skinny guy, I didn't know. Had he seen my face, under the helmet? Had he realized I'd followed him from the closed bar? Who else would be there after closing but the owner? Would the skinny guy tell the police? My heart felt hot.

I was without a ride. I ducked under the highway bridge and along a major thoroughfare. I walked for a mile. Miami is not a town with cabs roaming in the rain. But I found a small, closed bar in a strip mall and I took shelter from the rain in front of it. Every responsible barkeep has a taxi app on his smartphone, and I used mine to find and electronically hail a vacant cab.

I sat in the back of the cab and shivered from the rain and thought, Why did they kill Steve? Steve was kindness, and goodness, and bad jokes, and a round of drinks for the bar. I would have to tell my parents. He'd asked me for help and I'd said no. I'd failed him, utterly. My thoughts were a jumble: guilt, fury at the killers, fear I'd be caught. The CIA taught me to think clearly in a dangerous situation but it was as though my brain had abandoned me.

I had the driver drop me off a few blocks from Stormy's with a very hefty tip, paid in cash. I watched the cab pull out of sight before I took a step. I slowly walked toward the bar. Half the street was closed, the police working Steve's murder scene. A forensics team, hurrying in the rain. Not much traffic but the late-night crowd—there's always a late-night crowd in Miami, even on Sunday—was a thin gathering along the edges of the police barricade.

My bar stood dark—it looked deserted. The pools of light near the entrance were turned off. I had left those on, I was sure.

I didn't see Steve's friend.

I didn't see the police interviewing anyone.

And her Jaguar was gone.

Still three blocks away, I turned and walked over one street. I went to my bar's back door. It was unlocked. I went inside; I left the lights off and locked the door behind me. I hid the gun I'd taken from the driver—it might have been the weapon used to kill Steve. I went upstairs and in the dark I hid the gun in a safe. I hid the dented motorcycle helmet under the bed.

Very quietly, and in the dark so the cops outside wouldn't notice, I came downstairs and I gently tested the front door. Locked.

She was gone.

I went back upstairs, again without turning on any lights. I dried off and put my rain-wet clothes in the dryer and turned it on. I put on pajama pants and a T-shirt from the bar (IT'S ALWAYS SUNNY AT STORMY'S!). I took a deep breath. I turned on the TV and put it on the classic movies channel, turned up the volume. Then I flicked on the upstairs light. I scrunched my hair into a bedhead tangle.

Me turning on the lights didn't go unnoticed by the police. Within a minute there was an officer and a detective knocking on the bar door. I went down to answer it.

"Sir?"

"Yes?" I said. I sounded sleepy, or a little drunk.

"There's been a shooting about forty-five minutes ago. Did you hear the gunfire?"

"No," I lied. "I just woke up. What…what happened?"

The detective told me there had been a man shot to death on the street. I said I knew nothing. I said that I'd closed the bar promptly at midnight and then gone straight upstairs and gone to sleep, because I wasn't feeling well. My story was hard for him to dent. I hadn't heard a shot; I had the TV turned to an old movie, which, along with the pattering drone of rain, lulled me to deep sleep. Or if I'd heard a shot, I hadn't recognized it as such. He talked to me and around me some more, lots of questions. We stood in the bar, me dressed for bed, the police puddling rainwater on the floor.

"The ID on the man was Steve Robles. You know him?" the detective said.

I let some of the emotion I felt bleed out. "Oh, hell. Yes, sir. I know Steve. He's a regular here. Oh God, no."

"Was he here tonight?"

There had been no mention of another witness, certainly not one here in the bar. So she had said nothing. So I gambled, and if I was wrong I'd be spending the night in jail for lying to an officer. "Yes. But he left when I closed." And yes, I knew I shouldn't lie, but I couldn't tell the police I'd chased down his murderers and maybe killed them both. I thought of the video feed of Daniel, sleeping in his crib. I couldn't risk losing that sight.

"He's a really good guy. Everyone likes him. Who would do this?" I asked.

"He didn't argue with anyone here tonight?"

"No. Argue? Steve is very easygoing. Everyone likes him. Who would…did someone see him get shot?" I asked.

"A man driving by saw him lying on the sidewalk, called us."

So she didn't call the police. And maybe from the street you couldn't see Steve's body if the Jaguar was still parked there.

"I can't believe this." I went and got a glass and poured a shot of bourbon. I needed to play the part of the rattled barkeep. The bottle clinked, clinked, clinked against the glass as I tried to steady the pour.

"Sir, please don't drink that right now."

I took my hand away from the glass. "Sorry, this is just very upsetting."

"He leave with anyone?"

"I don't know, I didn't see him go. I cleaned up before I closed because there wasn't any crowd. I was in the back and he just hollered he was leaving. I said goodnight to him. Then I locked up and went upstairs and turned on the TV." Lies. "He rides his motorcycle here. He only lives a few blocks away." Truth. They would know this from his wallet. And I let my emotion show, how distraught I really was, my friend was dead and my face crumpled. "I can't believe this." Truth.

"What kind of motorcycle?"

"I don't know…he let me ride it with him once." Lie, but my prints might be on the bike. My prints were not in any files, though, the CIA had made sure of that. "I don't know about such things." Lie.

"There's no motorcycle out there."

"But…he parks it out front. Under the awning when it rains. Always."

The cop showed me that the bike was gone.

"You think someone shot him for a stupid motorcycle?" My crumpled face crumpled more. He and another officer began to confer.

"It's a vintage bike…" I said, half to myself in shock. The officers stopped, turned back to me. "A 1968 BMW R60US. I remember now. He said they're kind of rare." And soon enough the police in North Miami would be checking the license plate on a rare motorcycle and soon enough the two police departments would talk. The two officers conferred again and wrote down notes and one searched on his phone. They love a motive, no matter how small. Motive is all.

The other detective said, "You live above the bar, sir?"

"Yes, sir."

"And most nights you're open until three?"

"But not on Sunday. I close at midnight."

"I couldn't stand to live where I worked." Everyone was an expert about your business these days. I blamed the Internet.

"It's not for everyone," I said. I was not a witness, and I was not acting suspiciously. The detectives talked to me some more, probing to see if I had any holes in my story. It was not a hard role for me to play as the devastated, shocked friend. Finally they left.

I stared out at the empty street. The Jaguar. I couldn't remember her plates. Maybe she'd simply run as soon as I was gone. She'd said something about ten million. That was a lot of reasons to vanish.

The heavy man's words rattled in my head: *You don't know what you're messing with! Tell her it's for her own good.*

I picked up the glass of bourbon. I drank it slowly.

You're something, aren't you, Sam, he had asked, and I'd given him the wrong answer.

3

THE CALL TO my parents the next morning went like this:

"Mom?"

"Oh, hi, Sam."

"I have some bad news. Steve Robles was shot in front of the bar last night."

Murmurs of vague shock, dismay, then, "What kind of bar are you running?"

"What?"

"You have people getting shot at your business."

"It wasn't like that, Mom. It wasn't a bar fight."

A long, painful silence. "Well. I suppose in his security work he knew unsavory types."

Then I lied. "The guys who shot him stole his motorcycle."

"He survives wars in Africa and then dies at home for a material possession." This was followed by a lengthy diatribe against modern life and humanity's need to cling to objects. "Oh. He was such a handsome man."

"The funeral is in a few days."

"Oh. Well, I'm afraid we can't be there. We're both scheduled to speak at a conference in Dallas later this week on global relief initiatives."

"Mom," I said. "Steve saved our lives, do you remember that?"

"Of course I do." She spoke to me as though I were mentally

slow. "But the conference, we can't cancel. It's a chance to do good."

I often felt my mother and father didn't know the difference between doing good and doing the right thing. "I'll represent the family, then." I couldn't keep the chill out of my tone.

"I'll send you money for some flowers."

"No need, I'll take care of it, Mom."

"Well, then, put your name first on the card, if you're paying for it."

I closed my eyes. "I have to go, Mom, I just figured you and Dad would want to know."

"I'm glad you called. Will we see you soon when you're back in town?"

"Sure. Of course. I'll bring over Daniel."

"Daniel. Yes. All right, honey. I'm sorry about Steve. I need to go work on my presentation, so I'll help you later." My mother often did this, used "help" as a verb when it didn't quite fit. I'd learned to ignore it. We told each other we loved each other and then I hung up. The relationship was one I wanted to improve, but it was strained. I had materialized in New Orleans a few months back, no longer working for a London consultancy that was a CIA Special Projects front (Mom and Dad never knew I was CIA), without a wife (I'd told them she'd left me, but actually she was in a coma in a secret government hospital), and with a child they didn't know about. A son named for my lost brother, whose death was the giant crack in our hearts and our family. Once my mother said, "I'm not sure you should have named the baby for your brother. It feels like bad luck now." You would think losing their oldest child would create a tighter bond with their youngest; but they'd pushed me to a comfortable arm's distance since Danny died, as if to say, *Thank you, Sam, but no. We were hurt very badly once and don't care to be hurt again. So we'll just be involved with you a bit less, if that's okay. Insurance policy. Nothing personal.*

The police came again, asked me more questions. I stuck to my story. I wondered if they would find a record of Steve's mysterious client. The news sites stuck to the theft of the motorcycle as the motive. Nothing else emerged. I wondered what the police would think if the ballistics from the heavy guy's gun didn't match the bullet in Steve's head. I couldn't be sure which gun had been used on him. It would be an odd open question. Maybe they'd assume the murder weapon had been dumped.

I lifted fingerprints from the gun using tape and powder, scanned them into my laptop, and then had nowhere to send them. I couldn't go back to my friend August in the CIA and ask him to run the prints; I didn't work for him anymore. I supposed I could ask my friend Mila. But then I would have had to explain my actions, and I was already in trouble with her and my mysterious benefactors, known as the Round Table, who'd given me the bars and liked for me to serve as their private agent now and then. But asking Mila to do this would raise questions from her. The police had identified the two men, the dead one and the one hanging on to life, unconscious. The one I'd run over with the motorcycle.

The one who could wake up and possibly identify me.

So I waited to see what the news would bring. I drove by Steve's house; the police were there, then his family. The police would find out who the woman was. It was best to stay away.

Four days after he died, Steve was buried in a beautiful old cemetery on 8th Street, also called Calle Ocho once it stretches into Little Havana. I noticed a mix of Anglo and Cuban names on the tombstones. Steve's dad was Cuban; his mother was Anglo. The plot belonged to his parents and he was joining them in the final slot. I could see on the stone that his father had died fifteen years ago and his mother only two. Their plot was behind a huge mausoleum and we were parked in a line down a little side road. His family was represented by two cousins—male twins with narrow faces and narrow throats and narrow bodies—and some older aunts and uncles; they were weepy. Paige, one of Stormy's regulars who seemed to know everyone's history, told me that Steve's branch of the family did not get along with the rest, he'd mentioned it to her more than once, he had no use for his own blood ties.

The cousins looked bereaved not only for Steve's murder but that the fissure would never be fixed. I heard one say to an old aunt, "I thought we could mend fences. I was waiting on him."

You can't do that, I thought, because we don't have forever.

Most of the other mourners were the regulars at Stormy's. Most of them Coconut Grove folks who walked to the bar every night or so, treated it like a second home. Older guys, a couple of women in their forties, me. Six of us, and a young, solemn priest from St. Hugh's in Coconut Grove, where Steve went to Mass.

At the end, while the priest murmured final prayers, I saw a car stop down away from everyone else. The Jaguar. And the honey-voiced woman got out. She stayed by the car, like a curious bystander. She looked at me, then looked away and walked over to another grave, as though paying her respects. I stared at her; she stared back at me.

"Sam," Paige, the bar regular, eased close to me. She was fortyish, smart, pretty, always well dressed, favored Sauvignon Blanc, never had too much to drink at the bar. She was a daily regular, sometimes social, sometimes just with a book to keep her company. I knew from what others said she was a former librarian and maybe didn't have to work due to family money. I sensed a bit of murkiness in her background, something that no one talked about but only around. Steve had introduced her to me this way, less than a minute after meeting me: *She's a librarian named...Paige! Clearly she had a calling.* Note the past tense, never explained. And Paige shot right back: *I'll be happy to teach you to read so you can sharpen your sense of humor.* She took charge in the midst of the numbing grief, organizing a post-funeral gathering for the regulars at Stormy's. "Will you have the bar open now?" she asked.

"No," I said, watching the woman. "I mean, not right now. How about we meet there in an hour or so?"

"You want everyone to stand around for an hour on the patio?" Paige's tone was a little dry, annoyed.

"Paige, please. Something I have to do for Steve. Alone."

"Well, we've all got to go home and get our potlucks anyway," she said. I nodded and she went back to the regulars. I stood apart and watched the narrow cousins and the weepy aunts and the regulars toss flowers onto the grave and then they roamed back to their cars, clearly separate groups. They all left. I walked a fair distance away from the gravesite and sat on a stone bench.

I waited. I pulled a bottle of Red Stripe, Steve's favorite beer, out of my suit's pocket and watched the workmen tuck Steve's coffin into the ground. I set the bottle next to me and finally the woman came and sat on the bench with me, the cold bottle between us. She didn't really look at me; like me she watched them pile dirt on Steve. I don't like the idea of being sealed up in the dark. I hope I get cremated; pour me out to ride the wind wherever it takes me. I reminded myself to tell Leonie, my son's surrogate mother, to honor my wishes.

The woman spoke first. "A motorcycle. Two Colombians, down from New York for no clear reason, killed Steve for his motorcycle. And then one killed the other."

"Maybe you should give a statement to the paper."

"You are a good friend." Her gaze met mine. "A very good friend."

"You're not," I answered. "I don't think you're his friend. You're his client. I'm his friend."

"I wasn't his friend. I'm so sorry for what happened to him. I am so sorry." Her voice cracked slightly and she cleared her throat. "But I couldn't be tied to his death in any way."

"You knew they were hunting you."

"No...I thought they were following me."

"Who are they?"

"I don't know them."

"Then who sent them?"

She said nothing.

"You don't know who wishes you harm?" I asked.

"It's over. I got the message."

"It's over for Steve, that's for damn sure. One of the men talked about you."

The color tipped from her face. "What?"

"He said that it was for your own good."

She shuddered. I watched her. People decide to keep a secret, a terrible one, for really only two reasons. Because they don't want to be hurt, or they don't want someone they love hurt. "It's over," she said. "Neither of us can go to the police."

"I thought they would have found records that he was working for you."

"I asked him to keep none. I signed no contract. I paid him in cash."

"What did you want him to do for you? Protect you? Find something for you? What? I heard you mention ten mil-lion…dollars?"

She twitched. "I hired him for protection, but I stopped doing what I was doing, so it's over. I'm not a threat to anyone."

"Don't you dare lie to me," I said. "He wanted me to be his inside man. His spy. You don't need an inside man just for a pro-tection job. So you hired him for another reason."

"Please let it go. Please. I can't bear the thought of someone else getting hurt. So let it go now." A bit of fire crept into her voice, like she was used to getting her way.

"I told him no."

She seemed to relax and I added, harshly: "Of course, that was before. Is that why he wanted to meet at my bar? Let me see you, then pitch me again?"

She shook her head. "I simply told him I needed to see him and he told me to meet him at the bar that night."

"There will be a record of that call."

"On his phone, yes. Not on mine. I always called him on a throwaway I bought for cash in Little Haiti." And even now she looked over her shoulder, as if worried she was being watched. I saw no one.

"What was so urgent? He hinted that he had been threatened in some way. You said something about money. I overheard you."

"It doesn't matter now." And then she wiped a tear from her eye. "I am so sorry about him. I left him, dead in the rain. I ran like a coward. I have never been so awful in my whole life." Her voice began to shake. "I didn't have to come here today. It was a risk for me. But I couldn't *not* come. Do you understand that?"

I didn't know if her tears were genuine. I couldn't tell. But the pain on her face seemed real. "The story could still fall apart if there's any surveillance video at the complex in North Miami. I had on the helmet, so my face won't be seen. But they'll know someone on a bike followed them."

"Maybe they'll think it's a third thief."

"Yeah, it takes three to steal a bike." I stared at Steve's grave. You might wonder what the conversations will be like after you're in the earth, people talking about you, and this wasn't one he ever could have imagined.

"I'll keep my mouth shut," she said.

"I'm sure you will."

She studied my face. "Why didn't you tell the police about me?"

"I didn't care to explain my own actions."

We listened to the wind hiss in the trees, the distant honk of a horn. The steady traffic on Calle Ocho was just a hum, like the soundtrack to a dream.

"It's not a normal man who chases after gunmen," she said quietly.

"It's not a normal woman who doesn't call the police and vanishes after a man is shot."

"So we're not normal," she said. "What are we?"

"I'm just a bartender." I held up the bottle. "Gonna pour this on his grave when they're done covering him up."

"Is that all you're going to do for him?"

I didn't answer her.

"I mean, you took off after those men. And now one of them is dead and the other is in a coma. He might never wake up." She put her gaze down into her lap. "But if he does, I suspect he won't talk about me. But he might tell the police all about the guy who chased him from the bar."

That left me silent for five long beats. It doesn't take long to fill a grave; the workers were nearly done. The bottle I'd brought for Steve sweated in my hand. "Is that a threat?"

"No. A gentle, well-intentioned warning. Get out of Miami."

"I own a business here."

"It doesn't appear to be thriving. Cut your losses and go, Sam."

"Who are you? Why are these bad guys after you?"

"I admire that you went after those two creeps. Seriously. It's a rare quality. But…No one can help me now, all right? I'm not going to endanger anyone else. I'll handle it myself." She stood.

The workers finished with the grave. They moved the floral tribute from the regulars, who had gone in together on a spray of chrysanthemums, and the roses from the narrow cousins, onto the grave. The banner on the regulars' spray read THIS ROUND'S ON ME. Steve always bought the first round, with a stirring motion of his finger. He never failed to be generous.

She watched the banner flicker in the wind.

"This is a celebrity town," I said. "It's easy to find incredibly competent personal security, brokered by big firms. Why Steve? Why a small one-man shop?"

She didn't answer.

"But you needed more, I'm guessing. Did he have a certain skill set? Something in his background?"

She didn't answer.

"Maybe it was because he was slightly down on his luck. He might not ask so many questions."

She stood. "Might I join you in pouring that beer on his grave? I can't make this right for him, and I liked him."

"Who's behind his death?"

"I actually don't know," she said. "Believe me or not." She started walking toward the grave and I followed. We studied the fresh earth, a new blanket for Steve. I've been around a lot of deceptive people. I *am* a deceptive person, when I have to be. And deceivers often try too hard to convince you. Mostly what I read off her was frustration—I saw it in her closed fists as she walked, her slight hunch, the whiteness of her lips pressed together, the rise in that honeyed voice. Frustration that Steve was dead, that she couldn't stop it.

You can do a lot with frustration. It can be a rich fuel.

I opened the bottle. "Steve," I said. "I'm sorry. And—what's your name?"

I hadn't yet asked her. She'd hardly given me a straight answer. She should have said "Jane Doe." But this was ritual, standing at the grave of a man who'd died trying to help her, a powerful, primal tug, and by going after Steve's killers I'd earned the right to ask.

She said, very softly, "Cordelia."

That better not be a lie, I thought. Don't you dare lie to me at this moment.

"...and Cordelia and I are sorry. Sorry this happened to you. I wish I'd thanked you properly for saving my life all those years ago. My brother and I talked about you, Steve. Like you were a real-life G.I. Joe."

Cordelia stiffened next to me. I continued: "You were like the man my brother would have been if he'd had the chance. I enjoyed talking to you. And isn't that really what a bar is for? The talking. The unburdening. Listening to you was never a burden." I glanced at her, the beer ready to pour.

Cordelia said, "I'm sorry, Steve. I'll make the person responsible pay. But it may be a long wait." Then she went silent.

"Who's responsible?" I said.

"I don't know. Yet," she said.

And then I upended the bottle of beer, watched it foam on the ground. I thought of doing the same, years ago, on an empty grave. A marker waiting for the return of my brother's body. He never came home.

Lager inched through the soil. Whoever wanted him dead could drink a beer. For the moment.

"Steve. You were right," I said to the marker. "You were totally right. I was...*something*."

"What does that mean?" she asked me.

It was my turn not to answer a question. I set the empty bottle against Steve's stone.

Cordelia gave me an uncertain look and said, "Leave Miami for a while. Good-bye, Sam." Then she turned and went to the Jaguar and got in and drove away.

I went to my car—a nondescript gray Honda I'd rented when I arrived—and followed her.

If I was something, it was time to start acting like it.

4

TAILING SOMEONE YOU'VE just had a talk with is very difficult. She drove into a nice shopping district in Coral Gables and I was right behind her. She turned onto Aragon Avenue and lucked into a parking space close to the Books & Books bookstore. I honked and drove past her and she waved, almost reluctantly. So she thought I'd said my good-bye for the day.

I turned at the next intersection and parked in a pay lot one street over. I hurried back toward Aragon and on my smartphone called Paige. "Can I swap cars with you right now?"

"Why?"

"It's about Steve. You can have mine for the day." I told her where to park and where to meet me.

"Um, okay. I was about to buy ice to take to the bar..."

"Paige, never mind that, please, it's important."

"I'm on my way," she said.

If Cordelia drove off, I'd risk the follow and see where she went, and call Paige to meet me. But I stood in front of the store, which was sort of U-shaped and had a central courtyard with pa-tio tables with big canvas umbrellas. Books are one of my few relaxations and so I'd been here twice since coming to town, buying some recent bestsellers and a book on Miami history rec-ommended to me by the owner, a nice gentleman every customer seemed to know. I stood on the edge of the entryway and through

the courtyard I could see Cordelia get a very large coffee and begin tapping on her phone. She came out and I stepped back into
the shadows. She sat down at one of the outdoor tables, studying
her smartphone's screen.

You have to learn the maze, the old burnt man had told me
during my CIA training. My instructors had felt I didn't listen
well so they sent me off to talk a few times to one of the Special
Project legends, a man who had worked undercover time and
time again. Until an enemy caught him, burned him, made his
face into a melted candle. He lived in a CIA-run hospital. His
voice sounded like smoke and I thought, Why are they sending
me to a guy who failed? Who got caught? They didn't even tell
me his name.

What maze? I'd asked. To be polite.

*When you're pretending to be someone as an inside man, then
there's a maze you navigate to get in and then get home safe. Find
the map.*

I don't understand.

*Of course you don't. That's why they've sent you to me. Now,
listen...*

What's your maze, Cordelia? I wondered.

Then I committed a crime. I pulled out a smartphone Mila had
sent me several weeks back, even though the Round Table hadn't
given me a job to spy on anyone. I tapped an app. It scanned every phone in the vicinity of the store, relying on a software bug in
the SIM chips that had not been publicized or fixed. There were
sixteen active mobile phones in the store.

A list began to build on my screen. Phone numbers. As the
software (illegally, I presumed) accessed provider databases,
names began to appear next to the phone numbers.

It was gear like this that made me wonder who the Round
Table really were, who I was working with.

The seventh name that appeared next to a matching number
read CORDELIA VARELA. I slipped an ear-bud plug into the phone,
and then the ear buds into my ear, and I listened to her conversation.

5

I HEARD CORDELIA say, "I know where you're all going. The house in Puerto Rico."

Then a young man's voice: "Don't come, Cori. You're not welcome. It doesn't concern you."

"I want to know what is happening."

"As you appear to be selectively deaf, I'll say again, it doesn't concern you. Stay in Miami. Please."

"The ten million," Cordelia said. "Where did that come from? Where did it go?"

"Cori, you need to leave this alone."

"I'm trying to help the family."

"You will end up hurting the family. Stay at home."

"Stop talking to me like I'm a little girl."

"Stop acting like a little girl."

"I'll stop if you'll stop." From my vantage point I saw a flush of anger color her face.

The man on the other end of the phone laughed. "What am I supposed to stop?"

"Whatever you've gotten us involved in that coughs up ten million dollars in cash. I saw the money. I want to know where Papa got it."

His voice was weary. "The rest of the family wants you to leave this alone."

"I don't care," she said.

"You are sticking your nose in problems you can't understand. I am asking you to stop. Don't come to Puerto Rico. Stay home. Feed the hungry and get kids educations and do all that good work you do."

"I'll stop asking questions if you'll tell me the truth."

The man sighed. "Where are you?"

"The patio at the bookstore."

"For God's sake. Come home and we'll talk about this."

"I don't understand how you could do this to our family. To Papa."

For a long moment there was silence and I'd thought he'd hung up. "Papa doesn't want you to know about his business. *I* don't always know about it. There's a reason for that. So respect his wishes and stop asking questions." And then the man hung up on her.

Cordelia turned off her own phone and set it on the table next to her coffee and put her face into her hands. I watched. Then she reached for her coffee and I could see her hands shaking, ever so slightly.

6

Paige arrived about ten minutes later, driving past me in a ten-year-old white Lexus, and Cordelia hadn't yet left the courtyard. I gave Paige my keys and she took mine. "What's this about, Sam?"

"It's about finding out what got Steve killed. I don't have enough to go to the police."

Paige's eyes widened. "You're playing at detective?"

"No, nothing so dramatic. But the person knows my car and doesn't know yours. Okay? I just want to find out where she goes. I don't know her name."

"You're actually going to"—then she air-quoted with her fingers—"tail someone." Paige pronounced this like a verdict of insanity.

I handed Paige my keys. "The bar keys are on the ring. The alarm-system code is 9999. You all can go in and help yourselves to beers or drinks, but keep the Open sign off and I'll be there soon." I hadn't reopened the bar since Steve's shooting. I knew the regulars would want to gather, but I had zero interest in serving beers to the curious vultures who'd never graced Stormy's before and were only there to eye the brick sidewalk where Steve died.

"Sam…" Paige started. She liked to argue, but she stopped. "All right. Don't dent her."

I retrieved a pair of sunglasses and a dark hat from my Honda; in case I had to follow closer, I didn't want Cordelia spotting my face. I thanked Paige and she took off in my car. I saw Cordelia get up and I ran to the Lexus. I wheeled the car around, cap and sunglasses in place, and she was listening to her phone, standing at her car door. I slowed and she figured I wanted the parking slot. She got into the car and revved out onto the street. I followed her. She turned onto a major road, LeJeune, and headed south.

I let a couple of cars get between us. She stayed in Coral Gables. It's a town of nearly fifty thousand people, so it's bigger than most visitors realize. She drove into the Cocoplum area. Very nice homes—big ones, usually only four on a U-shaped street. She was waved through a guardhouse and I followed, and I guess because I was in a suit and in a Lexus the guard waved me through too. I saw no sign that these were private roads. I stayed back and saw Cordelia turn and go down another road, to a second guardhouse. How exclusive was this area? I wondered. I followed, a silver Lincoln now between us. The Lincoln got stopped, then waved through.

I got stopped. I lowered my window with an apologetic smile.

"What's your business here, sir?" the guard asked.

The trick with these guys is to never, ever challenge their power. I held up a wallet. Mine. "Cordelia dropped this at the bookstore over on Aragon, where we were just at," I said. "She left before I did and the clerk who found it told me and I'm trying to catch up to give it to her and my phone's dead. Didn't she just come through in her Jaguar?"

He studied me. The Lexus and the nice suit helped. I said, "Or you could call her to come fetch it, and then she can just drive back up here." I put the barest emphasis on the last phrase, like it would be a chore for her. "If she doesn't mind. Or I'll just be quick. You can time me."

"All right, sir," he said.

"You need me to leave my license with you?"

"No, that's okay."

The bar went up and he waved me through.

There was one street. Lined with huge palm trees and spectacular landscaping. The house numbers started at "1." The numbers
were the only small aspect of the neighborhood. Each bend of the
street held three or four massive homes. Every home looked like
it should be on the cover of a design magazine. They were incredible. I grew up with relief-worker parents and I'd seen more
poverty in the world's backwaters than most Americans do and
I could not wrap my head quite around this grandeur. They all
faced the bay. Driveways of stone, some with elaborate geometric
patterns. Some had large privacy walls, others had a dense growth
of sculpted foliage that hid as much as a wall would.

I zoomed forward and saw the Jag turn in, then the silver Lincoln. Huh. I wasn't the only one following Cordelia. I saw a
uniformed guard wave in Cordelia, then the Lincoln, then shut a
gate behind them. Cordelia had a shadow. Someone keeping an
eye on her, or someone arriving home at the same time? I drove
past. I made a note of the house number and U-turned it.

I thought, Why does she need protection when she has all that
security around her?

The obvious answer was: the people watching over her were
the danger.

I drove back up the road, gave a friendly wave and a thumbs-
up to the neighborhood gatekeeper, then drove back to the bar.

7

YOU'RE SOMETHING, AREN'T you, Sam? I felt as though I were too many somethings: Father. Bar owner. Former CIA operative. And private spy.

When my three-year CIA career was destroyed, I'd found a surprising set of allies: the Round Table, a private, secret group of do-gooders around the world, apparently financed by a wealthy few. They'd given me the bars as cover to search for my missing infant son—and I'd found Daniel and rescued him from his kidnappers—and then wanted me to be their pocket spy. I'd agreed, with some reluctance. But I'd run afoul of them, gone against their wishes in a bad job in Las Vegas, and my handler—Mila—was injured and recuperating. I was running the bars for them, but they'd given me no further covert work, aimed me at no more bad guys who were beyond the reach of the law, who'd slipped through the cracks of justice. Mila's husband, an arrogant Englishman named James Court, blamed me for her nearly being killed and he'd made it clear that I was unwelcome. They had given me the bars, and they could take the bars back, presumably by force or through threat. But Jimmy, as Mila called him, hadn't fired me from the Round Table, and he'd left me alone.

Every manager at my other bars had been wrongly convicted of crimes, and owed a debt of their lives and their freedom to the

Round Table. They knew that each bar was a safe house. I didn't know how many other pocket spies the Table had other than me and Mila, or if I alone needed to use the bars. Too much of the Round Table remained a mystery to me.

But I didn't have a manager to help me with a covert job in Miami.

I'd have to recruit my own help. Paige, maybe. She had motive to help me and seemed unencumbered by regular employment. But I didn't know if I could trust her. I'd see if she'd told everyone about me borrowing her car.

I parked Paige's Lexus behind the bar and went in the front door. A half dozen of the regulars stood sipping drinks and eating off paper plates, and casseroles and salads they'd brought lined the bar. I thought it was a nicer remembrance than many people got: not fancy, but heartfelt. I suddenly needed to be around people; it's not an emotion I often feel. I have gotten comfortable being alone. But I needed to be with people who knew Steve. I thought it might quiet the flame in the back of my head, the one that said, *Make the bad guys pay.* That said, *Do something to protect yourself before Coma Thug wakes up.* It was better to remember Steve, to think of the man he was. There were toasts, and funny stories about Steve from years past, and I felt a sharp pain in my chest. I wanted to tell them about the Steve who dragged me from a car on a bomb-ravaged road in central Africa. But I couldn't.

Because I had made a decision at his grave.

By early evening only Paige and I were left and I knew why she'd lingered, and it wasn't to help me clean up. Paige passed on her usual Sauvignon Blanc and drank a Red Stripe in honor of Steve. I handed Paige back her keys. She pocketed them and slid my keys back to me. I got a glass and poured myself a Red Stripe.

"You didn't tell the others I was playing at detective."

"I didn't want to embarrass you," Paige said. "Did you find this woman?"

"Yes."

"Does she know something about Steve's death?"

"I don't know yet. This might be related to Steve's work."

"I don't see why you don't call the police," Paige said, her voice rising. Her hands closed into fists.

"This might be…delicate. He wasn't killed over his motorcycle."

"You better call the police."

"And that might get more people killed. Including me."

"Oh, please, Captain Drama. Do I look like a turnip truck just went over a speed bump and dropped me off?" Paige raised an eyebrow.

I stared her down.

"Please be kidding, Sam." She toyed with the pearl necklace she wore. Her voice lost its mocking tone.

"I don't want to say anything yet. I might ask you for help."

"Help?"

"Like borrowing your car today. That let me find where this woman lived."

"Um, okay," Paige said.

"And Paige?"

"What?"

"I know you don't know me well, but I don't overdramatize. I think Steve could have gotten involved in a very bad situation. But I don't want to go to the police with no evidence, with no proof. I don't want to get sued, lose the bar."

She sipped at her beer. "Why you? How do you know how to…follow someone?"

And now I told my first lie, because I couldn't tell her I was ex-CIA or about my current work for the Table. "Steve worked private security." Then I paused, let the weight fill the air between us and said, "I used to be in the same business."

Paige nodded, said "Ah," as if that explained it all.

"If I find hard evidence, you know I'm going to the police. I promise I will. But don't call the police for me; let me handle that when I have enough to hold their interest. Otherwise they dismiss me as a crank."

"All right," Paige said, but she didn't seem to want to look at me. "I'll help you. But I don't see how I can."

"You're a librarian and you grew up here. I don't know the background of the town. Or have the connections. The ability to do fast research. You have that."

"Research." She looked away from me. "I can't help you there. I can't go on a computer."

"Why?"

She ran a finger along her beer bottle. "Do I look like a criminal?"

"Um, no."

"Well, I'm not supposed to touch a keyboard for another two months. Part of my deal with the district attorney."

"What exactly did you do?" I was surprised.

"You weren't here for the local headlines. 'Rogue Librarian,' the press called me, although my favorite was the columnist who called me 'Naughty Librarian.'" She took another sip of beer. "A patron at the library, I got suspicious of him...lurking around the children's section. He never did anything you could say was wrong, I just had a bad feeling about him. I thought he was taking pictures of kids on his phone, but when I challenged him, there weren't any pictures." She cleared her throat. "So. I hacked into his home computer. I found a ton of pictures of kids. Awful things. But that was still breaking the law, using the library's computer that way. He got arrested but I got suspended. Vigilantes are not popular with the police."

"That's why you don't work?"

"Yes. I thought they would hire me back when the suspension ran out...but my job's not waiting for me. And I haven't looked for another job. It's hard to be a librarian these days and not touch computers."

"I don't want to get you in more trouble."

She studied her beer glass. Paige was a kindred spirit, I thought; she'd answered a flame in her own brain, to stop a bad person, same as I had.

Paige looked up at me. "I want to know why Steve died and I

want whoever did it to pay. In full. So. You want to know about Miami, fine, I'll be your research assistant. My family has been here since the town was founded. I'm old-school Miam-a." She pronounced the last *i* like it was an *a*.

"But you don't touch a computer," I said. "I don't want you in trouble."

"Mmm, let's see what we need to do."

"Thank you."

"To Steve," I said, and we clinked glasses. She finished her beer and went home. I relocked the door behind her.

I went to my laptop and did a property search on the address to which I'd followed Cordelia. I didn't want to give Paige a name to research, not yet.

According to the public records, the mansion was owned by the Varela Family Trust.

I went to a popular social media site and did a search on Cordelia Varela.

She went by Cori—the man on the phone had called her that as well—with her friends, of which she didn't have many, at least on the site. I paged through the pictures. The About page told me she had a bachelor's degree in finance from the University of Miami and had started a charity called Help with Love. I did an online search for it. Help with Love—which to my twisted sense of humor sounded more like a dating service—had as its focus reaching out to kids at risk and giving them guidance to make solid choices and complete their educations. She helped finance smaller charities here in Florida, as well as in Africa, the Middle East, and South America—all with the idea that charities in those areas could do immediate good.

Cordelia Varela was listed as the CEO and founder. She was young, close to my age of twenty-six. Young, I thought, to be heading a large charity. I knew that from my own parents' long careers in relief work. Either she had managed to convince people early on to give her money, or she already had money. The size of the mansion suggested the answer.

No mention of family in her bio on the charity's website.

I did a search on "Varela Miami" and then got the hits. Reynaldo Varela. Multimillionaire owner of a large aviation cargo company with worldwide reach. He gave very few interviews, but he'd given one when Cordelia—apparently the youngest of his three children—launched her charity. Reynaldo Varela was a man of few words, though. He announced support for his daughter's charity; his air cargo company, FastFlex, pledged its backing as her first corporate sponsor.

The hits piled up. A Varela wing at a local modern art museum, specializing in painters from the developing world. The Varela Children's Clinic, in the economically depressed Little Haiti. The Varela Aviation Museum. The Varela Everglades Initiative. Donations to private schools of all stripes, to the Miami library system, to the symphony, to the university. Reynaldo Varela had made a lot of money and thrown a lot of money.

"That's the Miami way," Paige said when I called her and asked about the family. "If you make it, and you want instant respectability, you donate. A lot."

"Was he not respectable?"

"Yes, but cargo is not a glamorous way to make your millions." She hesitated. "And there were rumors..."

"I love a good rumor."

"Well, he and some Russian pilot built FastFlex from nothing. They flew those big old Soviet-style cargo planes around Africa and the Middle East after the Eastern Bloc collapsed. The very nasty rumor was maybe they flew guns into war zones, for both sides. Not that Varela was an arms dealer, no, but he was profiting off bloodshed. You know, the type of activity people picket your corporate office for. He sued some newspaper that suggested he was a dealer the UN nicknamed 'Lord Caliber.'" She laughed. "Nothing ever proven, and it was bad public relations for him for a while. But I know his company flew tons of supplies in for the US Army during the war in Iraq, and that was dangerous work, and that was all over the news here, and that was also when he donated lots of money. You'll sometimes see their planes at the airport. FastFlex, they have that red and green logo."

I hadn't heard of the company, or the family. But a word jumped out at me: "Africa." Where Steve had spent so much of his for-hire career. "The Varelas, are they in the news a lot, given all this philanthropy?"

"No, they're very low-profile. You rarely see them on the society pages. Usually because it's the wife that pushes for that, and he's gone through three of them. They all died. And one of his kids died."

"That's…awful."

"It is, but, you know, he didn't *murder* them. There was never a suspicion of that."

I thought of Cordelia in a house where tragedy was such a frequent guest.

Paige went on: "I remember, I met him once. Miami is smaller than you think. He made a big donation to the library system. I met him at a reception for all of three minutes. He seemed very nice. Rather imperial, but also quiet. He didn't look like a guy that anyone would nickname Lord Caliber. That's a family that keeps to themselves. Maybe with good reason. Tragedy builds a fence." She lowered her tone. "You think they had something to do with Steve's death?"

"Don't jump to a conclusion. The answer is no."

"Is there anything else?"

"No, thanks for this. Much appreciated."

"I could dig into them more, if you want." If this was dangerous work, she wasn't afraid.

"You're not supposed to be on a computer, Paige."

"Ask me questions, I'll tell you no lies. I need to help…this would make me feel like I was helping." Paige had been a bit snappish. We'd lost a friend. I thought maybe she was just taking it hard. This was as close to an apology as I would get. She didn't want to show she'd suffered a loss.

"Okay. Find out anything about them you can, but don't let anyone know that you're looking."

"Helping Steve. I want to…" And then she stopped. Her voice didn't break. But I had this feeling there were tears on the other side of the phone. I didn't really know what had happened between her and Steve before I met them.

"Sure. See what you can find out about the family." We hung up after agreeing to touch base the next day.

Find the map, I'd once been advised by the burnt man. The map started with the Varela family.

I leaned back. The Varelas were serious money and lived in a security-obsessed area. I found an interview online when Cordelia started the charity and read it carefully. She mentioned a twin brother, Edwin, who'd died a few years ago, the inspiration for her work with the less fortunate.

He'd been kidnapped, presumed dead, never found. I could assume the tragedy had marked the family—explained the abundant security.

I'd lost a brother. I knew how that pain felt.

I could call Cordelia Varela at Help with Love, tell her I knew who she was. She didn't want to be known. It might be best to not let her know yet. She could shut me out.

I went to the newspaper's website for the latest on the investigation in Steve's death. The police still said—at least to the press—that the motive was theft of his collectible motorcycle. The guy who'd fallen from the fire escape was a Colombian, Alberto Chavez. The guy in the hospital—Coma Thug, as I called him—was Carlos Tellez. Also from Colombia. Neither had a criminal record and both were in the country legally, having arrived via New York. There was no suggestion that they were in the stolen-motorcycle business; or that they traveled to Miami for any other reason. The only oddity was mention of a matchbook found in Coma Thug's pocket, from a nightclub in Washington, DC.

In the business we call stuff like the matchbook "pocket litter"—the everyday items on a person that could tell you a bigger story. He'd entered the United States in New York, stopped off in Washington...and then come to Miami. The resources of the Round Table might be able to unearth more information about them. I wouldn't ask Paige. These guys—and presumably their associates—were killers, and I'd have to keep her at a safe distance.

No mention of surveillance or security cameras on the North Miami property having been used to catch a glimpse of how the men died. If there was security film footage, the authorities would know for sure there was a third party—me—involved. Someone who rode the damaged bike, then escaped on foot. They might start calling cab companies. There would be an electronic record of my phone, a mile away, hailing a cab. But it had been four days. The police would have acted by now, I thought.

So I might only have as long as Carlos Tellez—Coma Thug—stayed unconscious and silent to avenge Steve. Because if he woke up and said: *The bar was closed. A man came out of the bar and followed us and that's who ran over me and killed my buddy*, well, then the suspect list would be...just me. Tick, tock, says the clock.

The next step was trying to find out more about what Steve did in working for Cordelia Varela. Since Cordelia's name hadn't come up in the investigation, I doubted he'd leave an easily found trail to her as a client. Or the news would have been full of his connection to the wealthy Cordelia Varela.

A knock at the bar's door.

I waited. The knock came again.

"We're closed," I said. "Death in the family."

"Then it is good I am here." Mila's voice came from the other side of the door.

8

I TOOK A deep breath and opened the door.

"Sam! How are you?" Mila came inside—no luggage—dressed in black jeans and a dark shirt and a black leather jacket too heavy for Miami. She looked and sounded healthy. The last time I'd seen her, she'd been recovering from multiple surgeries, drugged, her husband and I barely restraining ourselves from killing each other. Me accusing him of betraying the job that nearly got me and Mila killed, him daring me to prove it. Which I couldn't. And I couldn't really badmouth her husband. Mila was, if anything, loyal.

"I'm fine," I said. "How are you?"

"Nearly back to work," she said. "What's going on?"

"Just trying to keep the bar here afloat."

"You have no manager here."

"I barely have a bar."

"Jimmy tells me what a good job you have been doing." Jimmy hated me, but I think even he'd figured it was best to sing my praises until he found a way to usher me out of their lives. He knew Mila cared about me, as a good friend, as a colleague. This enraged him. I don't know quite how I felt about it. Her absence in my life felt like a hole, a persistent shadow, but I had Daniel to focus on, and that was best.

"This bar is a challenge. I might be here for a while."

"Any problems beyond the bar?" She met my gaze. "You've had a death in the family, after all."

"Oh, I just said…"

"Sam. After the problems in San Francisco during the Downfall incident, we set up a search program. Anytime there is a crime recorded near one of the bars I get an alert. A man died on the street here a few nights ago. I've been waiting for your call to explain what has happened."

I wanted to tell her about Steve. I hesitated. The Round Table wanted me on a leash.

Her gaze was unwavering. So I told her. Everything.

She sat down on a barstool. Normally Mila moved with an athletic grace. Now she was a bit slower. I might have been the only person who noticed. She was still recovering from her nearly fatal shooting.

"You have put yourself in a difficult situation," she said.

"They killed my friend."

She offered me a slight nod. "Yes. I understand the impulse. But you are supposed to be stronger than that. For Daniel."

"Are you here to tell me to not pursue this?"

"That milk has spilled. This man in the coma, he could know you followed them from the bar?"

"When he finds out the motorcycle came from the bar, he'll figure it out. And so will his employers."

"His employers may have figured it out already."

I shrugged. "What I did is pretty atypical. The employers may not know how it went down on the sidewalk. They might think there was a reason for Coma Thug to take the bike, to give a simple motive to the crime. He could have crashed it and been hurt. They can't be certain."

"Unless he wakes up."

"Unless he wakes up," I said. I didn't much like where the conversation was going. Maybe I'm a hypocrite. It was one thing to strike out at Coma Thug when he or his buddy had just murdered Steve. It was something else to go into a hospital room and kill a defenseless man. I would rather know who he worked for, why he killed Steve, than kill him for the sake of revenge. Let him rot in jail, it was a better punishment.

"So what do you do?"

"I stop them before they can find out about me."

She measured my resolve with her gaze. "Let us see first," she said, "who they are. Who sent them."

"Thank you. I have prints off the murder weapon I can send you."

"You have the weapon. Of course you do. Give it to me."

I went upstairs and got it from the safe and handed it over.

"And I will make calls," she said. "I will have our people dig and see who these men are." She then surprised me. "And how is Daniel?"

"Fine."

"I thought…" She hesitated, and that was very unlike her. "That…if you didn't mind, assuming that we resolve this problem, I might come soon to see Daniel. In New Orleans."

"Um, sure. Obviously I'll be in Miami a while longer…"

"It is really to see Daniel," she said quickly. "Of course, I mean, I would like to see you. I am seeing you. Right now. Of course. But I am missing that little boy so much. So much." Then she suddenly went silent, as though she'd spilled a few words too many.

Mila had risked everything to help me find and save Daniel. I loved that she loved my son. "Of course. I'll call Leonie, tell her to expect you."

"I flew down from New York today, Sam. I need to head to Los Angeles to see Jimmy. I could take a flight to New Orleans, it's on the way, tomorrow," she said. "I know Daniel's…caretaker…does not like me, but…I will stay at the apartment above the bar in New Orleans. Not at your home. I will not stay for long."

"I'm sure that will be fine." Leonie didn't care for Mila—the feeling was mutual, Mila always worried that Leonie, who knew how to create new identities for people on the run, would vanish one day with Daniel—but for Daniel's sake I expected they could treat each other with civility.

"Will Jimmy be meeting you there?" I asked. I'd prefer him nowhere near my son.

"No, no, just me. Jimmy is very busy."

Very busy using the Round Table for his own purposes, I thought. Just like last time. No matter who gets killed, or who gets hurt. But I said nothing. She wouldn't have believed a bad word against Jimmy, the man who'd saved her life years ago and brought her into this hidden world. Jimmy the golden boy. Only I knew the truth about how ruthless and ambitious he could be.

"Okay. Do you need a place to stay? I can go to a hotel and you can have the apartment upstairs."

"I have a hotel, thank you, I'm fine. And I need to go make those phone calls."

"Thank you, Mila."

"It will be okay, Sam."

She left without a handshake or hug. I watched her get into a rental car and pull away. I was glad to have her on my side, but I suspected her help would come at a price.

I called Leonie and left a message for her that Mila would be visiting and I'd like her to have all the time she wanted with Daniel.

So. The funeral was done. The police investigation was stalled or slowing. Steve's house was six or seven blocks away. I knew he worked at home. Maybe now I could pay a visit.

I stuck my set of Israeli-made lock picks in my pocket and headed out.

9

I SAW THE CAR I'd noticed at the funeral driven by the narrow cousins parked in a shallow, C-shaped driveway in Steve's lush front yard. I parked in a church lot a block away and waited; I could see his driveway from there. Forty minutes later, close to dinnertime, the two cousins left in the car. They'd been packing up Steve's belongings, preparing his house to go on the market, I presumed. If they were heading out for dinner I'd have some time alone in the house.

I left my car in the church lot and was inside the house in one minute. Steve had a security system, but it hadn't been activated by the cousins. I closed the door behind me. I could see half-filled boxes. I feared that some important link to Cordelia Varela had, unrealized, unseen, already been packed up.

The house was bigger than a single person needed and I thought this explained why he spent so much time at Stormy's. There wasn't a lot of furniture, even before the narrow cousins arrived to clean house. Pictures of Steve with his parents still hung on the walls. The cousins had already boxed up the plates and the silverware in the kitchen, which gave me hope they weren't bringing dinner back to the house. They hadn't yet tackled Steve's surprisingly large number of books on his shelves. You pack up belongings more slowly in grief, I think. It took my parents a long time to put away my brother's stuff: his books, his clothes, the photos of him and the friends he always made at our many stops around the world, the paperbacks on his shelf, the video games stacked next to the television. His pocket litter, the bits and pieces that defined his life. It felt like giving up hope, although we'd seen the video, we'd seen him die.

I stopped in front of the bookshelf; it reached from floor to ceiling. The books were mostly history, from all parts of the world. On the top two shelves there were many books about Africa. Nonfiction, short-story collections, poetry. He must have loved his time there. The library made me feel I'd underestimated him again.

His bedroom had been packed up as well, the bed stripped. Clothes were sorted and piled, one under a sticky note marked DONATE, one under KEEP. Inside I saw shirts I'd seen Steve wear and my skin felt cold. Another box kept financial papers, credit card accounts, bank statements. I took a picture of the credit card account numbers and of the bank account numbers on my smartphone. It might give me a trail to follow.

Client files. I paged through them. He'd worked security for high-dollar fund-raisers, law firms, visiting celebrities. The files were alphabetized and Cordelia Varela wasn't listed.

But fund-raisers? I paged back through the tabs listing the client names. HELP WITH LOVE. Cordelia's charity. He'd worked security at a black-tie event there several months ago. I took the file.

But what I wanted to find was a hiding place. Bathrooms are always good choices and nothing had been packed in there yet. I carefully searched the space below the sink. Nothing. The cabinet above the toilet. Nothing. I opened the medicine cabinet. He had a few prescriptions. No surprises.

Except for the hair gel. I'd never seen Steve wearing hair gel. I picked up the squat container and shook. A clatter. I opened it, and inside the empty container was a blood-red rectangular plastic chip. I held it up to the light. The label read *Gran Fortuna Casino, San Juan, Puerto Rico*. Those rectangular plaques were often used for very high denominations—think ten thousand dollars and higher. I looked for the number but instead there was a letter on it—X. No money denomination. And a short serial number, in the corner, very small. Weird. I'd never seen a casino chip like this.

I pocketed it. Put the hair-gel container back in the cabinet.

I made another fast pass through the house. Nothing.

Then I heard the front door opening. The cousins. I stepped out past the closed curtains, onto the back porch. Waited for them to speak.

But they weren't saying anything. Silence.

Not the cousins, then. Someone else. I had no desire to get into a fight or try to subdue and question someone inside Steve's house. I wasn't armed. There was a better way.

I moved, silently, to the stone wall and went over. Snuck through the neighbor's yard and back out onto the street.

I went back to my rented Honda. The cousins' car wasn't parked out front, so it wasn't them. I waited. Ten, fifteen minutes. I saw a man come out of Steve's backyard. He was thin, with dark hair and wearing a really unfortunate beige jacket that looked like it had last been popular in the '70s. Had those come back into style? I guess so. I wear good suits at the nicer bars I own but normally don't pay attention to such trends. It wasn't really jacket weather, so I figured he had a reason to wear it other than warmth. He hurried down the street and got into an older but nicely maintained Mercedes.

He drove. I followed, at a discreet distance. He went to Little Havana, not far from the cemetery where we'd laid Steve to rest, and he parked and went into a small Cuban restaurant. It was a two-story place, brightly painted in yellows and greens, with a red staircase going up the side. I circled the block and parked on a side street where I could see the front door and the staircase door.

And I waited. And I waited. And I waited and called Mila to spell me but she didn't answer her phone and I thought she might well have left Miami already. I cussed the guy out under my breath but I didn't want to leave for fear I'd lose him. I didn't want a restaurant, I wanted a house, an address where I could find out more easily who he was.

At eleven that night, on the dot, my target came back out of the Cuban restaurant and he got into his car and drove away. I followed him, keeping back a couple of cars—not hard with night traffic in Miami.

He drove over to Miami Beach, where, if I had any sense, I'd own a bar and rake in the cash from the beautiful people.

He pulled in at the Corinthian. It was one of the oldest, most iconic Miami Beach hotels and a few years ago it had undergone a massive renovation costing hundreds of millions. We both had to wait in a long line of cars, driving up one of the few inclined driveways in Miami—it was an artificial hill—while a squadron of scrambling valets dealt with the crowd. A lot of people arriving, not all of them hotel guests—the Corinthian being a dining and nightclub destination in itself. I pulled up into the massive porte cochere, which the valets organized with the intensity of air traffic controllers, yelling, pointing, making sure the Range Rovers, Maseratis, and Teslas didn't nudge one another. My Honda was the most modest car, by far. You always have to wonder how much money is in Miami and where it all comes from.

I saw my target undertip his valet, and then head into the hotel.

10

I FOLLOWED HIM down a long marble hallway, several people between us, staying back, until he reached a huge lobby area with a
vast open bar on the right, the floors aglow with soft green light.
On the opposite side of the lobby was the entrance to a nightclub,
more exclusive, with a roped line of optimistic partygoers already
formed. He walked right up to the bouncers, dressed in his nerdy
jacket and his pants that were a tad too short, and the bouncers
and the stylish hostess nodded at him and let him pass.

I did not expect that. They knew who he was. I heard a woman
in the line say, "You must be kidding me."

I hurried into the line for the nightclub, a place named, according to the massive gold sign on the wall: (Or). Or what, I thought.
It was an unanswerable question. How did one pronounce the
parentheses? I was still in my funeral suit—dark Armani, sans
tie—so I was dressed appropriately. I wear very good suits when
I'm at my fancy bars but didn't break out this particular suit ever
at Stormy's, only for Steve's funeral. But I was a guy without a
girl, and you know how that works at a hot club. I'd get denied.
Not to mention I knew a high-end club like (Or) would have reserved tables. I surveyed the line. Tourists, who might not have
known their hotel concierges could have gotten them tickets or
onto a guest list. Lots of young women, in very short skirts and
very high heels. The Miami look. You'd think the medical money

in this town would be in plastic surgery, but I think it must be in twisted or broken ankles. But no way I was getting in on my own with no reservation. I needed a strategy. I needed that jewel, a confused tourist.

There were two beautiful women in front of me, maybe a couple of years younger than me. They spoke French to each other, glancing around with the excitement that comes only from being a tourist. They were stylish: pretty but dark dresses instead of the neon Miami color palette, skirts slightly more modest. One with black hair, one a brunette. They consulted each other, glancing at their papers.

A reservation slip, or a ticket.

An advantage of having grown up all over the world was that I had to learn new languages fairly quickly. Lots of developing countries are Francophone. I tapped the brunette on the shoulder and smiled when she turned to me and said in French, "Pardon me, I don't wish to bother you, but I couldn't help but overhear you speak French. Welcome to Miami. Is this your first time at this club?" My accent was clean enough to let them hear I wouldn't massacre their native tongue.

"Thank you, yes! You are American? Or maybe Québécois?"

"American."

"Where did you learn to speak?" They could have said, "Congrats on speaking French," and turned their backs on me. But they didn't.

"All over," I said. "I lived in Senegal and Côte d'Ivoire and Haiti as a child." We chatted, in rapid French, while we waited and I told them about other clubs, restaurants, places to avoid. Their names were Rébeque and Justine. Rébeque had lovely black hair and eyes, Justine was the brunette. I'd spent so much time with the regulars at Stormy's—none of whom were my age—I realized I hadn't really talked to a woman my own age, face-to-face, in two weeks beyond asking her what she wanted to drink or if she wanted to start a tab or why my friend was dead. Cordelia was my age, Mila was a few years older. I pushed the thought of both of them away.

"Do you know how long the line takes?" Rébeque peered down the line, which hadn't moved in the past ten minutes.

"Oh, no, I think you are in the wrong line," I said, pointing at her ticket. "You have bought a table, yes?"

"Yes. The concierge at our hotel made us a reservation."

"There is another line, usually, if you have the ticket," I said.

The two women glanced at each other. "Where do we go?"

"I'm not sure, but I'll help you find it."

"But then you'll lose your place in line," Justine said. The queue behind us had grown substantially—guys in overdecorated shirts, wearing sunglasses as midnight approached, groups of women clustering together, inspecting one another's makeup, doing their best to not look impatient. To not look like it mattered or not if you passed the steely eye of the hostess and the bouncers.

I shrugged. "I'm probably not going to get in anyway."

For a moment their delighted smiles dimmed. "But why?" Justine asked.

"I'm a guy, alone. No way will the bouncer let me in—I thought the crowd would be so much smaller this early." Time to play a card. "Could I pretend to be with you two? They'll believe it with us all speaking French together. And the drinks are on me." Considering a beer or a vodka and cranberry juice can run twenty bucks at a place like this, it wasn't an idle promise. Even if their reservation covered drinks, I'd figure a way to treat them.

Rébeque and Justine were delighted to take part in a minor deception. They linked arms with me as we found the VIP line and we drew close to the gatekeeper's inspection and I murmured in French to them ("I hope this works") and Justine whispered back, "I'm sure it will. We'll make it work," and then she kissed me on the cheek for show while Rébeque batted eyelashes at the bouncer as she handed him the reservation slip for two and he checked it against his list.

He waved us in, even though we were three. (Or) was very new and shiny and dazzling. A vast dome, flooded with programmable colored lights above us, forming and breaking gorgeous patterns, like a church ceiling by Michelangelo on acid. A large middle section, two VIP sections above the main floor. Electronic dance mixes swirled over the space—as we entered boomed Deadmau5 and Kaskade's nine-minute remix of "I Remember," with soaring angelic vocals. (You own enough nightclubs, you hear a lot of electronic dance music, and you can name that tune in five beats.) Halos of fog, DJs with an array of laptops, sunglasses on as if their screens blinded them. Crowded, but not yet to the point where you couldn't see across the entire room. We were taken to an upstairs table near a bar. I gave the waiter Justine's credit card and mine and told him to transfer the charges from hers to mine. With the ladies' approval, I ordered French Champagne. At the end of the VIP section bar I could see the guy in the jacket, sitting alone. But he wasn't facing the bar, nursing a drink. He had turned the barstool around and was sitting, and watching, and I let my gaze track his.

Not far from the bar was another table, with a man and a woman, the two of them in their own world. The man was about thirty-five or so, broad-shouldered, arms heavy with muscle, hair black. He wore a fitted suit to show off the physique. He was listening to the woman but tuning her out at the same time: he had a bored, indulgent look. Like he'd had a lot of practice.

The woman was a stunner. Brown hair, cut in a pixie style, in a short, glittery dress. She had her hand on the man's knee and was whispering furiously in his ear.

I glanced back at the man in the jacket who'd kept me waiting on a Little Havana street for hours. I cordially hated him. He sat, watching them. Waiting for them to finish? Or waiting to be summoned, like an errand boy, I suddenly thought. They didn't want him at the table, not just yet.

I figured he'd either be bringing them whatever he'd found—had I missed something valuable?—or he'd be bringing a report. Who sends someone to burgle the house of a murdered man and then makes him wait on a barstool?

Did you kill my friend? I wondered, watching the pair. *Did you order the Colombians to kill Steve? What's your connection to Cordelia Varela?*

Champagne, perfectly chilled, arrived. I toasted Justine and Rébeque. They were laughing, glancing around the club, slightly amazed at how cool and hip it was. But Justine frowned.

"You can tell they're not letting in guys yet," Justine said. "Way too many women here."

"I don't want to interfere with your evening." I wasn't the right kind of guy for them to meet anyway. They'd done me a favor and I needed to deal with my targets. "Thank you for helping me get inside."

Justine gave me a smile. A warm smile. My throat went a little dry. She was so pretty and nice. Like most modern men I try to be a bit more analytical than that...but she was. "Please don't go. You saved us from the purgatory of the line and you're a gentleman. Sam, we're very glad we met you."

I tried not to notice the promise in her voice.

"So where are the people you are looking for?" Rébeque asked. I glanced at her in surprise.

"Did I say I was looking for someone?" I said with an awkward smile.

"We're not idiots, Sam," Justine smiled. "I start grad school in architecture next semester, and Rébeque is a lawyer. It was clear you didn't just want to get in here to scope the scene, or just to flirt with us. You had the determined air."

"Yes. I'm looking for someone."

"A girlfriend?" Justine raised an eyebrow.

"No. Just some people I am curious about."

"What are you, a detective?" Rébeque asked, smiling over her Champagne flute.

"No, but I used to be a spy."

They laughed at my oh-so-funny joke.

I didn't know what else to say. Rébeque and Justine drank Champagne and the music swelled, although not many were dancing. The club's lights were dim and broken flashes of light swam across the darkness. The pixie haircut drew back from the big guy and he reached out and grabbed her wrist hard. I didn't like that. But she wrenched it free and said something to him, and he then he put his large hand, very gently, on the side of her cheek. He spoke and she listened.

Then he gestured over the guy in the jacket.

II

I saw the jacket leave his spot on the bar and approach them. He sat down next to the big guy, across from the pixie haircut, and leaned forward so they could both hear him over Radiohead's classic song "Kid A" remixed into a dance number. I watched.

"Is that them?" Justine asked. Her knee brushed up against mine.

"I think," I said.

"Ah, is the cute woman your friend? Clearly she's not interested in you." Her knee stayed put. I didn't move mine either.

"Who's the big guy?" Rébeque asked. "He's handsome, if I'm being clinical about it."

"I don't know either of them," I said.

"Ah. So the short man in the unfortunate jacket." Justine sipped at her Champagne. "He has caught your eye."

"I had a friend who died recently," I said. And at this they both set their glasses down and looked at me seriously. "And that man might know something about his death." I felt I could be honest with them. They were smart and nice. I needed allies. Even if only for ten minutes.

Justine and Rébeque looked at each other and then at me. "Are you making this up?" Rébeque asked.

"No." I watched the short man speak with the couple. The woman with the pixie haircut felt the weight of my stare and then she looked toward me. I broke the gaze and refilled my new friends' flutes with the excellent bubbly. I looked up and she was watching us, and then she put her attention back on the jacket.

The big man was nodding, happy with what he was hearing from the jacket. Not the pixie. I could see her tenting her cheek with her tongue, angry, then leaning back.

So the big guy likes what he's hearing about Steve's condo, the pixie doesn't, I guessed. She leaned close to the jacket and spoke a few words. He shrugged and got up and went back to his spot at the bar, reclaimed the barstool.

"I could go," Rébeque said, "and ask him to buy me a drink."

"Absolutely not," I said. "He could be dangerous."

"In a crowded bar? With dozens of witnesses around?" She definitely sounded like a lawyer, ready to argue her point.

I didn't look at the other table and I said, "What are they doing?"

"Not sure," Justine answered. She had turned her back to them, but Rébeque could watch.

"They're talking. That woman seems distinctly unhappy."

I glanced up at the pixie just as she drew a finger across her neck.

"Actually," Rébeque added, "she seems a little murderous."

12

THE BIG GUY shook his head in answer to the woman's cutthroat gesture.

Maybe they're just joking and not contemplating a second murder, I thought. People make gestures all the time that don't mean anything. But. The jacket had broken into Steve's house. And I felt sure that either the jacket or the big guy was the man Cordelia spoke to on her phone, when I wiretapped her at the bookstore café. A brother. They'd both referred to "Papa."

This was the thread. This was the way into the maze. I could feel it. If these were the bad guys, then they were in conflict. Disagreement was a door-opener, an opportunity.

Justine figured it out too. "Hey, Sam. We need to give Rébeque a reason to talk to the short man. She needs to feel—what is the phrase?—extra. A third wheel."

So she nuzzled my neck, put her hand on my back.

"This is a bad idea," I said, catching my breath. Justine's mouth traced along my jawline.

"I feel so uncomfortable," Rébeque said. "You two are making me feel unwelcome. I should go and give you privacy." Her voice sounded almost merry.

Justine turned my face to hers and gave me a gentle kiss. I let her do it. Then I kissed her back, very softly, so it could feel like we were just playacting. It had been a long time. She was smart and beautiful and I could be dead soon like Steve.

"I don't normally do this while assisting people in tracking geeks," Justine said. But she kept her lips close to mine. Her mouth tasted of wine and mint. She laced her fingers in my hair.

"It's appreciated," I said.

Rébeque made a grand show of setting down her Champagne flute in irritation. "Now you ignore me for a guy you just met. Some friend," she said in loud, heavily accented English, and shrugged in that Gallic way that conveyed to any onlookers her deep annoyance. She walked toward the bar, recovered her dignity, and placed herself next to the jacket, a wounded look on her face. I decided Rébeque would be quite the performer in the courtroom. Juries must love her.

"I suppose," Justine said, her mouth close to mine, her finger against my jawline, "you need to spy on those tiresome people."

I wanted to say, *I'm a dad. My first wife was a traitor. I used to be a spy. You don't want to get close to me.* But I said none of that and just said, "I suppose I do."

She said, "Nuzzle my neck and you can look over my shoulder."

I did. Her neck, lightly perfumed, smelled so good, of honey, of flowers I couldn't even name. The big guy and the pixie were still arguing, but it had shifted in its heat: the pixie was lecturing the big guy, using her fingers to count whatever grievances she had.

I leaned back from Justine, smiling.

"If you're really chasing that woman, I'll be disappointed," Justine said.

"I'm not."

"I leave Miami tomorrow." She glanced over at Rébeque. "Unless I don't."

"You have school, Justine."

"It's not starting right away."

"Rébeque is talking to that man in the jacket. He has bought her a glass of wine."

"And you are stuck here with me. The man in the jacket has no chance. Rébeque has a wonderful boyfriend back in Lyon."

"And you?"

"And I don't." Her mouth was close to mine again. Her hand was on my knee. I glanced over her shoulder and saw the pixie slap the big guy.

Hard. I heard the impact of flesh over the thrumming beat of the music.

13

THE BIG GUY stood, but not in a threatening way. The security guards around the reserved section took several steps toward the big guy's table.

The big guy shook his head, almost sadly, and rubbed his cheek and the pixie didn't seem to know what to do after the slap. She stumbled away from him, and she stormed past us, glancing once over at the jacket, who had no eyes for her and was loudly testing his high-school French on Rébeque, who was pretending to be charmed by his linguistic incompetence.

I wondered what I'd seen.

I sat down and the big guy had cast his gaze around at every man who looked inclined to come to the pixie's rescue. Including me, for the briefest of moments, but I wasn't a threat because Justine was playing with my hair, and I turned my face away in the dim lights.

When I glanced at him again, the big guy was alone, at a table full of expensive wine and with seats around it. Lost in thought. Maybe his heart was broken. Maybe he was thinking about Steve Robles dying in a pool of rain and blood.

Then I saw him gesture toward the jacket and Rébeque. He might not be used to being alone, or he might be ready to move on to the next woman and I thought: *No, no, no, come back to us, don't do it...*

But Rébeque did. She went and sat down with the jacket, shook hands with the big guy, who stood to greet her with a polite smile. The jacket sat on the big guy's right and Rébeque, very smart, sat next to him rather than next to the big guy.

The jacket poked the slapped cheek of the big guy and shook his head and the big guy shrugged, but didn't look happy. However, he put a polite smile on for Rébeque. A natural host.

"I don't like this," I said. "These could be dangerous people."

"Rébeque is a lawyer," Justine reminded me, as if this imparted an ability to deal with the unruly. "She'll be fine. So. What do you do?"

"I own a bar here. Several, actually. Including two in France."

"Very cool! In Lyon?"

"No. Paris and Strasbourg."

"Tragedy." Justine smiled at me again, and how long had that been: a woman looking at me and not wanting anything more than my company? Mila, with her endless agendas; Leonie, wanting me to grant her a special, permanent place in my son's life. Lucy, my ex, with her catalog of lies, even when she said she loved me.

"Yes, it is. I've never been sorrier I don't own a bar in Lyon."

"No, I meant, final night. Like in a book. I meet an interesting guy my final night here."

"You say that only because I'm totally using you and your friend."

"Ah. We'd come in here and some guy would try to pick us up, then find out we were French and make bad jokes about chain smoking or surrendering too easily. I thought the guys in Miami were more sophisticated." She laughed.

"I don't like Rébeque hanging out with these guys." My fear for her had turned into a fist in my chest. "It's a bad idea."

"It will be fine," Justine said.

I glanced over again. The big man was leaning forward, elbows on knees, talking animatedly to Rébeque, who was laughing politely. She had a fresh glass of wine set in front of her.

This went on for forty minutes. Rébeque and the jacket danced once, then the big guy and Rébeque danced, but he didn't seem too into it. As though distracted. Then they returned to the table, drank wine and spoke some more, then the big man and the jacket got up and they all said their good-byes. I kept my back turned to them.

Rébeque slinked back to our table.

"I've been a wreck," I said as she sat down.

"Ah, they're harmless," Rébeque said. "The handsome guy is named Galo, the fashion failure is Ricky."

"I have to follow them," I said.

"Ah," Justine said. "You and your obsessions."

"I'll be back," I said. "Stay and have fun, I've covered the tab."

Justine gave me a doubtful look. "You're not coming back, Sam."

"I am."

She touched my jaw with her fingertip. It felt wonderful. "Well, we'll see. Take the ticket with you, so you can get back in."

"Thank you both so much," I said. I kissed Justine on the forehead and I hurried out of the club. I'd lost sight of Galo and Ricky and then I spotted them, separating, shaking hands at the valet station. I decided to follow Galo.

It was a ten-minute wait, given the crowds. I'd given my claim ticket to the valet and then I returned to the corner of the porte cochere, pretended to study my phone's screen while the two men spoke softly. Once Galo laughed. Ricky shook his head. I got an old-friend vibe off of them. They paid me no mind.

Our cars arrived roughly at the same time, delivered by the swarming flock of valets. Ricky got into his old Mercedes; Galo got into a newer Porsche; I followed him out of the lot. I hung back, just barely keeping him in sight.

I followed Galo's Porsche to an Art Deco apartment building on South Beach. The crowds on the street were thick with those wanting to see, and wanting to be seen. (This modern need for attention from total strangers confuses me.) I watched him go inside. Okay, an address, I could do something with that.

But I thought of Justine and told myself, *Go see her.* Just to say thanks and good-bye. I wheeled back to the Corinthian. I got back into **(Or)**; the bouncer remembered me—"French dude!" he laughed—and waved me in. On the dance floor, I could see Justine and Rébeque dancing with a pair of young guys. The guys were well dressed and probably had nice, normal jobs. Justine didn't see me. She gave her dance partner a polite smile, but not as nice as the one she'd given me.

I watched for a moment, full of regret, then I went back to the valet station and I went home. I hadn't reopened Stormy's since Steve died and I thought of the money flowing like a river into (Or), probably earning more tonight than Stormy's cleared in a year. I could charge twenty bucks for a beer and see if I could catch up.

I went upstairs to the humble, slightly shabby apartment. I wouldn't have wanted Justine to see this dump anyway, I thought, not after the glamour of the Corinthian. I sat on the edge of the bed. I could feel her lips against mine. We'd wanted each other and that was okay. I was twenty-six, divorced from a traitor, with an infant son, and chasing murderers. What was I doing with my life?

14

I FELL BACK on the bed and thought, *Give up the bars. Hand them back to Mila, quit working for the Table, figure out something else to do with your life.* Then I thought of Steve, laughing. My brother, pleading for his life on the grainy, low-grade video. Helping an innocent young man in New York whom some very bad people wanted me to kill in an unholy exchange. A woman in San Francisco, whispering *Help me* before all hell broke loose and people started trying to murder her.

Was I more moved by the unexpected dangers people faced, or the feel of Justine's lips against my own? Duty or life?

Back in my brain the fire lit. I got up and went to the computer. I had an e-mail from an address I hadn't seen before, an address that was mostly random letters and numbers. It was a report, a summation of press clippings about the Varela family, from newspapers, magazines, news services. Librarians never sleep, I guess, especially ones on parole. She wasn't supposed to be on the computer, but the e-mail wasn't signed, there was nothing in the address to suggest it had come from librarian-turned-criminal-mastermind Paige. I opened the report and my gaze locked on the words "Galo Varela."

He was Cordelia's older brother; no doubt the one I'd heard on the telephone tap. He was a senior vice-president at FastFlex, his father's cargo transport company. He had been arrested twice for fighting when he was younger, both times acquitted—this wasn't from a news report, but a personal note from the rogue librarian, who'd made some phone calls to those in the know. He'd also been valedictorian of his class in an expensive private school, played football for the Miami Hurricanes, although not as a starter, and trained as a pilot before getting his MBA. Made sense when your family was in the aviation business. Galo had been groomed for success.

He must've known Cordelia hired Steve. Was he behind the Colombians? Why kill a man hired by his own sister?

I scanned the articles Paige had pulled. Reynaldo Varela—who went by "Rey"—had three children: Galo, Cordelia, and Edwin, the son who'd been kidnapped and killed. I studied the photo of Edwin from the newspaper; you could tell he was Cordelia's brother, the resemblance was strong. Rey had been married, and widowed, three times. Unlucky in love. He had a stepdaughter named Zhanna from the final wife. A quick summary told me he'd built his company with a Russian business partner, flying cargo on routes between Europe, the Mideast, and Africa after the Cold War on surplus Russian aircraft behemoths such as IL-76s and Antonovs. Those planes were the hardy workhorses of the Soviet Air Force, and Rey and his partner made runs where they dodged missiles and customs and kept the planes together with luck and glue. They flew cargo such as flowers and fish and medical supplies. FastFlex eventually expanded and settled their base back to his hometown in Miami, flying runs to South and Central America and the Caribbean and the western coast of Africa. He'd kept the company family owned and bought out his Russian partner, Sergei Pozharsky, and poured a lot of money back into the business. He'd flourished in a big way. He'd slowly built his millions and been generous back to the city—all confirming what Paige told me earlier. He had a good quote from an article, when asked about running an airline: "Cargo does not complain like passengers do." It made me smile, for a moment. Not a lot else. Nothing really about the man, what had driven him to build this business, what he was like in the wake of losing three wives and a son.

I wondered who the fiery pixie was. There was no mention that Galo was married. A girlfriend? I looked up the address in South Beach on the online property tax records. Twenty-four apartments in the building. No Varelas listed as owners, no names I recognized. Some names looked corporate.

I took out the casino plaque. This might have been what Galo sent Ricky to look for; I'd just found it first. Maybe this was my ticket to getting inside the maze of the Varelas.

———

My lessons from the inside:

The burnt man said, leaning forward, "When you're an inside man, you have one job. Find the thread."

"The thread?"

"The thread. You are pretending to be something you are not. You are not on a stage. You are in a maze, a labyrinth. You have to pick up the thread that leads you out of the maze, like Perseus in the old myth. You go into the maze, you kill the monster, you follow the thread out."

I blinked. "The monster was called the minotaur."

"Yeah, I know. But concentrate on the thread." Here his voice rose in a hoarse whisper. I wondered if his vocal cords had been singed. "It's the information, or the person, that takes you into the maze, all the twists, to get to the heart of what you need. Either the person you need to bring to the CIA, or the information we need, or the object we need. You pick up the thread. The thread takes you into the heart of darkness and then leads you home."

"Um, in the story, Perseus didn't pick up a thread to find the monster. The thread was his way of getting out."

"It works both ways for an inside man," the burnt man said.

"So what's the thread?"

"It can be a person. A guide. Someone you make trust you. Or information that makes you irresistible to the people you're infiltrating. Makes you golden. Hey, wasn't Perseus's thread golden?"

"I don't remember. This is your story, you should know."

He leaned back and his eye stared at me from his ruined face. "You think this is a waste of time."

"No, sir, I don't. I'm just trying to understand."

"Inside man, you got to have attitude. You're not there to play a part. You're there to get in, get what you came for, get out. It might take you five minutes or five years."

I laid back on my bed. I thought of the burnt man and what had happened to him the one time he didn't take his own advice. I wondered what Justine was doing with the guy who'd moved in after I left. I wondered if I might ever see her again. No, probably not. For the best.

There was one way to find out what the chip was worth.

Go to Puerto Rico and see what happened when I tried to redeem it at the casino.

I undressed and I went to bed, my thoughts full of Justine and Cordelia Varela and the regulars at the bar, mourning Steve, the rounds to be bought no more, and that little flame in the back of my brain burning to put the world right. But what I dreamed of was Coma Thug awakening and pointing at my picture, and the taxi driver telling the police he'd picked me up carrying a motorcycle helmet less than a mile from Coma Thug's broken body, and Cordelia Varela sitting in a courtroom and saying, *Sam lied to the police, where do I even start?* So many ways for my life to unravel, because I had to fix the world, make them pay for Steve. That night I dreamed of the strong hand pulling me and my family from the wrecked car, flames along the side of the road as the scrubby grassland began to burn, jets rumbling above as the besieged airport emptied. In the dream I reached up toward one of the planes and in the weird bent physics of dreams Rey Varela looked down at me from the window.

Come on, Sam, let's hurry. Don't cry. It'll all be okay, Steve said.

My life was still a debt unpaid.

15

THE NEXT MORNING I called in a favor.

I called the CIA.

Or rather, I called a back corner of the CIA, where my oldest friend in the agency, August Holdwine, was a fast-rising star. He and I had both worked for Special Projects, a group that sounds like they might design databases or handle career day at Virginia high schools. What they handle are dirty jobs. The ones that can never be owned or claimed. Because they tread on the territories of law enforcement or overseas agencies. I called August at a number he'd given me for emergencies and left a message.

He called me back in ten minutes, even though it was a Saturday. "How's the kiddo?"

"Daniel's great. He's awesome."

"You could send me a picture now and then of my godson."

"I don't really want his photo going into a CIA archive because I sent it over the official wires."

"He might be the only baby in the world who already has a CIA file, Sam, it's fine. I have a home e-mail account you can use."

August had sent Daniel a onesie from the University of Minnesota—where August had played linebacker—and I told myself to remember to have Leonie put him in it and send a picture to his godfather. The bribery involved in espionage isn't always what you expect. "All right. I need a favor."

He waited to hear it.

"The old Sam Chevalier identity," I said. "Can you reactivate it for me?"

Long pause. I waited.

"Why?" he asked.

"I might need to travel under a different name, briefly, and have a different credit history." I'd decided redeeming the chip as Sam Capra might be too dangerous. Plus, if there was money tied to cashing in the chip, I didn't want it going to my bank account. Better to act under a different name.

"Don't you have these bars to keep you out of trouble?"

"I'm not in trouble. A guy who saved my family during our relief-work days, he got killed. The police aren't doing much. I have a lead but I don't want the bad guys to know my real name if I get too close to them. Because of your godson."

It's awful to use your child as a trump card. "Sam Chevalier," August repeated.

"The talented yet not exactly noble Mr. Chevalier holds dual citizenship with Canada and the United States but travels on a Canadian passport. I used that name as a cover on a few jobs in Hungary and Czech Republic. He's ex–Canadian Army, muscle and enforcer for smuggling rings. I need him to have a credit history and passport and charge cards, and pocket litter active over the past two years. I'll wire you the money to fund the charge cards. The person connected to this already knows me as Sam, I can't suddenly use a different first name."

"That Mila friend of yours, she could arrange you a new name, couldn't she?" August knew of Mila, but he had no detailed knowledge of the Round Table. He only had suspicions.

"First, don't sound jealous, and second, that would be illegal, August." I pretended to be shocked at the thought.

"And you as ex-CIA using a CIA-sponsored identity isn't? Totally illegal. I could lose my job."

"There's no risk. Just file me as an informant, then, using the identity. Or consider me a freelance contractor you hired. Whatever is less paperwork."

"Like I would commit any of this to paper. This is a bad idea, Sam."

"It's Mr. Chevalier to you, sir."

"Sam, honestly. I can't. You're not a contractor."

"Pay me a penny and I am."

He went silent and I waited for him to decide. "I don't know, Sam."

"Okay, listen. If I get any interesting intelligence out of this—I mean, come on, they killed a guy with an overseas security background and I think his history had something to do with his death"—(I really have no shame about small lies)—"then I'll give you all I learn."

"And then I have to rinse and clean the product so it looks legit." Product equals information in August-speak. The information has to come from a credible source. That was not necessarily someone who was thrown out of Special Projects and who asked to borrow a retired ID.

"It's just sitting there, no one's using it. No one will know."

He said nothing and I pounced, like a salesman knowing the yes is on the prospect's lips.

"Look, August, you simply say you reassigned the Chevalier cover to someone who's still undercover. Encrypt the file, reclassify it. My name doesn't have to come anywhere near it. Then when I'm done, you delete the reassignment notation, as it was a misfile, an accident. Please. They killed this guy in cold blood; he was just trying to do the right thing. Let me get enough to give the police an anonymous tip. They won't know how to find me, and Sam Chevalier won't exist. If I get caught, I'll fall on the grenade. Say I hacked the system using an old password, I reactivated the identity, you had nothing to do with it."

"This really matters to you."

"It does."

"All right," he said. "I'll do it. I'll have a passport, driver's license, credit cards, and bank accounts updated for you. I'll have the Oliver Twists"—this was Special Projects' team of very young, very capable, and very deniable hackers—"create a financial history for you. You'll have them tonight."

"I'm in Miami. Please open the accounts there. Thank you, August."

"I miss you, man," he said. Like I mentioned, I don't have a lot of friends. August had filled the role my brother Danny had in my life after Danny's murder—though no one could ever replace Danny—but our time working together was past. August had his life; I had mine. He had a brilliant career; I had this. Running bars and trying to settle scores for those who couldn't. I'd not been able to take the credit for bringing down the people who'd framed me and driven me out of the CIA, but August helped me destroy them and he was the one who looked like the golden boy to the agency.

And I was fine with that. As long as he did what I wanted him to do.

"I miss you, too," I said. "When this is done, come to Miami and have a drink. It's the worst bar yet."

He laughed. "You mean it's not all elegant joints like your place in Manhattan?"

"Sadly, no." I thanked him again and said my good-byes. Then I wired the money to a Special Projects account at a bank in Virginia so he could fund the accounts. That was a problematic paper trail, but I'd worry about erasing it later.

August was better than his word. That afternoon, I was behind the bar watching the World's Worst Bartender—a nominal employee who had actually arrived for his shift, and was managing to pour wine badly for Paige, splashing half of it on the napkin—when a young man came in and walked up to me with a package. He wore a suit and he looked tired. "Sam?"

"Yes?" I said. "That's me." Paige said nothing. The World's Worst struggled to get the cork back in the bottle.

The courier handed me the package. "From your friend in a special place."

"That was fast."

"I flew down at your friend's request. If you could first inspect and see that all is well?"

"Come with me for a minute." We went upstairs and I opened the package. Passport. Three credit cards. Bank accounts, including one close by at a small regional bank. A Florida driver's license with a false address. The two photo IDs used old CIA pictures of me. I'd only been out of the agency for several months. I didn't look very different, although I had been a very different—more trusting, naïve—man when the pictures were taken.

"Perfect. Thank you."

"Then I'm done."

"Would you like a drink?"

"No, thank you. I have a flight waiting for me at the airport to take me back to your friend. Oh, and this." He pulled a teddy bear from the bag. "Mr. Holdwine said you would deliver this to a certain individual."

I smiled. "Tell Mr. Holdwine I am very grateful to him." The courier nodded and left.

I studied my face on the passport. Sam Chevalier. I played a part when I played him, and he wasn't a particularly nice guy. I thought of Galo and his intense stare, of the dark-haired woman and the fire in her eyes. I thought of Steve, dead in the street. I thought of the two men who'd been sent to kill him.

Going back into the game was like putting on an old coat, one that felt familiar and yet you're not sure it will still quite fit.

I went back downstairs and Paige said, "Does this have something to do with our project?" The World's Worst had gone outside, where there were a couple more customers.

"Yes. Can't say more right now. I need to go clothes shopping."

She frowned. "Why?"

"Because I need to look a little seedy. A little down on my luck." Sam Chevalier did not wear Armani.

"Standing in this dump, you're halfway there."

"My clothes don't exactly suit where I need to go."

"There's a resale shop a few streets over."

"You want to go shopping with me? We can leave him in

charge for an hour." I nodded toward the World's Worst, who'd reappeared in the doorway.

"All right."

Paige and I went and bought the clothes, the second step of camouflage, of being seen as someone new. When the ever-tasteful Paige held up a shirt or a pair of pants and said, "Ew," I'd buy it. When we got back, I went upstairs. I used the new credit cards to make my flight reservations for the next day. They worked fine.

I went into the bathroom and washed my face and looked at myself in the mirror. I could feel the Sam Capra I'd promised myself I'd be take a little step back, into the shadows. Someone else moved into the light. A new me, a pretend me. I was Sam Chevalier again.

16

THE NEXT MORNING, I flew from Miami to San Juan, Puerto Rico. My new driver's license evoked no suspicion from the TSA agent. I wasn't bringing a gun with me so there was no extra paperwork. I did not take my fancy, loaded-with-spy-apps phone—if it were examined, I couldn't explain it. I took a regular phone. I looked, um, sharp: a tropical-weight suit, slightly worn, the cuffs close to being frayed. A loud purple tie, not fully knotted at the throat, a yellow shirt that was a little too close to canary-bright. There was a lot of gel in my dark-blond hair. I never put gel in my hair. But it wasn't my hair anymore. It was Sam Chevalier's.

The flight took off and I closed my eyes and the burnt man danced up from the darkness.

"You live your legend. You are that person. You react, think, act as that person. It's not acting. It's a brain transplant. You get a new brain in your body."

"I know."

"Don't sound impatient with me, Sam."

"Every few months," I said, "my family moved. To a new country. I was continually the new kid. I could reinvent myself however I wanted. I could be the brainy, quiet kid in Senegal. I could be the loud, athletic kid in Thailand. I could be the loner in Haiti, I could be gregarious in Belarus."

"You're not special. Don't be overconfident," the burnt man said.

"I'm not overconfident. I'm motivated."

"Because bad guys killed your brother? Motivation would be going to Afghanistan and killing them yourself. That's motivation. Not just signing up for the CIA and taking on this."

I stared at him. He was crazy. His words made my skin itch.

He glanced down at a file. "So, Oscar nominee, your legend is that of Sam Chevalier."

"Yes, sir."

"Sam Chevalier is a life invented, first in Langley, then on the streets of Prague or Moscow or Jakarta or Dubai, wherever he needs to go."

"Yes, sir."

"Tell me who you are."

I recited. "Born in New York to a Québécois father and an American mother, raised mostly in Albany and Montreal, joined the Canadian Army, was turned out of that army a couple of years later."

"Don't give me shit I could read in an obituary! Tell me who he *is*."

I lowered my voice. "My parents were professional, but drunks. They're assholes."

"Why don't you have a more Canadian accent?"

"I went to school in Albany, my mom's hometown. They split up a lot but never divorced. We were the family that never quite jelled."

"And why did you go into the Canadian Army instead of the American Army?"

"I thought it less dangerous. Less likely to be sent to the middle of a war. I don't like danger when I'm not paid enough for it."

"And then?"

"I smuggled. Contraband, not drugs, black-market goods." I steadied my gaze. "I'm a practical guy. The Army didn't approve but they didn't bring charges. They just showed me the door. I had the goods on my superiors, you see. They were involved."

"It doesn't sound like I should cross you, Mr. Chevalier." His voice was mocking.

"I take care of myself first." And I had a weak little grin, the kind I'd never have on my own face, and I flashed it at him.

"And that..." said the burnt man, "is the difference in these two Sams."

"Something to drink, sir?" the flight attendant asked.

"No thank you, sweetheart," I said, which is not what Sam Capra would have said. The flight attendant moved on and I stared out the window. I hadn't used the ID in two years. Sam Chevalier had been out of sight. That could be a problem, but I didn't have another option. I reminded myself of every detail of his past jobs, felt myself settling into his skin, then blanked my mind, like an actor taking to the stage who needs to react and portray the character as though it's a soul he's always inhabited.

When I landed in San Juan, the day was warm and sunny, the sky a faultless blue. I rented a car and drove to the Gran Fortuna. I felt uneasy. I had no backup, and no plan beyond redeeming the chip and seeing what happened. I'd packed for a stay, and I'd reserved a room at the resort. It was a beautiful hotel, with views along the edge of Old San Juan. I could see two massive cruise ships docked. I valet-parked and went inside and checked into my room. I stayed in my cut-rate suit, checked the hair gel, and slipped the casino chip into my pocket.

I headed back down to the lobby. A tour group milled, from the Northeast, judging by the thick stew of New York and Boston accents that I heard. They spilled into the hotel casino and I followed them. The casino was smaller than I expected, fitted into one side of the hotel's first floor. More slot machines than anything else, but gaming tables offering blackjack, poker, roulette. I walked through the casino, assessing the security presence, eying the cameras, the guards, the exits, wondering what would happen when I tried to redeem the chip. What would be handed to me? Money? An offer to transfer funds to an account? Then why not put the value on the chip? Would I be handed an object? And how had Steve gotten this chip? That was a question that nagged.

I headed toward the casino cage.

Then I glanced past a group of tourists and I saw them. Cordelia. Her brother Galo. Sitting at a table near the bar, beyond the casino area, heads close together, talking. Cori looked unhappy, but then I realized I'd never seen her look happy. I moved so they couldn't see me. They spoke, she shook her head, he got up. He didn't go to the bar or approach a server, he headed toward the hotel's front entrance, pulling out a phone. I saw she had a small carry-on bag by her feet.

Why were they here, and together? They must have known about the chip. But I cautioned myself not to jump to conclusions.

I faced a split-second choice: Approach her now, try to redeem the chip, or follow them. She was alone, no Galo, and I didn't know when I could talk to her again. I chose her.

I went and sat across from Cori. I thought she was going to jump out of her skin as I smiled at her.

"Hi, Cori." I used the nickname I had no right to know about.

"Sam?" She took in my hair, my cheap suit that didn't stack up to the Armani she'd last seen me in, my bright-purple tie, and the clashing shirt. "What are you doing here?" She glanced toward the front of the hotel, where Galo had gone with his phone. "You need to leave."

"I need to stay," I said. "Your brother Galo sent a man named Ricky to search Steve's house."

She went as pale as milk. "I don't think so—how do you know?"

"Because I got there before he did. Then I followed him back to a nightclub in Miami Beach. Galo was there."

She looked stunned.

"Why are you here?" I asked.

"Please go."

"Did your brother have Steve killed?"

She looked horrified. "Galo didn't—he wouldn't. Please. Go."

I made my voice gentle. "Do you think I'm stopping or giving up? I don't."

Her mouth worked. Her eyes went past my shoulder. "Go. *Leave.* Now."

"I'm going to find out why Steve died," I said. "And you're going to tell me."

"I don't know." Cori's mouth turned into a smile and she leaned forward and kissed me. On the mouth, with more heat than Justine had. I was too surprised to move. I felt her fingers explore my gelled hair, her thumb caressed my ear; the kiss got more real. Then she leaned close and whispered, "Play along. I'm saving your life."

17

Cori." A voice behind me. Male, surprised, a little annoyed.

She leaned back and smiled over my shoulder. "Ha-ha, well, I have another surprise."

Another, I thought? Cori continued: "I asked my boyfriend here for the weekend."

I turned and saw Galo behind me. He was a big guy up close, solid throughout, broad-shouldered. He wasn't smiling, but he didn't look angry. More like confused.

"You must be Galo," I said. I stood and offered him my hand and thought, Maybe he saw me kissing a French girl two nights ago, across a darkened club; does he remember my face? The club was dark; we were a few tables away from his.

"Hi," I said. "Sam Chevalier." I said the last name carefully, and a bit loudly, so Cori would know it. "I've heard a lot about you."

He shook my hand, a bit wary. "I can't say the same. I didn't know you had a boyfriend," he said to Cori.

"We've all been keeping secrets, Galo." Her tone was edgy, nervous.

Now he risked a smile, as if he didn't have a choice. I got up from the seat he'd occupied and sat on the arm of her chair, gestured at the leather seat. He sat down, taking my measure. "How long have you two been an item?"

"Not long," she said. I let her take the lead; a lie was better coming from a sister than a stranger. "A few weeks."

It's one stress to be undercover, it's entirely another to be making up such a story as you go along, and it's blood-freezing to let someone else be writing your fiction for you. The burnt man would have had a tantrum at me losing control of the situation. *I'm saving your life,* she'd said, so she knew the terrain better than me. I kept my mouth shut.

"And what do you do, Sam?" he asked me. The smile was still on his face, but he wasn't amused. The protective brother, I thought.

I had to answer before Cori said *He owns a bar.* The worlds of Capra and Chevalier must not come together. "I do freelance security work."

"What does that even mean?"

"Mostly in Miami it means that I'm an extra bodyguard, local, when needed."

"Like for celebrities?"

"Sure, sometimes."

"Like who?"

I named a boy band that had toured through Miami recently, a young actress who was dating a Miami Heat player. I shrugged like it was no big deal.

Galo studied me. "So, how did you two meet?"

"This feels like an interrogation," Cori said. "Rather than a 'Hi, nice to meet you.'"

"It's just that kind of day," Galo said with a tight smile. "Sam, you got a sister? You know how it is." Galo winked at me. His shock at my unannounced appearance seemed to have passed and he'd decided, I suspected, that the quickest way to find out what he wanted to know about me was to be my new best friend.

"It's okay, hon," I said. "I get it. Actually we met because Cori didn't hire me. I bid on a job for one of her charity functions and I got outbid." I smiled affectionately at her and she smiled back, nervousness dancing behind her eyes. "So I asked her to coffee to see if I could bid again on another job, and…well…we liked each other." I cracked a smile at Cori.

"I guess you'll get the contract," Galo said.

"Not so far," Cori said. "Having seen what it's like to work with people you care about, I actually think Sam may not work my charity's events." She gave me a sweet look and I smiled back at her. I guessed it was somehow a jab at her brother.

I shrugged. "I can live with that."

Galo seemed to study her words like they hung in the air. "Cool," he said. "Sam. It's nice to meet you. I'm just surprised Cori didn't mention you."

"Like I said, we've all been keeping secrets."

He flicked a smile.

Cori said, "Sam, it's a family get-together this weekend. But I wasn't invited. So when I arrived here at the hotel—which our father partially owns—the concierge called Papa and he sent Galo to come…fetch me."

"Are we intruding on a private time?" I could imagine the burnt man saying: "*When* you enter the maze is as important as *how* you enter it. Avoid times of heightened suspicion. Don't ever seem to be a coincidence." I was breaking the rules left and right.

Galo's phone rang. He glanced at the screen and excused himself, a few feet away.

"What's going on?" I whispered.

"What I just said. Family meeting, shutting me out."

"Does this have something to do with the ten million I heard you mention to Steve?"

She gripped my hand. "Don't mention that. Please don't." She bit at her lip. "Look, I'm going with my brother. You need to fake stomach cramps or a migraine and stay here."

"Yeah, that's gonna happen."

Galo got off his phone call. His smile was dim. "She's brought you to meet the family. I've set it up so you can. Papa can't wait." He glanced between the two of us.

"Just because you don't bring someone special home to meet

Papa," she said, "doesn't mean I shouldn't." Her arm went around me. "Of course, I bother to date. To meet new people."

Galo made a noise. She was making some kind of verbal jab at him that I couldn't read, old business between them. Siblings love to complain about the other's choices. My brother and I had been the same way. I tried not to dwell on those memories. I missed Danny terribly. We'd each been all the other had in our nomadic childhoods, our parents busy with their work.

"So, Sam. Since my questions sounded like an interrogation to my little sister, I'll turn it around. What has Cori told you about her family?" Galo asked.

And then this felt like the tightrope, the point where the wrong word would truly get me in serious trouble. I could feel the shadow of the burnt man on my shoulder, watching me, coaching me.

"Enough to know maybe I should stick close to her." I made my voice a little challenge. Not intimidated. Not diplomatic. Not particularly smart, given the delicacy of the moment. Blustery, full Chevalier.

The hospitality faded. "Has Cori made you think she has some reason to be afraid of her own family?"

"No."

"I would hate for you to think so poorly of us. Cori's upset over a very minor issue."

I held up my hand. "Hey, I don't want to cause a family squabble. I'm here for Cori, not trouble. Really, this was the free weekend I had, I didn't mean to cause trouble."

"Galo fixes every problem," Cori said. I could hear bitterness in her tone. "Doesn't every family have a fixer, and don't you get fed up with them now and then?"

Galo ignored her and studied my face again. "Sam. Would you excuse me and my sister for a moment? Get yourself a drink at the bar."

Cori didn't release my hand. "I don't think so. Tell Ricky we'll leave in a few, Galo. We'll see you at the car." She stood and basically dragged me along with her, away from him, into the casino.

"That went well," I said. "Do they even know that you were targeted by the Colombians...?"

She ignored me. "Do you already have a room?"

"Yes. Why are you and he at this hotel? At this casino?" It had to be about the chip.

"I told you, we own part of it," she said in a rush. She let go of my hand. "You cannot stay. You *cannot*. We'll tell them you got sick, that you ate bad food on the plane..."

"Cori!" Galo called across the bar. He held up a phone. "Papa's called again, he wants us back at the house and he sounds impatient. Let's go." He cracked a smile. "C'mon, Sam. Meet the family. As Papa just said, 'Let's have a look at you.'"

"Sounds great." It actually sounded foreboding. But I smiled. I took Cori by the hand and she stumbled after me as I followed Galo.

18

THE JOB WAS already going badly. No backup, having to tell Cori the backstory in public, where I could screw it up, going into the countryside, away from the city, no idea what I'm facing.

Her fingers entwined with mine, Cori sat next to me in the backseat of the limo, apparently theirs, not hired. Galo sat across from us. When we climbed into the limo, Ricky was there, having abandoned his jacket for a blazer. I assumed he was armed. He glanced at me but gave no sign of recognition. He closed the doors and got into the driver's seat.

"Who's this?" Ricky asked. He didn't offer the deference of a typical employee.

"Cori's got a boyfriend," Galo said. Ricky watched me in the rearview as we headed into the snarl of San Juan traffic.

"Congratulations. You make a nice-looking pair," he finally said. I might have detected a hint of sarcasm. Did he recognize me from Or? Dark there, but how dark?

Galo brought out a smartphone and began tapping at it. He glanced up at me once and I thought I heard the very soft click of the phone taking my picture.

"The last name is Chevalier with a *c* and an *h*. Do you need me to spell it for you?"

He cracked a smile. "I don't know what you mean."

"You just took my picture."

"No, my phone makes all sorts of odd noises. It's old and crappy." He glanced up at Cori. "That's a hint, you know, my birthday is coming up."

"The way you've acted, like I'm really going to buy you a gift."

"I think I'm being very welcoming, Cori. I bet I look totally charming next to Papa and Zhanna." He smiled at me, like we were sharing a joke.

I suspected he was e-mailing my photo and my name to his father. Get me checked out. If I made a big fuss, I might look like I was a threat. If I was just a boyfriend, then I needed to be just a boyfriend.

I'm saving your life, she'd said with a kiss. She wouldn't be kissing a guy she hired to protect her, a bodyguard. Not the new Steve, if one of them was behind Steve's death. I had to be a boyfriend. Not a threat. Just here for her.

Cori put her head on my shoulder.

"You didn't fly out this morning with Cori, Sam," Galo said.

"I caught a ride on a FastFlex cargo flight," Cori explained. A little too quickly.

"I was tied up on a job until late," I said.

"And I like surprises," Cori said. "You know how much I like surprising you, Galo."

Galo put away his phone and I got the sense her words somehow scalded him. An old sibling grudge, an unfunny joke between them. "And you know how much I hate surprises," he said. "No offense, Sam."

"None taken."

"What did you do before you hired yourself out as a bodyguard?" Galo said. "Is there such a thing as bodyguard school?"

"I worked in Europe." I didn't elaborate. "Before that I was home in Canada. In the Army, then I was out."

"And what did you do in Europe?"

"Nothing exciting. The transportation business."

"What a coincidence," he said, as if it wasn't. "That's our business."

"I worked for people on a much smaller scale than FastFlex." I could feel Cori's gaze on me, wondering how much I knew about her family, what facts I might throw out, where I might trip.

"You took a room at the resort?"

"Yes. I thought it best in case I needed to give you all family time." Or myself an escape hatch.

Cori shifted under my arm. "I'll have your things sent to the house."

"No, I think I'll keep the room," I said. "I don't want to over-stay my welcome."

"Are you sure we haven't met before?" Galo said. "I think I know your face."

Oh no. I shrugged. "Do you ever go out to nightclubs?"

"Now and then."

"I often have to work security in the crowd at some of the bigger ones, if a client is there."

"Like Miami Beach?"

"Often." And I wondered if he was remembering two nights ago, a French young woman joining his table because I was half a couple making out at ours. I was really regretting those kisses with Justine. But they'd seen dozens of faces at Or. Right? Would they remember me?

"Galo," Cori said. "Be nice."

He smiled like he didn't want to be nice. Something major was going on here with this family, and Cori wasn't invited. And then suddenly we were. It could only be to keep an eye on us, to suss me out and see if I was some kind of threat. *Galo fixes every problem,* Cori had said. I was definitely a problem.

"Zhanna's the family party animal," Cori said. "You'd probably see her at a nightclub."

"This is your sister?" I asked.

"*Stepsister,*" they said in unison, stressing the "step." "Not a blood relation," Galo added, as if I didn't understand the concept.

"But more like our father than either of us are. Funny how that works out," Cori said.

"And you two are half-siblings, right?" I asked.

"Yes. Papa was three times married, three times a widower,"

Galo said. "He's unlucky in love." The same words I'd thought. Or...something worse.

"So three children, counting Zhanna?"

Silence all of a sudden. "Four. I had a brother, Sam. A twin. I hadn't mentioned him to you before. He died a few years ago."

It was a mistake. I'd forgotten about the lost twin for just a moment, caught up in the conversation. She should have said, "Don't forget Edwin," and Galo might have thought nothing of my slip. I could see the sudden doubt in Galo's stare at her, then at me. Edwin was a detail she would have shared with a serious boyfriend.

I squeezed Cori's hand. She looked at me and she was a very good actress because she looked like she really regretted not having told me. "It's painful. Very."

Behind the windows the tropical landscape unfolded as we took Highway 22, toward the western coast of the island. The mention of family deaths made everyone go silent for a few minutes.

"I'm guessing Cori's either complained plenty about our stepsister," Galo said, "or said nothing." It was a first attempt at seeing what she'd told me.

"She's said very little about you all," I said before Cori could answer.

"Well, that's a relief," Galo said, and in other circumstances it might have been a joke.

"Zhanna is a lovely name. Am I pronouncing it correctly?" I asked.

"She'll be sure to find fault with it even if you say it perfectly," Cori said, and she and Galo both laughed and for the first time, really, they looked like brother and sister.

"She's Russian. Zhanna is Russian for Jane," Galo said.

"Don't refer to her as a stepsister; she hates that. She hates that she doesn't have the Varela blood," Cori said. And then she and Galo said, together: "Jealous Z," like pronouncing the word "jealousy," and then they laughed.

"Galo, do you work for your father?" I asked. If he was going to interrogate me, it was only right I return the favor.

"Yes. I'm the chief operating officer of FastFlex." Then he gave his sister a meaningful smile. "How much has she told you about this weekend, Sam?"

"Nothing, except," I said, truthfully, before Cordelia could answer, "this was the weekend for me to meet everyone."

Her hand tightened on my knee.

"It's family business. A summit meeting of sorts. It's awkward because Cori doesn't work for the family business, so she wasn't asked." His smile stayed steady on me.

"I'd be happy to keep her distracted," I said. I could almost see Cordelia wince out of the corner of my eye. I didn't care about being on Cori's good side; she was stuck with me. I wanted to lessen Galo's suspicions.

"Well, we might ask you to take Cori back and have fun at the casino. On us, of course." Yes, I thought, after you've checked me out and convinced yourself I'm not a problem.

"I'm not going anywhere," Cori said. "So stop talking like I'm not here, boys."

19

WE NEXT TOOK a rural highway and then some private roads, and at the top of a small mountain there was their island home. The house was grand. Beautiful stone, a cross between a Mediterranean villa and an old Spanish castle. The house commanded a view of both the ocean and the surrounding hillsides, not far from the surf town of Rincón on the northwestern coast. The sky above it was clear and blue. Fortress Varela, the island version. We drove onto a driveway, past a large automated gate. We all got out and I looked around, smiling like the slightly callow guy who has just realized how truly rich his girlfriend is. I let the look linger on my face, sell my basic harmlessness to them.

Ricky drove the limo away from us and parked near a four-car garage, then walked back to us. A couple of youngish guys who looked like they doubled as bodyguards followed him from the garage and said hello to Galo and Cori and looked at me with a quick assessment. They wore holsters under their lightweight jackets.

"Your family gatherings include guards?" I said to Cori. I laughed, a little nervously.

"Today's does," Ricky said. "I need to search you."

"What is this?" I said to Cori with a half-smile of surprise.

"Ever since my brother was kidnapped," she said, "my dad is very security-conscious around people he doesn't know."

"Kind of useless to search me now. You should have done it before I got into the car," I said to Ricky. Very Sam Chevalier. He greeted my logic with a sour frown.

"If I found something I didn't like," Ricky said, "I wouldn't want to deal with you in public, in front of a nice hotel. I'd deal with you here. Where no one is at."

"Watching," I said. "We're actually all *at* here right now. And they are watching." I made my smile friendly. I need not appear too bright.

"Scaring me with grammar," he said.

"I'm just exact," I said.

"Exactly a jerk," Ricky said.

"Ricky, that's enough," Cori said, but he ignored her and glanced at Galo. A sign. Maybe, that Ricky was loyal first to Galo, not the family.

"You watch too many movies, Ricky," Galo said, breaking the tension.

I obligingly raised my hands. He patted at my wallet but didn't ask me to remove it. Then his fingers brushed at the two rectangles of plastic in my front pocket, probing with his fingers. He didn't reach into my pocket. "Two keys to my hotel room," I said, in a low voice. "Don't tell Cori's dad."

"Give me a key," he said.

"What is going on?" I said to Cori. "You're kind of freaking me out."

"It's okay. They need it to get your bags and bring them here," she said.

Wrong, I thought. They could have a hotel employee bring my bag down before we left the hotel. What they want to do is search my room. Which is exactly why they hadn't let me bring my bag along. They had an excuse. She laced fingers with me. "Don't mind."

"I said I'd keep the room. I've paid for it."

"Daddy will reimburse you. Galo wants you here."

They want me close to watch me. Not allow me to come and go from their compound. I'm a prisoner. Excellent. I'm inside. The burnt man would be so proud.

"All right." I slid the key—it was a bit thinner than the rectangular casino plaque—out of my pocket and handed it to Ricky. The casino chip stayed where it was.

Then I saw her. The dark-haired pixie from the bar with the furious eyes, who'd mimed cutting a throat. She stood on the large stone porch that led up to the home's grand entrance. She wore a business suit instead of a dress of slinky silk. Dark jacket, pants, a creamy white shirt. She looked, somehow, more dangerous. More seductive. She was like a flame, the kind that could make you forget a good woman like Justine or Cori for a moment and ruin your judgment.

"Zhanna." Cori kissed her stepsister's cheek, Zhanna did likewise. It was ritual, I thought, not warmth. "This is Sam Chevalier. My new boyfriend. My stepsister, Zhanna."

I stuck out my hand and for a moment she studied it as though unfamiliar with the custom. Then she took it, shook it, let me go. As though my fingers were soiled.

"Hi, Zhanna," I said. Her gaze went over my unsubtle clothes, my hair, my gaudy watch.

"I'm delighted to meet you, Sam. Cori has said absolutely nothing about you."

"Same here, Zhanna," I said. It was calculated, that moment, being undiplomatic.

I speak fluent Russian and pronounced her name correctly but she said, "No, it's Zhanna."

I repeated it exactly as she pronounced it.

"Almost, not quite. Zhanna. Try again."

I said in Russian: "I hope this time I say your name correctly, Zhanna. Please inform me if I don't."

Her jaw dropped, then quickly her mouth closed. Her smile looked stung. Cori stared at me. Galo broke into laughter.

"Or," I said, switching back to English, "I could just call you Z. That way we don't misunderstand each other."

Galo laughed again. "She didn't tell me about him either. I guess she didn't want to scare him off."

"I don't scare," I said with a smile. But I could feel the shift. If

Zhanna was on the attack, Galo would be on Cori's side, even if he hadn't been five minutes ago in the limo. Sides drawn. I wondered whether this family was in a permanent state of war.

Zhanna's smile didn't waver. "This one is younger than most of your conquests, Cori." Her Russian accent was nearly gone, but I could hear the barest hint of it.

"Oh, like I have conquests, Z."

Zhanna said, "I guess I should have said strays."

"That's what I am," I said, meeting Zhanna's gaze. "A stray." I winked at her. "Don't be all jealous, Z."

My insolence nearly made her drop her false welcoming smile. She kept it in place, barely. I was unexpected. She didn't like surprises. At least not right now.

Galo put a hand on my shoulder and steered me toward the house. "Welcome. We really don't bite."

"With everything going on between us, Cori, this was not the time to bring a guest," Zhanna hissed behind us. She was bad at whispering.

"Now you all know what it means to be surprised," Cori said with a hint of satisfaction. I pretended not to hear.

I followed Zhanna, with Cori and Galo, into the grand foyer of the big house. The burnt man would have smiled: the large stone entrance did look like it could be the doorway to a maze. Your brain sizzles when you enter the heart of darkness, the headquarters, the inner sanctum. You've made it this far, stepping carefully along in your dance of lies. I felt a bright chill climb my spine.

Four steps into the foyer I stopped as suddenly as if I'd wandered into a church service. On the walls hung three grand portraits—not photographs, but actual paintings, enormous yet delicate. Three beautiful women. The first was tall, dark, regal, riding a thoroughbred, eyes of black satin. The second was lovely, petite, a pale blonde standing in furs before an expanse of snow, eyes of sky blue. The third was a brunette with generous curves, impeccably dressed, with a bouquet of flowers in her hand, walking in a field. The loveliest of the three, which was saying a great deal.

Her smile was warm. It was a face so much like Cordelia's, I studied it.

The three Varela wives. I wondered if the placement of the portraits was intentional, or if this was just the expanse of wall that could hold the huge paintings. A reminder of loss, or a reminder of division. Odd that they would be displayed together. One had the sense of...trophies. I saw each of the three siblings, step and half, pause before their own mother's portrait. A moment of homage, a moment of...missing their mother. My mom was still alive but we didn't really talk. That was a shame, but I seemed powerless to change it. I knew it was a cheap excuse. At heart I was a disappointing son and I knew it. But with my parents' work I had been in places where suffering seemed to hang in the air—coastlines ravaged by storm, villages abandoned during war, fields emptied by famine—and this house felt the same in some way, marred, ruined, by a deep well of tragedy.

"Your mom was lovely," I whispered to Cordelia. She'd taken my hand and I wondered if it was for the charade or so we could give each other a boost of courage. We were in a very dangerous situation—clearly, from her warning—and we didn't yet know how much we could count on each other. She looked at me and I could see fright on her face; she was deathly afraid here in her own home, and then she slipped the merry little mask back on with a smile. The *meet my boyfriend, everyone, I'm so excited* expression.

"Mum was," she said. "She grew up near Canterbury, England. She was a model in London when she was young." I glanced at Zhanna and Galo; they were still looking at their moms' pictures. "All those were painted at Papa's houses. Galo's mom, here. Zhanna's mom, painted when Papa had a house near Moscow, he had a lot of Russian business deals then."

Zhanna glanced away.

"And my mother, well, not in England, but at Papa's house in Johannesburg. When FastFlex started to grow, they were doing many flights across Africa."

I thought of what Paige had said, the rumors that FastFlex and Rey Varela had flown all sorts of weapons and arms into those unstable countries. I wondered again if Steve's path had ever crossed Rey's.

"He doesn't have those houses in Russia and South Africa anymore," Zhanna said. "Just this one."

Zhanna coughed and Galo turned away from the portrait, as if resisting the pull of the past. You couldn't help but feel you were sliding under Rey's thumb here. This display didn't seem like a memorial.

We followed Galo away from the three portraits. Rey Varela was here. And I wanted to look in his eyes, see what I saw.

We walked into a large den. Magnificently furnished in what I'd call Grand Caribbean: dark woods, local art, a beautiful mahogany bar. I ran my hand along the smooth wood. Beyond the bar were family photos, less intimidating than the portraits. Galo, Zhanna, and one of Cori and her brother Edwin together, smiling, laughing, leaning on each other's shoulders.

"Where is he?" Zhanna said. "He was here a moment ago." She went to the windows. "Kent? Where is Papa?"

A fortyish man, dressed in a fine light suit and wearing dark sunglasses, came to the door. Then I noticed his thin white cane, gently moving in front of him. He was blind.

Zhanna touched his arm. "Kent, we have a guest. Cori's boyfriend. He's over by the bar." She guided him toward me. And I noticed all the brittleness she seemed to show the world—in the nightclub, in the driveway—vanished. She looked at Kent with a real tenderness.

Kent smiled and said, "Well, hello, boyfriend." He did not sound particularly surprised. He extended his hand.

I moved forward, took the blind man's proffered hand. "Hello. I'm Sam Chevalier," I said.

"Kent Severin." He was balding, with light blond hair, a granite jaw, a strong face. His accent was soft, Southern. His handshake was firm. "A delight to meet you. Cori needs a boyfriend."

"You're funny," Cori said. "Where's Papa?"

"I guess he went upstairs," Kent said. "He was certainly anxious to see you all…"

"Sweetheart, wait here," Cori said to me. "I want to find Papa and talk to him about you first…it'll be better that way." And Cori left, and her brother and her stepsister followed her. Presumably to watch the fireworks if their papa wasn't pleased to have a weekend guest. But I thought this was more for show.

"Have a seat, Sam," Kent Severin said. "I'm also Zhanna's boyfriend, by the way. She's not good at introductions."

Boyfriend? I thought. And where were you when your girlfriend was at the nightclub the other night? It didn't seem like a brotherly/sisterly night on the town for Zhanna and Galo. I'd thought, mistakenly, that they were an arguing couple, ending a relationship. There had to be another explanation.

"I'm glad I'm a welcome surprise, at least to you," I said. "I don't mean to intrude on family time, but Cori insisted. I understand there's some sort of family meeting."

"Cordelia is good at getting her way." Kent didn't sit, but he lingered near the windows, and he completely ignored my comment about the family meeting. "I'll save the interrogation regarding your career, your schooling, and your honorable intentions for when the whole family is here." He laughed softly. "The Varelas are a demanding lot. Fiery. But they all love each other and they mean well."

"I'm sure," I said, "that Cori is worth any number of grillings."

"She's a wonderful young woman."

"How long have you and Zhanna been dating?"

"Almost a year." Kent leaned against his cane. "But I've worked for Rey for many, many years. I've known Zhanna since she was a teenager and a handful of trouble. I never paid any attention to her until a year ago. Life happens."

"What do you do for Mr. Varela?"

"I give him advice," Kent said. "Basically he brings me his problems—how do we expand our routes, how do we deal with troubling regulations, how do we improve security—and I help him find a solution."

"And are Cori and I being here problems?" I might as well keep up the slightly callow persona I was crafting.

"You're very blunt." He kept the gentle smile in place.

"I can tell there's a lot of tension between the siblings. I don't want to add to it," I lied.

"No, you're not a problem. And Cori is a joy. It's a misunderstanding between her and her father. Easily fixed."

He kept the smile in place. "What do you do?" His curiosity seemed to burn in the air, despite his promise to wait and ask my particulars when the family was present.

"Same business as you. I give advice. Just on how to stay safe. I own a security company."

"Interesting. You don't sound old enough to be a former police officer."

"I used to be in the military. Will that not be impressive enough to Mr. Varela?"

He ran a hand along his cane. "The kind of guys she goes for usually want to start solar-panel or granola or sustainable-farming businesses—often with Cori's money. Security is a brave new territory for us with a Cordelia boyfriend." He sounded cordial, but a hint of malice tinged the gossipy words. But then he laughed. "I'm a big Cordelia fan. We all are. She's a genuinely good person."

"So what is Mr. Varela like?"

"He's very strong-willed. He's...but you should know...ever since he got sick, I mean, it's all been...different."

I started to say, *Sick?* but Cori would have told a boyfriend if her father were seriously unwell. So I shut my mouth.

Zhanna raced back into the room. "Kent, he's *gone*. Papa's gone, we can't find him."

Kent pulled out a smartphone, said to the screen, "Call Rey." He listened at the phone. "He's not answering."

I looked out the window. Steep hills and gulleys marked this side of the property, small trails winding down toward a crescent of shallow beach and a curve of a small inlet, stunningly blue. "Maybe he went to run an errand," I suggested.

"He has people for that," Zhanna said, clearly indicating with her tone that I was an idiot. "He has me. Maybe he's having an episode…"

I didn't ask what that meant; better to be seen as immediately helpful rather than inquisitive. "Is the property large?" I asked.

Zhanna took a break from her concern to smirk at me. "No, we built this huge house on a postage stamp."

"Yes, Sam, it is," Kent answered, more politely. "Hopefully he hasn't wandered away. Let's spread out, let's find him." Zhanna took his arm and hurried him out of the library, leaving me behind. "Wait here, Sam!" he called.

Presumably I was useless, as I didn't know the property. Or I wasn't trusted. He'd wandered away? Perhaps the sickness wasn't physical.

I went to the French doors and then out onto a large stone patio. In the distance, past the hills, was a bright-blue smear of ocean. At one side of the patio were steps, winding down out of sight, to gardens bright with blooms. I figured I might as well help and I hadn't seen anyone searching in this direction.

I headed down the steps.

20

As I WENT down the stone steps I could see the chaos that was creeping into the garden beds — weeds, wild growth so heavy with blossoms that they bent under the weight.

The staircases wound away from the house, putting me out of sight of the Varela home. In the distance I could hear muffled cries that sounded like *Papa*. Cori and Zhanna, calling for their wayward father.

I stopped at the end of the stone stairs. The last few were broken, ending into soft grass and the more level stretch of the hillside. Another set of stairs on the opposite side of the knoll led down to the beach. Farther down the grass was a dense growth of small trees. He hadn't come this way, at least. Unless he'd gone out into the wilderness, and with two of his children arriving, surely not…

Then I heard it. A cry. Soft, quickly muffled. For a moment I thought it a trick of the wind.

Caution kept me from calling out Mr. Varela's name. The suddenness of the cry being stopped. Something was wrong.

I ran onto the grass. I moved away from the stairs leading to the beach toward where I'd heard the sound. The short trees grew thick here and the scrub was patchy, but I could see tracks in the dirt, two sets of prints, one dragging a foot, the other heavier. Heading downhill, threading through the trees, curving toward the neighboring hills and another stretch of beach.

I followed.

Forty seconds later I saw them, down the hill from me, weaving through the scrubby trees. An older man, in dirty white slacks and a torn guayabera shirt, being hurried along by a much bigger man dressed in camo pants and a dark-green shirt, shoulders thick with muscle, dark hair clipped short. Maybe thirty. He powered the older man—I recognized him as Rey Varela from Paige's clippings file—down the hillside, the old man clutching at the scrubby, bent tree trunks. With one hand the bigger man guided Rey Varela; his other hand held a knife. No sign of a gun, but that didn't mean anything.

I ran after them, at full speed. Only slowing to scoop up a rock because I had no weapon.

As I closed in on them, Mr. Varela turned, saw me, his dark eyes widening, and he cried out again. Moaning, talking, saying words I couldn't make out.

Giving me cover to approach.

The kidnapper didn't turn toward me, but he shoved Rey Varela and told him to shut up. At the last second he heard my footsteps, but I jumped and slammed my feet into the kidnapper's back. He and Rey stumbled and fell as I rolled past them.

I saw the knife, bright steel, in the kidnapper's grip. He let go of Rey Varela and scrambled back. I threw the rock, hard, he dodged, but it grazed his head, bloodying his hairline. He retreated back to where Rey Varela crouched and then he grabbed the old man by the collar of his ruined guayabera.

And then he smiled at me.

He slammed Rey Varela's head into one of the small tree trunks. The old man fell to the ground, stunned. It was ruthlessly efficient. The kidnapper never broke eye contact with me. He needed the old man down and not escaping; there was a tree and so he used it.

My throat went dry. Odd he didn't use him as a hostage, a shield.

"You're not one of them," he said to me, in a soft voice.

I didn't know what that meant. Then he started trying to kill me. The kidnapper came at me in a feint, trying to draw me out into the open where I had no tree to shield me, where he could catch me and slice me open in clean silence. I dodged back. But retreating uphill is dangerous, especially when you can't see a root or a stone or a patch of treacherous loose dirt that can trip you up.

I snatched another rock from the ground. It didn't fit into my hand as neatly as the first one.

"Eddie?" Rey Varela called, dazed, his temple bloodied by the tree. "Eddie?"

The kidnapper ignored him and concentrated on me. He held the knife in his right hand and made a grab for me with his left. If he slowed me for one second, he could stab me or open my throat.

I parried, smacking his hand with the rock.

I wasn't letting go of this stone yet.

The kidnapper reversed his hold and slashed with the knife, missing me, catching the air. When the knife swept past and his reach was to my left I drove the rock toward his throat. He stumbled back, surprised. I missed crushing the larynx but it hit him hard and he grunted. But then I didn't see his other hand jab toward my neck. He clawed at my throat and I swung the rock toward his head, hoping to shatter his eye socket or his jaw before he could stab me.

But the loose dirt of the steep hillside beneath both our feet gave way and I slid past him. The knife caught me along the shoulder, cutting through the light blazer into my skin, my blood bright against the canary-yellow shirt.

It hurt and I was on my back, the sky and the knife above me, and he reached for my throat. I could see my own blood on the knife's edge and I hammered the heel of my hand toward his face. He blocked and parried me with his free hand, not risking me getting a grip on his knife, using sharp, sudden *muay thai* punches against me. Not what you expect to see in a street thug. I grabbed the wrist of the hand that held the knife and I sank my teeth hard into it. He screamed. He was bigger than me and ropy with muscle but as my teeth sank he dropped the knife.

It fell to the ground. He tried to grab for it and I used a *sok ti* elbow slash across his eyebrow, the blow cutting his flesh, bloodying him. He howled in rage and I slid away from him, dodging his grab as he tried to seize me. He forced his hand over the dropped knife before I could reach it.

Now I was the one in retreat.

I was still sore from chasing Steve's killers and I ran toward Rey Varela, thinking, *Get him up, get him out of here while the kidnapper's down.* It is always a different fight with a noncombatant in the mix. I reached for the old man, and the kidnapper was blinded by the blood gushing into his eyes but he heard my breathing. He'd recovered the knife and made another slash at me, opening my jacket's back through to the skin. The pain was bright and hot. I whirled to face him.

His eyes and his nose were bloodied. He raised the knife again, telegraphing that he intended to slash, and I slammed my fist into his damaged face. Then into his guts and a kick into his groin. He stumbled back. I had him reeling. I just needed to grab the knife.

Then Rey Varela changed it all. Bloodied and confused, he bounded onto the kidnapper, a rock raised in his fist. The kidnapper slashed at him, and the old man cried out, dropping the rock.

"Hold it!" the kidnapper yelled at me, caging Rey in one arm, scrabbling to his feet. He had the knife at Rey's throat. I stopped.

"Hands up, get on your knees, or I cut his throat."

I obeyed his orders. I heard the trace of a Russian accent in his ragged voice. I could read a code in it; he'd underestimated me, he was afraid he was going to lose. But to kill me he'd still have to get close. I could wait for him to move.

Rey Varela's eyes bulged, not in pain but in rage. "I'm gonna kill you for this, gonna kill you..."

"Shut up, old man," the kidnapper said. "Now," he said to me, "he's coming with me, to have a quiet chat with some friends of his, no one wants him dead. You understand? Last thing we want, all right? Lay down flat and stay still and be quiet and you'll be okay."

"All right," I said. Rey's eyes met mine.

I understood his look: *Get ready.*

Rey seized the attacker's arm, then bent back, getting the knife away from his throat a few more inches. I threw myself at them, slamming my fist into the kidnapper's face, yanking down his arm, pulling the blade away from the old man. Rey fell, slipping out between us.

But the kidnapper head-butted me and my brain exploded. He caught me to one side of my nose, worse than a fist being thrown. I staggered back, falling, and he was on top of me, the knife raised. The bright gleam of steel was the last thing I was going to see.

I grabbed his wrist but all the leverage was on his side. The blade was inches from my face. I saw a rock bounce past the kidnapper's shoulder—Rey Varela throwing it, trying to hurt him.

My gaze locked with the kidnapper's. His eyes were brown. His mouth was set in determination. It was nothing personal. The blade inched closer to me. I thought of Daniel, and I'd like to say that my love for my son powered my strength but instead I felt my muscles start to give and the life I wouldn't share with him spun before my eyes. And then I heard two shots; the kidnapper's head turned toward the sound and he fell. The knife nearly cut me as he went down, but not because his hand guided it. Just gravity.

He fell and I could see the wet hole above his eye. He looked surprised.

Rey Varela was on the ground, clutching his cut and bleeding arm, blinking.

Ten feet away I saw Galo Varela slowly lower a gun. Staring down at us, shock creasing his face. Then running toward us, yelling, *"Papa!,"* calling for the guards. I heard Cori scream too. Screaming the way she did when Steve died. Then it stopped, because she saw her father and I were both still alive.

Rey leaned over me. He looked about seventy, his hair bedraggled, his gaze blank and confused. I wanted to tell him to sit down, but my whole face hurt.

"You saved my life," Rey Varela said to me. "But who the hell are you, kid?"

The blood pulsed from my shoulder, my brain felt rattled in its cage of skull, and I fell back down in the dirt when I tried to stand. The sky spun. Rey leaned into my face, studying it as though wondering whether he knew me, asking Galo, "Who is this? Is this Eddie?"

21

MEET THE FAMILY.

One way to make that important first impression is to save the father from abduction and see the brother kill a man to save you.

From my bed, I looked through the stone-framed window at the lovely blue sky. The day was still quiet.

Too quiet. No sirens. No police officers came to my room to question me, to take my statement.

The sheets were cool against my body, the high-thread-count kind you find in a luxury hotel. Towels under me to catch any bleeding past the bandages. A doctor, a longtime and trusted family friend of the Varelas, had been summoned. He was in his seventies, English, tanned, and gentlemanly. He stitched up my shoulder and tended to my back (which was a very shallow cut) and inspected the head-butt bruise on my cheek. He brought painkillers instead of a prescription pad.

"I am pretty sure there are hospitals here in Puerto Rico," I said to the doctor as he worked on my shoulder and back. He took a sip of whiskey when he was done and then offered the glass to me and I took a sip as well.

"There are indeed. Excellent ones."

"But I don't get a ride to a hospital."

"Horrifying lack of privacy at a hospital." The doctor said this to me in a tone of maddening reason, as though I were a five-year-old asking why I couldn't go out to play during a hurricane.

"They're not going to call the police, are they?"

"I can't say."

It occurred to me it might be good for the police to understand how badly I was injured. That Galo's killing of the kidnapper was justified to save me.

"It was self-defense," I said when he finished stitching me. "That guy getting killed, it wasn't my fault." I needed to sound like the scared, in-over-his-head boyfriend.

"Rey will tell you how this is handled, Mr. Chevalier, and I suggest you listen carefully to him. You don't have a concussion, so you should be able to understand his reasoning." A slightly wry tone shaded his words.

"Who would want to kidnap Mr. Varela?"

"He's a very wealthy man," the doctor said. As if that was all there could be to it. "Kidnapping is a very sensitive subject here. After Edwin. You understand."

"I guess."

"The police were ineffective. It was as if Edwin vanished from the face of the Earth, pardon the cliché. So if Rey doesn't think they need to call the police, they won't."

"But…Cori…there could be a threat against the family…" I'd thought the threat to Cori came from *inside* the family. Ricky searching Steve's house for Galo, Z and Galo arguing to the point of her slapping him, this big secret meeting that excluded Cori…

What if I was wrong?

"I am going to give you very important advice, Sam. Please follow it. Rest for a couple of days, then go home. Your cheekbone's not broken, the bruising will heal, the cuts will heal. The family will be grateful to you and no one can be grateful like a Varela." He rubbed fingers together: money. "And keep your mouth shut. That above all else. Keep your mouth shut."

"You knew Mr. Varela in Africa," I guessed.

He nodded. "Yes. I used to work with the UN. I decided to retire here." He washed up, threw away his gloves. I got up and washed the sticky, dried blood from my hands. He stood in the bathroom door, watching me.

"The UN…" I said.

"My paths crossed now and then with Rey and his partner. They can be very charming."

"You mean when they smuggled arms?"

"Rumors. All I ever saw unloaded were food and medical supplies." The doctor's voice got a little harsher. "You were a bit of a surprise." He glanced aside at me. There are some other scars on my body. I've picked them up like hipsters find tattoos. "You helped Rey, so you're the golden boy for the moment."

For the moment.

A knock sounded on the door. "Is he decent?" Cori called.

"Yes," I said.

She stepped inside and she held a dark T-shirt and a pair of loose athletic pants, with a drawstring waist. "Not the dressiest. Galo's extras, he's bigger than you but loose clothing might be best with the bandages. Your baggage is coming from the hotel. But your suit is blood-soaked, ruined, and so…" She stopped and she looked at my bandaged back and my bruised face and her mouth twisted.

"It's okay. Thank you."

"You saved my dad," she said, her voice breaking.

"It's okay."

"None of this is okay, Sam." She drew a steadying breath.

The doctor told me and Cori he'd want to see me again in two days, or I should see a friend of his, a doctor back in Miami who could keep her mouth shut about unexplained knife injuries. Cori thanked him and kissed him on the cheek and he seemed embarrassed. "Cori, I'm going to check again on your father before I go."

"Thank you." She looked to me. "Papa's not badly hurt, but he's very confused."

"And the assailant?" the doctor asked. "I don't want to know details, I just want to know if it's handled."

"It's…handled." Cori nearly choked on the word. She glanced

at me as though she were afraid I was going to ask unneeded questions. Or maybe she was afraid I was going to simply leave. Would they let me? *Great to meet y'all, but I've had quite enough for the weekend, thanks! Let me out.*

"All right," the doctor said. I heard the putter of a boat in the inlet. I looked out the window. A small boat, returning. I couldn't see who was in it.

"They took the kidnapper's body out in the ocean," she said. "To get rid of it." The words sounded like they tasted bitter in her mouth. Then she looked at me, at the doctor. "No jury would convict Galo...saving his father, saving his sister's boyfriend..."

"No jury would," the doctor agreed. "Your dad's resting in his room?"

She nodded.

"I'll go check on Rey. He took a couple of hard blows there and added onto what he's already dealing with..." The doctor shook my hand. "You're a brave young man, Sam. You take care. Remember what I said." He walked out and shut the door behind him.

The silence between us was thick. "So," she said. "What did he say?"

"To do exactly what your father tells me. I'm going to put on those clean clothes," I said. She handed them to me and turned around to look out the window. I shrugged off my bloodied underwear, and socks, slipped on the exercise pants. I stayed barefoot, since she hadn't brought socks. The T-shirt, built for Galo's wide shoulders, hung a bit loose on me.

"Okay," I said, and she turned around and gathered my discarded cut-and-bloodied clothes. "We'll get rid of these." She couldn't look me in the face. I touched her arm.

"We may only have a few minutes before the family descends on us, Cordelia." I made my voice a low growl. "You are going to tell me everything, right now."

22

She shoved my clothes into a trash bag. "I asked you to stay at the hotel. You don't have to be involved."

"Way too late, and you're a liar," I said, and she looked up at me, stung. "You *want* me involved. You kissed me when you could have pretended I was a stranger bothering you in the casino. But no. You told your brother I was your boyfriend, it made your family nervous that I was here with you, so they bring me here to have a look at me. And now I'm nearly killed and I'm supposed to hush up a death." I shook my head. "Now. Tell me what is going on here."

"I'm not a liar. I didn't engineer this. Sam. Just...I was trying to protect you because I didn't know what you might say to my brother. Steve was already dead, I didn't want you hurt. I'm sorry."

"Are the people responsible for Steve's murder the same people who tried to take your father?"

"I think so. They must be."

"You think. Does your family know Steve was killed working for you?"

"No. They didn't know I hired him."

"At least one of them must. Galo sent Ricky to his house."

"Maybe they found out, but there's no way my brother could have..."

"Your brother just shot a man an hour ago." Maybe Galo didn't shoot him just to keep him from killing me, I thought. Maybe Galo shot him to shut him up. But why would anyone stage a kidnapping of his father from the family retreat? Was that designed to throw off the scent of suspicion?

"That's different," Cordelia said.

"What did you hire Steve for? I know he did a job for your charity a few months ago."

She swallowed, sat down on the bed, glanced at the door, made her voice a whisper. "Papa's company routinely donates to the charity I run. He's been very generous." She licked her lips. "About six months ago, he started slipping. Mentally. We thought he was just forgetful, but the doctor here said it was probably dementia. Papa refused to see a specialist. Sometimes he'd be just fine for weeks, then he'd be out of it. And I mean, *out* of it. Thinking one of his wives was still alive. Thinking he was still flying planes back in Angola and Congo and Rwanda. We kept it quiet. For the sake of FastFlex. Papa said he didn't want anyone in the company finding out. Galo and Z and Kent were going to start, you know, transitioning Galo to be the CEO, retire Papa. But Papa got mad, fought them. He didn't think then he should give up running the company. So they backed off, a bit, but Papa knew he'd have to hand over the reins."

She took a deep breath for composure. "Two weeks ago, he called me and asked me to meet him at FastFlex's office by the airport. He seemed out of it. Confused. When I arrived, he took me to a storage facility we own, he said he had something to give me. He had a...large crate of money, basically. Ten million dollars, in cash, he wanted to donate, to help the kids I help. I told him, Papa, this isn't how you give me money for the charity, and he kept insisting that I was to take the money...I mean, who stores cash like that? In a warehouse? Not a legitimate business, right? You keep it in a bank. I'd never seen so much cash in my life and it scared me. He told me to take it and go. Like I was going to rent a truck and shovel it in the back. He started to cry and he sat down on the money. I asked him, where did the money come from, all this cash. And he said, from the underside of the business."

"The underside."

"Yes. And I asked him what that meant, and I called Galo to come over there and then, and Zhanna showed up, and she freaked that I'd seen all this cash. Galo got there and saw it too, and Z told him to leave, to wait outside. And he did, like she was in charge. Zhanna said it was cash moved from a South American government, they were a client. Well, I researched it, and it's not legal to bring in a massive amount of cash like that and not declare it. Zhanna told me that it was a special case, showed me all the paperwork. But…who moves cash like that? And Papa thought it was *his* to give, not a client's. Galo waited for me, walked me to my car, and told me to go home, and I was so upset I did. Later when I pressed Galo on it he claimed it wasn't my concern, it was a private FastFlex matter. They'd moved it, he said, just like Zhanna, for a client. Then Papa claimed to forget he'd ever brought me there, or shown me. I knew my family was lying to me. Lying about ten million dollars." Her voice shook in anger and frustration and she blew out the tension with a ragged sigh.

"So you decided to find out where this cash came from. You hired Steve."

"Yes. He'd worked for me before, security at an event where there was a jewelry auction…and I remembered he'd had a background working security details in Africa. That was where Papa started FastFlex. I thought…" She looked at the door. The family still hadn't materialized, probably hovering around Rey and the doctor. "I've heard the rumors. I've seen the newspaper articles that accused Papa of running weapons into war zones. He's always denied it and nothing was ever proven, and more than one government tried. But then…he talks to me about the 'underside' of the business, I thought, maybe it was true. But if it was true, I thought it was in the past and he's done so much good for people…what if it's not in the past?"

"You wanted Steve to investigate your own family's business."

"Yes. Just a bit. If they were doing something illegal then…I wanted to know."

"Why? You'd be complicit."

Her mouth moved. "My brother vanished four years ago. What if Edwin was taken because of what they're doing? If Papa is giving up the company to Galo and Zhanna, then this is time to stop doing anything illegal."

I considered. "They're moving cash under the radar. What else do you suspect?"

"Nothing. I have no idea what else they might be moving."

"Why would your father risk a very successful, legitimate business to be a smuggler?"

"I don't know."

Downstairs I heard voices. "What did Steve find out?" I asked. "Because I didn't find any reports on your family or FastFlex at his house, and he worked from home."

"I asked him not to keep records. To tell me everything verbally. I just wanted to know, I didn't want evidence. I wasn't going to the police and I didn't want Steve to have evidence the police could take. He'd just started, and he was digging into Papa's past in Africa. He said someone might be trying to bribe him to stop…"

Bribe. The casino chip. I got up, dug through the bag of bloodied clothes. Found the chip, slipped it into my pocket.

"What are you doing?"

My back was blocking her from seeing. "Nothing. My spare hotel key." I stood, dropped the bag to the floor. "Yet someone knew Steve was investigating your family's business."

"My family wouldn't kill him. They *wouldn't*."

"Cori," I said quietly. "They're covering up a death right now."

"Someone came after Papa. It's someone else, someone outside of the family. An enemy."

"Unhappy clients, maybe?" I said. "If Galo and Z and your dad are doing something illegal, then there must be clients. Who might be unhappy your father tried to give away a large amount of money that wasn't his? Or competitors? Someone in the same line of smuggling who wants to get rid of your father. But why now?"

"Oh God," Cori said, putting her face in her hands.

I leaned close to Cori. "The kidnapper—he told me he didn't want your father dead, he wanted to take him to chat with his friends." She looked up at me. "And the man who fell from the roof, he said this—I assume he meant getting rid of Steve—was for your own good. That's what made me think it was your family, after I saw Ricky go to Galo after he searched Steve's house."

I took her hands in mine. "What do you want to do, Cordelia?"

"I want my family to stop breaking the law. I want them to be safe."

And I wanted whoever ordered Steve killed. Maybe it was this outside group, maybe it was her family. She couldn't see straight about it. My head ached. "Do you want my help?"

"I would but I'm afraid of you, a little."

"Why?"

"Sam, I know you saved Papa today…but you *killed* that other man. The one who shot Steve. He fell off a building, the news said. Am I supposed to think that was an accident?"

"I didn't push him. He panicked, he fell. I wanted him alive to talk, Cori. Do you think I'm some sort of killing machine?" I nearly laughed and then I thought, This is why you're alone. You kind of are what she's afraid of.

"The other one, you did try to kill. You ran him down with a motorcycle."

She thought I was a cold-blooded killer. "Cori. He fired right at me. I didn't have a choice, I didn't have a weapon other than the bike. If someone is after your family, I can help."

"I'm not playing the naïve baby of the family anymore, Sam." A new toughness was in her tone. "If we can find out what they're doing, or who they're doing it for…then we can force them to stop." Her voice went low. "What if this has been going on for a while? It's been a curse on us. My mother, my brother, my father's wives…maybe this is why so much tragedy, so much pain. It has to stop, Sam."

She ran a charity. She was an idealist and thought the world could be a better place. She was just like my parents. And I admired them all, but I felt like their optimism could blind them to the darkness in the world. And how hard it was to banish that darkness.

I leaned back from her. "I saw Galo and Zhanna arguing at the Or nightclub at the Corinthian a few nights ago. Zhanna seemed very upset, she even slapped your brother. What's that about?"

"I have no idea." She looked startled. "You're spying on my brother?"

"I was following Ricky after he searched Steve's house. He met them there. Could you find out what happened?"

"I can try." She squeezed my hand. "It might have been about me. I'd told Galo I was coming to Puerto Rico, even though I wasn't invited."

I thought of Z, miming the cutting of a throat.

I said, "We have to get our stories straight. Details we could be asked about independently. Where our first date was, our second date, and so on."

She nodded. "And why you haven't met any of my friends yet, why I kept you secret…"

I stood and brought her close to me. "Fine. Kiss me."

"What?" She looked flustered.

"I'm supposed to be your boyfriend. They cannot suspect, especially now, after this, that I am anything else. If we kiss in front of them, it can't look awkward…" And then she put her fingertips along my jawline and went on her tippy-toes and kissed me. It was a good, long kiss, the kind that breaks you in together, much better than the one at the casino for Galo's eyes. Soft, then open, then harder, then gentle again. When I opened my eyes, she opened her eyes, studied my ugly, bruised face. And she smiled.

"Okay," I said. "That'll work."

Then she kissed me again. "For good luck," she whispered.

"We'll need it to help my family get out of this."

Was she using me, or was I using her? Or both? The problem was—I liked Cordelia. She was smart and lovely and stronger than her family knew. I felt she was a generous person. I believed her story. Her family was shady, she wasn't, she was trying to save them. If she was using me, it was because she was alone, and where else could she turn for my kind of help? I was her weapon to save her family, and she was my gateway to finding the person behind Steve's death. I guess I had a look in my eye, appraising her, and she blushed and leaned in and kissed me again. Gently, with nothing to prove.

"I wish…we were meeting under normal circumstances." Her fingers were against my jaw, then ran up to the bruise on my face. "Thank you for saving Papa. Thank you."

I smiled. No matter what—I had her gratitude for that. "If we get through this it will be normal circumstances," I said. And then I'd have to tell her that Chevalier wasn't my real name and that I wasn't exactly who she thought I was. That could be a problem. A bridge to be crossed when reached.

She gave me "Dating Cordelia Varela 101"—her friends, her schooling, her ex-boyfriends. She whispered most of it in my ear, fast. The CIA taught me to retain and remember information like this quickly. I closed my eyes, committed the details to memory even though my brain was fogged by the pain.

"You don't look well," she said.

"Don't forget to call me honey. Or sweetheart. Or whatever you like."

She touched the side of my face. "You're a 'babe,' I think."

"Babes are helpless and innocent."

She took her hand away gently. "Always an exception to the rule, babe."

"I need to make myself something to eat or drink. I fought on an empty stomach."

She helped me to the door, and I let her think I was weaker than I felt. The pain would fade, in time. She wanted to protect her family, even if they were criminals. I had no such compunction. Let them think me helpless and hurt. Let them think they owed me for the blood I shed. Steve had found out very dangerous information about the Varelas before he died. He'd asked me to be his inside man. He'd had a plan in mind to penetrate this family, unearth its secrets. But what?

I was the inside man now.

23

So what does a family do after they've covered up the killing of a person? The Varelas apparently huddled up in a meeting in Rey's room and we weren't invited.

Cordelia led me to the impressive stone-floored kitchen. I poured a big glass of water and she pulled a covered dish from a massive refrigerator.

"This is a Puerto Rican chicken stew. One of Papa's favorites. Do you like chicken? Of course you do. You barbecued chicken for me, on our fourth date," she said to the empty kitchen. She seemed to talk so that I would not.

I drank the water and joked, "Good job doctor did on the stitches, I'm not leaking anywhere," and she laughed, the jagged giggle of nervous release. She told me to sit down, I looked pale, and that she'd heat the food up for me. I thanked her.

She set a hot bowl before me, and I slowly began to eat. The stew was delicious, rich with the spicy taste of *sofrito*, thick with potatoes and green beans. On the wall across from the table was a large antique map of what looked like this section of the coastline, on the western side of Puerto Rico. I saw Rincón and Aguadilla on the map.

She followed my gaze. "Ah, this land belonged to the first Mrs. Varela, Galo's mom, it had been in her family a long time. Her father made those maps. Aren't they cool?"

I studied the terrain. It's always good to have an escape route.

Galo entered the kitchen and we finally had an audience. He glanced at me for a moment then went to the refrigerator. He touched my shoulder in silent thanks as he passed me. I looked up at him, a bit scared, as though I didn't have words. Then he opened a Dos Equis and sat across from Cori and me. Cori was drinking a glass of red wine and I could see her hand shake, ever so slightly, when she lifted the glass. Everyone was self-medicating.

It's awkward to make small talk with a man after he's killed someone. It changes you. The air around you seems different for a while. Television and movies make us think, usually, that it doesn't. They don't want to slow down the action for reflection. But it twists your heart, your brain, even if it was justified. You played God. You took away something that cannot be given back. It makes a little hole in you and puts a ghost there and you have to learn how to live with it. I had dreamed of the falling thug every night since he fell—I didn't know him or like him and he'd helped murder Steve. But that was how I had to be different from him; his death had to matter to me. The dreams would fade soon enough.

If Galo was bent on the inside, the dreams would never start.

Galo kept his hands cupped around the cold beer. He looked scrubbed; his hair was damp from the shower. You want to get clean after death; I understood that.

"Thank you," I said.

He took a deep breath. He wasn't used to this, his history of fighting as a kid aside. He looked tough but he had the muscles of an athlete, not a thug. He looked a bit lost.

"Oh, Galo," Cori reached for his hand.

His voice was steady. "I've thought of all the ramifications." As if the recent events could be analyzed, plugged into a spreadsheet, with a happy result. "You thanked me. Fine. I thanked you. Fine. You don't bring it up again, okay, Cori?"

"Okay."

"You don't bring it up again," he repeated, looking hard at her. Trying to be tough. She met his gaze without blinking.

She squeezed his hand. Now he looked at me. "We have no idea whether we can trust you, Sam."

"You saved my life. Why would I tell anyone what you did? I'm not an ingrate."

"You asked the doctor about calling the police," Galo said. And I thought: I have his life in my hands. I could make his life so hard with a phone call. Because even if it was justified, they'd gotten rid of the body. That itself was a crime.

I had a part to play, and I needed to be pitch-perfect. "Cori says we're not bringing in the police, and I'm fine with that. I want whatever makes Cori happy. But I have a question. You could have just dumped the body off the property, phoned in an anonymous tip or left him where someone was bound to find him. The police would have done the work of identifying him, maybe even learning who he works for."

"You thought about this? All the angles?" And sometimes, I remembered, a scared man is much more dangerous than a calm one.

"I try to consider all the options in a dangerous situation."

"Like you, I have to consider all the options." He took a sip of beer. "You come here. Unannounced. All hell breaks loose. You're a stranger. A secret."

"He's not a stranger to me," Cori said. "And you all have been keeping a lot of secrets from me."

"Zhanna and Kent are checking you out, Sam. Thoroughly," he said.

"Okay, point one? I'm the guy who saved your father."

"*I* saved my father." He almost looked embarrassed. "I've never shot anyone before."

"Oh, Galo," Cori said. She sounded like her heart was breaking. She put both her hands on his.

"I'll be all right," he told her.

"How can any of us be all right?" she said.

He could see where she was aiming the conversation. "Do you

feel well enough to walk with me for a moment, Sam? Sit out on the patio and get some fresh air?"

"Yes," I said. I pushed away my empty bowl.

Cori stood as if to follow.

Galo said, "Doctor said the kidnapper injected Papa with a depressant. To keep him quiet. I think that's part of his confusion. He's resting, but he wants to see you."

Cori glanced at me and then left the kitchen. I got up, gingerly, and followed Galo out onto the stone patio. The breeze from the sea—where it was logical to presume the kidnapper's body now rested—had grown in strength and the cool air felt good against my face. I was at their mercy. Hurt, worn out, trapped. I sat down heavily in the chair. From there I could see the small slice of beach.

"Did you find anyone else?" I asked.

"You mean was the kidnapper working alone?"

"Yes."

"No. Ricky and the guys and I searched the property. But it's a lot of acres."

"Did you find a car? He must have had some means of escape. Keys? A phone? An ID?"

"We didn't find a car," he said, as though he'd followed the train of my thought. But he didn't fully answer my question. He still didn't know if he could trust me. "He was taking Papa toward the beach. We didn't find a boat, either. So I'm guessing he had a partner waiting in a boat for a signal and the partner took off when he didn't come back."

Possibly, or they hadn't looked in the right place. I would find it, then, if there was something to be found. I'd figure out a way.

"What have I gotten myself involved with?" I asked him. "I could have gotten gutted helping your dad."

"You didn't seem the type when we met. Not the serious soldier."

"I was trying to be funny and charming. I wanted to impress you all. Being a bodyguard doesn't normally bowl over the young woman's parents." I tinged my voice with shame.

He looked at the ocean, then looked at me. "I do want to thank you. Man to man. For saving my papa."

"Technically I think you saved him."

He shook his head. "No, we both did. Together." Yes, I thought, and it'll make a bond between us if I play you right. "You kept him from taking Papa. Thank you."

"You're welcome. You saved my life too, Galo. He would have opened my throat if you hadn't stopped him. So thanks."

His own throat worked. You know when you first make friends with someone, real friends? You find that thread that binds you there. He *had* saved my life; I was in imminent danger from the knife. I had saved his father's life and he wanted to believe I was a good guy. In crisis we want to trust, even when it's hard. "Yeah. Okay. We need to talk about that."

"All right."

"I did my duty to my dad. I don't let anyone hurt the people I love."

"I respect that, Galo."

He looked down into his beer. "We'll offer you money. Not to ever say anything to the police. You'll be well taken care of."

The burnt man would have loved this invitation. I let five long seconds pass. "You don't have to buy my silence."

"You seem like a guy who appreciates money. No offense."

"None taken." I pointed at the bandage under my—his—T-shirt. "I fell down the stairs while walking with a knife. Freak accident. My face hit the edge of the stair. Fortunately I'm going to be okay."

"You're very cool and collected. Funny that the guy who gets hurt is the calmest," he said.

"Everyone else is panicking," I said. "Right? Kent. Zhanna. Your dad. Because you stepped up to the plate and did the right thing."

He watched me. I'd guessed right. The others were distancing themselves from him, even if they didn't know it. Natural human response. There's a reason warriors underwent purification rituals when they came back from killing on the hunt.

Death makes us uneasy, even when we don't want to admit it. "Galo."

"What?"

"When the shock wears off, and it will, don't doubt that you did the right thing."

He tried to smile. It didn't quite work. He wasn't ready to smile yet.

I made a decision. *Sometimes you have to rock the boat,* the burnt man had told me. *You have to do the unexpected and see what happens.* Then he had said: *You're too young, Sam. You're so young. If these new kinds of criminals weren't so young too, we wouldn't have to send kids like you.*

So, Burnt Man, here was my bit of unexpected. "Let's go search again, along where he took your father. Maybe we'll find something we missed."

"All right."

We walked across the patio, down the steps. Galo said, "You were incredible. I saw it when I was running toward you and Papa. You fought like you were trained."

"Some of it was Army training." I waited and he waited. The dance of lies moved into a new rhythm. They were in trouble. They needed me. And so I would be there. "And I worked for a man in the Czech Republic. He got me special training, he made sure all his people could take care of themselves."

"Who was the man? You said you worked in transportation."

"Nobody." I managed to look slightly ashamed. "You wouldn't know him."

"In Prague?"

"Yes."

"Tell me. If I can trust you, then you can trust me."

"His name is František Lada," I said. This was part of the official Sam Chevalier cover. Lada was a moderately successful smuggler, using a legit company as a front, and he was also a CIA informant. His cooperation protected him and his operations. "He's in the export-import business. There are unsavory types around, it can be rough." I kept my face neutral.

We searched along the pathway. I saw nothing. We reached the scrubby incline where I'd caught up to the two of them.

"Did the kidnapper say anything to you?" Galo asked.

I hadn't told him yet that the kidnapper claimed an intention of not harming Rey. First, because the kidnapper might have been lying and second, because the Varelas might be more likely to tell me who their enemy was if they felt the enemy could not be reasoned with. They'd seen a man nearly kill me, brutalize their father. If Cori's theory was right and these were unhappy clients, then the Varelas might try to reason with them and shut me out. Let the Varelas wonder a bit longer who was after them.

"No one will bother you or Cordelia." He bit at his lip for a moment. "I'll protect you, whatever it takes." He was trying to figure out who he was now, how he lived with what he'd done. I could use that.

I walked the scrub and the loose soil and the rocky places where I'd fought the kidnapper. Glanced at Galo. He was farther down, looking in the grass. I slipped my hand into my pocket, palmed the casino chip. I had no idea of the consequences of what I was about to do. It was a bit like a scientific experiment. The unexpected.

"I think when you're okay to travel," Galo said, "you should get Cordelia out of here. She already told me she won't go back to Miami without you."

"I don't know if I can promise that. Cordelia feels shut out, and she's not going to stay that way anymore. She's seen too much today." His back was to me. I kicked at a clot of dirt, snapped the chip in half, shoved one half of the chip into the mud, covered it partially back up. Dirt grimed the red. You'd have to look for it. I moved away, circling to the left, putting the other half in my pocket. After a few moments, Galo hiked toward me, circling toward the right.

"Um, this Lada guy," I said. "I understand you want to check me out. But maybe you could not tell Cori I worked for him?"

"What's wrong with him?"

"Nothing," I said, knowing that he would therefore definitely check out Lada.

I could see blood on the ground, drying. I grubbed around in the dirt and found a bullet. I didn't have to fake the wince. My whole body ached, badly. The pain radiated out from my shoulder. I stood up. "You might want this back."

"Thank you." And he came over and he touched my shoulder, the uninjured one. A reassuring squeeze, a pat of friendship.

"Ouch," I said.

"Sorry, sorry."

I saw Zhanna hurrying down toward us. "What are you doing?" she asked.

"Trying to figure out who the kidnapper was," I said. "It was a violent fight, there might be something…"

She stared at me. "I'm in charge of security. I'll take care of this. I already went through…"

Galo held up the bullet. "We have to be more careful. Sam found this."

She seemed unimpressed. "I'll search here, not you."

"I'll search here," I said. "Are you going to tell me who the kidnapper was? I mean, these people could come after Cori next. Or me. I want to know what I've gotten involved with. Who is behind this?"

"How would they know about you?" she said.

"How did they know Rey was here? Or that he was alone?" I countered.

"Help us, Z, come on," Galo said.

"Aren't we all on the same team?" I said.

She snatched the bullet from Galo's hand.

"So who's behind this?" I asked again.

"We don't know," she said.

"I think you do." I moved away from where I'd planted the chip, down past where we'd fought. Zhanna, still in her suit but with blood along one sleeve—I presumed it was Rey's, from the knife cut he'd taken—searched along where I'd hidden the chip. It was red, even if smeared with mud.

Galo moved down toward me. "She's territorial," he whispered.

"I noticed."

"But she'll respect you for finding that bullet she missed."

I'd respect her if she found what I'd left. It took her four minutes. Galo was five feet away from me and I saw Zhanna suddenly kneel down in the mud. She pulled the broken chip free, cleaned it. Stared at it. I glanced at Galo. He had his back to her.

Then I turned back and she was watching me. The chip wasn't in her hand.

She said nothing, then she started searching again.

She must have stuck the chip fragment in her pocket. She would either know that it might have been the chip that had been in Steve's possession, or maybe the kidnapper had visited the casino. It would create questions. Perhaps suspicion.

I'd just thrown a little bomb into House Varela. I'd have to see how long it took to detonate.

After twenty more minutes of searching we went back up to the house. Zhanna kept glancing at me. Wondering. Had I seen her pocket the chip? Was she going to talk about finding it in front of me? I started to feel like I'd made a mistake.

When we reached the stone patio Kent and Cori were waiting for us. So was Rey Varela, dressed in a bathrobe, his arm bound. His head was bandaged where the kidnapper had shoved him against the tree. He blinked at me. Pointed. "You. I don't know you."

"No, sir," I said.

"This is Sam. He is the guy who saved you, Papa," Galo said.

"Why?" Rey said. "Why would he do that?"

"I need a why?" I said to him, and he laughed. It was a curiously empty sound.

"Everyone needs a why," Rey said.

I pointed at Cori. "I did it for her. You're her father."

His gaze went from being blank to being knowing. He crooked a small smile.

"What were you doing?" Cori asked us.

"Searching for clues. We found a bullet. Nothing more," Zhanna said.

"Zhanna stuck something in her pocket," I said. "I saw her."

Everyone stared at me. But I stared at Zhanna.

"Z?" Galo said.

She shrugged. "Yes. It's a part of a chip from the casino." She produced the muddied, broken plaque.

"That's a high-dollar chip," Galo said.

"Maybe he was gambling earlier," I suggested.

"At our own casino?" Cori's voice rose. "It's half a chip."

"The half with the serial number is gone," Zhanna said. She handed it to Galo.

"What denomination is it?" I asked innocently.

"The denomination is on the missing half," Zhanna said after a moment.

"Aren't they color-coded?" I asked.

No one answered me.

"Do you think someone goes and gambles at a casino before attempting a kidnapping?" Cori asked. "Seems odd."

"Unless he's getting paid with the chip for services rendered," I said, testing a theory. "It's broken. Maybe he got half the chip when he took the job, and the other half when he delivered Mr. Varela."

It got even quieter, the family silent as the grave in the Caribbean breeze.

"No one delivers me," Rey said, to no one. "I deliver things." Cori patted his arm and for a moment he smiled at her.

"Or maybe it was yours, Sam," Zhanna said. "You were at the casino this morning."

"I didn't gamble," I said, hoping no one would suggest I empty my pockets.

"Why would you hide that, Zhanna?" Kent asked in a gentle, understanding tone. "I'm sure you had a good reason."

"We don't know much about Sam," she said. "And I think that

maybe we shouldn't quite trust him yet. So I didn't want him to know what I'd found."

"It's great to feel appreciated, Z," I said. "Thank you for that."

Galo went over and talked to Kent and Zhanna in a quick whisper. Everyone looked at me. Kent nodded, went back inside, led by Zhanna. I saw Kent speak to his phone, but couldn't hear what he asked it to do.

"Wait here," Galo said. He looked tense.

"What's the matter?" I said.

He shrugged. "Kent just needs to make a couple of phone calls."

"Maybe we should go," Cori said. "Take Papa back to Miami right now."

"No," Galo said. "We're not doing that. We're safer here."

I looked at Rey. "Are you all right, sir?"

His gaze met mine. "Fine. Of course I'm fine. That little punk, he couldn't have taken me if he hadn't shot me up with a drug to make me woozy." Then I noticed he was leaning on Cori.

"Maybe go back to bed, Papa," she said.

"No, I wanted to see this boy. Say thank you."

"You're welcome," I said. A minute ago he hadn't remembered me.

He looked at Galo. "This one, too, he's tougher than I ever thought he'd be. Pulling a trigger. Like a man."

"Can we not talk about it, Papa?" Galo said.

"Galo has to stay clean," he said to me, as if this made sense. I just nodded.

"A boy like you," he pointed at me, "that's a good boy. You help keep Galo clean." His words slurred slightly and I didn't know if it was a leftover from the sedative. He turned to Cori. "Him I like."

"Yes, sir." I didn't know what else to say.

"Let's go back to bed, Papa," she urged.

He raised a finger toward me. "That boy. He fought for me. Give him some money, Galo."

"I don't want your money, sir," I said.

"Of course you do."

Cori led him away. Zhanna reappeared on the patio, this time with Ricky, who gave me a grim stare. "Come with us, please, Sam," Zhanna said. I'd made a gamble when I tattled on her, and it had failed.

I followed them back into the house.

24

ARE THEY GOING to kill me? I wondered. I felt like a man walking to his execution. Not to freedom.

I followed them down a hall and around a corner to an office that faced not the ocean but the courtyard. Before we got to the door I could hear the soft drone of a computerized voice. Reading out Sam Chevalier's Canadian military record.

Kent sat in front of a computer. I listened to that computer read out my fake history, and then Zhanna told me to sit down. I sat on a small couch. Cori appeared in the doorway, looking miserable, and sat down next to me.

Zhanna settled into a heavy leather chair, Galo stood by the window, and Ricky stood by the door. This was a war council.

"Have I done something wrong...?" I began.

"Sam," Zhanna said, not smiling. "I am security chief for FastFlex. So answer our questions truthfully and honestly and we will all be happy. Cordelia, you met him when he bid on a security job for you? And he didn't get the job, but he asked you out socially."

"Yes."

Galo looked at me. "Sam says he used to work for a guy named František Lada in Prague. Kent, you know who Lada is?"

I shot him a look of annoyance, playing my part, and Galo shrugged. "Sorry, man."

"Not personally," Kent said.

I let myself blush and continued to stick to polite fictions. "Mr. Lada's an importer." True enough, that was the legitimate business that served as a cover for Lada's more lucrative activities.

"Do we have any friends in Prague?" Zhanna asked.

"Guy named Gajda," Kent said. I knew Gajda's name. He was like Lada—a legit businessman who might sometimes cross the boundaries of the law but was bigger and better connected in the Czech government than Lada. "Rey flew goods for him from Africa to Prague back in the old days."

"Check with him, see if he knows Lada. I want to talk to this guy," Zhanna said.

Kent made the phone call. Gajda did indeed know Lada and called him a couple of choice names. However, he arranged for Kent to speak to Lada in a matter of minutes on a secure line.

Sweat dampened my back. If Lada didn't validate me...I'd be exposed. What if August couldn't have reached him or he was no longer on the CIA payroll? I wondered if I could fight my way past them. On the desk were a keyboard, scissors, a heavy glass statue, some corporate award from FastFlex, a framed photo of Zhanna. I could kill with any of those...This all blazed through my brain in five seconds.

"You," Zhanna said to me, "not a word during the call. Remain silent."

"Or what?" I said. "You'll go all security chief on me?"

"Mind your mouth," Ricky said.

"Where were you during the kidnapping attempt, ace?" I asked, and his face reddened.

"Stop this, gentlemen, please," Kent said.

Zhanna dialed the number. Mr. Lada came on the phone. He coughed, sounding like he had a cold. "Hello?"

"You don't know us, Mr. Lada, and I'm not giving you my name. But I appreciate you talking to me," Kent said. Interesting, I thought. Zhanna was the security chief but Kent asked the questions.

"Mr. Gajda insisted as an old friend," Lada said. "Only for him do I talk to a stranger."

"We're his friends, and we appreciate your courtesy."

"Forget the diplomacy. What do you want to know?"

"Did you once have a man named Sam Chevalier work for you?"

A few beats of silence, then he said, "Yes. He worked on my security team. Sometimes my shipments need...protection."

"I just e-mailed you a photo of him, Mr. Lada. Did you see it?"

"Yes, that's Sam. His hair is little longer now. He had military cut when I hire him."

"And how was he as an employee?"

"Reliable. Very smart, much smarter than usual muscle. Good with languages. He spoke French fluently. Also some German and Russian."

"We know about his not-very-good Russian." Zhanna frowned. I smiled, since I wasn't supposed to talk. "How do you think he came by it?"

"In Canada Army. Trained as translator but got thrown out. Him having some Russian was reason to hire him, I deal with Russians a lot."

Zhanna and Galo exchanged a glance. "Why was Sam thrown out of the Army?"

"He said fighting with other soldier and also he did little smuggling on the side while in the Army and they don't like that. They show him the door."

I stared at my knees as though too ashamed to look at Cori.

"Sam was a good fighter?" Galo asked.

"I never saw him in boxing ring, if that's what you mean."

"Then what do you mean?" Kent asked.

"So...one night some competitors try to grab a shipment Sam was in charge of watching. Two jerks with guns, Sam was alone and unarmed. The two jerks both ended up in the hospital."

Now I winked at Zhanna. She looked away in disgust.

Lada cleared his throat. "But not a bragging man. Pay him well. He likes his money. He likes his women. I liked him. If you are hiring him you are getting a good man."

"Discreet?" Kent asked.

"Dis...what?" Lada's English was only so good.

"Could he keep his mouth shut?" Galo asked.

"Ah. Very, the shut mouth. Very dis...creet." Lada said the last word like he was tasting it.

"And when did you last see him?" Kent tilted his head toward the couch where I sat. He knew exactly where I was, had heard the shift of my legs against the furniture.

"Little over a year ago, I guess."

"And he only worked protection for you?"

"Well." A sniffle. "A bit more."

"It's all right, Mr. Lada. Mr. Gajda vouched for us, remember?" Zhanna said.

"Well. Okay. There was a guy trying to screw with my business. Some idiot in Turkey, trying to disrupt my routes. He wanted a cut. I don't know how to say this, you know, diplomat like. Sam found out who the Turkish guy was and convinced the guy to leave us alone."

"Convinced?" Zhanna stared at me. This time I didn't wink.

"Yes, Sam convinced him. Guy not problem no more. He go off to bother someone else."

Zhanna raised an eyebrow at Cordelia. Galo reached out, touched Kent's shoulder with a pat. For them it was like exchanging a look, a sign to say, *That is interesting*.

I put my innocent schoolboy gaze back on my feet.

"Did you ever think Sam was a cop?" Kent asked. Now the questions were getting good.

Lada laughed. "No, never. Not a cop. Nothing like that. Not customs, or for government. Just a kid who got out of Canada Army and knew how to solve my problems for me."

"Why did he stop working for you?" Kent asked.

"He moved. To London, I think. I don't know what he did after working for me. He don't send Christmas cards."

I studied the room. Zhanna looked annoyed, Galo looked relieved, and Kent was impossible to read behind his dark glasses.

"Thank you, Mr. Lada," Kent said.

"You tell Gajda I answered your questions. He owes me. You see Sam, you tell him I said hi and the beer is still cold here." And Lada hung up.

Kent turned off the speakerphone. "I don't have to see your self-satisfied smile to know it's there, Cordelia. But you didn't know he'd worked for a smuggler."

"Import-export," I corrected, as if it mattered.

"No," Cordelia said. "But I knew Sam was a good man."

"It's a bit tidy, isn't it? You meeting him, and him having this background. Then he's here when we need him. It's neat as a pin," Zhanna said.

"May I speak now?" I said.

"Of course, Sam," Kent said, as though the idea of me being silent was my own. He was always so measured, an interesting counterpoint to the ever-brusque Zhanna.

And then I gave the thread leading into the maze a hard, hard yank. I wanted to shake the hiding monster. Because here was the brutal truth: either the attacks on Steve and Rey were the work of an outside enemy, or they were the work of a cold-blooded someone in this room who wanted both Cori and Rey out of the way. And the someone in this room could *not* own up to being the culprit—the rest of the family would take him or her down. A line had been crossed. "The kidnapper told me something interesting."

I studied their faces for a hint of reaction. Saw none.

"You chatted during your fight?" Zhanna asked, disbelieving.

"What did he say, Sam?" Kent said.

"I'll get to that in a minute. Let's stop dancing around," I said. "You're acting like idiots."

Silence.

"You're under attack. Someone tried to take Rey and was willing to kill to take him. And note that they made their attempt today. When you're having some big secret confab about your family's business problems. The one involving the ten million in cash that Rey tried to give Cori, the ten million Cori wasn't supposed to know about, the money that's made her think that there's something very dirty under the family business."

They all stared at me.

"We explained to Cori that the ten million was just some cargo…" Kent began.

"If you insult my intelligence once more, blind man or not, I will take your cane and shove it up your ass."

Silence again.

"Pray continue," Kent said after a few moments. "I won't insult your intelligence again."

"The ten million is the reason for this secret meeting, for shutting out Cori, for the old man nearly getting hauled off down the beach. Elephant in the room acknowledged," I said. "Now. I know there's a big bad problem here and it's just gotten worse. So either I can help you with it—because I want to help Cori, because I care about her—or Cori and I can leave and we'll never mention it again. But you'll never see her again, period, because she's not going to hang around you all and hope there's not an eventual bloodbath." And I looked at Zhanna, because I thought she was the most dangerous person in the room.

Silence again, as if no one wanted to debate me.

I stood. "I'm not here to solve your problem, I'm here to solve Cori's. But as of the moment of the attack on your dad, I think those problems are the same."

"What do you think you can do?" Galo said.

"Find whoever's after him. But I suspect you already know who it is. Tell me."

"We don't know for certain," Zhanna said.

"Then tell me who the suspects are. He had a very slight Russian accent. Have you pissed off some Russians?" I looked particularly hard at Zhanna.

No one answered. I counted to ten inside my head. I turned to Cori. "You see how much they value you. And your dad."

"We'll deal with the problem ourselves," Zhanna said. "Although your offer is appreciated."

"Did Cori hire you?" This from Ricky.

I met his glare with my own. "Hire me for what?"

"Hire you to be her bodyguard," he repeated.

You mean like Steve? I wanted to say. He knew about Steve, and so did Galo. But the rest of them? Perhaps not.

"No," Cori said. "I didn't." She leaned over and took my hand.

"I'm exactly what I said I was," I told them. "Since I nearly got killed for your problem today, you want to tell me and Cori the truth about the ten million?"

Kent said, "It's a confidential business matter and you need not worry about its legality. I'm sorry if that bothers you, Cori, but it is, and we're not going to talk about it with you. For your own good."

I laughed. "You see, Cordelia? Your father's life in danger, and still they're closemouthed." I wagged a cocky finger at Galo and Zhanna. "Here's something to think about. Your kidnapper had half a casino chip. If someone else here has the other half of that chip, then you know who's behind the kidnapping."

They all stared at me and then, as I hoped, glanced at each other, except for Kent, who didn't move. "I mean, you might conduct a search."

"That's ridiculous," Kent said.

"It's such an unusual way to pay. I presume if you redeem the chip, you get the cash. It would be easy for any of you to arrange that, since the casino is a family business. You're not going to bring a load of cash with you. You don't want it traced to you. Back when I worked for Lada I got paid in all kinds of hard-to-trace ways."

"Why would any of us want Papa kidnapped?" Zhanna said.

"Don't play that card after you don't report a death to the police." I'd planted the seed of doubt. "It's just a suggestion. I'm tired, I took a beating, and I'd like to go back to my room." And I got up, and Cordelia and I left, and no one stopped us. I went back to my room and she said, in an unhappy whisper, "You shouldn't have told them you knew about the money."

"I yanked on the thread."

"What?"

"It's just a phrase." I lay down on my bed, Cori next to me.

"Are they going to come in here and kill me?" I said.

"No," she said. Her breath was close on my cheek. "I don't think so."

"You said they were incapable of violence before."

"They know smugglers in Prague," she said. "I don't know my own family right now."

"Do you think they'll look for the other half of the chip?"

"Probably, because you've scared them now. But this is someone outside the family, Sam."

"I'm glad you're all so sure."

I excused myself to the bathroom. I hid the broken chip, in a better place than Steve had hidden his. I flushed the toilet for cover.

When I came out of the room I crawled into the bed next to Cori and I closed my eyes. I needed to sleep. Everything hurt. Now we'd see what they would do.

25

I AWOKE THINKING about death. About Coma Thug, the thudding of his body as I ran over him with Steve's motorcycle. His buddy's scream as he lost balance and fell four stories to the pavement.

The light was dim in the room, the sun sliding below the horizon, purpling the clouds. Twilight. Cori, who had been curled up next to me when I fell asleep, was gone. An evening breeze drifted through the window. I'd slept the rest of the day away.

I ached, horribly. I trembled with thirst. I decided against a painkiller; I needed to be sharp. I got up, washed my face, went to the door.

They'd locked me in. Not a good sign.

I sat back down on the bed.

Something had changed. Maybe Coma Thug, who might have worked for whoever the kidnapper did, had awakened. Carlos Tellez. He was my own personal time bomb, ticking away in his bed. If he died I was pretty safe. If he lived, it depended on what he remembered. What he wanted to say to the police or what message he could pass to his employer. I had to find the connection between Coma Thug and Rey, or whoever was after Rey and Cori. It didn't matter if it was a family member or someone else who killed Steve. That was who I wanted.

Except it would matter to Cori. She'd try to stop me if it was a family member. I'd deal with that problem if it got serious.

Locked in the maze. *You'll think you can't get out at some point, but you can,* the burnt man had said. *You can't always fight your way out. Sometimes you will have to negotiate.*

Did I have a chance to negotiate? I'd done them a favor.

Then came a knock on my door, the sound of the doorknob unlocking, and I said, "Come in."

Zhanna stood in the doorway. She wore a dark dress with bright indigo flowers. She looked stunning. She flicked on the room's main light. "Did you have a nice rest?"

"Yes," I said. "Thank you."

She stepped aside and Ricky brought in my suitcase that I'd left at the Gran Fortuna. He set it down, hardly gave me a glance, and then he walked out.

"Thank you, buddy," I called out to him. He vanished down the hallway. Charming as always.

"Never mind Ricky. You made the guards look bad. They didn't protect Papa and you did." Zhanna leaned against the doorway, smiling in a way that seemed designed to make me uncomfortable.

"So if I'm okay, why am I locked in here?"

She shrugged. "That's my fault. I have a security mentality."

"You're mad at me because I mentioned the chip you found."

Zhanna let three beats pass. "No. I would have done the same if I were you. I thought you might have planted it."

"I didn't even know your family owned a casino until Cori told me at the hotel. I sure didn't have much time to gamble up to an interesting amount."

"But then I decided you made a good point. A payment made half on taking the job, half on delivering Papa."

"A casino chip's an unusual way to pay."

"Kidnapping is not a job one writes out a check for," she said.

"How did you decide to go into security work?" I asked.

"I joined the Air Force out of college, was an investigator. Family tradition. My father was in the Air Force, in the old Soviet Union."

I remembered a detail I'd read in the history of FastFlex. "Your dad was Mr. Varela's business partner. Sergei Pozharsky."

"Yes."

"That must be awkward."

The slightly friendly smile dimmed. "How so?"

"When your father's partner becomes your stepfather."

"My father...we were never close. And then there was the plane crash..." She shook her head at her past tragedies. "Papa— Rey Varela—took care of all of us, of me and my mama...even though Mama was never easy to live with." She said this with the gravity of a person who has endured many trials.

"I'm sorry."

She waved it away with a flick of her hand, like her lost family didn't warrant much reflection. She had a new family, apparently one she liked better.

"How's your stepfather?"

"*Papa* is resting." I couldn't miss the emphasis. "He wants to talk to you." She gestured to the hallway.

I followed her, and then saw Ricky, down the hallway, waiting for us. Zhanna put her hand on my arm, the uninjured one, and kept a grip on me as we walked. "You saved Papa." This announcement wasn't for my benefit.

I said nothing.

"Unlike do-nothings who are paid good money," she said to Ricky's back. I saw his spine stiffen for the barest of moments, but he didn't break stride.

"Fifty acres are a lot to cover," Ricky said. "Ten bedrooms are a lot to cover."

"Your paycheck is a lot to cover," she said, still to his back.

"Then it's good you don't pay it."

Did he work for her or Galo or Rey? I wondered. It might be good to know where his loyalties lay.

"Everything's about to change, Ricky," she said.

Ricky shrugged. "Not everything. You're still a pain."

So clearly he didn't work for her. Her mouth was a thin line; she wasn't mad, she was enjoying the little duel with him.

"Ricky," she said, "maybe Sam can show you the moves he used to defeat the kidnapper."

"Sam was actually about to get his throat stabbed before Galo saved him," Ricky said. "I don't need to study his moves." His voice was grating, a bit whiny, cold.

"Do we have more guards now?" I asked.

"No. Papa doesn't trust anyone else on the island. We could fly in some from Miami but he said no."

So. Just the four, and now they'd be on high alert.

"So thank you, Sam. I don't think earlier I thanked you," Zhanna said this last bit with the barest tone of apology.

"You're welcome."

Ricky glanced back at us, a frown on his face. "You're welcome too," I told him. He ignored me.

At the end of the hall we reached a staircase and we went down to a foyer that divided kitchen and dining room. The dining room was large, with a massive wooden table of deep mahogany. Behind it, on each wall, was art. Modern stuff, but clearly inspired by the scenery of the Caribbean. At least there were no dead wives watching us. Cori and Galo sat at the table, and Kent sat next to Galo.

"Ah, the hero awakens." Galo tried a smile that didn't quite work. Cori got up and took me from Zhanna—who'd let go of my arm as soon as we'd entered the dining room—and steered me to a chair between her and Galo.

"Do you feel like eating?" she asked. Her grip on my arm was strong, purposefully tight. Danger signal, I thought.

"Yes," I said. "I'm starving."

"The doctor said you should eat," Cori said. "We're having steak and salad."

Kent nodded at me. His dark glasses masked his eyes.

"Wine?" he said. I saw he and Galo and Cori all had glasses, and an opened bottle of dark-red Zinfandel stood on the table. Galo looked tired, as though the weight of shooting a man had firmly settled on his shoulders. Cori seemed tense. Zhanna drank from a bottle of black tea, fidgety.

"No, thank you, just water. I'm thirsty."

What do you talk about when no one wants to talk about

the dead man? Or whether it's safe to walk outside. The Varelas talked about sports and weather and audiobooks. Ricky and another guard brought in the steaks, baked potatoes, and bowls of salad. I ate my steak and said little.

Find the map, the burnt man had told me. The ancient map of the family, in this case. Zhanna was the stormy seas on the map, always looking to be slighted, looking for an excuse to love, an excuse to be angry. Kent was steady, a lighthouse. When he spoke they listened. Cori was the distant island, a bit apart from the others. And Galo? I couldn't decide. He was in a way the center, the bright sun, by the force of personality that not even his disquiet over having killed a man could eclipse. But he seemed tugged, like the moon, trying to please them all and pleasing no one. I drew a little map in my head. Varela-land. I was the dragon, in the corner of the sea, the unseen danger of the unknown.

We'd just finished eating when Rey Varela came in and stood near Galo, surveying the remains of the dinner, and said, "I want to talk about today."

His eyes didn't seem dulled by sedative or dementia. He stared right at me.

26

He looked like a faded lion.

We followed Rey Varela into the living room. He walked toward a large, ornate carved chair, gorgeous polished mahogany with a towering back lined with antique scrollwork; it looked like a throne. Before he sat down he came to me and asked, "Are you all right?" He reached out toward my purpled face—the bruise had deepened as I slept—but he didn't touch me. He frowned, looked over at Galo. I wondered if they'd already talked about the shooting.

I risked a smile and shook his hand. "Yes, sir."

"Good. Your bravery won't be forgotten." Rey Varela wore a black bathrobe and black pajama pants. He seemed frail and strong all at once: frail from the physical travails of the day, strong from a heat inside himself. This was not a man, I guessed, easily scared or bent. He eyed his children with a knowing gaze. I noticed his glance lingered longest on Cordelia, his mouth working, as though uncertain of the words.

He released my hand from his grip and he sat in the thronelike chair. The rest of us sat on the more comfortable, softer seats that were arranged in a semicircle around Rey. Cori sat next to me. Zhanna and Kent were on my other side, Galo across from us and next to them.

Rey said, "I need to talk with all of you about what has happened. And what we're going to do about it."

Zhanna said, "Papa, while we're all grateful to Sam for what he did today, I think if this is family business it should stay private. Just family. And this isn't for Cori's ears either."

I looked at her. "You want me and Cori to leave? We will. But you have to tell us who's attacking the family."

Rey crooked a smile at me. "I like you. But you don't set conditions."

"Then I don't have to tell you what the kidnapper told me. It might affect your decisions here today."

Rey shifted in his seat, wiped a finger along his stubbly chin. "This doesn't concern Cordelia."

"That ship has sailed, sir," I said. "Cori knows. I know. So that dance is done." I looked at all of them. "Ten million dollars you can't explain, even with assertions and faked paperwork. You're all a bit dirty, except there seems to be this big concern that Galo not be."

Rey's mouth narrowed. "You said the kidnapper said something to you. I don't remember him saying anything."

"You were drugged and had taken a couple of hard hits," I said.

"Well, I still threw a rock at him to help the fight. I still got it. No matter what my children think of me."

"Papa…" Galo began.

Rey held up a hand. "What was said?"

"Uh-uh. First you tell us who is after you."

He just stared at me, but then Zhanna interjected, "We don't know for certain." Then Rey glanced at her, as if annoyed she'd even bothered to answer me.

"Is that money stolen?" I asked.

"Of course not," Zhanna said. "We're not thieves."

Rey studied me. He seemed to decide. "Here's the thing. I'm stepping down; the kids can run the company. So they can decide whether or not they need you."

You could feel the tension shift in the room. "Stepping down?" Galo asked.

"Yes." An odd little smile touched his lips. "You killed a man for me."

Galo looked down at the floor. "Yes, sir."

Was he going to pat his son on the head? Tell him he appreciated him saving his life? Ask him how he was holding up?

Rey said, quietly, "Glad you grew a pair, but that was a mistake. We could have learned who he was."

Galo looked up from the floor, his mouth twisting. "But he was going to kill you and Sam."

"He would have killed me if he wanted me dead. Why bother dragging me to the beach?"

"I didn't want him to hurt you or take you, Papa."

"It was a mistake. You cannot have bloodied hands, Galo."

"It's a little late for that, Papa. I shot a man." Galo's voice rose.

"Get over it," Rey snapped. "Honestly. Today you get to be shocked. Tomorrow, stand tall. Be a man." He glanced at Zhanna and she smirked back at him, as though a message had passed between them.

In that moment, I felt for Galo. The room was so silent it seemed like none of us knew how to breathe.

The smirk wavered on Rey's face. "Men try to shoot me sometimes when I load the planes, when I taxi down the runway in the hellholes in Africa. You think I sit around and think about it and feel sorry for myself? No."

"Papa, you don't fly anymore," Cori said, but he waved away her words.

"Yes, sir," Galo said, barely a whisper.

"Better you than him, eh?" Rey said.

"Yes." He cleared his throat. "Whoever it was, they'll send someone else."

Silence.

"What is clear is that we are under attack, and a change must be made," Rey said. "It's time."

"Change," Galo said. "Yes, sir."

"I've run both the businesses for far too long," Rey said. "I'm a target because I am seen as weak for some reason. Although I'm not."

"Of course not, Papa," Galo said.

Both, he said. *Both the businesses.*

"And because I am seen as weak, we are seen as weak," Rey said. "So. I'm passing what I've built to the three of you. Galo. You will take over FastFlex as CEO."

"All of it?" I could hear the incredulousness in his voice.

"Yes."

I saw Zhanna tighten her grip on Kent's hand. Kent tilted his head up slightly, as though listening to words no one else could hear.

"Thank you, Papa." But Galo sounded hesitant. "I thought...given what has happened. We might sell the company and shut down the..." He stopped, withered by his father's sudden glare.

"Sell? Never. Don't you want what I've built for you?" Rey's voice became harsh. "Maybe I could give it to Zhanna if you don't want it. She's tougher than you in some ways."

"I do want it, but..."

This was painful. Watching him play one against the other.

"Take it or don't." Rey seemed bored now.

"Yes, Papa, I'll be CEO." But in those few words I thought I could hear Galo longing to be free. To do something else. I'd been there. *Aren't you going to go into relief work like your parents and your brother, Sam? Oh, no?* And the implicit suggestion that I was somehow selfish for wanting a life of my own.

Now that he had a yes in response to his insults and his offer, Rey gave up a smile. "If you mess it up or lose it I will haunt you forever. This is your duty."

"Yes, Papa." Galo was now a CEO of a multi-million-dollar concern, but he didn't sound that thrilled.

"You will take care of your sisters. Both of them."

"I can take care of myself, Papa," Cori said. "You don't need to be patronizing."

"Zhanna," Rey said, ignoring her, "you will run the security. Kent will run operations." And then he spoke to her in Russian: *You will run the na levo, you understand. Na levo* was a Russian slang term for "under the table." The underside of the business.

An odd joy filled her eyes. Then her gaze slid to me, and she remembered my Russian.

"What did he say to her?" Cori whispered, and I just squeezed her hand in response.

Galo had caught the meaning. "Papa, we all love Zhanna but...please don't divide up the company like this."

"You can't have it all. We need her," Rey said, and Zhanna smirked. I wondered exactly what Rey meant by *need*. "Think, Galo. You cannot have it. Be smart. I'm protecting you." He turned to Zhanna. "Galo can never know the details of the security work. Always. Protect the family, Zhanna, as we've protected you."

"Protected her?" Cori asked. I could sense Cori's anger rising. Nothing was changing, except that Galo and Z would be running the business—both the legal and the illicit.

"I mean...what is the word," Rey said, confused. "We took her in."

Zhanna nodded. A bit smugly, I thought.

"Cordelia," Rey said, "I need you, sweetheart. I need you to keep running the charity and I want you to be safe until this...problem blows over. Then I need you to take care of me. You have to put me someplace where I can rest until I'm better. Maybe here? Find attendants we can trust who won't talk. And Sam. Maybe Sam will bodyguard me. He is like me, aren't you, Sam?"

I could only nod. What did he mean?

"You take what you want! You fight for it!" he yelled at me. I glanced at Cori. His grip was slipping.

"I'll take care of you, Papa," Galo said.

He waved a hand toward his son. "No. Not you. You run the company. Run it well. Keep it clean. Zhanna, keep them happy."

Who was a security chief supposed to keep happy? *Them.* The presumed clients?

"Papa, of course I'll take care of you," Cori said. Steel in her voice. "But you have to tell us, you have to tell me, who does that money belong to? What are you doing?"

Rey didn't answer.

"Papa?" Galo, Cori, and Z all said it as one.

Rey didn't answer.

"Rey, are you having another spell?" Kent's voice cut through them all, like a knife.

Rey stared. "Please don't break your sister's heart, Zhanna."

"I don't know what you mean," Zhanna said, and for once I believed her. She frowned in confusion.

Rey pointed at me. "You. You're the key."

"I'm what?" I said.

"To keep Cori safe. Z, let him be. There is no need for her to be involved. She must not know."

They were all silent now. He'd pitted them against one another, issued his demands, and they'd all agreed. The power of a parent.

Rey stood. "I'm hard on all of you. Zhanna, Galo may fight you because you're not blood." He coughed. "I want you to know. I love you like you were my own. I want you to know you are a Varela, no matter the last name."

"I know that," she said, and her voice was very small.

"Where is Eddie? I...I have to give him something." Rey looked around the room.

"Edwin is dead, Rey," Kent said quietly. "Remember?"

"Dead? Show me a grave. Show me..." And he put his face in his hands. "You all hate me. You all hate me for what I've done."

"Papa, no, we don't." Galo and Zhanna and Cori were all standing but I thought I was the only one who saw the little gleam in Rey's eye. I blinked and it was gone.

Rey caught me looking.

"You didn't run away from the fight. I like that in a man." And then he said, "Last week, it was, in Kinshasa, I got into a fight. A fistfight with a man who tried to cheat me on my payment for the weapons..."

"Not last week, Papa," Cori said gently. "There were no weapons."

Lord Caliber, I thought. Well, well, maybe there was truth to the rumor.

"Last week, yes, and…" His voice trailed off and he was quiet. Cori moved next to him and patted his back. "No. Of course. I am kidding you." He tried to laugh. His mind was sliding from here to there.

"I think perhaps Papa should go to bed," Galo said.

"I want Cori to take me upstairs," he said.

"I have something to say first," Cori said. She turned to face her brother and stepsister. "Whatever you're doing…you have to stop it."

Galo shook his head. "Cori, we can discuss this another time."

"Is moving this money worth this? Papa nearly dies, Galo kills a man. He'll have to live with that forever." She swallowed. "I realize…maybe you have to disentangle yourselves from whatever this is, moving this money. But start. Now."

They all stared. "Or what?" Zhanna said quietly. "You'll go to the police?"

"No, but…"

"Then you'll do nothing." Zhanna stood. "I'll put you to bed, Papa."

"No. Cordelia. Please." He looked at me. "You come too, Guard Boy."

Great. I had a new freelance job. I followed Rey and Cori out of the silent room.

He looked at me again, glancing back at me as we headed up the stairs.

"Sam is a good guy," Cori said.

"How good? No one is good enough for you." Affectionate teasing in his voice. For a second it seemed like his mind was back entirely.

"He saved you, Papa. If we'd lost you…"

"Oh, never mind that. I hate that I need saving. When I was young…I could fight for myself then. I didn't need some kiddo."

"Now you really sound like an old man. Shall I get off your lawn next?" Cori said.

He laughed.

She didn't. "The cash, Papa, where did it go after you showed it to me?"

He stopped in the hallway. "I told you. I got confused. I thought it was money I could give. We moved it for a government in South America. It's a secret. The paperwork was handled legally, though, with the Internal Revenue Service. They had a reason for moving the cash physically back into the States and I got…confused. You must believe me. You must stop asking questions about this part of the business. We've done nothing wrong."

I didn't buy it for a second. Who needed cash moved like that? Okay, maybe a government, for some reason if they wanted a payment that couldn't be traced. Maybe someone who needed cash for bribes. Drug runners. Terrorists. Criminal syndicates. Smugglers. My mind began to spin.

"The kidnapping attempt today makes me not believe you." Her voice rose. "Edwin. Papa, does this have something to do with Edwin's kidnapping? It has to. It must."

"No. No."

"You could have died today, Papa. I am not giving this up."

"Do you love me?" Rey said.

"I love you," she said. "And you know I love you, and that I am a good daughter to you. But you're endangering yourself…"

"You trust me?"

"Yes," she said, a little more uncertain.

"This Sam," Rey said. "We trust him?"

"Completely."

"I will talk to him." It was as though I wasn't standing there. "Cordelia. I want you gone until this danger is past. It won't be long. Sam fought for me; he will fight for you."

"I won't go. You can't make me."

"I know you want to help us. But you cannot." His frail voice turned to steel. "I will cut off all contributions to your charity. It will fold. I'm by far your biggest benefactor. Help me and I'll keep the money coming. Fight me and it's gone."

"Papa, you wouldn't…the charity does good work…"

"Yes. I know. But you come first."

Cori said, "Be honest. Have you had me followed since I found out about the ten million?"

"Followed?" Rey sounded confused, and not from his illness. "Why?"

"Two Colombians, maybe?"

"I have no idea what you're talking about," Rey said. "Why would I send anyone from Colombia to follow you around?"

"Cori, what do you mean?" Zhanna asked, suddenly appearing on the stairs. If she had sent the Colombians... Cori was showing her hand that she knew about them.

"Go back, Z!" Rey yelled at her. "This is private."

With the barest dignity, Zhanna turned around and retreated down the hallway.

"She's like a worm in the fruit," he said, as if his kind words to her earlier were forgotten. Or more likely, I thought, insincere. He's using everyone in this family, I thought. And now it's starting to show.

"If you dislike her, why do you give her the most dangerous part of your business?" I said.

He blinked in surprise. "I know Russian. I know what you said to her," I told him. "*Na levo*. The underside. What is it?"

He shook his head at me. "Very clever. Like my Cori." He laughed. He patted my chin. "Zhanna is tough. Galo is smart. Only Cori is tough and smart. Good match, you two."

"You have a strange way of showing your kids that you love them," I said bluntly.

"We as a family can stop this," Cori said, defiance in her tone.

"Cori, I will give you until tomorrow to prepare to leave. To go someplace far away. For us to be sure this Sam is all right. But if you do not, I will end support for your charity. And your other donors will wonder why your own family has turned their backs on you."

"Maybe I'll go to the police," she said.

"And you will get your sister and brother and me and Kent all arrested. We got rid of a corpse today, my darling. I can't make your mind unknow that. But we'll all face charges. And I will never"—here his voice broke—"forgive you."

"Is it money laundering? Who are you moving this cash for?"

He took her face in his hands. "You are the smartest and the bravest," he said. "If only you would take it over. But I wanted to shield you. You have no taste for this." He looked at us both. "When you're good at something, you never get to leave it. Success is a prison."

She stepped away from him. "Papa…"

"Good night, Cordelia," Rey Varela said. "Go where you like. Australia, Thailand, Canada, I don't care. But you will go. Now. Where's my wife?"

27

STUNNED SILENCE, THEN Cori murmured, "Papa, you're tired. You're tired."

"Quit nursemaiding me! I am a man! I fought...I fought my way out of the worst hellholes in the world...me and Sergei, they'd shoot the SAMs at us"—and for one moment I thought he'd said my name, but realized he meant surface-to-air missiles—"and we'd dodge them, and the warlords, buying the loads of guns and the rifles, paying me in the diamonds... paying me in diamonds that could choke you...I stared down those bastards, those animals...I'm not afraid of my own children...I did..." His voice faded, like an old lion's feeble roar. "I did what they made me do. Where is my wife? Where is your mama?"

"She's dead."

"Oh," he said. "She is. They all are."

"You are tired, Papa. Come. I'll help you," Cori said. "Sam, maybe go back to your room."

I nodded.

A few moments later Cordelia knocked on my door. She'd wiped away her tears but her eyes were reddened. Her mouth contorted.

"I hate crying," she said. "I hate it. I hate him, too."

"No, you don't," I said. "He's your dad."

"But he's changing into something that is not-my-dad," she said. "*What* is my dad now?"

"What he's always been," I said. "You just haven't seen it."

I didn't intend the words as a slap, but she recoiled. Then she nodded. "He was always driven. Sometimes not kind. He's always played us against each other and we've known it."

"Yet tonight you played along."

"Listen to him...he's losing his grip on reality. He's like a stranger. It's worse at night. He's better in the mornings. Tomorrow maybe he won't feel this way."

"What can I do?"

"According to him, you can take me out of the country." She laughed a jagged giggle. "Actually, I have an idea on what we should do."

"What?"

"Kidnap him." She stared at me, unblinking, her mouth a firm line.

I stared back.

"I'm just stealing the kidnapper's idea. We take Papa, we keep him somewhere until he tells me the truth about what the company's doing. Galo and Zhanna won't dare call the police. We use him to strike a deal with them."

"And where do we keep him?"

"They have no idea that you own a bar with an apartment above it," she said. "It's not like we have to take him at gunpoint. I'm saying take him with us and then force them to tell us what's going on."

"I don't know, Cori."

"I think it's a brilliant plan."

"Okay," I said. "Let's think about it. I need some fresh air, you want to come?"

And she took my hand and we went downstairs and walked out into the cool of the stone patio. I liked watching the sea, at night. It seemed deeper and darker and more dangerous then, but the breeze was a gentle rub along our skin.

"Kidnapping. It brings back all the pain about Eddie."

"You think they're related. Now and then."

"Yes. I don't know how, but yes. This family. We keep so much…hidden away. Do you know," she said, "Galo stood here while his mother committed suicide? Right here."

"Suicide."

"She swam out into the ocean. Drowned herself. I think she didn't want Galo to find her or see her dead. So worse, he saw her choose to die." She sat down on the edge of the stone. "Eddie is dead somewhere. He might as well be lost in the ocean too."

I took a breath. "Your dad used to move arms and weapons into war zones. He could still be running illegal weapons. It could be any kind of contraband, and it's much harder to catch, because he's hiding it, somehow, under the legitimate cargo he moves…I don't want you to underestimate how dangerous this could be. Eventually you may have to go to the police."

"I'm not going to go to the police. If I can get them to listen to me—"

"They don't take you seriously," I said. She'd put a sheen of love on them all, but I could see them for what they were. Galo, determined to protect his family and be a good son—and he'd been willing to kill to do so. He'd seen his own mother commit suicide here, killed a man himself and then hid the body. That could rot a man's soul. Zhanna, cruel and petty, so desperate to prove herself as one of the Varelas, greedy for a role and willing to take on the illicit work. Kent—well, who knew? His loyalty might have once been Rey's, but now it might be Zhanna's. Cori's protests were nothing, because they knew she wouldn't betray them to the police.

A small little plan began to form in my mind. Sometimes the maze turns in an unexpected way, and you have to tighten the thread that leads the way out.

"Your dad said he'd talk to you tomorrow. He's had an emotionally unhinging day." I took a step toward her. "Maybe we think about what he said. Take a trip somewhere."

She started to shake her head. "And what about Steve? Look, we have the same enemy, Sam. Whoever grabbed Papa has to be whoever ordered Steve's killing. They can't get away with it."

"We go, but we don't," I whispered in her ear, giving her a reassuring hug.

She leaned back from me, searching my face.

Kent walked out onto the patio, his white cane moving softly in front of him. "Cori? Are you here?"

"What?" she snapped. "Yes. Sorry. Sam and I are both here."

His cane tapped against a chair and he pulled it to himself and sat down. "A very long, trying day."

Cori sat next to him, took his hand in hers. "The others are too bound to Papa, but you're not. Whatever they're involved in, get us out of it."

I admired Kent because he didn't throw us a denial, none of that *I don't know what you mean* junk. "You act like that can be done instantly. And you don't understand what's at stake...what we're asked to do..."

Cori crossed her arms. "Kent, who's trying to hurt Papa? Who hurt Edwin?"

"We don't know that's connected, Cori." He took a long breath.

"Seriously?"

"If I told you that it wasn't, would you believe me?" His voice went low. "Your father made a lot of enemies in Africa. Edwin, I have always believed, was a payback for that."

Cori was silent.

Kent leaned back. "I know you think I'll always take Zhanna's side, but perhaps not in this case. In this case I am worried about you, and your safety, and keeping your charity running." He stood with quiet dignity. "And Cori, please, don't judge him. Trust me—he has tried to do right by you. You want this to end—stop asking questions that no one is going to answer for you. You said he could stop this? Well, apparently, so can you. Do as your father asks...until it's calm again. We're setting a simple trap. It will catch the people who are bothering us. And then it'll be over."

Cori didn't speak.

"Good night. Sleep if you can—the guards are on alert; they'll keep us safe."

When Kent left, she whispered, "I think we go with my plan. Take Papa with us."

Maybe, I thought. We'd see how tomorrow unfolded. But tonight, I had work to do, work Cori couldn't know about, so I just smiled and gave her hand a reassuring squeeze.

28

My body ached, but I couldn't sleep. My long nap in the afternoon after the fight meant I was awake, watching the moon, thinking through the twists and turns of the day.

Ricky had followed me back to the guest hallway after I said good night to Cori.

"I can find my own way back to my room," I said.

"You think you're cute," Ricky said. "You're not."

"You're right. I'm not. Of course, getting into actual fights will reduce one's attractiveness."

He didn't smile. He always looked angry. "Cordelia is a bit flighty. She'll throw a guy like you over. And what will happen to you then, huh? Knowing all you know. It's never good to be a security risk."

"Wonderful then that the Varelas have you on their side," I said.

"Sam. Look, I'm sorry. You and I, we don't have to be snapping at each other. We can get along." He offered his hand and reluctantly I shook it. "I've been around this family a long, long time. They've been very good to me. But Galo knows what loyalty is. Cori, I'm not sure. She has a weird idea about what's right and wrong."

"What's right, like not smuggling money?" I said.

"Your Lada guy in Prague, how much he move a year?"

"A few million in counterfeit cigarettes and software, mostly."

"That's nothing. And I don't mean in terms of cash. What the Varelas do is far more. Far more important."

"Important."

"What they do affects the whole world," he said in a whisper.

I started to make a joke and then I didn't. Ricky's face was grim. "Why are you telling me this?" I asked.

"Because it's important work. Good work that saves lives. That helps keep us all safe. And because Cordelia could screw it up. There might be a lot of money in it for you to keep her busy. Keep her mind off the family business. Occupy her time even after the current crisis chills down."

"Is this a message you're delivering on someone's behalf? Maybe Galo's?"

"Galo wants his sister happy. Cori needs things to care about. That could be you. You could keep her occupied."

"Message received," I said. "If Cori wants me she'll have me. If not..."

Ricky flexed a smile. There was an emptiness in his gaze that unsettled me. His breathing was sharp and shallow behind the smile. In his mind, if Cori didn't want me...then I knew too much. Buy me off yet worry about me talking again, or kill me.

"Thanks for the escort, Ricky. I get so scared wandering around this big old house by myself."

"Go rest up from your fight, big man," he said. "Who knows what tomorrow will bring?"

I stepped inside the room and he shut the door.

There is no walking away knowing what I knew now. Message received.

So it was time I made myself super-useful to the Varela family. I checked where I'd hidden the other half of Steve's casino chip, dangling down the bathtub's drain, tied with a piece of thread to the plug. It was still there.

I didn't have a weapon, but I'd packed—in case there was a bit of trouble—a set of Israeli lock picks, hidden in a false compartment in my shaving kit. I removed them and assembled them and slid them under the mattress on my bed. I laid out fresh clothes on the chair: black slacks and a dark mock turtleneck, long-sleeved. I'd packed these decidedly nontropical clothes in case of (a) nightclubbing or (b) stealth. Okay, mostly stealth.

In my boxers, with my shoulder and back still heavily bandaged, I eased between the sheets. To wait for the house to sleep.

The family had had a long day, and finally the house felt settled in its uneasy quiet. After a moment I went to the door and opened it. The hallway was empty. No more guards. I went back and I dressed in the black clothes and slipped the lock picks into my pocket.

29

I KNELT BEFORE the door to Kent's office and picked the lock.

I opened the office door. The lights were out and I shut the door behind me and relocked it. I didn't turn on the light. I re- membered the arrangement of the room from sitting on the couch while they'd called Lada. The office had been set up for a blind man, so the layout was simple, nothing between desk and door to impede Kent. Five steps and I could feel the edge of the desk. Ran my fingers along the Braille keyboard, traced the cord to the lap- top. I suspected he probably used his computer more with voice commands and used the keyboard only when necessary.

I opened the laptop. It wasn't passworded; he'd just set it to sleep and it awoke with a gleam of light. He kept a lot of programs open, which made sense if he was using voice com- mands—simpler to know that the program was already up and running rather than waiting and hoping it started up properly. I would have to be careful not to change any settings or close any programs.

I checked first his search history on his browser. There were searches for "Sam Chevalier" and for "Lavrenti Nesterov." Then in the gleam of the light from the screen I saw, sitting next to the laptop, was a driver's license from Florida. Lavrenti Nesterov was the kidnapper. They hadn't thrown his ID out with the body. An address in Miami. Not a Colombian, like the guys who'd killed

Steve. Maybe that meant something, maybe not. The only interesting search result showed he'd been a decorated police officer
who had resigned from the force. There had been accusations
of improper behavior, kept vague, but no charges filed. But he'd
stopped being a cop.

Nesterov. Russian. Zhanna was Russian. But there were many
Russian expatriates in Miami. Coincidence or not?

Kent had done a property search on the Chevalier name in Miami. He'd found the fake social media pages August had set up
for Sam Chevalier—who didn't have many friends and whose last
status update was nine months ago.

But then I saw there was a short call history in another text
window on the screen—the call history for the phone I was using
as Sam Chevalier.

The Varelas had friends in important places, like my prepaid
phone carrier.

They had my phone, too. I picked it up and slipped it into my
pocket. A small act of defiance.

On Kent's e-mail account I found he'd sent notes to people
in Moscow, Budapest, and Prague, asking if they knew of a Sam
Chevalier—all time-stamped earlier this afternoon. FastFlex,
thanks to having a Russian founder and first having served eastern European routes, had lots of contacts, but I didn't recognize
any names. No e-mails about me to anyone in Miami—yet. If
they were thinking of getting rid of me, they wouldn't want local
people remembering they'd asked about me. Or maybe they were
accepting my story, finally, bolstered by Cori.

But no further queries about Lavrenti Nesterov. It suggested
to me again that they knew who'd sent him, that he was simply a
hireling. And that the Varelas knew that.

I looked at Kent's incoming e-mails. The most recent was from
an account simply called "Nanny." The e-mail read: *I will ask re
your request on Chevalier.* Below was Kent's original e-mail: *Ask
the guests about the name Sam Chevalier. Extras for those with
provable information. Might need a new spacesuit.*

The guests? Extras? Spacesuit? That had to be a code.

I searched the computer for "Steve Robles." No matches. But that proved nothing.

I found spreadsheet files, but every one of them was passworded. A whole series of them were titled "Transport Schedules." I couldn't see into how money was moved here, or how any illicit profits being run under the legitimate businesses were tracked. One was a list of charities, tied to Cori's work.

Then I saw it, on the corner of the desk. A smartphone. I turned it on. The app that was up was a Cyrillic phonetic keyboard. Lavrenti Nesterov's phone. I went to his text messages, all written in Russian. There were messages exchanged with only one number, with a Miami area code, from yesterday and then again earlier in the day:

> Lavrenti: Arrived in SJ. Following him. He's at his house in the hills.
>
> Miami number: Our demands have to be made clear.
>
> Lavrenti: They will comply to get him back.
>
> Miami number: What will you do with him?
>
> Lavrenti: I have a place for him where I can question him.
>
> Miami number: Good luck.

Then a gap in time. Then Lavrenti texted, after the attack:

> Have him but there is a problem. I need you to come to SJ.

But that was a lie. Lavrenti was dead by then. This was Kent's trap he'd mentioned.

> Miami number: Where? When? There's nothing on the news.
>
> Lavrenti: Because they want no police. Meet me tomorrow at 12 noon at Castillo San Cristobal, plaza on the street near the entrance.

So the Varelas were setting a trap.

They couldn't question Lavrenti, but they could question his accomplice. I knew Castillo de San Cristóbal was the biggest of the ancient forts that abutted the coast, in Old San Juan, designed to protect the island from invaders.

I had a few choices. I could text, in Russian, that it was a trap, not to come, then delete the whole text conversation so the Varelas wouldn't know what happened. I could do nothing. I could capture the accomplice myself, before the Varelas did, and find out who was behind the attack. And maybe find out who was behind Steve's murder.

Or maybe I'd work my own trap. *I have a place for him where I can question him.* The whole tone of the conversation suggested the accomplice wasn't here to help in the kidnapping. Lavrenti probably drove his own car or boat.

No sign of car keys along with Nesterov's wallet. No receipt for a rental car in the wallet. So where was the getaway vehicle, to get Rey away from his family? It had to be close by.

This had become so much bigger than Steve. The Varelas were doing something seriously dangerous, crimes beyond killing Steve. *What we do affects the world,* Ricky said by way of warning. I didn't think he was exaggerating.

That odd message haunted me. *Nanny. Guests.* I needed to know what that code was.

I carefully repositioned the windows the way I'd seen them and closed the laptop. I put the Russian's phone back where I found it. I kept mine in my pocket.

I left the office unlocked and shut the door silently.

And then I went back to my room, and out through the window.

30

I CREPT ALONG to the edge of the roof. The wind off the sea was loud, which meant no one might hear me but I might not hear anyone approaching. I made it to the edge of the roof and studied the courtyard below in a flickering gleam of moonlight. The compound itself wasn't bathed in light—there were lights aimed out at the periphery, away from the house. I figured the Varelas didn't want their own bedrooms flooded with glare so they couldn't sleep. I lay there and watched the guards.

Two of them circled the house, staying along the stone walls that faced the road and the side that bordered the cliff overlooking the beach. I watched them, timed their orbits in my head. The other two guards—well, one at least presumably would be asleep. That left Ricky. I could tell by their strides that neither guard on duty was Ricky. He was the leader and presumably the most dangerous one. So where was he? Inside the house? Maybe opening doors, finding my room empty.

Maybe searching for the other half of the casino chip.

I didn't feel so clever all of a sudden. If he found my bed empty, then he'd raise an alarm, and I'd have to run.

I decided it was worth the risk.

I felt stiff from the bandages. I would have to be careful how I moved. If I opened my wounds and bled on the courtyard stones, it would be a telltale clue that I had been there.

I had a three-minute window when the guards weren't in sight of the wall where I would descend. Three minutes, to climb down stone, in the dark. The glow of the lights wouldn't help that much with the nuance of where to place foot and finger.

I watched the guards make their turns, the window of time opened, and I swung my legs out from the roof, found a place to settle my feet. And began to climb down.

If I slipped, I was dead or crippled. I got a sure grip with my hands, one at a time, as I let go of the roof. Hunched like a spider, I put my feet lower on the wall, found the stray bits of stone that could give me enough purchase.

I clambered down the wall. The constant wind from the ocean had worn the stone; some of the places my feet found were only stubs. I wore a pair of shoes that had a dressy top but a sole designed for gripping. Leonie had them custom made as a gift to me, presumably to help keep me alive in a dangerous situation.

I heard the wind die, and then the soft tread of a guard. My three minutes were up. I was still twenty feet above the courtyard.

I froze, trying to melt into the shadows. The clouds hugged the moon. I felt a tightness on my bandages. Barely enough space, and strength, to hold my balance. I risked turning slightly, to see the guard's progress.

He'd stopped to light a cigarette.

I could see the ember glow, then vanish, hidden by his head. No doubt the guards were wired on tobacco or caffeine or the thought that they'd failed in their jobs earlier and could not fail again.

My hands felt like they would cramp. *Hold, hold.*

The guard started to walk off. I could trace him out of the corner of my eye from the glow of the lit cigarette. He kept going, and I slowly continued my scrabble down to the courtyard. I stepped onto a stone pane that fronted a window, then eased myself down to the ground.

Where was the second guard? His orbit should have crossed with the smoker's, but I hadn't heard him. So either he was about to arrive, or I'd missed him.

I crouched low against the stone. I heard the second guard speak for a moment to the first guard, asking a question.

I was caught. One leaving, the other coming. I had to go now, before the guard came around the corner. Which he could do at any second.

I was on the same level as the stone patio where I'd started my search for Rey, but about forty feet away from it, between the ocean and the road. I listened, heard the guards chatting, then bolted toward the protective stone wall and clambered up and atop it. If I was going to be spotted, it would be there, as I stood on the wall.

I heard them chatting, then the rush of the wind.

So I jumped from the wall to a low-hanging branch of a tree, whipped low by the constant sea wind.

I don't recommend this after you've been pummeled in a fight.

I felt an ache in my side open up as I dangled, holding on to the branch. Not the stitches. The sore ribs. I kicked my legs up, caught them around the branch, and began to shimmy down. I reached the main trunk and eased myself to the ground.

Still too much light around me. I hurried into the deeper darkness. Toward the sea. I stopped before I reached the beach. Because there could be a guard there, I realized—if Galo felt sure the kidnapper's approach had been by water, then they might try again. I waited in the undergrowth, watching the silvered light on the sand.

And then I saw him. Galo. He had broader shoulders, a bigger build, than any of the guards. He was patrolling the beach. Protecting his own. I moved back. Hard to sleep after you kill a guy. And it's sad I know this.

I remembered the antique maps in the kitchen, made by Galo's grandfather. I could follow the coast up, toward the road that crept past the house. There were rocky cliffs, shallow inlets, areas where the land eased down to the sea. I didn't think the kidnapper had brought a boat. Too many complications, too easily spotted from the air when the family raised the alarm.

I tried to think about how I would have done this.

He'd come alone.

He had one person who was his confidant, who wasn't here with him—maybe his version of Mila. I figured he'd kept it simple and brought a car. Boats, alone, were a hassle.

I thought the kidnapper would want to get Rey into a car unseen, and then get him onto the road. But Ricky and the guards hadn't found one, so it was well hidden.

I headed into the heavy growth. I used my phone's flashlight application. It gave off a tiny glow but I shielded the brightness with my palms.

Eventually, heading downhill, I found a path. It was overgrown, neglected. Then I found a fence. I climbed over and the path became smooth gravel, and led to a boat dock. Empty. Beyond, a house loomed in the dark. Not as large as the Varelas', but a good size. All the lights out. The driveway stood empty.

I frowned. I'd made it to a neighbor's property. And it would be a risk to park there, if they were at home…although maybe they were part-time residents, like Rey. Surely the guards would have checked here, would know if the neighbors were around or not…but the guards were from Miami, like Ricky. Maybe they didn't keep tabs on the neighbors. It was a fair distance from the Varela property. I circled the neighbor's house. Dark.

On a back patio I carefully let the light play along, keeping it away from the windows. I didn't want to scare anyone into calling the police. Patio furniture, outdoor kitchen, bar, a pool…and then, a metal sign leaning up against a wall. A For Sale sign from a high-end global real estate agency, showings by appointment only. It had been tucked nearly out of sight.

This house was for sale. I wonder if the guards knew that, in that quick search they'd done before being recalled back to the Varela house to help get rid of the body and stick close to Rey.

I went around to the garage. There was a lock on the garage door; I knelt and studied it. The lock had been neatly cut and put back into place so that it looked, to the casual viewer, secure. I unhooked the lock. Slowly I raised the door and it creaked in the quiet of the night. I stopped. Waited. No response from the house. I slowly raised it again, enough to wriggle under the door.

I played the light around the three-car garage. It was empty except for a GMC Yukon SUV, with darkened windows. I tried the driver's door. It opened, unlocked. The keys, ready, dangled in the ignition. Ready for a fast getaway. I climbed inside. Nothing else in the front; in the back, the seats had been folded down. A blanket lay spread next to a large aluminum case. I opened it. An expensively stocked medical kit, not so different from the ones you might see at an agency safe house. A syringe preloaded with adrenaline. Smelling salts. Bandages. Adult diapers. Plastic cuffs. Thick tape, to bind the mouth and the hands. Another syringe, preloaded, labeled with a brand-name tranquilizer. It might have been the same dope that Nesterov had given Rey.

This was a mobile unit in which to put an old drugged man in the back and keep him still until he reached wherever they were going. Nesterov had taken a gamble that this high-end property wouldn't be shown for the brief span of time he hid his car here.

I opened the glove compartment. I found a rental agreement for the Yukon from a rental car company office in San Juan. In the name of Lavrenti Nesterov of Miami. There was also a Glock 17 9mm, loaded with a high-capacity magazine, thirty-three rounds. I found a pair of keys with a Miami airport lot parking ticket attached; this must be his regular car back home.

Okay. So this was it. He'd been here alone. No driver waiting for him. The person he communicated with was back in Miami, presumably, and coming here to fall into Zhanna's trap.

But now I could have a trap of my own. I had his car.

We could kidnap him, Cori had said. Well, actually, now we could. I wasn't sure I'd tell her about this. Not yet.

I put everything back where I found it. I wiped it down. But I put the Glock, the tranquilizer-loaded syringe (capped, of course), and the two sets of car keys on the floor. A little pile of useful treasures. I thought of trying to sneak them into the house. But if I were caught with them, it was a death sentence.

I found matches in the garage and I burned the car rental documents with Nesterov's name on them. Because I was going to use this car, and I didn't want it tied easily to his name.

I crawled back out into the windy night and lowered the garage door as quietly as I could. I sat against the garage door and listened. The wind rose again, the smell of rain thick in the air. I didn't want to get caught in a storm. Drenched clothes would be impossible to explain. I was running out of time, out of night.

I headed back the way I came; I'd threaded a needle getting out, and I thought it unwise to vary my approach on the return. So down I went on the path, then I hit the fence and the overgrowth that marked the Varela property line, and then into the scrub. Along the water, where the shore turned stony and the waves washed eternally. Then the smooth stretch of the Varelas' private inlet, the small, narrow beach silver in the broken moonlight.

Galo was gone. That meant an extra pair of eyes back at the compound.

I began to sweat as I approached the wash of light that illuminated the area of the stone wall and the stairways. I looked at the time. I'd been gone for forty minutes.

With Galo back, what if one of them were permanently stationed in the courtyard? It would be impossible to avoid being seen.

But I couldn't wait out here.

I shimmied back up the tree I'd climbed down in escaping. My chest and ribs felt tight; I could feel a bit of blood sticking to the back of my dark shirt.

I climbed into the blast of light, edged out over the branch. No yells of dismay, no screamed orders to halt. I peered at the house. I could see one guard turning on the other side, walking out of sight. No sign of the other.

I put my feet down on the wall. I dropped and scrambled down the side. My feet touched the courtyard. And I could see, edging around the other side of the house, the one closest to me, the lit cigarette of the guard who smoked. I was seconds from his view.

I was trapped. If I ran, he would see me. If I stood still, he would see me. I had five seconds to decide.

I walked toward him. "Hey," I called, in a harsh whisper. "It's Sam. It's Sam."

He reacted instantly, the cigarette dropping from his mouth, rushing toward me with his gun extended.

"Calm down!" I said.

"Get on the ground! Now!"

I obeyed him.

The other guard—now I could see it was Ricky—came running. Galo came out from the carport and I saw a thin gleam of light; he'd been inside the garage.

"Ricky, please tell this guy not to shoot me," I said.

"What are you doing out here, Sam?" Ricky's voice was frosty.

"I was looking for one of you. And trying not to wake up the house," I said.

"Stand up, Sam," Galo said. "Slowly."

I obeyed.

"Man, you scared me," the guard said, and then he went silent at a glare from Ricky.

"Search him," Galo said, and Ricky gave me a thorough patdown. I was glad I'd left the goods I'd found behind. He found nothing in my pockets, front or back, except for my smartphone. "He's clean," Ricky said to Galo. He checked the phone. "No recent calls or texts."

"Put your hands down, Sam," Galo said, sounding mildly annoyed.

"Didn't we take your phone earlier?" Ricky said.

"Cori gave it back to me," I said. Lie, lie, lie. If she were asked about it, she'd have to have the presence of mind to play along.

"Why are you all dressed in black?" Ricky said.

"That's what Cori laid out for me," I said. "It won't show the blood if my cuts start bleeding again. Back home in Canada these are nightclubbing clothes. I know they're not so much here in the tropics." I shrugged.

Ricky made a little hissing noise. Like he didn't quite believe me. And then I thought, *He really might just shoot me, here, in* front of them all. *Sorry, Cori. Your boyfriend just made too big of a mistake. Find a smarter one next time.*

"Why were you looking for us?" Galo said.

"I woke up and couldn't sleep because I slept so much this afternoon, my injuries are hurting, and I looked out and down by the inlet I thought I saw a light."

"Check it out," Ricky told two of the guards. He turned to me. "Like a flashlight on the beach? Or a boat's light?"

"I don't know. Just a slash of light. Small. Maybe even like a smartphone's light. I saw it twice."

Galo studied me. "Is that all?"

"No, it's not," Ricky said and he punched me.

It hurt. I dropped to the courtyard, the stones scraping my palms. My jaw ached. I tasted blood and a beat in my head pounded like a hammer striking stone. I threw up a little on the ground.

"Stop it, Ricky, he's in no condition…" Galo started.

"You're an idiot. Next time I'll just shoot you," Ricky said to me.

"Ricky, enough. Leave him alone."

"They don't learn unless you teach them," Ricky said, and the odd singsong in the way he said the words was chilling.

"I wasn't thinking," I lied. "I took one of those painkillers and I wasn't thinking straight." I offered a hand to Ricky. "You're right. I'm sorry."

"I'll be glad to hit you again when the painkillers wear off," Ricky said.

I looked at Galo, wiped away a trace of blood from my lip. "I want to talk to you."

"About what?"

"I'm kind of mad. Not at you. The guy…you know."

"No point in being mad at a dead man."

"Well, he nearly killed me. So if you go hunting for the people behind this attack, I want to be part of it."

"Don't you have my sister to babysit?" Galo asked.

"Don't you have an airline to run? I think you were given one tonight."

He laughed, softly.

Ricky made a noise. "We don't need your help. And it's a security issue, so you don't discuss it with Galo. Only Zhanna. In fact, you need to talk to Galo, you come talk to me first."

"He has to stay clean," I said. "You're right. I'll just keep saying that."

The two guards returned. "No sign of light. No sign of a boat," one of them said.

Ricky glared at me. "I guess your brain's addled by that blow you took."

"It's been a long day," I agreed.

"Good night, Sam," Galo said. "Maybe you should take another painkiller so you can sleep."

"Maybe I should. Good night."

I started to walk toward the house. And they watched me, and I realized I absolutely must go straight to a door that was already unlocked. One I would have unlocked. Right? So I wagered the best choice was the kitchen, where the lights gleamed. I didn't look back at them but I imagined a bullet striking me if I guessed wrong and I went up to the patio and opened the door and the kitchen was warm, the smell of coffee rich in the air. They were drinking coffee to stay awake. I carefully shut the door behind me and then I could see Galo watching me through the glass, talking to Ricky.

I went back to my room. In the bathroom I undressed and I turned on the shower and locked the bathroom door. And I dialed a number in New Orleans.

31

Yes?" Leonie sounded sleepy. I'd called her on a spare prepaid cell phone I bought for her, often changed. Not on my home number. I didn't want this traceable.

"It's me. Sam. Hi. Sorry I woke you."

"Where have you been? I thought you would call…are you in a shower?"

"Long story. Is Daniel okay?"

"Yes, he's fine." A pause. "And so am I."

"Good. Good."

"You sound stressed."

"I am in some trouble and I need to speak to Mila."

"Of course you do." Leonie could make words feel like blades when she felt slighted. "Well, she's not staying *here*." Leonie resented the influence Mila had in my life; Mila thought I was insane to let Leonie, who'd come into our lives under dubious circumstances, be in Daniel's life. But that was the reality: Leonie had been the only mother figure Daniel had ever known, the person who had always been there for him. And she'd begged me to let her stay in Daniel's life, and I could not make my heart say no. She loved Daniel and he loved her. Leonie and Mila cordially resented each other and would politely cut and snarl while Daniel played between them, stacking blocks. I wondered how it might affect him as he got older and I told myself, *You should be there.* "She's staying at the bar."

"I know. I need you to call her and patch her into this call. And then get rid of this phone afterwards."

"Why don't you just call her directly?"

"Would you please just do as I ask?"

"Yes, Your Lordship. Hold on."

Mila was on the line a minute later. "Thanks, Leonie," I said. "Kiss Daniel for me. Give him a big kiss."

"What the hell have you gotten yourself into? Are you in jail?" Leonie said.

"Off the line," Mila said. "I will take care of it."

"I want to know what is happening! Sam! You can't keep doing this, you cannot get yourself into these situations and expect me..."

"Leonie. You are going to get me killed," I said. "Off the line." She got off the line.

"Situation?" Mila said.

"Get to San Juan. Get two adjoining rooms, or a suite, at the Gran Fortuna Resort in Old San Juan. If they're sold out, get as close to there as you can."

Four seconds passed. "Understood."

This was weird; normally Mila, as my handler in the Round Table, gave me the orders.

"I need full research on a Russian living in Miami named Lavrenti Nesterov. He's a former cop who tried to kidnap Rey Varela today. He didn't fight like a cop, though. He's had training. I want to know who he works for now. Also trace this phone number..." I fed her the number Nesterov had texted. "But it may be a throwaway phone." Then I gave her his address from the driver's license I'd found in Kent's office.

"And where is this fighting ex-cop now?"

"He's not a worry."

"I see."

"And could you check on the account activity at a bank, on a savings and a checking account." I gave her the bank statement numbers I'd photographed at Steve's house, from memory. "I want to know if there have been any unusually large deposits, or a pattern of deposits."

She made a noise, copying down the numbers.

"I am at Rey Varela's house on the western coast of the island," I said. I spelled the name for her. "If the Round Table has anything on this man…"

"He was thought to be this so-called Lord Caliber," she said instantly. "But it was never proven that Lord Caliber was indeed simply one man. It wouldn't have surprised me if many arms dealers tried to work under that name. It sounded fearsome."

Not surprising that she kept up on international crime syndicates. They were sort of her hobby. "Two other names, I would love to have backgrounds. Kent Severin. He works for the Varelas' cargo company; it's called FastFlex. He's blind. And a guy named Ricky. Hired security, a thug." I gave her Ricky's car model and license plate, from memory. "He may have a tie to a restaurant in Little Havana at this address." I fed her the street address where Ricky had waited for almost four hours before meeting Galo and Zhanna at the nightclub.

"All right," she said. "The fingerprints of the Colombians you gave me. The men were former Colombian Army; they had minor criminal records in Bogotá. Theft, nothing major. Then they both dropped out of sight ten months ago. One had been reported missing by his family, but he re-contacted them after the report was filed. He told them he had a new job in America."

Odd. I wondered what it meant. They'd been doing something, working somewhere, but out of touch with their loved ones. Somewhere near DC? One had a matchbook from a bar there. The thought was unsettling—they could be tied to someone in the government, or to the dozens of contractors who worked for the government.

"Sam…"

"Just please get here."

"And do what?"

"I need you to help me kidnap someone." I had the barest kernel of a plan, but I wasn't sure it would work.

She responded to this announcement not with disbelief but with a sigh. "I shall be breaking laws left and right for you."

"It's for a good cause."

"All right. Can I call you on this line?"

"Yes."

"Fine, Sam. I'll see you tomorrow. I'll be on the first flight I can get. Will text you my flight arrival time in a coded message." She hung up.

I turned off the shower. I erased the call from my log. I texted Cori: Thanks for getting my phone back for me. Just so she'd know to lie if she was asked.

I crawled into bed. This had been one of the longest days of my life. The Varela family drama made me think of my own blood ties: my distant parents, my lost brother. I missed Danny so bad it hurt. I closed my eyes against the memories and finally I slept the kind of sleep my body craved, the window softly lit with the glow of the lights turned outward, toward the darkness.

32

I AWOKE TO gunfire.

I pulled myself out of bed and looked out the window. The sun was just up, the sky clear. Below in the courtyard Rey Varela fired his gun, hooted with laughter, fired it again. I couldn't see what he was aiming at.

I was already in a T-shirt and I yanked on khakis. I ran down the stairs, into the kitchen, out onto the stone patio. He smiled at me.

"What are you shooting at, Rey?"

"Birds."

Cori and Zhanna appeared on the patio, disheveled with sleep. Ricky and Galo, presumably exhausted from their night vigil, didn't appear.

"He's shooting at birds," I said.

"Papa, put up the gun," Zhanna said. "We are not starting our new day this way."

"It's mine," he said as I took it from him, making doubly sure the clip was empty and there was no round in the chamber. I nodded at them and handed it back to him.

He's better in the mornings, Cori had said, and I couldn't help but feel he was out here to cause trouble. Sometimes the elderly are as rebellious as teenagers.

"Come inside, Papa," Cori said.

"Come inside," he mocked her. "You two go inside. Let me talk with my new friend here."

Neither of his daughters moved.

"I'll behave," he said. You could see it, the odd mix of charm and bravado that must have served him well in building his business.

Cori steered Zhanna back inside.

"You know why I had kids?" Rey asked me.

"No, sir."

"Because I had wives who wanted kids. I never wanted them. I used to see little starving runts running around in these godforsaken villages and I'd wonder why, why did anyone bring a kid into this rotten world? Then you have them and you understand why."

"Yes, sir." I understood, but Sam Chevalier had no children.

"My first wife...people, do-gooders, busybodies, they sent her pictures of kids. Dead kids, dying kids, kids blown apart by weapons all over Africa. Because they thought I brought the weapons. Part of why she killed herself." His voice trailed off. "Kids. They're always trouble. But what can you do? They're the future. You got to make them useful."

I had no answer to this. "The do-gooders thought you were the so-called Lord Caliber."

He snorted. "Even if I was, what did that have to do with my wife? She never hurt nobody. Poor Galo. He stood there and watched her walk into the ocean. Explains who he is, why he's got to rescue everybody all the time." He snorted and changed the subject by inspecting the fresh bruises on my face, and the leftover ones from yesterday. "How you feeling this morning?"

"I'm okay."

"Did you take painkillers? They dull the mind. I was just telling Natalia...well, no, I mean, I told her when she was alive, 'Not so much with the pills.' That didn't work. She killed herself with the pills." I guessed Natalia was Zhanna's mom, wife number three. Suicide number two.

"I'm sorry for all your tragedies." Nothing else to say.

"Sometimes I get a little confused."

"We all do," I said.

"You feel up to a walk?" he asked. "They won't let me walk alone anywhere anymore."

"Yes, sir."

I followed him across the stone patio, past the fire pit. Halfway down the steps to the beach stood one guard, the one who'd had most of the night off. The guard had a whistle in his mouth, presumably to rouse the household at any sign of danger. As we walked past him, Rey flicked out a finger and knocked the whistle from the man's lips.

"You look stupid. Get up on the driveway."

"Yes, sir, but Zhanna…"

"Do as I say."

Did he not remember last night? He'd given up command to his kids. Rey sailed on past and I glanced back at the guard, who shrugged and put the corded whistle back in his mouth. And stayed where Zhanna had apparently ordered him to be.

The clouds hung low and gray over the water. We went down the stone stairway, past the area where we'd fought the assailant.

"You could have used a whistle yesterday," I observed.

"If I ever have to whistle for help, don't come save me," he said.

We walked along the sand to a flat rock that abutted the water. He set down his coffee on the rock. Then he sat, the breeze ruffling his thin strands of hair.

"Who's after you?" I thought it was worth a shot. You never know; unguarded, he might tell me.

"A wealthy man can have many enemies." His gaze met mine, bemused. This was a man who'd cut million-dollar cargo deals in jungles, shantytowns, bombed-out airports. He would only respect forthrightness.

"It seems to me life started getting complicated here when you showed Cori the ten million dollars."

He glanced at me.

And here I played my card. "It's the ten million. Either some-one is upset with you that you showed it to her, or you stole it."

"Here's all you need to know: a slice of that money will be yours if you take care of Cori."

"Why trust me? You don't even know me."

"Because I don't trust anyone. Ever."

"You just handed over the company to Galo and Zhanna. Odd that you don't trust them."

"We'll see what they do with my trust."

Trust. Then I put it together, wove the strings of what I'd learned here into a thread. "The family knows you showed the money to Cori, and someone in the family told someone else. Without your permission."

He watched the sea. "It's a hard thing to feel your mind slip away at times. Right now I know you, and where I am, and who's around me. And then it's like my brain is in a time machine and my first wife is still alive and coming down those steps. Or I forget my own name. My time's running out. I used to say I'm running out of runway, you know, to take off. And I shouldn't have shown Cori the money but I wanted her to have it…"

I studied the foam of the surf sliding onto the beach.

"So the money's yours?" That meant everything we'd been told about the money was a lie.

"Yes." But he didn't look at me. "I'm not going to risk Cori. I can't take another…" And he didn't have to say *Edwin.*

I stayed quiet. For all his scoffing at the trials of having chil-dren, I could hear the pain in his voice.

"You can't know what's it like. To lose someone to kidnapping. The not knowing…every night I would go to sleep and know that somewhere my boy was either dead or wondering when I would use all my power and money and influence to find him. Waiting for me to help him."

But I did. Not Sam Chevalier. Sam Capra did. My son, Daniel, kept from me after his birth, used by a criminal syndicate as a pawn to get me to do their bidding. He was already a few months old by the time I first saw him, held him, and I could never make up that time. My brother, Danny, kidnapped in Afghanistan as a relief worker, held for days, his throat finally cut on a grainy video.

I knew what it was like. But I couldn't say so. I preferred not to dwell on any similarities between the Capras and the Varelas. That was a mirror too close.

Rey kept talking: "...back when Sergei and I flew in Africa, no one would have touched us, or my kids—because of our friends. You don't piss off the nonelected president or the warlord. But I didn't have enemies then; I was everyone's friend. I need better friends now." He lit a cigarette, coughed. "Kent and Galo and Zhanna, they hired the best detectives money could buy. I know people in the CIA"—and here my heart jangled and my blood dropped a degree or two—"because every Cuban in Miami, they know someone who knows CIA. Did you know back in the day, when we were going to kill Castro, that the CIA Miami office had the standing of a foreign office? The CIA's not supposed to work on US soil, right?"

"I believe I've heard that," I said.

"So after Castro comes to power, the CIA treats Miami like *foreign soil*. Thousands on payroll, lots of funding for companies that could turn into fronts for the CIA if needed." He shrugged. "They poured all that money into south Florida, like it was the front line of the war on communism. And for nothing. Castro, the bastard, stayed put." He stared out at the blue of the water.

"Did they fund you? Before you were flying in Africa?"

"The government used to look at me, flying arms into Africa, and hold its nose." He'd just admitted he dealt arms. He kept his gaze locked on the ocean.

"But if you couldn't find Edwin, with all your money, all your contacts...then you and your family were up against someone more powerful than you."

He blinked at me, then looked again to the blue of the water. "You're a good match for Cori. She's smart and she doesn't give up. It can be very annoying."

"Who is after you?" I asked again. "Because I'm not going to let what happened to Edwin happen to Cordelia."

"Too many men would have run from the trouble. You ran toward the trouble. I am like you, Sam, you are like me. I want you watching Cori. I want you to take her away today. Now." He tossed the cigarette onto the beach, scooped sand atop it to smother the ember. "I sent some friends of mine for a follow-up talk with your friend Mr. Lada. They...leaned on him. Tried to punch holes in your story. He stuck to it, apparently even after they burned him with a cigar."

I stared at him in horror.

"Oh, don't worry, he's fine. He'll just have a few days of quiet rest at home. If he needs a bit of cosmetic surgery I'll make sure he's taken care of."

Poor Lada. I felt a hot stab of anger, but I kept my face very still.

"Does that make you angry?"

"You did," I said, "what you had to do. I don't like it, but I understand it..."

"Okay. So. Take Cori today, yes, don't wait around. And I'll pay you very, very well."

"Yes, sir." He was trying to get me away from the action. But he'd also given me an excuse to not be here, and I needed to take it.

Now to get Cori away from here, and to meet Mila.

Because there was going to be another kidnapping today. But this time, I would be the kidnapper.

33

We took a spare car—an older Lincoln Navigator—and I pulled onto the road, heading north toward Aguadilla. It would be around a two-hour drive to San Juan. No one followed us.

"So are we going to, um, grab my dad?" Cori said.

I wondered if the car might be bugged and I shook my head at her. I turned on the radio. Near Aguadilla we parked at a scenic overlook along State Road 2 and I went through the car carefully while Cori stared out at the blue of the Atlantic and the smudge of Desecheo Island.

No bug. We could talk.

"I found the kidnapper's car. We're going to use it. But not to take your father. Instead we're going to get the kidnapper's accomplice before your sister and your brother do."

"That sounds more dangerous."

"Cori, your father will tell us nothing. The kidnapper's accomplice could tell us everything."

After a moment she nodded. "How?"

"I need you to do exactly as I say, Cori, if you want to protect your family and protect yourself. Are you all right with that?"

She nodded after a moment. "I trust you totally."

"Okay. I'm keeping the promise to your dad to keep you out of danger. But I need you to drive this car, and I'll drive the kidnapper's."

"How on earth..."

"I snuck out last night, found the car, snuck back in. This was a professional job. The car had knockout drugs, a medical kit."

Her eyes widened. "You are something else. So what's the plan?"

"You may not like it. But you've reached the point of no return."

"What?"

"You have to...well, to be blunt, burn this house down."

She shook her head. "It's made of stone and Papa will just buy a new one."

"I mean your family. To save them, you've got to ruin them."

"What?"

I crossed my arms. "They have a legit business and a dirty one. The dirty one, whatever they're smuggling for people—this ten million, whatever else, it has to go. Make it a disaster for them. Unprofitable. Make them *want* to give it up."

"I can't hurt them."

"It might be one of them trying to kill you off because you know about the ten million."

"I can believe a lot of bad about my family except...that they would try to hurt me."

Sometimes you have to be blunt. "Eddie. What if he found out too? What if this was why he died?"

She swallowed. The thought had to have lodged in her mind already, poisonous, a sickening seed, ready to grow. I just poured water on it.

"What did we say before, back at the bar? Every game must have a winner." I remembered the abandoned checkerboard. "Someone wants to win here, very badly, and doesn't care who gets hurt."

I saw the tears edge her eyes but she didn't cry. I kissed her, gently at first, and then hard. She kissed me back. I did not expect this. How long had she felt penned in a cage by crimes she couldn't even name? The wild mix of anger and resentment and love she must have felt toward her family.

She broke the kiss as another car drove past us. "Sam. Sam. Can you guarantee no one gets hurt?"

"I won't hurt anyone unless I'm forced to. But if one of them killed Steve, and we find that out...I won't protect them."

"But you won't go to the police."

"I won't go to the police," I said. "One step at a time. First we find the Russian's partner."

"And what do you get for this?"

"Justice for Steve. And very likely justice for your brother. And freedom for you."

"And when it's gone..."

"They can't start it up again. This has to be a final solution." I didn't threaten. I didn't explain. I wanted to see if she could wrap her head around the idea. "It's huge. Ricky said it affects the whole world. Your dad even said it was a prison for them, they can't get free of it. This isn't just about Steve anymore, Cori."

"For Eddie," she said, after a moment. Almost a whisper to herself. Her gaze met mine. "All right. What do you need from me?"

"I am going to grab this partner of the kidnapper's before your family does. Could be a partner in the smuggling, could be the owner of the ten million, could be an angry customer. Zhanna and the guards will have a plan to trap this person at a rendezvous they've set up. But we trap the person first."

"I don't know how to do any of that." She looked shell-shocked.

"I do."

We got back in the car and drove to the neighbor's house. The Yukon, and the gear I needed from it, was still there. Cori watched me ready the car; she stared at the medical kit in the back. I went inside the house to see if Nesterov had left anything else of interest or any other clue as to who he worked for. Nothing.

When I came out, Cori was in her car, ready to go. We took both cars to San Juan, heading east, me following her. Mila had texted me earlier; she would arrive in a couple of hours, on a flight coming in from Miami. It could well be the same flight as Nesterov's partner; it would be easier to get a last-minute booking on the midmorning arrival. We had very little time.

But the giant question mark was driving the car in front of me. How far would Cordelia go?

34

I LEFT CORI in my room at the Gran Fortuna in Old San Juan. "Can't I do something useful?" she asked.

"Tell me about Ricky's guys. They don't seem the sharpest pencils. How good of a team are they? Can they grab someone in the middle of San Juan and get away with it?"

"They're all ex-Army, from somewhere in Central America. Honduras or Panama. It varies. I have no idea of their level of training."

I pulled the broken casino chip from my pocket. Her eyes went wide. "You..."

"It was in Steve's house. I found it there. I broke it and planted the other half because I wanted to see how your family would react. Do you have a friend here you can trust? Someone who could tell us what you get if you redeem an unmarked chip like this one?"

She nodded. "Yes. I worked here a couple of summers when I was in college. I have a friend who got a full-time job here. I can ask her." She took the half with the serial number from me, studied it. Something lit in her face—anger, surprise—and I wondered how it would feel to realize the people in the world you loved most had kept the darkest secrets from you.

"She can't let anyone know who might alert your family."

"I'll make sure she keeps her mouth shut."

"I'll be back soon." I decided not to take the gun with me; but after a moment's thought, I slipped the syringe, capped, into my pocket. You never knew.

I left her at the casino and drove back to the airport to catch Mila's arrival.

I waited near the baggage claim as the crowd from the Miami flight came through, and then Mila was at my side before I realized it. She wore a dark suit, white shirt. Her cool eyes hidden behind large sunglasses.

"She is there," Mila said. "With the two men who look like they could bend you over their knee and snap you. Do not look. Just follow."

We followed. The woman was fortyish, an attractive, elegant redhead. The two men with her were in their twenties, thickly muscled, with the air of bodyguards. They boarded a shuttle to a car rental complex away from the terminal. We followed. They sat in the front of the bus; we went to the back.

"Who is she?" I asked as we sat.

"She's big trouble. Which means Lavrenti Nesterov," Mila began—and this was her way to say hello and give me her answer—"is not just a former Miami cop."

"What is he?"

"There was a Round Table file on him."

This was unusual. The Round Table is not the FBI or the CIA—they track people who may be of interest because they've fallen through the cracks left by the world's justice systems. "What about him?"

"He was spotted and photographed once with this woman. One of our people was following her."

"And she is?"

"One of the most dangerous freelance assassins in the world. Trained by former East German operatives, one of which was her father. She goes by the name Marianne. Nesterov was photographed with her in Ecuador, a month after he was dismissed from the Miami police. We were tracking her, not him, but after we got his picture from public records we ran a face-recognition program against our files and we found him with her."

"Why was an assassin meeting with an ex-cop?" We stopped at a rental car company, about half the bus got off. The woman and the two young men stayed.

"We believe he was one of her protégés. She has many. She trains them and they work for her. Sort of like how I have taken you under my wing, yes, Sam?"

"Not remotely similar."

"Marianne is franchising her expertise. She is the new model of assassination." Mila shrugged. "I dislike new business paradigms, myself."

"And Marianne sent Nesterov here on a job."

"One might surmise. Once we realized we had a file on him we pulled up her information—not that there is much of it—and I recognized her."

"I didn't know assassins did kidnappings and traveled with guards." Something was off here.

"Marianne does. She calls them her 'sons' or 'daughters.' As a former teacher I admire her dedication."

"And the Varelas think they're going to take this woman down?"

"I'm quite sure she realizes there is a trap. Hence the 'sons' with her today. Perhaps she has a trap of her own." The shuttle bus reached another, larger car rental office. Here everyone got off. Mila began tapping at her phone, using the rental company's app, speeding up her rental of a car from this same lot. We stayed outside.

"I don't suppose she would tell us why someone wants Rey Varela dead."

Mila glanced at me. "Don't underestimate her. She's worked for governments, we believe. Not just terrorists."

Marianne and her "sons" got their paperwork completed at the counter. The sons kept a steady watch on their surroundings.

"I want to talk to her," I said.

"Are you insane? Let her and this family hash it out. You have no reason to be involved."

"I want to know who wants Rey Varela dead and why."

"We have to take out both her and the sons," Mila said, "and I am not armed at the moment. And we need to ascertain where they're going to and…come, I'm a gold member, I have a confirmation." We followed as the trio headed toward the rental car lot, walking over to the section with the luxury SUVs. Seriously, what was it with criminals and big cars? There's no subtlety left in the world.

"Sam. No. We take them at their hotel."

I stopped. I'd nearly spoken to Marianne in German, thinking if I called her name out the shock of it would stop her in her tracks. And she wouldn't be armed, none of them would be. They wouldn't have had time to get the guns from their checked bags. But it had been foolhardy. Of course they could probably kill with their bare hands. But it would attract unwanted attention here in the rental car lot.

Mila proceeded to her rental. So did Marianne and her fake sons. I jumped back onto the shuttle, which headed back toward the terminal, calling Mila and activating my phone's earpiece.

"I'm following them," Mila said. "They're headed into town. Gray Lexus SUV." She fed me the license number.

"They have three hours before the meeting, assuming they intend to show up for it. They might be checking into a hotel."

I jumped off the bus and ran to my car. I paid the parking and bolted into traffic. I drove like a maniac, caught up to the SUV, catching up to Mila, staying close to them and slowing.

"I think she is suspicious," I said to Mila. "She brought these guys with her. She smells the trap. Why does her own protégé ask to meet in a public spot? The Varelas didn't realize the relationship between Marianne and Nesterov."

"So why did she come if it's a trap?"

"She might think Nesterov is captured and she wants to negotiate for his release. Maybe she is acting on behalf of the clients." Nesterov's words to Rey echoed in my brain: *We just want to talk to you.* Could Marianne just want to talk? Did you send an assassin—a team of assassins—to chat? Ricky and his team didn't quite look as professional as Marianne and her boys.

And what if there had been some other communication with the Varelas since we left? I only knew what I knew, and it made me uneasy to base decisions on incomplete information.

Mila broke through the whirl of my thoughts. "I have missed you. Daniel misses you too. He says 'Dada' to me. I am sure he adds a question mark."

"I miss him," I said. I should have told her to not mention my son on this unsecured line, but I also knew this was the kind of stuff she said to me that she didn't much like to say to my face.

"He misses you," she said again. "Why are we here?"

"They killed my friend." I let my car fall back from Marianne's.

"Revenge is never a good motive."

"Said the woman who took down the people who hurt her sister."

"I did that to save her, not to get revenge," she said quietly. "A world of difference, Sam."

"So if the Varelas kill me, you'll do nothing."

"Oh, Sam, you're funny. What happened to the person who shot me? You never did say."

I didn't answer.

"Well," Mila said, "I'm a hypocrite. Because anyone who kills you dies. Ah. An eye for luxury and convenience. They are turning into the Gran Fortuna."

I veered through the traffic, anxious to reach the hotel at the same time Mila and Marianne's team did. I pulled up to the porte cochere. Marianne and her people were already inside the lobby.

I tapped the phone, putting Mila on hold, calling Cori.

"What?" she said.

"Call one of your friends on staff…a German woman and two men are just checking in right now. I'm pretty sure they'll have requested adjoining rooms. I need those room numbers ASAP."

"I'm on it," she said.

I valeted the Yukon. Mila had already parked and was in the lobby pretending to be on her phone. I walked in and she turned

toward me and I saw Marianne and her guys picking up their bags
and heading toward the elevator. Rather, Marianne and one guy
did. The other guy branched off, headed for the stairs.

Splitting up. You don't put your whole team in an elevator in a
hostile environment. Standard precaution.

"Elevator, you," Mila said to me as I passed.

I didn't even glance at her. She headed for the stairs.

The elevator doors slid closed long before I reached them. But
the elevator next to it opened.

My phone buzzed. "They're in room 1212 and 1210; those are
adjoining," Cori said. "What is going on?"

"In a few."

"Do I call the police if you don't call back?" Her voice was all
steely control. I was glad.

"I'll call you back."

"Sam, please…"

I cut her off. I got in the elevator, joined by a couple who'd
forgotten something in their room and were blaming the other.

"I asked *you* to bring the guidebook," she said.

"*You* have the backpack. So you're supposed to carry it," he
said icily.

"You never remember anything," the wife snapped. They
pressed 12. The same floor as Marianne and the boys. Rotten
luck. I did not need witnesses.

"Then *you* can just go back down to the lobby and wait for
me," the husband said.

"No, I need to be sure *you* remember it," the wife said. "I
mean, sports might be on the TV; *you'll* end up slack-jawed sitting
on the edge of the bed and *I* didn't come to Puerto Rico to explore on *my* own…"

"That's so unfair," he said, and she glowered.

"*My* wife is in a coma," I said, into the gap of silence. "Pretty
sure she and I wish we'd been kinder to each other."

It shut them up and, better yet, made them eager to get away
from me. No one likes a good shaming.

We reached the twelfth floor. They turned one way and I

turned the other and the elevator next to us opened. I didn't look behind me. I had to assume Marianne and her "son" were off and walking behind me. Right now I couldn't rely on eyes; I had to go by sound.

Hand went into pocket, like I was grasping for a room key. I uncapped the syringe, careful not to jab myself.

I heard the voices, down the hall, of the couple. Him saying he was sorry, her saying she was sorry too. Well, I'd fixed one problem today.

The sound, behind me, of Marianne muttering in German, annoyed with the hotel. She thought the hall looked like it needed a cleaning. Ahead of me the housekeeping cart. The rooms were still getting readied for the new occupants or being serviced.

We moved past the housekeeping cart.

The sound, behind me, of the door closing behind the now-happy couple. I really should be a marriage therapist.

The door to the stairway opened.

But no one came out.

I was now between the stairway and the targets' door, and I had to believe Mila had won. But if I was wrong I might get shot in the back.

I spun and jabbed the syringe into Marianne's throat. But I didn't depress the plunger. "Might we talk in private?" I started to say in German.

The son reacted. He drew his gun. I could hear the merry chatter of two women from the room being cleaned.

I shook my head. "You don't want me injecting this into her," I said.

Behind me I heard Mila say, in English, "Let's take this into the room please."

I didn't risk a glance. "You have him?"

"I do. And his room key." Mila switched to German. "I'm sure, Marianne, you'd prefer not to dig a bullet out of his brain. In the room, please. We only want to talk."

I could see indecision play across Marianne's face. She didn't want to go in the room with us but she didn't want her man shot.

"Lower your weapon," I said in German to the son, and Marianne said, "Do as he says," in English. And the son did.

The housekeeper came out and smiled at the five of us and wished us good morning. I had my arm around Marianne, my hand hiding the syringe, turning her away from the housekeeper. Marianne stiffened as I nuzzled her affectionately and said hello to the housekeeper. Mila had lowered the gun to her target's back. His mouth was bleeding on one side, away from the housekeeper, and he kept his face turned in that direction.

The housekeeper gathered supplies and ducked back into the room.

"We are not friends of the Varelas," I said. "We want a meeting with you. No one gets hurt. It's just a talk. Because you are about to walk into a trap the Varelas are setting for you."

"I understand," Marianne said.

I pulled the syringe free and she winced. A thin dot of blood appeared on her throat.

"All right. Give me the key."

She was already holding the room key and she handed it to me. "Them first, then the two of you." I opened the door and Mila shoved her charge inside, then the second son, and Marianne followed.

I closed the door on the housekeepers' chatter.

35

Lᴇᴛ'ѕ ʙᴇ ʜᴏɴᴇѕᴛ. You don't want five trained killers trapped in a room together.

The room was nice for traveling assassins, I figured. Big-screen TV, a generously sized bed. Curtains open over the charm of Old San Juan. The view faced the harbor and the massive cruise ships docked there. I could see families walking along the dock. Normal families. Not like mine, not like the Varelas, not like Marianne's. Odd how we all live, side by side, in our different worlds.

"Marianne, I have no quarrel with you," I said, switching to English. "You are headed into a trap by the Varelas. They want you dead or captured."

"Who are you?" she asked. She had her hand to her throat. I still had the syringe in my grip.

"A friend."

"I suppose you think we became friends on the rental car bus." She recognized us. Her gaze went back to Mila. "I don't know her, either." She looked at the second son. "She must be good to get the best of him."

"I let down my guard." He mopped at his bloodied mouth with the towel his "brother" had tossed him. "I apologize."

"Actually, I told him I would hurt you if he did not stop fighting, Marianne," Mila said. "So, commend him for his loyalty."

"Facedown on the carpet, fingers locked behind your heads," I ordered the sons, and they obeyed, one of them giving me a murderous look and the bloodied one keeping his expression neutral. "Keep the towel under your mouth, I don't want blood on the carpet."

"Will I sound melodramatic," Marianne said, "if I tell you this is a highly regrettable idea?"

"Yes, you will." Mila searched the sons.

I searched Marianne. I found it in her pocket. A casino plaque, rectangular, red, with the X symbol.

Just like Steve's.

"What's this?" I asked.

"Just a casino chip."

"Why is there no denomination on it?"

"It's…like a party favor from the hotel. It's not worth much."

"I think you're lying to me."

"I'm not."

"Who gave it to you?"

"The hotel, when we checked in."

"They didn't give me one." I managed to sound both outraged and disappointed.

"Well, they don't want trash like you in the casino."

"Yes, that must be it," I said. "Maybe I'll keep it."

"So you're not only a kidnapper, you're a thief," she said.

I studied the chip. It was identical to the one Steve had. What were Steve's words to Cori that night at the bar? *I got a surprise in the mail*…and then he'd said a few words I didn't hear, and then *How did anyone know you hired me?* A bribe attempt, perhaps, to stay away from Cori. If he'd taken the bribe, he'd probably still be alive. I slipped it back into my pocket.

"You're a lousy cheat," Marianne said.

So, I thought. It's money. Play this carefully. Get her on my side. "I'll give you back the chip in a few minutes. Let's talk about what's important. Lavrenti. Your 'son' from Miami, the Varelas killed him."

"I suspected that." Marianne had the air of a schoolteacher

with little patience for stupid comments. "That syringe. I knew his plan. You found his gear."

"I, not the Varelas, found it after the Varelas killed him, in his car. I didn't kill him."

"So what's your interest?"

"I have a grudge against the Varelas."

"And I care why?"

"I want to know who hired you."

Marianne gave me a bemused smile. "Can we not pretend to adhere to standards of professional conduct?"

"Who hired you?" I repeated.

"Ask Rey Varela who's mad at him, get him to tell you." She apparently didn't like that I knew she referred to her protégés as her kids.

"If she dodges another question of mine," I said to Mila, "shoot one of her sons in his gun hand."

The men were following Marianne's calm lead, but at this I heard them breathe in sharply, and a flash of panic crossed Marianne's gaze.

"Before we get to a point of deep regret," I said, "let's get this straight. I have zero interest in you or your team. This is professional, not personal. And when we're done, we're done and we all walk away healthy. I'll even suggest you keep your meeting with Mr. Varela today, although it wouldn't surprise me if he sends his stepdaughter and his adviser in his place."

"I'm only talking to him," Marianne said.

"Did your client order the killing of a man named Steve Robles in Miami? If so, did you use two Colombians?"

"I don't have any Colombians in my employ, so if they were used in a hit, they're not my guys. I can't confirm what a client did that doesn't involve me."

"Did you ever hear your client mention a man named Steve Robles, or offer you the job of killing him?"

"No."

"Who is your client?"

"I don't know his name."

"What's the client's code name?"

She hesitated, and Mila said, "I can see the slightest callus on this one's right forefinger. That's his gun hand." She lowered her weapon toward him.

"Mr. Beethoven," Marianne said.

"Is Mr. Beethoven one of the Varelas?"

"I cannot be certain."

"And where might I reach Mr. Beethoven?"

"There's a throwaway phone in my jacket pocket," she said. She wore a thin, dark cotton blazer. Carefully, I leaned forward and reached into the pocket and took it. There was one number in the call log.

"Answer a question for me. Who killed Lavrenti?" she asked. "Which one of the Varelas or their men?"

"I'm sorry, I don't know." I wasn't going to give her Galo; he'd saved me with that shot.

"He was a very promising student," she said. And I thought I detected a hint of sadness. I suppose you don't take just anyone off the street and train them to be a hit man. Was she close to her charges? Would she be motivated by revenge? I wasn't going to tell her, *Hey, you trained him well: he nearly killed me*. Best left unsaid.

I tapped the number. It was a Miami area code. Marianne kept her gaze locked on mine. It rang twice, then a bright young female voice said, "New Horizons Dental Care, we put your smile first! How may I help you today?"

"Mr. Beethoven, please."

"For when did you wish to make an appointment, sir?"

"Tomorrow at five p.m. That's the only time I have available."

"May I have your name, sir?"

I clicked off the phone. "So when I do an Internet search on New Horizons Dental Care, I'm not going to find an actual office, am I?"

"You know as much about the client as I do," she said. "Mr. Beethoven, the dentist." She risked a smile. "It's frustrating isn't it? Good enough to take me and my team unawares but not to get the information you need. If I knew it, I'd tell you. I've never compromised a client but I've never been taken this way either."

"What are you supposed to offer Rey Varela?"

She closed her eyes for a moment, as if betrayal of her professional code caused her actual pain. "It concerns…part of his business. He is giving it to his stepdaughter to run. This is unacceptable to his clients."

"Why?"

She shrugged. "They know he is not well. They will not accept Zhanna as his replacement."

I felt stunned. How had they known about him putting Zhanna in charge of the underside of the business? He had only announced it after Nesterov's attempt…which meant logically Rey had decided to put Zhanna in charge and discussed it with someone *before* last night. That could be anyone in the family. Who could have secretly told the clients. "You learned about Zhanna's new role very quickly."

"Perhaps my client's information," she said, "was better than yours. Lavrenti was only told to detain him. So Varela could be reasoned with. The remote house in Puerto Rico was considered an easier grab than his house or office in Miami."

"Did your client kidnap Edwin Varela five years ago?"

"I have no knowledge of that. So. Who killed Lavrenti? I read it in your face that you know."

Professional to professional. I wasn't going to argue. I couldn't betray Galo, so I lied. "A guy named Ricky. He works for the Varelas. You will know him by his very retro jacket. They dumped Lavrenti in the ocean, by the way."

A coldness settled in her eyes. "And where is Mr. Varela? At the house?"

"He was injured in the attempt. The Varela security team will try to take you at Castillo de San Cristóbal. Probably they'll simply try to force you into their car, or if they don't take you then they'll just want to talk."

"What *are* you?"

"Right now, I'll be your backup. You are going to keep your

appointment with the Varelas. I'm going to wire you, though, be-cause I want to hear the conversation. Your boys will stay here with my partner. If you tell on me to the Varelas, my partner shoots them."

She frowned. "The magnitude of the mistake you're making is quite remarkable," she said. But Mila had brought a full set of surveillance gear, and she let Mila wire her while I watched her sons.

36

CASTILLO DE SAN Cristóbal was a massive fort on the cliffs overlooking the Atlantic, on the northeastern side of Old San Juan—a gigantic redoubt built to protect the island from the British and the Dutch. Everyone back in ye olden days wanted San Juan and Puerto Rico. Spain, for hundreds of years, was determined to not lose the gateway to the Caribbean trade. Hence the stunning forts of the old city. During World War II the fort had added concrete pillboxes in case the German navy attacked Puerto Rico. Tourists wandered, a few alone, most with groups from the cruise ships, walking with tour guides in traditional costume—the women in lovely hoop-skirted dresses of pink and yellow and white, the men dressed in what most Americans would have thought of as Revolutionary War garb: tricorner hats and long jackets and breeches with stockings. One of the hoop-skirted tour guides told the story of the language of the fan, snapping a gorgeous decorated fan open and closed, fanning herself with a variety of flourishes in a hidden language that could be interpreted by a suitor so he'd know what she wanted him to do: flirt more, go away, wait for her husband to leave.

The plaza opened up from the hillside, facing Old San Juan. Above it was a large incline that led to the fort proper. I'd been here, once before, with my parents during a break from an assignment in Haiti, and my mother constantly made us feel guilty that we were enjoying a beautiful day in a clean, functioning city while people back in our temporary home were trapped in squalor. I remembered small turrets that faced the ocean; Danny and I had played in them, pretending to watch for both Sir Francis Drake and Nazis—we were historically inexact.

Marianne would meet the Varelas on the plaza courtyard, bordering the street.

I was parked along Calle Norzagaray, uphill a bit from the open courtyard, a sign in English and Spanish on the dashboard marking that I was a hired driver. Behind me were more of the colorful buildings with balconies that were the standard in Old San Juan.

The Yukon's windows were darkened—I'm guessing the high-end luxury car rental market has to always be prepared to rent to a celebrity. But I had a dark cap and dark glasses—left behind in the car by Lavrenti—and Mila's makeup on my bruised face. I watched, one earpiece in my right ear tuned to Mila, the other in my left tuned to Marianne's wire. I had no intention of ordering her men dead—but Marianne didn't know that, and I wanted Mila to know how this rendezvous unfolded.

So at the appointed time, Marianne walked to the plaza.

And then I saw Galo and Kent and Rey get out of a car and walk toward her. No sign of Zhanna. Or Ricky. They had to be close. Rey seemed fragile still; Galo kept a hand on him. Kent walked next to them, his white cane moving in front of him. He didn't like to be guided unless it was necessary. I was surprised to see Galo and Rey making a personal appearance.

Marianne waited.

"I figured my associate would not be here," Marianne said.

"He won't be," Galo said. There was no waver in his voice. Rey centered himself before her, Galo to his side, Kent two steps off, his sunglasses aimed sightlessly at the sky, listening. "We're here to talk with you. Nothing else. We don't want trouble."

"You should know we're being observed," she said.

"As you are, by our people," Kent said. And now I knew where Zhanna was.

"Given yesterday's events, your clients entrusted me with a message to deliver to you. From your clients: You do not hand off our mutual business to Zhanna Pozharskaya."

Rey said, "It is mine to run. That has always been the agreement."

"The clients do not trust your stepdaughter."

"How did anyone know I was making a change?" Rey asked.

She shrugged. "Phones can be tapped, e-mails monitored. Offices bugged. Mobile phones are shockingly insecure."

Who is her client? I wondered.

"Zhanna is perfectly capable of running the business."

"Your clients don't agree. They know what she did, and they don't like her for it. She is not...stable."

"Unfounded," Rey said. Galo looked confused; Kent was calm. But he always looked calm. "What do they think she did?" Kent asked. He tapped the cane against the stone, twice, and I took that for a show of anger.

"I cannot answer questions," Marianne said. "I can only deliver the message. This isn't a negotiation. Galo can run the legitimate side of the business. But the underside will be run by someone of the client's appointing. Someone that you will accept."

"And if I say no, you try to kidnap me again?" The rage shone in Rey's voice.

"This is no different than shareholders not agreeing with a new CEO's appointment. It is a business matter. But it is not up for negotiation. She cannot run it."

Rey started to sputter, and I thought of the pride and arrogance I'd always heard in his words. He would not take this lightly. Galo put a calming hand on him. A big group of tourists wandered past them, being broken into three smaller groups by their costumed tour guides. Kent kept his head tilted upward, as though listening to the sky. He pulled the cane close to him.

"We could simply shut the business down," Rey said. "Walk away from it. The clients could do nothing."

Marianne looked at him. "Again, this is a message. Not a negotiation. Message delivered." She paused. "Now. A new item on the agenda. Which one of you killed Lavrenti?"

Silence. I could hear the wind hiss between them.

"Are you so afraid of me?" she asked, in barely a whisper.

"You bore me," Rey said. "Go away, lady."

"You're cowards," she said. "Good-bye." And she turned on her heel and began to walk away, back toward me.

Kent started to follow the click of her footsteps, his cane swishing in front of him, taking Rey's arm.

And then the shot rang out.

37

MARIANNE STAGGERED, SHE screamed.

The people in the plaza, intent on their tours, glanced around and then realized, as if one, what they'd heard. The firing of a gun in a public space.

People scattered, parents huddling over their kids, guards running, weapons drawn, tourists and families going over the stone walls or running back down the hill.

Images swimming in front of me: Kent blindly lurching after Marianne, his cane swinging, Galo knocking Rey to the ground and covering him, a shield of good-son flesh.

She ran toward me, in the Yukon. And then there was Galo rising, making sure his father was all right, his gaze following her through the scattering crowds.

"I'm shot!" she screamed in German. "I'm shot!" Most people collapse at this point. The pain is terrible. An assassin trained by former East Germans is made of sterner stuff.

I lost sight of them all as people fled. Then I saw Marianne, running, clutching at her jacketed arm, toward the Yukon. She clambered into the backseat.

Galo hurried after her. Thirty feet away.

I didn't have to be told. I revved the engine and sped down the street. In the rearview I saw him climb into a BMW, firing up the engine.

I couldn't let him see me.

"Sam, respond," Mila said very calmly into my earpiece.

"Marianne's shot, being pursued," I answered.

Marianne cursed in German from the backseat.

I took a hard, screeching right at the bottom of the hill, narrowly missing a tour bus that was trying to inch forward. Onto Calle San Francisco. On my right was a block of charming little restaurants and shops, on my left Plaza de Colón, with a big statue of Christopher Columbus and tour groups wandering among small booths selling crafts and food and souvenirs. I laid on the horn and the pedestrians scattered. Ahead of me stretched Old San Juan—narrow streets of blue-gray cobblestone, crowded colorful buildings, full sidewalks. Not ideal for a chase. I leaned on the horn and hurtled forward, people scattering out of my way, blasting past a church. The buildings were brightly painted, most with balconies, and in some ways the architecture reminded me of home, back in the French Quarter; maybe San Juan and New Orleans were of an age. Weird what registers during your fight against panic.

I glanced in the rearview and saw Galo, three cars behind me, honking and gesturing like mad, desperate to catch me. And then also a cop, on a motorcycle, trying to catch Galo.

I didn't need this.

It got worse. I came up on Plaza de Armas, one of the more congested sections of Old San Juan, full of tourists and artists. I dodged the Yukon around them, screaming out the window that I had a sick woman in the car.

"Here, turn here!" Marianne ordered. I turned right onto Calle del Cristo.

"No, the other way, idiot!"

Now I was driving the wrong way on a cobblestone street, past buildings of tangerine and turquoise. I saw a sign as we approached the cream-colored Catedral de San Juan Bautista. I remembered it from my childhood visit, because the beautiful church held the mausoleum of Ponce de Leon and I remembered thinking then, *Well, I guess no Fountain of Youth for him.*

"Sam, where are you?" Mila said in my ear.

"Wrong way on a one-way street!" I yelled.

"Hurry, take a left...before you get to the cathedral. Go down the hill." Marianne ordered me.

The road was clear.

"Slow down, there's always cops around here," she said.

Right on cue, another motorcycle cop was approaching me. Waving at me that I was going the wrong way. Typical tourist, I hoped he'd think. No sirens yet. In the back mirror I couldn't see Galo. Or the other cop. I could see the bright yellow El Convento Hotel ahead on my left, catty-corner from the cathedral.

And on the corner were four cops, both on and off their motorcycles, chatting. The motorcycle officer I'd seen approaching from the direction of El Convento pulled alongside. I quickly made the left turn, waving in apology at them, them waving good-naturedly at me, one reminding me in Spanish to watch for the signs.

"Go toward the gate! Puerta de San Juan," Marianne told me.

I remembered calling it the Red Gate from an earlier visit as I turned down the tree-canopied street. Because it was painted a vivid scarlet.

And slammed on the brakes.

Across from the cathedral was the Museo del Niño, and a large group of kids were marching single-file across the street onto which I'd just turned left. They went across, chained together holding hands, one smiling at me with her front teeth missing.

One of the cops looked right into our windows as we were stopped. I waved as we waited on the kids. I lowered the window. Don't let him notice the woman in the back is hurt, I thought.

"Sorry, officer!" I said in my best German-accented Spanish. The cop waved back.

Marianne murmured a pleasantry through gritted teeth.

The cop nodded. "Look out for the signs, sir."

"Yes, sir," I agreed.

"Enjoy San Juan."

I will, I thought, as long as your radio doesn't tell you to be looking for a Yukon, leaving a shooting scene.

We waited. The chain of children seemed to go on forever. Then the police suddenly had fingers at their earpieces, murmuring into their radios. They mounted the motorcycles and revved off behind us.

Then the last child and the last chaperone went by and I drove slowly past the houses of green and pink and blue, toward the bottom of the hill, then over toward the *puerta*. Bright-red against the gray of the massive fortification.

It was a surviving gate from the days when San Juan was a walled city.

"Don't drive through!" Marianne said. "The other side is a walking path. You can't get out, it'll be blocked off, and there are always police."

Lavrenti's gear for kidnapping Rey was still in the Yukon. Marianne had had the presence of mind to put one of the adult diapers under her jacket on the wound, to soak up the blood. She wasn't bleeding too badly.

I got her out of the car, left the engine running, the keys inside. "Can you walk?"

She nodded. I put an arm around her. Her black jacket covered the blood.

"We'll be noticed," she gasped.

"I'll support you," I said. "We'll be okay."

We went through the ancient gate, through the old fifteen-foot wall, onto the Paseo de la Princesa. Above us the wall rose nearly forty feet. Ahead of us was the sparkling blue of San Juan Bay.

A stunning view that I had no time to appreciate. If the police stopped me with a wounded woman, I was done.

38

WE STROLLED. CALMLY. In a non-attention-attracting way.

We made steady progress down the esplanade. If anyone looked too closely at us, Marianne laughed, as though she didn't have a care in the world, then she gritted her teeth together so hard I could hear them grind. I glanced over my shoulder. I saw one blotch of blood painting the stones. We walked steadily, past couples, families, solo adventurers. A couple of security men chatted and ignored us as Marianne giggled and fake-cooed in German.

"You're such a good actress," I said.

"Shut up," she said. "You have ruined my day."

The cops must have pulled Galo over, gotten him instead of me. And what would he tell them? Did he see my face? If he had... I was done.

"Those bastards," she said. "I was just the messenger."

"I'll take you back to the hotel," I whispered to her as we reached the esplanade's end at Plaza del Inmigrante, a large cobbled area not far from the cruise-ship ports, and a few blocks from the Gran Fortuna. "We can tend to you..."

"Screw you, you got me shot!"

Why do it? She'd delivered the message. It was an enormous risk to shoot her in public, to bring attention to the Varela family.

"Who trained you?" Marianne said. "They're idiots. You

should have been one of mine. I could have made you into something."

"Sam, Sam?" Mila said into the earpiece.

"I will tell Mr. Beethoven I delivered the message," Marianne said. "And then I am done with these people."

"The hotel..."

"No. Drop me off here. I will call a friend in San Juan. I have friends everywhere." Her voice broke. "Do not hurt my kids. Please."

"I promise you we won't. But you can't go to a hospital."

"No. My friend will get me the help I need, quietly."

"I'm sorry, Marianne." It was strange to apologize to her. But we were both professionals. At least, I had been once.

"You do not hurt the boys. You let them go." Sweat beaded her face. I pushed her behind a building, out of sight of the pedestrian traffic.

"They won't be harmed. I don't think I feel comfortable leaving you hurt..."

She slapped all the sympathy out of me. My ears rang from the blow. She put her mouth close to my ear. "You can't kill me here on the street. But if you hurt the boys, I know your face. Your name is *Sam*; I heard it through the earphone. And I know the face of your woman. I know her accent; she's Romanian or Moldovan. I will find you both if I have to, find out who you work for. So don't give me a reason to hunt you down. I have lots of sons and daughters around the world that I've trained. You do not want to make my family mad."

Then I did an unkindness. I jabbed my fist, hard, into where her bullet wound was. She nearly crumpled from shock. "And now you hear me. I knew about you and Nesterov before you even showed up in San Juan. I have resources you can't imagine. If you come after me or mine, I will come after you, Marianne, and I will kill you." Our voices were whispers in each other's ears. "Do we understand each other?"

She made a noise of assent.

I gave her back her cell phone. "I'll tell your sons to call you."

She turned away from me. I hurried back toward the Gran Fortuna, thinking the whole time that Galo, freed from answering police questions, could be looking for me. I could feel my phone vibrating with texts.

I redialed Mila. "Let the guys go."

"I'll leave them a small knife that they can cut themselves loose with," she said. "It will take them several minutes and by then I'll be gone. What happened?"

I explained. "There's a tie between Marianne and Steve. Someone was paying them both with a casino chip." I glanced over my shoulder. No sign of the police or Galo. "We have to find out who that is. And if the Varelas saw me, I can't go back to Cori."

"Did they see you?"

"They didn't know the Yukon. I was wearing dark glasses and a cap. Galo might not have gotten close enough to me to see."

"*Might* not? That's a risk, Sam."

"Not if Cori lies to them and tells them I was with her the whole time."

"Will she lie for you?"

"Yes. I think so."

"You think. Sam, we need to pull back."

"I know too much about them. They'll come after me. I have to see this through." I'd reached the hotel. Mila was in the lobby. I nearly fell into her embrace.

"Are you hurt?"

"No."

"What do you want me to do?"

"Go back to Miami. There's nothing more here."

"I don't want to leave you, Sam."

Her husband, I knew, would hate that she said that, even if it was only a professional statement. I looked out over the casino, the crowds. Bells rang from a slot machine, and from the bar reggaeton music blared. For some reason I didn't feel like looking at her. "Why didn't you tell me you were married?"

Mila blinked in surprise. "What did it matter?"

"It didn't. Except it's the sort of thing you share with your...friends."

"I didn't know you so well, Sam. I didn't know if once you had your child back you would stick with the Round Table, working with me...I don't really talk about my personal life."

"But I knew you worked with a guy named Jimmy, and he'd recruited you after you had to go on the run," I said. "How hard would it have been to say, 'Oh and he's my husband'?"

"It wouldn't have been hard at all, but I didn't do it." Her voice grew a little cool. "I don't think I really owe you an explanation."

"Fair enough," I said. "You don't. It's your business."

"You and Jimmy don't like each other."

I had to be careful. "I think he's taken advantage of situations to build his own power base."

"Ah. So then he is like every executive in every company in the world."

I hated that she described him with that veneer of respectability. "Not quite the same. He's more like a military commander who doesn't care how many troops he loses. As long as he gets what he wants."

"But that is what commanders are supposed to do, yes?"

"You really don't know what kind of man you married, do you?"

She crossed her arms. "Maybe I knew exactly who I married, Sam, and that is what bothers you."

I ignored that last stab.

She shifted the topic. "You asked me to do checks on Kent Severin and a guy named Ricky, and Steve Robles's bank accounts."

"Yes." Following Marianne meant we hadn't had time to discuss this.

"Steve Robles was clean. No unusual amounts. Irregular deposits, since he was self-employed. But nothing suspicious."

I felt relief. He hadn't taken a bribe.

She got brisk. "Kent Severin grew up the son of a US diplomat.

Like you, he spent a lot of time wandering the world as a small child. Then flight school, and he worked as a pilot for FastFlex. Retired after a crash here in San Juan."

"Here? A crash?"

"Yes, and that was when he was blinded. He retired, obviously, got his MBA and went to work for the corporate office, no police record. His bank accounts match his pay at FastFlex. No suspicious financial trail, no unusual payments or purchases. No hidden accounts. No sign he is dirty at first glance."

"And Ricky?"

"Oddly—nothing interesting on him yet."

"There's a regular at the bar. A librarian named Paige, who's good at finding out info on locals. I'll give you her phone number. See what she can find on him."

"Fine." She picked up her bag. "I'll see if I can get the next flight back. Are you sure you don't want me to stay? If Galo Varela saw you, you could be a dead man."

"That's true." I wanted her to stay, but I couldn't ask.

"Sam."

"What?" I stopped on my way to the elevators.

"Be careful."

I got on the elevator and the doors slid closed.

I found Cori in her room. She was frantic, pacing. "What the hell is going on? The news says there was a shooting at the Castillo."

"Non-fatal." I showed her the chip. "This was given to the messenger. Just like the one Steve had. Someone is paying people through this casino. What did your friend say?"

"She was off today. I called her on her cell and she's come in to help us... she should be here soon."

I turned on the television news. The coverage was confused as to whether there had been a shooting or it had been some sort of sick joke. No one had seen anyone bleeding, just a woman screaming, but she had run to a car and had not been found. Police were asking witnesses to come forward. No mention of the prominent Varela family.

"This is horrible," Cori said. "Who shot her?"

"I'd guess Zhanna. Or Ricky, probably from a roof on one of the facing buildings. Sending a message. No more negotiation. She maybe didn't like the clients saying she couldn't have the job your father gave her." But it seemed odd, literally shooting the messenger. It seemed unnecessary and would only enrage the mysterious clients further. Unless Zhanna meant it as sheer defiance, as a way to thumb her nose at the clients. The stakes must be extraordinary for Zhanna. I turned to Cori. "Your friend. How much can you trust her?"

"I helped Magali when she needed some money. I think she'll be discreet."

A knock at the door and I checked the peephole. A young woman in a suit entered, smiling uncertainly at Cordelia, glancing at me. Cori introduced me as her boyfriend.

"There has been a problem with someone following Cori. We're trying to figure out why," I told her as we all sat down.

"Why not call the police?"

"The family wants to keep it quiet."

"I'm not sure how I can help."

"Someone who was following Cori dropped a casino plaque from here. Rectangular, with an X symbol on it instead of a dollar amount. We also found a broken chip connected to another person we think was following her."

I saw Magali's throat tighten.

"I'm wondering what the chip means," I said.

"I've never seen such a chip," Magali said.

"It has the casino's name on it," I said.

"Maybe it's counterfeit," she said softly, not looking at us.

"Magali, please," Cori said. "You're not a very good liar."

"I could just take these chips down to the casino cage," I said, "and see what happens when I try to redeem them."

Magali wet her lips. "I don't want to get in trouble."

"I'll protect your job, Magali," Cori said.

I wasn't sure it was her job Magali feared for, but she took a deep breath. "I've only seen such a chip twice in my five years working here. When the first one was shown to me, I was told to summon a supervisor."

"And then what?"

"Well, the supervisor did an electronic funds transfer from a casino bank account to the redeemer's bank account. Two hundred thousand dollars. I guess people don't want to walk away with large winnings if they can't get to a branch of their bank here in San Juan."

"But then those winnings, those chips, would still have denominations on them," Cori said.

I watched Magali. She was nervous. "There's a serial number on the chip," she said, as if that excused the lack of a denomination.

"I guess that lets them tie the chip to specific transfers?" I said. "Is it reprogrammable, like a hotel key?" That is what you would need if one chip was worth two hundred thousand and another chip was worth three hundred thousand. It would depend on the payment you were making. She shrugged.

"Have you ever seen this kind of chip on the gaming tables?" I asked.

"No."

"So where do these special chips come from?"

"I don't know. Please, Cori, I don't want to get into trouble."

"You've said you've seen them twice. Do you remember the people who brought them?" Cori asked.

Magali bit her lip. "The first time, yes, it was a man. He had cold eyes. In his thirties. I've seen him here another time, with your brother, Cori."

I glanced at Cordelia. "Did he wear a jacket?"

"This is Puerto Rico, we don't often have to wear jackets."

"Kind of geeky? But scary, at the same time?"

Slowly she nodded. "Cold eyes."

Ricky. Cordelia frowned.

"What about the second person?"

She shrugged. "In his late twenties, early thirties. A bit taller than you. Gorgeous suit." She gave me an awkward smile. "You know, he looked a bit like you in the face."

Cori glanced at her, frowned at me. Like I'd told her a lie about myself.

"I mean, you know, clean-shaven, all-American." Then Magali bit her lip again.

"Ha," Cori said. "You mean all-Canadian."

Oh, yes, she still doesn't even know who I really am, I thought.

"I never saw him again," Magali said.

"When was this?"

"The weird creep about six months ago. The other guy, around Christmas a year ago. I remember because he wished me a Merry Christmas and I thought he was cute, and you don't see those chips very often at all."

"Was Galo with the weird creep when he redeemed the chip?" I asked.

"Oh, no. Galo would have talked to me. The guy was alone."

"Would there be a record of those transfers? I'd like to know what banks they went to."

Magali's nervousness returned. "I don't know that I can find that out."

"It's a computer record, Magali," Cori said. "And therefore searchable. Your job is safe, I'll make sure of that."

"All right. I'll try."

"Call Cori when you have the information. Thank you, Magali."

Cori gave her friend a hug and kiss on the cheek before Magali left.

"Ricky," I said, "is the weird creep. Just a guess."

"That makes no sense," Cori said. "Galo wouldn't pay him through the casino."

"Two possibilities. One, Ricky's also working for the underside of the business and this is how they pay him. Off the books." Rey was insistent Galo stay clean. "Two, someone else is using this as a payment system. Zhanna or Kent or even your father. Or another partner in the casino. Who are the other owners?"

"Some consortium. Omega Investments."

"Have you ever met anyone who works for them?"

"No," she said. "We're the majority owners." A sudden frost in her voice. "Ricky. And a guy who looked like you."

"That's ridiculous," I said. "It was over a year ago and I didn't know you."

A rapping at the door. We weren't expecting anyone else. I drew the gun and checked the peephole.

Galo. Looking broken and panicked.

39

IF HE'D SEEN me driving the Yukon…my cover was blown.

"Sam, Cori," he hissed at the door.

He'd known I'd had a room at the hotel already. As I reached for the doorknob I thought, *You'll know in his face in the first three seconds if he saw you or not. If he wants you back at the compound they saw you. Get rid of you like they did Nesterov.*

I opened the door, hoping I wouldn't have to kill him.

"Sam. You didn't answer my texts…" He practically fell into the room. I shut the door.

"I'm sorry," I said.

He went to Cori and embraced her.

"What's happened?" Her gaze met mine over his shoulder.

"We met this woman who was the kidnapper's boss. She delivered a message to us. And then she got shot."

"Shot!" Cori was very good.

"Not badly hurt, I think, she ran off. But Papa and Kent and I were right there and we could have been shot…Papa could have been shot." He didn't seem scared—more angry. "What do I do?"

Galo, trying to be whatever the family needed him to be.

"Who shot her?" I asked.

"I don't know. She knew…about Zhanna taking over the smuggling. The clients are spying on us." He spoke in a rush.

It was the first time he'd used the word *smuggling* in front of me. "Did your father talk about giving the smuggling to Z before yesterday morning?"

"Not to me—he might have said something to her. Or Kent. Or someone else. His mouth runs." He glanced at Cori.

"Where was Zhanna during the meeting?" I asked.

"Watching from a distance. On a roof. The woman ran toward a car—a man was driving for her—I tried to catch them, but they got away. And the police stopped me for honking and speeding."

"What'd you tell the police?" Cori asked.

"I thought I'd heard a shot and then this woman ran like she was hurt. That I tried to follow her, to help her." He sat on the bed. "Zhanna shot her, I think. She was the only one in position."

"Why didn't she go to the meeting with you?"

"She said we shouldn't all go if they tried to trap us. So she stayed on a roof to watch. The clients don't want Zhanna running the smuggling. I don't know how, though, how could Z have heard what the woman told us?"

"Parabolic microphone," I said.

"Like she carries that around with her?"

"Did she drive with you and your father?" I asked.

"She drove her own car," Galo said slowly. "I guess she could have had any gear in it she needed." He shook his head in anger. "Z wanted to send a message. She's not backing down from them. She'll get us all killed. What do I do, Sam?"

"That depends on who these clients are. I know the secret business, the underside, moves huge amounts of cash. What else?"

He said it as though the words were still hard to pry from his throat. "Papa has kept me out of it. Obviously, cash, since you saw it, Cori. Sometimes other goods, but I don't know for certain. I don't think it's drugs," he said, as if that would be worse.

"You could move millions in high-grade meth in small packages," I said. "Dealers would love to have a legit cargo company in their pocket."

Galo bit his lip. "If I knew, I'd tell you, I need your help, Sam."

"They've all gone back to the house?" I asked.

"Yes. Papa wanted me to be sure Cori was okay. And I wanted to ask for your advice," Galo said.

He hadn't seen me, then. I needed a calmer Galo. So I called room service and ordered plates of appetizers, hamburgers, chicken *mofongo*, strong Puerto Rican coffee, and whisky. Cori sat next to her brother, and she put her head on his shoulder.

"Tell me about Zhanna," I said. "Why do the clients object to her?"

"I don't know." He got up, paced. I thought of how they'd leaned together at the Or nightclub; she'd been angry and he'd tried to soothe her.

"Of course you do," I said. "You're family."

"That's the problem. Z has always preferred our family to hers."

"Her family is gone. You all and Kent are what she has left."

They glanced at each other. "Her father's still alive, Sam," Cori said.

"She said there was a crash…"

"Sergei was flying the San Juan to Miami run. With Kent, back when he was a pilot. They crashed on takeoff. Sergei was badly injured; he's never worked again. Kent was blinded by fragments of wreckage. Papa takes care of Sergei. Pays his bills. He lives over in Sunny Isles." I knew the area, between Miami and Fort Lauderdale, where many Russian immigrants had settled.

"She made it sound like he was dead. Was Rey her stepfather already when the crash happened?"

"No," Galo said. "About six months after, Natalia—that's Zhanna's mom—left Sergei and married Papa. It was awkward."

"More awkward than you know," Cori said, and I couldn't miss the annoyed, embarrassed expression on Galo's face. There was a history there with him and Zhanna. Maybe not a good one.

"We'd grown up with Zhanna; she was the daughter of our father's best friend," Galo said. "And then suddenly my stepsister. We were teenagers, it was awkward."

"Some friend your father was." I spoke before I thought.

Galo couldn't stand a criticism of Rey. "Papa took care of both of them. They had different needs. Sergei couldn't ever be a husband again to her. Papa could."

I couldn't keep the edge off my voice. "So if you were married, and crippled in an accident, you'd be fine with Ricky marrying your wife and taking in your kid in a matter of months?"

Galo didn't surrender. "I'd do my best to understand it. Especially if Ricky was taking care of me."

"So the clients don't want Zhanna. Who would they accept? You? Kent?"

Galo paced the room again and sat by me. "They want to appoint their own person."

"Meaning that they want to take over the smuggling business."

"Papa will never cave in."

"So he loses this business," Cori said. "That's for the best, Galo."

I hazarded a guess. "Maybe he *can't* give it up. He's under threat, something beyond money. Your father...owes somebody something. He told me that success could be a prison. This is what he meant."

Galo shook his head.

The food arrived and we ate in awkward silence and Galo said, "Sam, what do you think I should do? Papa says I can't be involved, but I have to be. I killed a man. I saw a woman get shot today. Papa can't solve this and the clients won't deal with Zhanna. It's all up to me." And he sounded beaten by it.

"You need to find out what they're moving," I said. "You're positioned in a way you can. That's our only hope."

"You want me to spy on Papa and Kent."

"Yes," I said bluntly.

"And then, Galo, walk away from it," Cori said. "There are other jobs, other companies."

"How do I do that? I give up the job I was groomed to do from when I was a kid? I can't do that to the family."

"It's fine with me if you do it," Cori said.

"Do you know how to not be rich, Cori?" Galo asked. "To do without?"

"Screw being rich. These must be the people who took Edwin. We can't make peace with them, not now."

"We don't know that they took Eddie," he said.

"Cling to your illusions much?" Cori said. "Please, Galo. These…clients don't want Papa, they don't want Zhanna. That means they might tolerate you. There's no way you stay free of them. Unless we just give them what they want."

"I can't give away our family business, Cori," he said.

Cori gave him a hard, unforgiving look.

We finished eating and Galo said, "Sam, would you walk me down to the car? Cori will be safe here, won't she?"

"I'll be fine." Cori's voice was stone. "I love you, Galo, please listen to me."

"I love you, too. Now, shut up."

40

WE WENT DOWN to the lobby. It was crowded, the casino was chiming.

Galo gestured toward two seats by a window and we sat, away from any listeners.

"Don't get me wrong." Galo's voice was low. "I love my sister. But if there's a traitor amongst us—it's her."

"What?" Shock colored my voice.

"Papa showed her cash she wasn't supposed to see, and she panicked. She called us. We panicked. Maybe Papa told her more than I know. Maybe she knows who the clients are and she called them."

"Why would she do that?"

"Because she wants us out of this business. She wants the clients just to take it over, take it away from me. She could think she's protecting me."

I kept my voice calm. "I don't think Cori's done that, Galo."

"She has you. Her protector. The timing is great." He looked past my shoulder for a minute. "Where were the two of you during the meeting?"

"We've been at the hotel the whole time." Was he truly suspicious?

"She thinks I'm behind all this," he said. "She thinks I'm the traitor."

His words made me draw back. "No, she doesn't."

"Of course she does," he said. "It's a simple proposition of who benefits. I benefit the most from reaching peace with the clients and being in charge of both businesses. I take over everything. Z and Papa and Kent and Cori all know it. They're all looking at me…" He closed his eyes. "I love them all and they think I could hurt them to get what I want."

"Galo—"

"I could never hurt my own family." He shrugged. "You can understand that. After we lost Edwin."

"I lost a brother," I said, suddenly. It was true of Sam Capra, not Sam Chevalier. But I knew what it was to be pushed away by the ones you love, to carry the burden of guilt. To be the one who tries to fix it all. I couldn't believe I'd said it. The burnt man would have slapped me.

"Was your brother older or younger?" Galo asked. He looked at me with new eyes.

It was best to stick with the truth so I didn't have to invent details or remember lies. "Older, three years."

"Eddie's three years younger than me. Did your older brother look out for you?"

I thought of Danny, under different skies—Africa, South America, Asia—standing up for me, dusting me off after I'd fought, punching a kid in the face who tried to best me by fighting dirty. "Yes. He did."

"How did he die?"

A terrorist beheaded him with a huge knife and videotaped it for the world. But instead I lied. "Stabbed. In an argument over religion." That was mostly true.

"Murdered," he breathed. "Don't you want to kill the guy who did it?"

"I could never find him," I said, "but it wouldn't bring Danny back."

"What was Danny like?"

"Strong. Protective. Smart. Better at team sports than I was. The kind of kid who made friends easily; everyone liked him."

"And you hung back. You were quieter. Maybe book smarter."
I swallowed. "True."

"You're like Edwin, then. And I'm more like your brother."
That might be more true than I wanted to admit.

"It's a special thing, watching out for your kid brother. It's like a test run for being a grown-up." He paused. "Edwin was kidnapped after a family dinner."

I stayed silent.

"I was supposed to drive him home and we were gonna go play basketball. He was a terrible player, couldn't shoot, couldn't guard. But we loved playing together."

My eyes felt hot. I didn't cry for Danny anymore. I hadn't in a long time. Tears didn't make people pay for their crimes.

"But Papa—who spent most of our childhoods flying other people's stuff back and forth among the world's hellholes—wanted me to work. So Eddie was by himself and those bastards took him, they took him when I should have been playing basketball with him." He stopped and seemed to wait to breathe again.

"They would have taken him some other time."

"Maybe. Or maybe they don't take him that day and they give up or maybe they don't take him and they get hit by a tractor-trailer on the highway ten minutes later and they never take him. I killed that man to save my papa yesterday, and you know what?"

"What?" I said.

"I slept okay. I used to think if I could find the bastard who took Eddie I'd kill him and it would change me; I'd be something awful. I don't think so. I think I could kill whoever killed Eddie and I could sleep like a baby. But they cut off his finger, his ear, so I'd cut off their fingers first. All ten of them. I know that sounds sick. But to me that is justice."

He stopped and I thought: He has said this to no one before. Not to Rey, to Zhanna, to Cordelia. He looked at me like he thought he'd said too much. We're only supposed to show so much emotion. Not more. Never more. It's so stupid. But a man has to be a man, especially around other men.

"My brother and I—I won't bore you with the history, but we only had each other much of the time," I said. I looked at my lap and then I looked at Galo. "My parents were—occupied. Busy, but not busy about us. I was a kid who got knocked around a lot. He was always there, to teach me how to fight, or to fight for me. He said that was the first rule of brotherhood."

"Our family only had two rules: don't ask Papa too many questions and don't talk too much."

"You're talking to me," I said.

"You bled for us. Like Papa's made us all bleed." And then he was quiet and I thought, All these secrets, all this family weight, it's crushing him. Making him scared and desperate but he can't appear to be afraid. And a scared man was capable of doing a lot of damage.

He saved your life, remember that, I told myself. *He saved your life. Save him if you can.*

"I'm glad you told me this," I said.

"So these clients, if they were the ones who took Eddie, I would never make peace with them. I wouldn't help them just to get what I want. You see that, right?"

"Of course," I said. "But you don't really know who took Eddie."

He shook his head.

I raised an eyebrow. "Your father could stop all this danger to your family in a moment, and he won't. Out of pride, or greed. You must convince him."

He stood. He wouldn't listen to anything against his father. "I won't. Papa knows what he's doing."

"And you're stuck doing what he wants."

"I want to get back to Papa." Discussion and honesty were apparently over. "We have to figure out a plan. You and Cori will fly out tonight on the jump seats?"

"Yes. What about you all?"

"Chartering a private jet tonight. You'll get Cori someplace safe?"

"Yes," I lied. I gestured at the casino. "The other owners of the

Gran Fortuna. What do you know about them, Omega Investments?"

The question surprised him. "Why?"

"I think they could be tied to the clients," I said. "Has it occurred to you all that they could have spied on you for a long while, to ensure your loyalty? Maybe Omega Investments is just your father's clients, hiding under a name."

"Why do you think this?" His voice rose in a slight panic.

"From what you have said, they know too much. They knew when Rey tried to give Cori the ten million. They knew when Rey decided to split up the company, even before you did." Maybe they gave casino chips to Steve, Nesterov, and Marianne to pay them off, but I couldn't say that. "They've got a hand in your shipping company, why wouldn't they have a hand in every Varela company, including the casino? How do you know they're not spying on us right now?"

His face reddened.

"You're wrong about Cori," I said. "But you can't trust anyone else. Not Z, not Ricky, not your own father. They've lied to you for too long, Galo."

"I have to believe I can fix this and save the company."

"Good luck." I offered him my hand and after a moment he pushed it aside and embraced me. He didn't know I was such a liar, he only remembered that he'd saved my life. He let me go and told me, "Take care of my sister."

"I will."

I watched him go and then I went back to the room.

"I feel like I'm in jail," Cori said.

I carried all the plates and trays from lunch, set them outside. Cleaned up the table. Then I sat next to her on the bed.

"What did he want to talk to you about alone?" She sounded mad she hadn't been included in the conversation.

"He's trying to protect you by keeping you out of the loop," I said.

"I think he has every reason to be behind that shooting," she said.

Now they were accusing each other. "He was there."

"And why is he there when Papa says he mustn't be close to the smuggling? Look at the past few days. The clients send a man to take Papa. Maybe to talk, or maybe to hurt him. Galo kills the man—so the man can tell us nothing. Papa freaks out and gives Galo the company. The clients send a messenger to say no to Zhanna. That messenger gets shot, and if one of us did it, then the clients have every reason to escalate against us. And this all works out perfectly for Galo. Now he's Papa's answer to shut out Zhanna and keep the company. Maybe he's behind the clients not wanting her. Maybe he knows more than he says. He could have been in contact with them." The words came out in a breathless rush.

"I thought he and Z got along." I thought of them talking at the nightclub. At first I thought they were conspiring together, but I wasn't so sure anymore. Maybe they were playing each other.

"They can't live without each other and they can't live with each other," Cori said. "God, this is a nightmare. Before Papa showed me that money I thought we were just a normal dysfunctional family."

I went to her and took her hands in mine. "We're going to beat your family back home and we're going to find the evidence we need to stop this war between your family and the clients. Maybe Galo will do as I asked: find out who the clients are. And I don't want a war because I think the last time there was disagreement, your brother paid the price."

"I didn't think you cared what happened to the family."

"Cori, I care about you. And I like your brother. And I frankly don't want to see anyone else die." I went back to the window, looked out over Old San Juan and the cruise ships. Hordes of passengers were drifting back to the docks, perhaps unsettled by the report of a shooting in the quarter. Families, mostly. Families, sticking together. "Shooting Marianne makes no sense to me. She'd delivered the message, they'd heard it. It put them all at risk."

"Zhanna must have done it out of anger. Maybe that's why the clients don't want her. Too unpredictable. Too hot-headed."

"Your father made reference to having protected her. I think he means took care of her, right?"

"I suppose."

She lay down on the bed as I watched her over my shoulder. "Are you in pain?" she asked. "You haven't had painkillers today. I thought the soreness would be worse the second day."

I did feel like a giant bruise. "I'm okay."

"You should rest. Let me check your bandages."

"They're okay."

"Sam, please."

I sloughed off my shirt and she took off the bandages from this morning and cleaned my wounds. Her touch was gentle. "You're flinching."

I was certainly not flinching, and I wondered: Does she want me on the painkillers? Maybe taking a nap? So she can go do something else? I hardly knew who I could trust anymore. I wanted to trust Cordelia so badly.

She changed the bandages—which weren't so begrimed—and I lay down. The room only had the one bed. She sat on the edge, watching me, then she touched my shoulder. "Sam?" she said softly.

I turned my head toward her and her lips brushed mine. Gently. I raised my head and kissed her for real, the kiss deepening, her small hand sliding behind my head, fingers tangling in my hair. Her mouth was warm against mine, needy, comforting.

Is this a trick? I thought. Because she senses your suspicions, because she wants to know more about your conversation with Galo? Did she want pillow talk?

And then I thought, with shame: *What, you sleep with her, you steal her family's secrets to tear them down and you never let her know your own? She's trying to escape from a criminal family and what are you? A guy who breaks plenty of laws in the service of good. Are you any better?*

Pulling off her blouse, her fingers working the button at my pants.

"Mistake," she said. "Big mistake."

"Yes," I said. We kept kissing. I imagined that we could have met under normal circumstances, through our mutual friend Steve. Like a regular couple. Drinks, dinner, dating, movies, laughter, lovemaking. Not lies and subterfuge and murder and theft. She didn't even know my real name. I couldn't use her this way.

"Cori…we shouldn't…"

"I know what I want," she whispered. "It's okay. I want you." She kissed my hair, my temple, my ear.

But you don't even know me.

My mouth went to her throat, her fingers to the back of my pants, pushing them down. This changes everything, I thought. It always changes everything. Please don't let this be a lie.

41

We were quiet afterward and she didn't ask me about her brother or her family's problems. The only question she asked was: "So who do you think the clients are?"

"Your father denies to the public, despite all the rumors and the Lord Caliber talk, that he ran weapons or contraband. But we know he did. That very profitable trade started the business and then he went legit with his cargo. But he still had those old contacts, and they knew they could tear down his real business if they went public with what he'd done." I went up on my elbow, traced a finger along her lovely throat. "Maybe they forced him to do them the infrequent favor. Some of those warlords and weapons dealers from the past are dead. Others are still in power. Others have ties to governments, to international crime syndicates, to terrorists."

She shuddered. "Yet he tried to give that ten million to charity. There is still good in Papa."

"Why would Kent have a list of names tied to your charity on his computer?" I remembered seeing the list.

Her eyes went wide. "He shouldn't. The charity is separate from the business."

"I saw it on his system when I broke into his office."

"I don't know why."

"We need to know. They could be using you, Cori, the same

way they're using FastFlex. You could be a legit cover for what they're doing."

She shook her head, turned away from me. "Using me."

"I'm sorry. Maybe there's a legit reason he has the list. But I doubt."

"I don't know how much more I can take," she said quietly.

"Did your dad ever give you money before? Directly for the charity?"

"No, I mean, he'd have the treasurer from FastFlex write a check and he'd say, 'Here you go, sweetie.' "

"But he gave it to you," I said. "He'd physically hand you the check."

"Yes. Of course. He liked doing that."

"We need to get back to Miami. If we can get Galo to find who the clients are, we can figure out how they're using the charity. We'll let the family think we're out of town. We're not."

She got up and got dressed in silence. No pillow talk, no murmurings in the sleepy, delicious afterwards. It had not been very romantic, and I felt we'd made a mistake.

We were about to head down to the lobby to check out when Magali came back to our room. She looked nervous and scared. "In both cases the payment made after the chip was cashed was sent to two Swiss banks. The accounts are numbered. I wrote them down for you." She passed me a slip of paper with the numbers. I studied them.

"Thank you." I handed her the chip I'd taken from Marianne. "Redeem this one."

"Are you serious?" Cori asked.

I shrugged, thanked Magali again, and she left.

"She wasn't here to hurt your dad, she was here to talk with him and someone shot her," I said. "She still gets paid. She won't want to admit to the clients she got kidnapped by me. Makes her look bad. This might tip in our favor what she tells them."

"You have an odd sense of honor," she said.

"I don't want her coming after me, or you, or anyone else."

We took a cab to the airport and instead of the passenger terminal we went to the cargo area. Cordelia got us "jump seats" on the FastFlex jet that was flying from Puerto Rico to Miami. Miami was the main FastFlex hub for delivery, and Cori showed them an ID that enabled us to hitch a ride. The equivalent of boarding passes were clipped to us; I felt like they were cargo labels. The plane was comfortable—a few seats, the rest of the fuselage given over to cargo. She sat next to me and leaned against my shoulder. I waited for pillow talk–style questions. But instead she just seemed tired, beaten down by the nightmare of the past two days.

The crew was closed off in the cockpit. The plane took off and arrowed out over the Atlantic. In the cargo netting I could see dozens of boxes with the FastFlex logo and its green-and-red corporate colors, with bar-coded delivery stickers.

"How does air cargo work? I mean, if you had to smuggle something in the system?"

"It's pretty simple. Each package is scanned as it comes off and on the plane, then scanned and sorted at entry points like Miami. Incoming international cargo and packages have to clear customs—you can hire a customs clearance service to help expedite it; there's always paperwork—and then they're sorted for further delivery. Not everything is suited for air cargo. Not everything needs speed. And there are restrictions, of course, on agricultural and biological goods—human remains and so forth." She looked at me. "But cargo moves fast. They don't want businesses to be slowed down."

"So how did they ship the ten million with no one noticing? One big package or several small ones?"

"A package would only be opened if there was strong suspicions about it. An anomaly shows up or something triggers a sensor: detecting a plastic explosive, traces of cocaine, radioactivity, something weird on the X-ray, et cetera."

Yet somehow the Varelas had built a flaw into their own system. A secret window. They had to have a shipping system that passed government muster and yet allowed smuggling.

I leaned close to her. She continued: "Most of the time smugglers have to go to a lot of trouble, hiding their illicit goods under manifests that look legit or moving illicit goods mixed in with legit goods that are heading to a real address. But if the transporting courier is in on the deal, that makes everything simpler, doesn't it? Much, much simpler. Hide inside a legit company's shipment and then cruise it through with a helpful customs clearance agent."

She stared straight ahead.

"So," I said, "if these clients were shipping bad stuff tonight from San Juan to Miami, how would I know? How would someone keep it out of the scanners, where an honest employee or customs official might report it if they saw something suspicious?"

"I don't know."

Drugs, diamonds, dirty cash, weapons. Those seemed the likely shipments, the goods that Rey Varela's old buddies would be most interested in moving. I doubted their interests changed much over the years. But how? I got up and walked into the cargo section. Every package in here might be legitimate. Probably the illicit traffic being allowed by FastFlex was a very small part of their overall volume. It had gone on for a long while without being discovered.

What they do changes the world, said Ricky.

I studied the packages. Sender's address, recipient's address. Checkmarks for packaging, speed of delivery, credit card or other payment information. A tracking number that was twenty characters long, starting with a letter. Many packages seemed more like regular courier fare: from banks, law firms, wholesalers, and many individuals sending to other individuals. Other packages were bigger: human remains in a casket returning to the mainland, flowers, fish, coffee. Some packages hadn't originated in Puerto Rico but had come on from elsewhere in the eastern Caribbean, countries along the northeastern coast of South America, such as Suriname and Guyana, and nations in western Africa, with Puerto Rico presumably a way station. There must be contracts with these governments for FastFlex to move the mail.

I left the cargo bay and sat back down next to Cordelia. I said, "Zhanna is the weak point. The clients won't accept her. Think. There has to be a reason. She knows the secret window they're using. Maybe she messed it up."

"She's done them wrong. She's mishandled a job. She's betrayed their trust. I don't know, those are just guesses."

"Or she's unstable."

"Zhanna's only crazy like a fox."

"Is she? She is obsessed with your father. The way she talks about him..."

Cori shrugged.

"Kent. Tell me about him."

"He's been with us forever. Papa hired him straight out of college. We took care of him after the crash. Smart, cool-headed." She paused. "You know, being blinded—it would break a lot of people. You could almost see him square his shoulders, decide to forge ahead with his life. I admire him in many ways. And dating Zhanna is no picnic. I think she really does love him, though..." Her voice trailed off.

The same crash, taking down Sergei and Kent. It had reduced one to a shell, a shadow in his own daughter's life, and slowly elevated the other.

"He and Zhanna seem an odd match to me."

Cori shrugged. "Zhanna's all fire and temper and Kent is a calming influence. And he might do nothing but work if Zhanna couldn't pry him out of the office now and then. She makes him have fun. They're good for each other." She had her head on my shoulder again.

I closed my eyes to take a nap. She held my hand when I fell asleep, and she was still holding it when the landing in Miami jarred me awake.

42

LATE AFTERNOON IN Miami. We got off the plane. I watched the cargo being offloaded, onto conveyor belts, onto flatbeds. The domestic cargo seemed to head one way, the cargo to clear customs another. Workers with handheld scanners swarmed over the carts.

"Take me into the facility," I said to Cori. Maybe we could see how the secret window worked.

We walked to the FastFlex warehouse and the guard nodded but didn't open the door. "Miss Cordelia."

"I wanted to show my friend the facility."

His smile faded. "I'm sorry, miss. Your brother and your father called. Absolutely no visitors right now. FastFlex employees only. They insisted."

"No worries," I said. "I'll get to see it another time, maybe."

We walked away.

"That...that has never happened," she said.

"They don't want us in there." I glanced back at the facility. I've broken into places before. But this was at the edge of a busy airport, running constantly, with armed guards and customs officials who took dim views of interfering with cargo operations. Knowing the secret window wouldn't necessarily lead me to the clients. I'd have to think of another way.

I held up Nesterov's keys. "Remember, I have his parking ticket and his car key."

"Let's search it," she said.

Nesterov was one of those people who helpfully wrote the lot number down on his ticket. We walked along the rows of cars, me pressing the Unlock and the Lock buttons and I saw the lights flash.

The car, a new sedan, was pretty clean. The car registration address matched the driver's license. He lived in Sunny Isles. Inside the glove compartment was a phone, a cheap one, a throwaway. I checked the call log. There were two numbers, both local. I showed them to Cori.

"Do you recognize either of these?"

"No."

I pressed the first one, held it up to Cori's ear so she could hear as well.

"Hello?" a man's voice said. The voice was raspy, a low baritone. "Hello?"

Cori closed her eyes, gestured for me to turn off the phone. I did.

"Who is it?" I asked.

"Zhanna's father. Sergei. But that's not his home phone number."

"Maybe he has a throwaway phone too."

"Why?... Papa has taken such good care of him."

"Yes. He stole his family from him."

"It wasn't like that."

"It might have been like that to Sergei. What's your relationship with him?"

"He's always been kind to me. I used to visit him a lot, with Zhanna, and then when he and Z didn't get along so well, I'd go see him. Take him old movies to watch."

"He's in touch with a man who tried to kidnap your father."

Cori wiped her face. "Let's try the second number."

I pressed it. It had been called several days before. I got a voicemail greeting, in Spanish: "Hello, this is Carlos. Leave a number."

Carlos. Carlos Tellez, aka Coma Thug? The man I'd run over with Steve's motorcycle.

Never be surprised at a connection, the burnt man told me. That's the whole point of going inside.

He'd called the Colombian, the day of Steve's death.

"What do we do?" Cori asked.

"I take you home so you can pack and we can get you out of here. Then I go to Nesterov's house. Then we go together to see your friend Sergei." Someone might have already been sent by the Varelas to check out Nesterov's place. They had his address off his driver's license. It could have been cleaned. But it was worth a try.

"No," Cori said. "I'm coming with you."

"Please go home and get packed. If I don't get you out of here, your family's going to freak. I need them believing I'll do what I say."

"All right," she said, finally. "I'll check Kent's computer at home, too, see if he has any more information about my charity there."

"At home? Kent and Zhanna live with you?"

"I still live with Papa. After Eddie vanished…I didn't like to leave him. Galo has the house next door. Zhanna has the house across the cul-de-sac. Kent moved in with her a few months back."

I remembered the three grand houses on the street, all facing the water. Rey kept his family very, very close. "Fine. When you're done, meet me at the bar."

We left Nesterov's car where it was. I pocketed his cell phone.

I walked her to her car and she kissed me, once, quickly, chastely. I headed to my car and got in. I turned on the radio after I'd paid my ticket and heard the newscaster talk brightly about a family shooting down near Homestead and then mention that the suspect in the Steve Robles murder had awakened from his coma and, to quote the reporter, "was speaking with police."

Coma Thug was in a coma no more.

43

My time had run out. It was my moment of reckoning.

All it would take would be for him to say, *We didn't steal that motorcycle; some guy followed us from the bar on it and he ran over me; he tried to kill me* and the police would be knocking on my door, asking me questions as Sam Capra, not as Sam Chevalier.

It might be best not to go back to the bar right now. Would the police question Paige or Mila if they found them there? I texted them both, asking if they were all right.

Paige texted me back: I'm at the bar and we have customers. Living, breathing customers.

I'll come by soon, I answered.

There was no response from Mila.

Nesterov's address led me to a house, a low, old ranch style close to Sunny Isles, in a relatively older neighborhood. I drove by. No cars in the driveway. It looked deserted. But if Nesterov worked for Marianne, she could have easily sent someone here to clean up after him, get rid of any evidence of their connection. No one else was missing Nesterov yet, as far as I knew. But there could be family members or a spouse or partner. I couldn't barge into the house.

So, knock on the door? No.

I watched the house. The curtains were drawn. Not a lot of flowers in the beds; it was spare, a bachelor's house.

So I waited for a neighbor to finish puttering in his yard and then I drove over to the parallel street, in front of a house that seemed empty. I cut through the back and then jumped the fence into Nesterov's backyard. A lonely grill sat on a concrete patio. A forgotten beer bottle on the table. I tried the back door.

Unlocked.

I tensed—someone else might be here—but I slipped inside. The décor was Spartan to the point of being ridiculous. A futon in a corner, a TV, a game console, and a card table with four folding chairs in the kitchen. It looked like temporary housing. He was an ex-cop here, presumably with a history, with connections. This looked like the home of someone who needed to run quickly.

I went through the kitchen and the dining room. No sound. No sign of human presence. Down the hall to one bedroom and found a small bed, unmade, and a laptop sitting on it. The other bedroom was entirely empty, just a closet door ajar.

I turned away and behind me I heard the closet open and when I turned back Mila leveled a gun at me.

"You scared me," I said.

She didn't lower the gun.

"Um, making me nervous with the pointing of the weapon," I said.

"We need to have a talk, Sam. I'm sorry."

"Yes, we're all quite sorry, Sam," a male voice said, and a rangy figure stepped out from the closet. James Court, also known as Jimmy. Mila's husband. The guy who seems to run all the secret jobs for the Round Table. I may have mentioned: We don't get along. At all.

I'd given Mila the address to investigate, and so she had. I just didn't expect Jimmy here.

"So, how are you?" Jimmy asked. He didn't offer a hand.

"I'm fine."

"Really? You look awful."

"I was in a fight."

"You've been very busy," he said. I glanced at Mila, expecting her support. She stared me down.

"Yes," I said.

"I think we've been very generous to you, Sam," Jimmy said. He was an Englishman, tall, lean, annoyingly handsome, dressed in dark slacks and a dark shirt. "We helped you recover your son. We gave you thirty-plus wonderful bars to run, as cover. We promised you interesting work that drew on your skill set."

I said nothing.

"And yet you persist in taking on jobs that aren't ours." He gestured with his head and I walked backward, back down the hall and into Nesterov's den.

"I was right to do that in San Francisco," I said, keeping my voice even, "and I'm right about it here."

Jimmy shook his head. "Let's not even get into whether you should be chasing after your friend's killers." I glanced again at Mila and her expression didn't change. Jimmy went on: "You are using a CIA cover for this job. You didn't even ask the Round Table to create an operational identity for you."

"You might have said no."

"We might have said yes, given that it was connected to Rey Varela, a man many people around the world are interested in. But you made a deal with your old friend at the CIA, and I wonder what you promised him in return."

There was no point in lying. Although, for one moment, I was sorely tempted. "I promised him any useful intelligence I found."

"And you were going to give us, your actual employers, what?" Jimmy said softly.

"Are you going to stand up for me?" I said to Mila.

"That's not my job, Sam," she said softly.

"I suppose not," I said. She was right. "I would have given you the same intelligence, Jimmy. I wasn't going to shut the Round Table out of anything I learned."

"Let's cut to the chase, Sam. Are you spying on the Round Table for the CIA?"

"Of course not."

"Yet you ask them for a cover identity. Who exactly do you work for?"

"Is this a turf war?" I asked. "Are you serious?"

"You're going to give the CIA nothing. Nothing at all."

"I made a promise."

"You made a promise to us as well, and over the past few months you have not kept it."

"Jimmy, how have I broken it?"

"You were to work only for us. Not for yourself, not for the CIA."

"You're like a person who thinks it's unfair an off-duty cop makes an arrest when he sees a crime happening," I said.

"You are not a cop, Sam. You are an employee, and I think you'd better start acting like it."

"What exactly is it," I said, "you don't want the CIA to know?"

"You certainly are not going to tell them anything about the Varelas or what happened in San Juan. I will feed you some information to appease your friend."

And it would somehow benefit Jimmy, I thought. "I'm not lying to him. I gave him my word. He went to huge risks to let me use the Chevalier name. He could lose his career over it."

"That's stupid of him, then."

"That's loyalty. I don't think you know much about it."

"Sam," Mila said.

"If you don't like me, fire me. Take back the bars," I said. But I was scared he might. I didn't want to lose the bars. I loved owning them. I loved running them. They were my ticket to the world. And what would I do if I wasn't a spy anymore? I wanted a normal life, I kept telling myself, a life with my son. But I can never see myself sitting at a desk. Or working at a computer or on a phone all day, or whiling away hours in meetings. I wasn't qualified for anything except being a knife in the shadows. It's very limiting.

"Maybe we will fire you," he said, "if you can't take orders."

"What are my orders, then? Mila told me to investigate the Varelas further, and I did just that."

Mila was silent.

"This Paige woman Mila says helped you, this librarian. Does she know about the Round Table?" Jimmy asked.

"Of course not."

"She simply thinks, what? You're a vigilante?"

"I swear, Paige knows nothing." I took a step toward him. "Are you threatening her?"

"Of course not." Jimmy's voice was silken. "I'm not the bad guy here, Sam. None of us are."

"Why don't you want the CIA to know what I know about the Varelas?" Then a feeling hit me, a shock of coldness deep in my gut. It couldn't be. "Oh, no. No. Is Rey Varela part of the Round Table?"

What did I know about them? I'd been told the Table was a league of corporate leaders and other interested parties who wanted to do good for the world, beyond the limits of the law, to handle enemies that that governments could not. They had been brought together years ago by the CIA but had walked away from the agency's control, secretly to pursue their own path.

"No, I swear to you, he's not," Jimmy said.

I said nothing. I didn't know if I could believe Jimmy on anything.

"But knowing what we know now, we're curious about him. About what else, who else, he could lead us to."

I looked at Mila. "I just heard on the radio that the man I ran over with Steve's motorcycle has regained consciousness."

"Can he identify you?" Mila asked.

"If he spotted me as having followed him from the bar. The police know I live above the bar. I would be the only suspect."

"Sam," Jimmy said, very softly, "did he see you when you drove at him?"

"I had on a helmet."

"Your prints are on the bike?"

"It was my friend's bike. I could say he let me ride it the day before."

Mila wandered toward the front of the house. She often got quiet when Jimmy went on these tirades. It was so unlike her. But he'd saved her from a million-dollar bounty on her head, he'd brought her into the Round Table, her loyalty to him blinded her. So I thought.

"The whole idea of the bars as safe houses," Jimmy said, "is that they remain safe. Which means you don't call attention to them. You don't call attention to yourself. The police look at you, they look at your business. It's very inconvenient."

"I guess you have to decide if what I've learned about the Varelas is worth it."

"You've learned more than what you told Mila?"

I smiled.

"Someone's here," Mila said. "Just parked out front."

"Out the back," Jimmy said. "We're not risking discovery here."

He was the boss, so we obeyed. We went out into the backyard and behind a small tool shed that was nestled in the back corner, the three of us huddled close together.

"Did you find anything inside?" I whispered to Jimmy.

"Later," he whispered back, in a tone of deep annoyance.

I heard the back door slide open. Footsteps across the concrete porch. Clink of glass, the door shutting. Someone cleaning up the forgotten beer bottles on the patio?

We stayed still. I could see Jimmy's hand on Mila's back. Mila stared at me. I looked at the dirt.

Footsteps again. Heading our way. We froze. I hated that we'd retreated; we were trapped. I tensed my legs in case I need to spring out and fight. But I just heard the slide of the shed door, a moment of silence, then the sound of a clang against the door of the shed.

I waited ten seconds and then I risked a glance around the shed's edge. Immediately I felt Jimmy's fingers in my hair, starting to yank me back in anger. But I saw enough.

Ricky, carrying something I couldn't see in his arms, heading back into the house.

He certainly liked to visit the homes of the recently deceased. I started to move and then I felt a cool circle of metal against my neck.

"Be still." It wasn't Jimmy's voice. It was Mila's.

I let two minutes pass. The gun stayed exactly in place. They were really scared I was still working for the CIA. This wasn't like Mila.

"I know him," I hissed. "He works for Galo Varela. He's here to find out who Nesterov worked for." I knew Mila wouldn't shoot me. I got up but stayed crouching behind the shed. She didn't shoot me.

"He won't find it," Jimmy said.

Meaning, I assumed, that Jimmy had already found the evidence. Or that there was nothing to be found. I heard a car in front of the house start up. Ricky, leaving. I peered over the fence. I could see him, pulling away quickly from the curb, eyes ahead.

"He's gone." I looked back at the happy couple. "You know who Nesterov was working for beyond Marianne? This mysterious Mr. Beethoven?"

"No," Mila said. "We don't. We'd like to."

I walked back into the house and then I smelled it: the combined stench of fuel and natural gas. The quiet hum of the microwave. And then loud sparking noises.

"Run!" I screamed, and Mila and Jimmy, following me inside, spun and ran. We bolted past the patio and started over the wooden fence when the house blew. The roof boomed and the windows shattered and the house seemed to shift on its foundation.

Then the flames, spread by the gasoline, started to accelerate.

"We can't be seen here," Jimmy gasped. The fence had blown apart, already weakened by age, planks of it lying on us.

We ran. Nesterov's house was now ablaze, a few neighbors drawn by the boom of the blast out in their yards, all apparently calling the fire department on their cell phones. I followed Jimmy and Mila one street over to a Mercedes. My car was parked farther down the street.

I headed toward it and Jimmy grabbed me. "Where are you going? Off to the CIA?"

"You said we couldn't risk discovery here. Shall we meet back at the bar?"

He nodded. I shrugged off his hand on my shoulder and headed toward my car.

Jimmy, for once, didn't try to stop me. We each got in our cars and drove away as the sirens began to wail.

My phone rang. Mila. "Jimmy wants to know everything you know about the Varelas."

Eventually. Instead I said, "Our friend who torched the house was cleaning up."

"But this is going to make Nesterov's disappearance that much more interesting to the police," Mila said. She had me on speaker and I heard Jimmy mumble a curse.

I saw them take a left turn. I waited until they were gone and I let more traffic pass and then I took a right, peering ahead through the windshield. There he was. "And bringing attention to Nesterov, it doesn't benefit the Varelas."

"Because he doesn't work for the Varelas," Mila said quietly. "He works for the clients attacking them. This pressures the Varelas."

"I think you're right," I said. "I can go and confront Ricky and Galo directly…"

"You will do no such thing," Jimmy said, exactly like I figured he would. Thanks, Jimmy.

"I'm supposed to get Cori Varela out of town," I said. "That's what her family's expecting me to do."

"Fine," Jimmy said. "Go. Pick her up, take her to New York, to our bar there. We can question her at length. You can write me a report on the Varelas. And only me, Sam, not for the CIA. We don't share."

"You don't want to bring the Varelas down. You want to know what they're smuggling."

"We want to know, true," he said.

"Why? You won't go to the police."

He laughed. "You haven't worked for us long enough to know what we'll do, Sam."

You'll use it, I thought. *Whatever the Varelas have built, like bees taking over another hive.* The Round Table wasn't just do-gooders, they were something more, the same way the Varelas

were more, and I was tired of not knowing. I'd taken their help at
my most desperate time, then I'd been in denial about what they
might be. They had done nothing but good—but who were they
really? If I let them take over whatever the Varelas were doing, I
was no better than Rey.

"That's true," I said. "I don't know what you'll do."

"You will, however, take Cori Varela to New York. For her
own safety, and so we can find out what she knows. As well, she
might serve as a useful bargaining chip, given the family psychol-
ogy about abduction."

I measured out my words. "I'm not kidnapping Cori. If she
wants to go to New York, I'll take her." But I wouldn't. I
wouldn't leave her to Jimmy's tender mercies. And I had learned
two pieces of information that Mila and Jimmy didn't know: the
fact that the casino chips were used, infrequently, as some sort of
covert payment system, and that Sergei, Zhanna's father, had contact with Lavrenti Nesterov.

"I don't think you know everything you think you do about
Cordelia Varela," Mila said. "Where are you?"

"I think I'm ahead of you," I lied. "I cut through a bunch of
cross streets to avoid traffic. What don't I know about Cori?"

"Her charity. It's an interesting setup. We had someone hack
into their computer systems. She gets money from donors. She
distributes money not directly to the needy but to other charities
overseas. She's like a clearinghouse for donations."

"So?" I was already tired of arguing with them.

"So we'd like to know more about these other charities, considering her father tried to hand her ten million in cash."

"You think she's cleaning the money and it's being disbursed
to, what, bad guys?"

"Perhaps. We don't know yet. Hence our desire to talk with
her."

"And what about Steve?"

"Who?" Jimmy asked.

I took a deep breath to steady my patience. "My old friend
they killed."

"Oh. Yes. Well, the thug that is still alive could be a problem. Wait, where are you?"

I hadn't followed them in their car. Instead I'd caught and followed Ricky. He was staying on side roads, which was making it hard to be unnoticed. I had to hang back much farther than I liked, risking losing him altogether.

"I stopped to get gasoline," I lied.

"Sam," Jimmy said.

"I am not meeting the CIA," I said. "I swear to you on my son's life I'm not."

This shut him up for all of five seconds. "I know you, Sam, even when you think I don't. You're following the arsonist," Jimmy said.

"Nothing gets by you."

"Sam..." He wanted to tell me to break off the pursuit; but he knew it was useless, so he didn't. Then he surprised me. "Be careful."

"I know what I'm doing, Jimmy, and I will tell you all."

"My wife is insisting that I trust you, and so I am," he said.

"Are you supposed to meet Cori?" Mila asked.

"Yes," I said. "At the bar, so yes, I'll be back soon. Paige is supposed to give me a report on what she's learned about the Varelas off the Miami grapevine of old and established families."

"We deal in facts, not gossip," Jimmy said.

"I think the Varelas' past has everything to do with their present," I said. "Then I'll get Cori out of town." I'm such a liar sometimes. Not really a good example for my son.

"See that you do," Jimmy said. "Mila will take over the surveillance on the Varelas."

"Fine," I said. I turned off the phone.

Ricky turned into a lot. The hospital where Coma Thug had been taken, and was now presumably chatting with the police. Maybe about me.

44

RICKY PARKED AND walked inside, carrying a bag. He pulled on a white medical jacket, and I could see what looked like a hospital ID clipped to his pocket. A very basic disguise.

I felt cold. I knew, instantly, why he was there, and now. Coma Thug talking to the police was not only a threat to me, but to his employers. Burn down Nesterov's house in case he had hidden evidence. Make sure the Colombian can't talk.

You tried to run him down. What do you care what happens to him? If he's dead he can't tell them about you.

I walked into the hospital. The entrance was crowded, busy, but I knew at that very moment my face was being recorded on a camera. Hospitals have more security than you first think.

I had no idea where Coma Thug was being kept. The police might have moved him, even. Ricky wasn't in the lobby. I checked the directory and saw the floor for the ICU. I took the elevator up.

At one end of the hall was a large waiting room, full of families and friends of the sick, hostages to fate. At the other end was a shut door, with glass in it, the portal to the patient cubicles. You would be admitted only if you had a family member inside.

Then I saw a stairwell door open and out came Ricky. He was twenty feet away from me, his back to me, and I turned and ducked into an alcove, where there was a soda machine and a linen closet. I risked a glance around the corner.

He headed away from me, toward the ICU, but before he reached the double doors he veered into a room marked Staff Only. He peered inside for a moment, as if making sure it was empty, then slipped inside.

The syringe I'd stolen from Nesterov's SUV in Puerto Rico—the one I'd stuck into Marianne's neck but not injected—was still in my pocket. I put it in my hand and hurried toward the door, hoping he'd have his back to me.

I opened the door, soundlessly. He was six feet away, searching through a locker, and before he could turn I jabbed him with the needle and injected the sedative. He stiffened and dropped a tablet computer he had in his hand. I shoved his head into the open locker and finally he collapsed.

I took off him the white jacket with the ID clipped to it. I felt a little weight in the pocket. A syringe, loaded with a pale yellow chemical. Well, well. This was no errand of mercy.

In the open locker I found a stethoscope—perhaps this was the prop he'd stopped to steal—and put it around my neck. I also found a pair of prescription glasses and I put them on. I dragged Ricky to a back corner of the room, where there was a cart of dirtied scrubs and towels and dumped him in it, covering him with the laundry. I would just have to hope he wasn't noticed.

I picked up the tablet computer he'd dropped. The open app was one for patient records.

I looked as much like a doctor as I might.

I walked into the ICU. The cubicle with the police officer stationed outside it was four down from the entrance. I didn't even glance at him, I stepped into the next cubicle. Inside, an elderly woman dozed. I counted to sixty, then stepped out, tapping at the tablet.

Then I walked toward Coma Thug's room. At the nursing hub was one nurse; he was on the phone and peering at a computer screen, not looking at me. I heard voices, raised in a slight hubbub, behind the curtain of a room down the hall; an emergency demanding the attention of most of the staff.

I tapped at the pad and nodded at the police officer, who gave me the once-over, and I stepped inside.

Coma Thug lay in the bed in front of me. He looked wasted, spent, his neck in a brace. He hardly noticed me.

I went up to the supply shelf, pulled off a strip of gauze tape and put it across his eyes. He moaned, put up a hand, started to cry out. "Hush and listen, Carlos," I said in Spanish.

He went very still.

"A man came to the hospital. He was here to kill you. To inject poison into your IV feed so you would die. I stopped him." I continued speaking Spanish. "You're safe for the moment. For a price," I said.

"What?" he whispered.

"Do not speak to the police about Steve Robles or anything about the motorcyclist you saw that night," I said. "Not a word."

"Are you here to take me away?"

Interesting idea. I paused. "Are you expecting to be taken away?"

"They'll get me out," he said. "They've already talked to the police. There aren't going to be charges against me."

"Who could promise that?"

He seemed surprised by the question, his mouth twisted. "Aren't you?..."

"Who is Mr. Beethoven?"

"I don't know that name."

Outside, I heard the cop's newspaper's pages rustle.

"I have the syringe the killer brought. I'm uncapping the needle." He writhed in the bed and I made my voice a whisper. "Think again. Who is Beethoven? Who does he work for?"

"Please, I don't know," he whispered. "My partner handles the business side. I swear I don't know. Please."

So he'd heard the name, at least. I didn't want him screaming. "Shhh. Shhh. All right, I believe you. Keep your promise. Nothing to the police about Steve Robles. Not a word. Or I will go to

Bogotá and see your family. They don't have a cop sitting outside their room." This was an idle threat, but he didn't know it.

His mouth worked. He was helpless, his body broken, bound to the bed. I never wanted to feel that helpless. "Do you understand me?"

"Yes."

"If you stay silent, I'll tell the police tomorrow it was your partner who killed Robles, and I'll give them the name of the man who was sent here to kill you. But if you talk, I'll tell the police you shot Robles."

"I understand."

I left the gauze taped across his eyes; he could take it off himself. I nodded at the officer as I went out and I walked to another room, an empty one, then I turned and left the ICU. Carlos Tellez did not scream out or cry for help. He was a businessman; he understood these arrangements. Part of me, a dark part, wanted to end him in that bed. Part of me knew it would mean nothing.

I went back into the locker room. Ricky was still out. I wiped the tablet computer and stethoscope clean of my prints, left the jacket, clipped the ID on Ricky's shirt.

Then I walked out of the hospital and drove to Stormy's.

45

Night had fallen by the time I reached the bar. Mila had the Open sign on.

I walked past the pair of couples drinking on the patio to find Paige inside and Mila tending bar. There was no sign of Jimmy.

"Hello," I said.

"I want to get the bar in order before you go," Mila said.

"Where's your husband?" I expected him there, ready to argue with me more.

"He's off doing," Mila said, "whatever it is he does. But he said he was trusting you at your word."

"Thank you," I said.

"Where have you been, Sam..." Paige started, and I raised my hand.

Oh, Paige, you don't want to know, I thought.

Paige glanced at Mila. No one else was in the bar.

"I like your new manager," Paige said. "She makes a forceful cocktail." She raised a martini glass instead of her usual wine.

"I see you've moved to the hard stuff," I said.

"I needed it."

"This librarian, her I like. She's the right kind of customer," Mila said. She gave Paige a smile.

Great, a mutual fan club. "I did the favor you asked me," Paige said. "Can we talk?"

"Yes." I took Paige upstairs while Mila helped a pair of customers who'd just walked into the bar. Paige turned on me when I closed the door.

"What are you?" she said.

"Sam the bartender."

"Whose compatriot happens to be some sort of a mysterious Russian woman."

"She's Moldovan, that's totally different."

"But you're not, like, an undercover agent. You're just...doing this."

"Yes. For Steve. Like you. You said you had some information?"

Paige took another sip of her cocktail. "Ricky Vega. Please be careful of him," she said.

"I already am."

Paige tapped a manicured nail against her martini glass. "I talked to friends of friends of friends, who went to high school with him and Galo Varela. In some corners, Miami is still a small town—people remember, and they know each other's family histories. Ricky and Galo grew up together, went to school together. Back before Rey Varela was rich, they lived in a tougher neighborhood. Ricky got bullied. A lot. Galo stuck up for him and Galo was bigger than every other kid and so everyone left Ricky alone. Then FastFlex took off and the Varelas were suddenly rich and Galo moved to a private school. Ricky got left behind." She swallowed some of her martini. "It got very bad for him, without Galo as a protector. Like—he was bullied so much that he went a little crazy. Finally Rey Varela got him moved to the private school where Galo was. Paid for him to be there. That's not cheap. Then they went on together to University of Miami, again paid for by Rey. Ricky studied criminal justice. Then he left Miami for a year, working up north, I can't find out what he did. I mean, I can't find an official record. His mother told people he was working in Virginia at a private security firm called Crossfire Protection. Then he came back and he's worked for the Varelas ever since, as a private bodyguard and errand boy."

This didn't seem to jibe, since I was sure Ricky was working for someone outside the family. But his loyalty to the Varelas should be rock-solid. Had I read the situation wrong? "So you think Ricky will be very loyal to the family."

Paige nodded. "To Galo and Rey, at least. But that's not the good stuff...while Galo and Ricky were in college, some of those kids who had beaten up Ricky, they ended up dead." Her voice lowered. "Four of them. In a year's time."

"What?"

Paige's usually steady voice wavered. "One in a car accident, he burned to death, up near Fort Lauderdale. One died from a drug overdose in Las Vegas. Two murdered, never solved. Those two had their throats cut in separate incidents. I mean, maybe it was a coincidence. Bad neighborhood, kids who had already been in a lot of trouble. But still."

"But Ricky had left that behind. Why risk it?"

"Because certain kinds of people can't ignore certain kinds of hurt and pain. Maybe it was the Varela influence, but Galo and Ricky were never even questioned. Please be careful. Please."

And I tried to imagine Galo involved in four murders. He'd seemed crushed by being involved in one killing. Or maybe he was just very good at wearing a mask, putting on a look of contrition. But this was information Paige got me that Jimmy and Mila couldn't have, not as quickly.

"Thank you," I said.

"You know who killed Steve," she said. "Don't you?"

"I might be close. And I think maybe you should get out of town for a while," I said.

"I'm not going anywhere," Paige said.

"It's gotten very dangerous for me. And that means people might come looking for me, and they might come here if they learn that I own Stormy's. At least stay away from the bar."

She took a long sip from her drink, a thoughtful look on her face.

"I'm close to finding out what I need to know to put them away," I lied. "I'll tell you everything then."

"All right. You know, I miss the library terribly. I miss helping people. This made me feel useful again."

"It's not the same as the library, but if all this works out would you ever be willing to run this bar?"

"Yes," she said. "I think I'd like that a lot."

"I promise you, I'll do my best to make that happen."

"Aren't you're the owner?"

"Yeah. I just have to survive," I said, and I tried to laugh.

"Well, do, don't try," she said in a prim librarian-stereotype voice.

We laughed. It sounded forced. "I need to make a couple of phone calls," I said. "Will you please excuse me?"

"I'll go help your friend Mila. I do like her, Sam. She's properly mysterious," Paige said, and she went downstairs.

I quickly repacked a small bag, tossing out the dirty clothes from Puerto Rico. I started up the computer, opened the browser, and opened the link to the Daniel cam. My son, asleep in his bed, his little mouth softly moving, maybe nascent words trying to get out. I wondered about his dreams. I watched him for five minutes and thought: *You have to do better than this.* He shifted in his sleep and opened his eyes and looked right at me and then he closed his eyes again and went back to sleep.

I closed the tab, erased the link from my browser history. I always do that. No one can know I ever look at him. Then I took Lavrenti's gun (no one had searched me on the FastFlex flight, being with a Varela) and I went downstairs. Paige was chatting up some customers with a new energy—a natural—and Mila stood by the bar.

"You're off to New York?" she said, glancing at my bag.

"Yes," I lied.

"I'll take care of things here with the Varelas. This is for the best, Sam."

"It's the best for Jimmy and the Round Table," I said. "They're not just a bunch of rich folks wanting to do good, are they?"

No one was near us. She could have ignored my question. She didn't. She looked at me and with everything we had survived

together it was the most nakedly intimate moment of our friendship. She said, very quietly, "No, Sam. I don't know what they
are but I don't think they're just a bunch of rich folks trying to
do good."

I believed her. Even though she was married to Jimmy, he had
not told her everything.

"You be careful," I said. "And please keep Paige out of trouble.
She's been a huge help to me."

She glanced at my carry-on. "That's a small bag for New
York."

"I have clothes and gear at The Last Minute." Just like here, I
had an apartment above my Manhattan bar.

"All right. Be careful."

"You too." I almost wanted to tell her the truth. That I had no
intention of leaving Miami. But I didn't.

I walked out to my car and drove to Cori's house. This time
the guard at the station to the neighborhood had my name, was
expecting me, and waved me through.

46

No one else came out to greet me on the driveway, just Cori. She got into the car with her bag and slammed the door.

"What's the matter?" I said.

"Just drive."

"Where?"

"I told everyone we would go to New York, like you suggested," she said. "I made us a reservation at a hotel over on Key Biscayne."

"What's the matter?"

"They're back."

"I know." I told her about Ricky and Nesterov's house and the hospital.

She dragged a hand through her dark hair. "You understand I've known him most of my life. The shocks just keep coming."

"He might not be working for someone outside. He could be doing your brother's bidding." And I told her about what Paige had found out.

"My brother had nothing to do with those deaths. I know him. You don't. He had nothing to do with it."

"So it's just Galo's closest friend that's the crazy one. You're right, that doesn't reflect on him at all."

"I know Galo. You know Galo, I mean, you saw how he reacted to...shooting that man. That's Galo. The real one."

"Okay, Cori."

"Don't you dare pretend to know my brother," she said.

"I won't. Did you find anything at the house?"

"Yes."

"What?"

"Let's just get to the hotel."

We drove across the Rickenbacker Causeway to a stunningly gorgeous shoreline hotel on Key Biscayne, checked in, and went to the room. Cori took a Coke from the minibar and then she handed me a printout from her luggage.

"Kent had a listing on his computer of many of the donors to Help with Love. He also had a list of charities and organizations that I in turn funnel money to in developing countries." Her voice was calmer. "Now. Most of the organizations I work with, they get funds from lots of other charities. These, though"—she'd marked them with a yellow highlighter—"these don't. I am their only donor, apparently, according to the notes in Kent's file. I checked out every group I send money to and I established that they had other donors when I started working with them.

"Sam, these recipients lied to me. Kent had their financials. How…how can that be? No charity can survive on a single donor."

"The obvious answer is your family is funneling money to these people. They're not charities."

"Why?"

"I don't know. But this has to tie in to their smuggling."

The anger was back in her voice. "I wanted to do good, Sam, I wanted to help people, and they've *used* me."

"I'm sorry, Cori. I am truly sorry."

I picked up my car keys, checked Lavrenti Nesterov's gun.

"Where are you going?"

"I'm going to talk to Zhanna's father. I think he can shed light on this."

"I'll go with you," she said.

"I think I'd better go alone." I pointed at the printout. "Can you figure out any kind of pattern in the payments? We need to know where your charity's money is going. Can you do that remotely?"

She nodded. "I brought my laptop."

"See what you can find out."

"Be careful of Sergei. I like him, but now I don't trust anyone."

"Do me a favor. Call him and tell him I'm coming. Tell him I'm your friend, trying to protect and help you."

"But..."

"I have an idea on how to approach him."

She smiled. "He loves coffee. That's how you approach him."

I kissed the top of her head and she hugged me. And then I left.

47

I DROVE UP to Sunny Isles, a northern neighborhood with new gleaming towers along the shoreline. I noticed roughly ten seconds after I crossed its borders that there were a couple of shop signs in Russian to go along with the English. I decided to take Cori's halfhearted advice and pulled into a shopping center with a Starbucks on the corner. I went in and got two decafs and while waiting in line heard three different conversations in Russian: two guys on cell phones—one asking a question about what to put into a PowerPoint for tomorrow's investor presentation, the other pleading with his girlfriend for a second chance. In a corner, two women sipping at waters discussed a new American movie, but in rapid-fire Russian. At least in this part of South Florida, the Russians had landed.

The address wasn't fancy—first floor in a solid brick building. A much grander apartment complex with Italianate architecture stood across the street. The rains had come, quickly, then moved on, and large puddles glistened in the moonlight.

I knocked at the door and a short, powerfully built man answered. "I'm here to see Mr. Pozharsky," I said. "I think I'm expected." He opened the door wider, no expression coloring his face. I gave him one of the coffees, said "Decaf," and he nodded his thanks. He gestured me inside.

The apartment was large but the furnishings were old, scuffed a bit. A signed Willie Nelson poster loomed above the television. I heard a motorized hum and I turned.

Sergei Pozharsky—Zhanna's father—sat in a wheelchair. The photos of him I'd seen, in Paige's research into the founding days of FastFlex, were pre-crash. In those he was tall, blond-haired, handsome. He would have been good on a Soviet propaganda poster, ready to harvest wheat with a red scythe, arms uplifted in fervor. Now he looked shrunken, broken. His legs were gone. Scar tissue began at his hairline and went down to his jaw and three seconds later I realized this was post-surgery: this was the improved version. One eye was covered by a patch. But he had thin, delicate fingers, the kind that must have been masterful on the controls of a jet, strong hands. He was wearing dark jeans, the empty legs sewn shut, and a Miami Heat T-shirt.

I thought, in a jolt, of the burned man who'd taught me so much about going inside.

"You are Cori's friend," Sergei Pozharsky said. His voice was raspy, like I'd heard on the phone.

"Yes, sir," I said.

He offered his hand and I shook it. He smelled vaguely of talcum powder and medicine and mint.

"I understand you like coffee, so I brought you a decaf," I said.

"Thank you." His Russian accent was noticeable but not thick and clumsy.

The attendant—Sergei dismissed him with "Thank you, Julio, we'll be fine"—vanished into another room and I could hear the murmurings of a television.

"So," Sergei said, and his jaw worked in kind of a funny way, like it hadn't been reset quite properly. "Why does a friend of Cori's want to see me?" He didn't sip at his coffee, and I realized he had no intention of doing so.

"I want to make you an offer, sir."

"An offer. I am no longer a businessman," he said. "I read books and listen to Willie and watch the silly people on the reality TV."

"It's about the Varelas," I said.

He glanced at the door where the attendant had disappeared. "Rey pays for my care. He takes very good care of me."

I spoke in Russian. "That's good to know."

His mouth worked and he answered in his native tongue. "Cordelia did not say you spoke Russian."

"Just enough to get by. Here's the deal. I know you know the guy sent to kidnap Rey in Puerto Rico. I want to know who he works for. I won't hurt you, harm you, nothing. I just want to know."

A man who made his living smuggling weapons and contraband into African war zones was not going to be easily rattled. He coughed, he laughed, very softly. "I like you," he said.

"Well?"

"And if I tell you nothing?"

"Then I will tell Zhanna that you have been in touch with the people who don't want her to have the job running the smuggling at FastFlex."

"My daughter and I are not close."

"But you'd like to be."

He studied me with the good eye. "Why are you so sure?"

"I think the Varelas' problems stemmed from a business relationship gone sour. It's you. I kept wondering who the enemy was, and the enemy was obvious. The business partner driven out. The husband whose wife was taken from him. The father whose daughter prefers another man as her dad. I think you've bided your time, Mr. Pozharsky. And now that Rey is sick, losing his grip on reality, you've decided to make your move."

His ruined face was very still. Then he scratched at his nose and I saw a hint of a smile. "What do you want from me?"

"Information. Are you the man behind the kidnapping attempt and sending Marianne and her thugs to Puerto Rico? Are you Mr. Beethoven?"

"I like Willie Nelson, not Ludwig Van," he said. He glanced again at the aide's door, even though we were speaking Russian. "Not here. I know a good place to talk. Down the street. Private."

"Yes, sir."

" 'Sir.' So polite. Cori said you were in the Canadian Army. I was an officer in the Soviet Air Force."

"Yes, sir."

"I like Canadians," Sergei said. "They are not afraid of the cold weather. Here, such babies, it drops into the sixties and they cry and put on old minks." He switched to English. "Julio! My friend and I going to café for blinis. Back soon."

Julio opened the door and studied us. "Is everything okay?"

"Yes, fine. Fine. I think this young man can push a wheelchair. We'll be back soon."

He wheeled himself into his bedroom and returned in a nicer shirt and a blazer jacket. He had his pride. I wheeled him down to the elevator. "I don't like Julio," he said. "He works for the Varelas, not me."

"You could fire him."

"And they could bribe his replacement to spy on me."

"I guess you couldn't ask Zhanna for help," I said.

He gave no answer. We headed outside and I pushed his wheelchair along the wide curve of the road, back toward the shopping center where I'd stopped at the Starbucks. There was a restaurant there, open twenty-four hours. St. Ekaterina's Café. There were a few others at the tables, finishing long workdays. He spoke in quiet Russian to the waitress, who looked tired and hopeless and yet managed a wan smile.

"So," he said, after our tea arrived.

"I want to protect Cori. If you're gunning for the Varelas, leave her alone."

"I have no wish to harm Cori."

I wasn't sure I believed him. He was connected to Nesterov, who was connected to the Colombians. But I didn't want him to know I knew all the links in the chain.

"I can understand why you hate her father. He married your ex-wife and your daughter sidled up to him. But you hate your daughter too? Why don't you want her running the underside of the business?"

"Would you want your child involved in such work?" he said quietly.

Our food arrived and we both smeared butter on the thick rye, then sliced the sausage and settled the little discs in the butter. We chewed on the open-faced sandwiches.

"I never got used to American bread." Sergei closed his eye in bliss.

"To answer your question, no, I wouldn't want my child involved in such work." And I thought, my heart cracking with terror, of Daniel deciding to follow in my footsteps. Doing what I did. I couldn't know about it, I'd never sleep again. He couldn't know what I did.

"Are you all right?" Sergei said. "You look ill."

"I just want to know why you sent Nesterov."

He swallowed a chunk of the sausage. "You assume I sent him."

"He was in contact with you. You're really not Mr. Beethoven?"

"That's his contact's name? No. Do I look like I am coordinating some big operation against the Varelas? I sit in a wheelchair all day and watch TV."

"Why was he in contact with you then?"

"If I tell you," he said, "you will go to the Varelas because you will be trying to earn the points with them. If I don't tell you, you will tell them anyway."

"Just tell me. If you help me, I'll help you."

"How? Grow back my legs, my face, my eye?"

"I'll help you get your daughter back."

He said nothing for two whole minutes, thinking, chewing, slurping at his tea. "You've seen Zhanna. She attaches herself to whoever is the most powerful. First it was me. Then when I was a remnant of the father she remembered it was Rey. When she came to see me in the hospital I heard her whisper to her mother that I smelled funny now. I could hear the disdain in her voice. Disdain, instead of a daughter's love or mercy. She will start sneering at Rey soon, as his mind crumbles. It's not coincidence that he begins to fade and she attaches herself to Kent."

"Is Kent the power behind the throne, then?"

"She believes so. She wouldn't have a chance with Galo. Too much dislike there."

"Why is that?"

He shrugged. "They've spent too much time around each other. They're not blood but they had to act like they were."

"I don't know what you mean."

"Two teenagers, forced to live together…must I draw a picture?"

"Are you saying they had a relationship? A physical one?" I thought of the comments Cori had made about surprises to Galo in the context of talking about Zhanna. And comments that Zhanna and Galo had made. Galo insisting more than once that Zhanna was not a blood relation. Hints of a fracture, but also hints of intimacy. I'd thought they were a couple back at the Or nightclub. She'd slapped him and stormed out. Then I thought I was wrong. I wasn't.

"I will say they are like the couple who can't live together but can't bear to be apart. You won't find Galo with many girlfriends in his past. Zhanna looms too large. But they can't date, they can't be together, it couldn't ever last. They collide for a while, they veer away, they collide again." He crooked a smile. "There are a lot of repeating patterns in this family." Yes, I thought. Of people cast aside.

"You were his partner."

He sipped his tea. "He bought me out, early. It was more money than I'd ever seen in Russia, that was for sure. I was a fool but I liked flying more than business meetings." He shrugged. "The spilled vodka. Or milk, whatever." He took another sip of black tea, then glanced over at the waitress, who was helping another table. He pulled a flask from his pocket and dosed the tea. Raised it to me, I nodded. Which was the only acceptable answer to Sergei. He spiked my tea. "So. Some clients do not want Zhanna in charge. I do not want Zhanna in charge, for a different reason. I want her free and clear of that family. They asked me to...coordinate the transition. No one knows the business better than I do. So. Nesterov is from here. He has gone to work for this German woman, but I know him, I know his family."

"Does Zhanna know him?"

"No. I have seen her fewer than a dozen times in the past twenty years."

"And they sent your friend."

"Yes. Who killed him? You?"

"No." I hesitated. "Galo. To save me, actually."

"I would have thought it was his nasty friend Ricky."

"One of them, maybe Ricky, wounded Marianne after she delivered the message that Zhanna was unacceptable."

"I heard," he said. "And Zhanna will never give up now. I know my child."

"I'm not going to say anything to the Varelas about you," I said. "But someone gunned for Cori. Was that you?" And I could see it—he wanted his revenge on Rey. He could have taken Cori from him. But why now? He could have killed or hurt Cori years ago. Why now? Because Rey would be less likely to strike back?

Sergei folded his napkin. "I did not try to hurt Cordelia. I would not."

"Nesterov was in touch with the men who killed the man she hired to protect herself."

"I had nothing to do with that."

I didn't believe him. "Who are the clients?"

He didn't answer. I asked again.

"I won't tell you that, Sam," he said. "Ever. There's nothing you can threaten me with. They'll take good care of me and if you keep your mouth shut, they'll leave you alone."

"I can threaten you with the Varelas."

"You could, and you could see what happens. See if they get madder at me, or madder at you for digging into their business."

He had a point.

He tossed money onto the table. "It was nice meeting you. I will wheel myself home."

"Don't be silly, I'll push you…"

"I don't want help from you or anyone else. Go. Let me think in peace."

I collected his money, and I paid for the bread, sausages, and tea, taking a few moments to settle the bill while he trundled outside. I followed him out of the St. Ekaterina.

"The food's my treat, Sergei," I said. On the street I tucked his money into his jacket pocket as he began to argue, "No, that's not necessary," and I felt the plastic brick of a phone.

I should have pulled it out and looked at it. It was just a phone. But I didn't think. Everyone carries one.

We were half a block from his apartment when the van pulled up fast behind us, its lights blinding me. I spun to face them and two men hurried out of the van. I'd left my gun in the car and I went into a fighting stance as they charged me, trying to get between me and Sergei.

But then they Tasered me and I didn't have much defense against that, the voltage dancing through me and they dragged me into the back of the van. Plastic handcuffs on me. I heard a man speaking, softly, Sergei answering. Laughing. A sack went over my head, but I heard the soft grind of Sergei's wheelchair, motoring toward home.

"You be a good boy for once," a man said in Russian, and I was a very good boy as they drove me away.

48

THE PHONE, I thought through my daze. Sergei had his phone turned on inside his jacket pocket, someone listening on the other end who he'd called while he was in his bedroom. Oldest trick in the book, and because he was old and crippled and one-eyed I was stupid.

My new friends didn't drive me to an abandoned warehouse or a dump of an apartment or the beach to put two bullets in me. After the van stopped, they carried me out of the car. I felt myself hurried up a flight of stairs—still outside—and then the creak of a door opening. They shoved me into a chair and they handcuffed me to it, and then and only then did they pull the bag from my eyes. They dropped it in my lap. It was a Miami Dolphins tote bag. I blinked against the dim light from the lamp.

A room. There were four windows across the wall, all with their shades drawn. I could smell spices and grease and so we were near a restaurant. On the other side of the shades was a soft rainbow glow of neon. But it was quiet. Not near one of the Miami nightclubs that didn't get started until midnight or later.

Four men. They were in dark suits and ties. All wore sunglasses that masked their faces.

One held a police baton and he twirled it, letting it arc past his leg like he really wanted to find a target for it. A taller man stood next to him. He searched me. He took my keys, the phone I'd taken from Nesterov's car, and my own phone.

"Mr. Chevalier, we'd like to have a talk with you." The tall guy next to the baton guy spoke in Russian. "Rey Varela asked you to protect his daughter. Bothering Sergei doesn't accomplish that goal. We do not like you because…we don't understand you. You are a stranger to us. So. If you want to protect Cordelia Varela, then I say now you take her credit card, go to Australia. Her father can afford it. We'll ignore you. Take anyone else you want to take along, to feel safe. Keep her in Sydney. She'll love it." He spoke like he couldn't quite string the words together and for a second I thought he was drunk.

I made no motion, gave no sign I understood.

"You do speak Russian, we are told?"

I nodded.

"You understand?"

"Yes." I understood more than he knew.

"Will you do this?"

"Why?"

"Do as we say and you'll be well rewarded."

"How do I know you'll keep your word?" I said in Russian. I didn't look at the tall man, I looked directly at the man behind him, curious if he, too, understood what I was saying. He glanced away and the tall man stepped into my line of sight, forcing me to look at him.

"Oh, you don't. But we will."

"Is this the part where you beat and torture me?" This I said in English, and he opened his mouth, and I said it again, quick, in Russian. I hung my head.

"Not…unless needed. Leave the day after tomorrow. Tell Rey you are serious about getting his daughter away from this situation."

"What's really going on here?" I said in English. "You're Americans. I can hear an American accent in your near-fluent Russian. Why are you pretending to be something you're not?"

Talk about awkward pauses.

"We *are* Russian," the tall man insisted.

"You want me to think you are, but you're not."

They looked at one another. "I want to hear that guy in the back," I said, and I jerked my head past the tall guy. "Say something in Russian. Right now. Tell me I'm a dumb, ugly loser. Tell me Merry Christmas. Tell me how to order a vodka."

"Say nothing to him," the tall man yelled in Russian at the others.

"Not very convincing," I said, in Russian. I looked at one of the others. And I cussed him out, thoroughly, insulting every parent, sibling, and child he might have had.

He bit his lip like he couldn't decide what to say.

The tall man punched me. Hard. It hurt. Then he kicked me in my cut shoulder and I thought I would vomit from the pain. I fell back in the chair.

"Do you understand what I said to you?" he whispered in Russian.

I nodded.

"Do as you are told."

"Iowa? Alabama? Where are you from, Fake Ivan?"

He Tasered me again. I fell back and felt my brain dance. Then they left me alone, filing out of the room, locking the door. I could hear a soft murmur of voices, a tone of whispered discussion. I pulled the chair to the window, staggering. Looked out. It was Calle Ocho, most of the signs in Spanish, and I realized this was the same place where Ricky had come before he went to meet Galo and Zhanna at the nightclub. I'd parked on that side road, directly in front of where I was.

The men came back in. The tall one was pissed. "We are going to let you go on your way."

I almost said, *How's Ricky,* but then I would be admitting I knew who their mole was. And they might kill me for that.

He punched me again. It seemed to make him feel better. "Now. You are going to do a favor for us, before you go to Sydney."

My lip bled. "Naturally."

"You are going to give this to Zhanna Sergeyevna." And he put a little bag in my lap.

"You want me to be your messenger? Your first messenger got killed, your second one got shot. No thank you."

He put the gun to my head. "I'd like to see some enthusiasm."

"What is it?" I asked, but what I thought is: They are very cautious how they deal with the Varelas. Why?

"It's encouragement to not pursue her new job."

"Well, if she doesn't take the job, can I have it?"

They all looked at one another. "Seriously," I said, again in English. "I'll take the job."

The tall man studied me for a full thirty seconds. "You're very funny," he said. "Work on your Russian; you are getting dumb with it."

They put the bag back on my bloodied head and hauled me down the stairs. The late-night street was quiet. No one noticed me being hauled like a sack of potatoes. They drove me back to Sunny Isles and set me down, uncuffed, in front of Sergei's building. They gave me back my keys and my phone, politely dropping them in my lap.

They drove off. I picked up the package and I walked to my car.

I drove to the very expensive hotel on Key Biscayne. It was three in the morning, but there was a valet on duty and he stared at my bloodied lip as I handed him the keys.

"Are you okay, sir?" he asked.

"Yes, I'm fine." A couple of other guests, returning from partying on South Beach, glanced at me and laughed. I probably did look funny.

I went upstairs and in the room found Cori, asleep. She had to be utterly exhausted.

Very quietly, I stripped and I washed the blood from my face and put a bandage on my chin. I opened the package. Inside was a mini MP3 player and a pair of ear buds.

I tapped the Play button. I heard a click and an official-sounding voice announce a date many years ago. Then a woman's voice, accented, speaking English: "Zhanna, please, no, have you lost your mind?..."

"Take the pills, Mama."

"No, no!"

"Take. The. Pills."

"I won't, you can't make me..."

"When I tell Papa you're nothing but a traitor, you've betrayed him...what will he do to you? I think he'll do like he did to the first wife. Was it really suicide?"

Sobbing. "Put that gun away, you won't shoot me, I don't believe it..."

"Mama. I will shoot you. You know I will. Don't act surprised. Now. You can suffer, or you can take the pills."

"I won't..."

"Mama. I will shoot you in the knees. I'll cripple you. Then I'll tell Papa what you did and he'll do the rest. He'll make you tell him who you work for." And her voice became slow, cajoling. "This is best, all right? Best for us all."

And then the sounds of a struggle, a woman screaming, her cries suddenly muffled.

The recording ended.

I sat naked, shivering, bloodied, on the tile floor. I listened once more. Then I went into the darkened bedroom and found a pair of boxer shorts in my bag. I slipped them on and hid the MP3 player in my bag and collapsed into the bed next to Cori, my mind whirling with matricide.

49

You look awful," Cori said.

"Good morning to you, too."

"Did you not sleep well?" She blinked at me. "Sam! You've been in another fight."

"Yes. You hit me in your sleep."

She sat up, touched my cheek with her hand. "Don't lie to me." She looked at me with real tenderness. I hadn't seen that in a while. *Cori, why couldn't we be two different people, without all this mess?*

"Both your family and the clients are insisting you get out of town. Do you like Australia? I hear it's wonderful."

"I'm not leaving you, or my family."

I called Room Service, ordered coffee and a continental breakfast for two. Cori nodded that that was fine. I wished painkillers were on the menu.

"Did you make any headway on your financial research?" I asked.

"No. I need to make some phone calls to Africa and the Middle East."

"All right. I'm going to ask you some questions about your family. But I don't want you to read too much into it, okay?"

"That sounds impossible."

"Tell me about Zhanna's mother's suicide."

"Why?"

I looked at her. "No reading into my questions. I'm just trying to figure out some threads here."

Cori sat down on the edge of the bed. "Natalia left a note. She had been unfaithful to Papa. She said she could not bear the guilt."

"Unfaithful with whom?"

"The note didn't say."

"How did Zhanna take her mother's death?"

"She was upset, obviously. She had to see a counselor for a while. But she had Papa, so she thought she had everything she needed. She doesn't much like damaged people. Her father. Her mother..."

"Yet she's in love with Kent. And someone as shallow as Z might see him as damaged."

"Well, Kent is useful to her," she said.

Gamble, I thought. "Did anyone ever treat it as murder?"

"No, Sam. Natalia was never well. It was a shock, but it wasn't, at the same time. Does that make sense?"

"Yes," I said. "I understand."

Breakfast came and we ate, and I drank the delicious coffee and I thought. Cori was quiet.

"Do you think someone killed Natalia?" she asked.

"I honestly don't know," I lied. Telling her I had a recording of Zhanna killing her mother was a bomb, and the clients wanted me to do their dirty work and set off the bomb in the middle of the Varelas. They were using me. I wasn't sure I was ready to be used.

I got up. "I need to run some errands," I said.

"They're going to think we're in New York. If they call me...do I pretend to be in New York?"

"Tell them you're safe, but we haven't left yet. I'll explain to them."

"Papa won't like you disobeying his orders."

"I think he might understand," I said.

She went into the bathroom and turned on the shower. I picked up Cori's phone. She had her family's numbers programmed in it, under Favorites. "Zhanna/Kent," one entry read. I called. Kent answered. I hung up. Another said "Zhanna Office." I tried; Zhanna's secretary answered, said Zhanna wasn't in this morning.

Zhanna and Galo once had something going. Galo lived next door to his father, as did Zhanna. But after their meeting at Or, Galo had gone to a South Beach apartment. One that wasn't in a Varela name.

Everyone needs an escape route.

I put the MP3 player and the ear buds in my pocket, and I left without saying good-bye to Cori. I thought I was doing the right thing, shielding her.

I would regret that later.

50

ZHANNA ANSWERED THE door, dressed in yoga pants and a snug exercise shirt. She frowned at me. "I didn't think Cori knew about this place."

"Cori didn't tell me," I said.

"Galo has a big mouth."

She made the rude throat-cutting gesture she seemed to favor when upset. "Galo didn't tell me either."

This she digested. "I thought you'd be on your way out of town by now."

"Can we talk?"

She let me in, slammed the door behind me.

"Shouldn't you be babysitting the princess?" she snapped. "That's your job."

"Last night I was given an audio recording of you killing your mother," I said.

She stared at me as I sat down. She laughed. She stopped. Then she laughed again.

I stared back at her.

"You must be joking."

"No. Would you like to hear it?" I held out the tiny player.

She slipped in the ear buds. Listened. Her face went ashen then surged red, as though every atom of blood in her body rushed to feed her brain.

"This is a lie." She poked at the mini player's buttons.

"You can't delete it that way. You have to do it when the player's connected to a computer."

She ran into the kitchen and shoved the player down the disposal. The ear buds dangled in her hand, like spaghetti noodles. The disposal made a horrible crunching, grinding, breaking noise.

"There are other copies, no doubt. You're breaking your disposal," I said. She stopped the grinding. She ran water into the sink like it made a difference. Then she turned away and she opened the refrigerator, studying the contents. She pulled out a bottle of dark tea.

"Zhanna? Did you hear me?"

She looked at me again. Then she pushed the horrified, anxious expression off her face. A calmness returned. The change was startling. She'd slid her emotional mask back on. "What do you want?" She even managed, crazily, to sound a little bored.

"Here's the deal, Zhanna. The clients are never going to let you run the smuggling. Ever. Shooting the messenger in Puerto Rico only pissed them off. They've gone nuclear on you."

"I didn't shoot her," she said.

But I kept going: "And I don't think the rest of the family is going to react well to you having killed your mother. So. Here's the offer. I can hide you where neither the clients nor the Varelas will ever find you. We'll set you up someplace where you're free from Kent and Galo and Rey. You tell me everything about the operation. What they're smuggling, who they're doing it for, why it's so important.

"That is my offer. If you don't take it, it's quite likely that the clients will crush you; Kent will leave you; the Varelas, the family who matters so much to you, even more than your own actual father, they're going to shun you. You're finished. So. One minute to decide."

She broke into laughter. "I'm not interested in your offer, Sam. You are a bad investment. And a terribly ineffective liar." She shook the tea, cracked open the bottle.

"I know about you and Galo," I said. "I've seen you together."
I didn't need to add that Sergei had confirmed it.

Ten seconds ticked by. "Or. At the Corinthian Hotel. I saw
you there," she said.

"It's over, Zhanna," I said. "Everything. It's over."

"No it's not," she said. "I'm golden. The clients will have to accept me." She took a big sip of the tea.

"You heard it yourself," I said. "They have a recording of you
killing your mother."

"It's a lie." It was the item she was least worried about and
I thought, She's a monster. The kind clothed in human skin,
masked by a lovely face and an engaging mind and a warm smile.
But underneath that, darkness deeper than night.

"You called her a traitor," I said. "You said she betrayed Rey.
And why would the clients have a tape of this? The one answer
is that your mother was their informant." I let the words hang in
the air. She looked at a spot slightly above my left shoulder. "I
think the clients keep a spy near this family if they can. To make
sure the Varelas are holding up their end of the bargain, not losing
their nerve, not wanting to stop the smuggling. It used to be your
mother, now it's someone else." Ricky, I was sure, but I didn't
say. "And you found out your mom was spying on your stepfather. You could have warned her, let her run or even let her quit.
Instead you killed her. You fixed the problem for your precious
stepfather."

The warm smile glinted like a knife. "I'm pregnant, Sam."

I stared.

"Don't you want to be the first to congratulate me? No one
will hurt me. I'll run the smuggling."

"Is . . . is that what you and Galo argued about?"

She ignored my question. She took another sip and coughed,
made a face. "I can't wait to have wine again."

I made my voice cruel. I wanted to break her; I wanted her to
take my offer. "Only Rey considers you family. And even he's using
you. You'd take the fall if the smuggling ever got exposed. Not
Galo. They don't much love you, Zhanna. There's no blood tie."

She ran a hand along her stomach and took another long drink. She recapped the bottle. "There will be."

So not Kent's child. "How do you know it's Galo's?"

"A woman knows."

She dropped the plastic bottle of herbal tea. It rolled to my feet and I picked it up and handed it back to her. "The Varelas all want to be free of you," I said.

"You...you are the worst liar I have ever laid eyes on," she said. Her voice slurred a little.

"Thirty seconds left on the offer."

She suddenly gasped for breath. "Morning sickness. My first time, thanks to you stressing me out."

"Stop faking," I said. It was just like her to play on sympathies rather than face the truth. She killed her own mother, I told myself. She has to see it's over.

And it was over. She fell off the stool, eyes rolling into whites. I caught her as she tumbled across the carpet. She convulsed, violently, in my arms.

"Zhanna! Zhanna!"

The convulsions worsened. Her eyes met mine, shocked, afraid. Her hands closed on mine. Then her eyes widened and the final choking convulsion took her.

I felt for her heart. Booming like it would explode. Then it went still in her warm chest. "Zhanna!" I called her name. Again and again.

She was dead.

I glanced at the bottle of herbal tea. Poisoned. Done in like her own mother.

And you touched the bottle.

I wiped the bottle clean. I pulled the mangled MP3 player from the sink. I put it in my pocket. I searched the apartment for any clue as to who the clients were, but this place was an escape, a retreat from the pressures of the Varela world. I found nothing—no laptop, no files, nothing.

I found a pregnancy test in the bottom of the trash.

But...why poison her if they were blackmailing her to resign?

Insurance? Or...the clients hadn't done this. Someone else had planted the poisoned tea.

Who knew about this place? Galo and Ricky. Who else?

I could run, I thought. Leave behind the recording, call the Varelas. Maybe Zhanna would look like a suicide. But then I wouldn't have the clients, and I was damned if I'd just do their bidding, the murderers who'd killed Steve. I wanted them put down, broken, out of business.

There comes a moment, the burnt man told me. There comes a moment you stick in the knife. And then he pointed to his ravaged face and said, "I missed my moment. I waited. Don't wait."

I wiped my prints from everything I'd touched and went downstairs to drive to the Varelas'.

51

THE GUARD WAVED me through, and Galo and Ricky stood in the driveway. My heart nearly stopped. If Ricky had seen me…he'd probably shoot me on sight. But as I got out of the car, he just gave me his usual unfriendly stare. I wondered whether he still smelled like hospital laundry.

"You're supposed to be in New York," Galo said. "Where's Cori?"

"She's safe," I said. "I got a visit last night. From the clients."

They both stared at me, and it took all my self-control not to glance at Ricky, measure his reaction. I was playing my part, being the messenger for his bosses. "I need to speak privately to you and Kent. Now. Is he here?"

Galo nodded. "None of us went into the office today, we're all working from home. Ricky, stay here." Ricky frowned but obeyed. I'm sure he knew I'd been grabbed and he wanted to be sure I followed my orders from his masters.

I followed Galo to the third house on the cul-de-sac—a massive waterfront affair, with a pier with two speedboats attached and a small fishing boat.

Kent was in the large living room, sitting in a large plush chair, tapping on a Braille keyboard attached to a laptop. I walked toward him and he said, "Sam, Galo," at the same time I announced myself to him.

"My walk or my smell?" I asked.

"Your walk," he said. "You're freakishly light-footed. Galo, Rey, and Zhanna are all stompers. Why are you here?"

I sat across from him. "You can't see the bruises on my face, but I got a visit. The clients who will not accept Zhanna running the smuggling."

Kent closed the laptop, put his hands at his side in the chair.

"And since the last messenger about firing Zhanna got shot, they decided this hireling who's hanging out with Cori and charged with keeping her out of danger...they decided I would be a good messenger now. So. They gave me a recording of Zhanna forcing her mother to take an overdose. I was supposed to play it for Zhanna to get her to step aside. I took it to her."

Kent got up, went to the bar, felt for a bottle, measured out a drink. Galo didn't move.

"And what did she say?" Kent asked.

"I'll tell you what she's decided to do. Where she's decided to go. I think you both want to know that." I let that threat hang in the air for a few moments. "But I want to know who these clients are. I want to know who is after me. No more dodging it."

I waited for Kent or Galo to argue or object to this demand and instead Kent just calmly said, "This is fascinating, but I certainly don't believe Zhanna was ever capable of hurting her mother. I don't like to comment until I've heard the whole story. Go on."

"Really," I said, "the bigger question is who has been bugging rooms in the Varela house from so many years ago, and keeping the recordings."

"Oh my God, oh my God," Galo said.

"That is a mystery," Kent said.

"The clients? Or a member of the family?"

Kent considered. "God, I hope not."

"So this is what I think. I think Zhanna's mother was an informant for the clients. She activated the taping. She could do that whenever Rey or anyone else with critical information she needed to know was there in the room with her. And maybe she was afraid of her daughter when Zhanna caught her spying. She didn't have the loyalty of her own child."

The silence was awkward.

"I suppose because she was, legally, a child, and accusing her would reveal they knew what was going on in this house—they said nothing. Or maybe there was already another spy inside they didn't want to risk. Someone had to hand them the recording. And they've kept it for all these years, until they needed it."

A thoughtful frown crossed Kent's face. He opened a drawer and groped for an item inside, then stopped. Galo rubbed his face with his fingertips, anxious, upset.

"Let's say she did this," Galo said. "Then the clients win. She can't run it."

I tossed the MP3 player onto the coffee table.

"What happened to it?" Galo said. "It's all chewed up."

"Zhanna panicked and tried to destroy it. I think maybe she's not so confident in your loyalty as you think," I said. "But the problem is that you have another informant already here."

"Who?" Galo said.

"Ricky. I think he shot the woman in Puerto Rico. I think he has been spying on you for the clients. Maybe for a long time."

"Can you prove it?" Kent asked.

"Tell me who the clients are, and I will."

Kent said, "Galo, perhaps it would be useful if you brought Ricky here."

"Make sure he's unarmed," I said.

Galo looked at us both, then left.

"So Ricky shot the woman who worked for the clients, same as him. That makes no sense, Sam," Kent said, almost gently.

I opened my mouth then closed it. I thought of the scene in the plaza: Marianne walking toward the three men, the stone fortress, the tourists in their little clumps, Kent's cane tapping, going still, then waving slightly, the tour guides in hoop skirts, flashing their fans in their secret language...

Then I realized it, with a jolt along my spine.

I said, "Ricky shot her because you signaled him to do so.

With your cane." I remembered. Taps, shakes. It struck me as odd that he was moving his cane during the conversation. He'd spent enough time in Puerto Rico to borrow the idea from the tour guides, who showed how the ladies once used their fans to send secret messages to their lovers. "Why did you...?"

"Because it would mean the end of the negotiations. The end of the chance of Zhanna running the smuggling," he said. "Really, I thought you were smarter. You're not."

And he was right.

Because no one expects to get shot by a blind man.

He raised the silencer-capped Glock up from the open drawer and with a steady hand he fired. I was five feet away. I vaulted over the sofa and he tracked the noise of my movement, my breath, the murmur of my palms touching the couch's fabric, the scratch of my shoe against the floor as I landed. I felt a bullet tear through my jacket, burning along the skin.

He fired again, the bullet hissing past my head, heating my ear. And again and again, firing steadily so I couldn't rush him without him scoring a lucky hit. I could only run away.

Splinters from a bullet hitting the edge of a doorway shot into my face. I stumbled, felt blood on my forehead. I ran into the dining room. And through the window I saw Ricky and Galo, running toward the house, Ricky holding a gun. Galo with a phone pressed to his ear, screaming Zhanna's name, for her to answer her phone.

No one was interested in what I had to say anymore.

I hit the back door. Ran out onto a wide yard, facing the bay. Kent couldn't see me, but he could guess where I went and within a minute or two they'd be on the wide lawn searching for me.

The Varela boats were on a private pier. I picked the smaller speedboat and slipped the ropes. I cracked open the ignition and hotwired it, staying low, keeping hidden.

I heard Ricky shouting. They wouldn't want to shoot, out here where the respectable folks would call the nice guard up at the gatehouse and report gunshots. It might buy me precious seconds.

The boat roared into life and I eased it back from the pier. Faster than I should have, I heard a tearing scrape along the boat's side. Then I sensed movement and glanced up. Ricky leapt from the pier to land in the boat, swinging the gun toward me.

I slammed a hand into his chin, an uppercut, and his feet lifted off the deck. We were clear of the pier but just backing into the bay. He fell, blood gushing from his lip, but he leveled a kick at my groin. He caught me on the hip and I fell, hitting the steering wheel for the boat, and we spun out, the prow now facing the water. He swung the gun toward me and we fought for it. I grabbed his hand, powering his aim toward the deck. He tried to head-butt me but he didn't commit and instead slammed my shoulder: but it was the shoulder that had been cut in Puerto Rico. Agony surged along my skin, but I pushed it aside and focused on the gun. He shoved me into the throttle as we grappled, and the boat revved ahead at full speed, the hotwire having bypassed the safety features. The boat veered into the bay, the throttle on full.

Ricky was strong. He was trying to aim the gun at my foot. I moved it and the gun fired, the bullet punching into the deck. Hopefully not *through* it. I hammered an elbow into Ricky's gut, got a moment of breathing room.

"Let it go, Ricky. I'll hide you like I can hide Zhanna. Galo will kill you for working for the clients."

He didn't answer, intent on fighting me. He broke free, still holding the gun, and in the background I heard the blast of a warning horn from another boat and hoped we weren't dashing into someone else's path. Our boat barreled through a wake, narrowly missing another speedboat—a woman screaming, the wake launching us into the air. Both my feet and Ricky's feet left the deck. I couldn't tell if we were taking on water or not; the world was a whirl between bay and sky and the fury in Ricky's face. I tried not to think that maybe he'd killed four people who had teased him as a kid. That kind of rage, that kind of anger, he wouldn't hesitate to murder me. There would be no deals, no surrender.

I heard the drone of another speedboat approaching but Ricky slammed us both back to the deck. Ricky hooked his fingers toward my eyes. I grabbed one of his fingers, twisted it back, broke it, and he howled.

Where was the gun? I saw it sliding down into the deck well and scrambled toward it. Then he was on top of me trying to bite my ear, his teeth closing more on my hair. I kicked him away and grabbed for the gun. Found a solid grip on it and then he looped the rope around my throat.

The rope was bright yellow; he'd grabbed it as the next weapon. He yanked me back, fueled by adrenaline. The rope scored my throat. I fired the gun downward and hit his foot, the easiest target, and he screamed again and we struggled. He tightened the rope and I made a choice of survival: I inched one finger, barely, under the rope to keep him from cutting off my air.

He yanked me, violently, toward the edge of the boat. I dropped the gun. We hit something else, I never knew what, and he slipped his grip on the rope. I forced my whole hand under the rope around my neck, then with my free hand lassoed another length of it around Ricky's throat. We were trying to strangle each other. The contest would be won by whoever didn't pass out first. I didn't like my odds. I tried to tighten the rope, but he pulled back from me in a panic and we both went over the edge, the rope binding us together.

The water was cold and yanked us along, me still gripping the noose around my neck, which kept me from total strangulation. Ricky flapped his hands at me but then I saw his eyes, wide and bulging in the froth of the water. He was dead, his neck snapped by the rope.

With one hand I was clenching the rope and fighting to free myself. The boat was moving too fast and dragging me along. I summoned all my strength and forced the noose wider and ducked my head out, every muscle in my body screaming. Free. The boat and Ricky tore away from me, heading out toward the open bay.

I had no flotation device, and exhaustion poured through me.

I heard an approaching boat and turned. Galo and Kent and another guard came up in the second Varela boat behind me.

The guard reached out and pulled me up onto the deck.

"Don't hurt him!" Galo yelled. "Let him explain, let me talk to him..."

Then Kent knelt down toward me and his hand found my throat. He said, "Oh, what are we going to do with you, Sam?" And the bright Miami sun went dark.

52

I AWOKE IN darkness and for the first few moments I thought, I'm dead.

I closed and opened my eyes repeatedly and the darkness held firm. No hint of light. It was all-consuming. I pulled in breath and my chest was tight; the air smelled of metal. I tried to pull up my arms and I could not. My legs—the same. I could not move.

Panic seized me—blind, surging terror: *I'm paralyzed and the Varelas buried me alive.* I started thinking of how slow death would be. Days, maybe, in this eternal blackness. It took every fiber of my being not to scream my throat raw.

"Help." I felt my mouth move to shape the word. "Somebody help me." My voice was a hoarse whisper. It seemed to echo in my ears. My mouth could barely function; it was as dry as sand. A sour chemical taste in my mouth.

I tried to calm my breathing. The air tasted slightly metallic. Then I noticed a slight hiss of air across my face. Constant. Unnerving. But air.

I tensed my fingers. They were inside...a glove? But I could move my fingers. I couldn't tell what bound my hands, but my gloved fingertips could register that they were resting against a smooth surface.

Why...why would they bury me with gloves on?

I tried again to lift my arms. Both were bound, at the forearm and at the upper arm. Encased in sleeves. As sensation returned, I could feel that my legs were encased as well. My feet, too.

I tried to do a sit-up. I was bound across my chest. My neck wasn't bound and I could lift it, but...my head was inside... something. I could feel it, like plastic, against the back of my head. Panic seized me again. My head...in a box? But I could feel the soft, insistent rush of air on my face; I could breathe.

I tried to listen. They hadn't killed me, I told myself, full of optimism and then the dark side of me whispered, *Well, this could be the start of a slow death. They don't want you to suffocate, that just takes minutes. Starvation and thirst, well, we're talking days. All in blackness. All while you cannot move.* But...I could turn my head, without restraint. I felt a fabric or mesh stretched across the top of my head.

I called out, again and again, and there was only silence in answer. I listened. I couldn't hear anything. The silence was as complete as the darkness.

Claustrophobia seized me and I struggled in vain. We all have our little fears, and when you run parkour you can't be afraid of heights. I'd lived in jungles with my parents, so I couldn't be afraid of spiders or snakes. But a guy like me, who runs and vaults and soars, what I cannot bear is to be trapped, pinned, unmoving. I fought down the wave of panic. To panic was to die. I had to think. I felt hazy, drugged.

But I was still alive. That was my hold, the idea that I gripped like an iron rung in a storm. If I was alive, I could get out of this. Somehow.

Unless they left you here to starve, to die of thirst, an unhelpful voice chimed again in my head. I strangled that thought. I closed my eyes. Maybe I slept. I didn't know. I just breathed and tried to stay calm and tried to not start screaming, because I was afraid I wouldn't stop. I thought of Daniel: *I will come home to you. I will get out of here.* Then thinking of him felt like a knife in the heart, because what if I never saw him again? What if no one ever found me? It would kill my parents after losing Danny, even with us not getting along. Mila, Mila wouldn't know what had happened to me. She'd come after the Varelas and maybe they'd kill her, too, or bury her alive like they had me. Cori. What had they told Cori? Leonie, she would have Daniel to herself. Just like I thought she wanted. At least he would be loved. My teeth chattered. I had to hold on to hope.

I think I slept. In my dreams I ran parkour under a huge, empty sky, flying between ivory buildings with perfect grace and strength, unbound, the world wide above and below and around me. Nothing to hold me, to imprison me. Perfect freedom.

"Sam?"

I was startled out of my reverie. Darkness again. I struggled against my bonds and the panic was like bile in my throat. In my delirium I thought of Coma Thug, helpless in his hospital bed, how I'd felt sorry for him, trapped and defenseless. How I wouldn't want to be him.

"Sam?" Kent's voice.

"Yes. Kent, please." I don't even know what I said please for, and then I was ashamed of the weakness. "Please."

"If you're thirsty, lean your head forward a bit. There's a plastic valve there. Gently bite on it and you'll have water." He spoke in a reassuring tone.

I did and cool, refreshing water filled my mouth. I could feel a plastic or glass surface against my forehead. I swallowed, drank again.

"It's only thirty-two ounces. Make it last for the next day or so."

Day? "Where am I?"

"When you need to relieve yourself, go ahead. There won't be a mess. The suit will take care of it."

Suit. A thought, a memory, fought through the haze of panic and drugginess. Suit. "Where am I?" I asked again.

"Well, that's a relative term. You're in transit. To a new life. Your old one is gone, Sam."

"Where is Cordelia?" I could barely form the words.

"She's safe. She's no longer your concern. Cori has seen the error of her ways. She sees that you've brought us nothing but pain and discord. You've done our family a favor at long last, Sam, even better than the one when you saved Rey. You made Cori realize we would have to come before you. So thank you for that, you dumb, stupid kid."

Two words he'd used felt like nails in my brain. *In transit*..."Where are you sending me?"

"To a place where you can share all your secrets. Like telling us who you really are and why you decided to interfere with our lives."

"I will be missed."

"I don't think the police will look hard for Sam Chevalier."

A new life, he'd said. They didn't want me dead, not yet. Mila would look for me. Of this I was certain.

That was a fight he would lose, I thought, now that I was calmer. Mila. Kent would regret hurting me if she found him. The thought of her was a lifeline. Line. Suit. He said *suit*.

Suit? No. What had I seen on the e-mail on Kent's laptop? "Spacesuit. I'm in a spacesuit."

"Very good, Sam. It keeps you alive and comfortable. The suits are similar to standard NASA issue, but of course they're not nearly as sophisticated. And the oxygen tank is bigger."

"Where are you sending me?"

"You'll see soon enough. Is it very dark to you, Sam?" Kent laughed. "I know what it is to be in the dark. I was afraid of the dark, as a child, and then I was in it permanently. It took me so long to adjust. Finally I did. I'm not sure that you're strong enough."

"I am going to kill you," I said.

"I'm just a harmless blind man," Kent said. "And you're just a kid who thought he was tough."

"You're Mr. Beethoven. You work for the clients. You hired Marianne. You're a traitor to the Varelas."

"I'm a safety valve for the Varelas. But that doesn't matter." A pause, and for a moment I thought he'd disconnected the communications feed in the suit. "You killed Zhanna."

"No. I didn't. Someone poisoned her tea..."

"You did it. We all know it."

"You did it," I said.

"I wouldn't. I loved her. Does that surprise you? I loved her so much."

"I didn't kill her."

"But you killed Ricky. You tried to destroy us, Sam, but you failed. The only reason you're alive is because we want to know where you came from. Who you are. We're sending you to a specialist of sorts. And if you're alive, Cori will behave, so Rey thinks. We shall see. I'm not going to talk to you again, Sam, at least not directly. Safe travels." A click of good-bye. Then instead of his mocking voice and blackness there was only...blackness. And somehow that was worse.

You are in transit to a new life.

They weren't smuggling drugs, or information, or technology. They were smuggling people.

Spacesuit. It had been mentioned in the e-mail to the person he called Nanny. Nanny had referred to "guests." I remembered it now.

And suddenly I yelled my throat raw. Could anyone hear me outside of a spacesuit or the container I was in? I had no idea. I was being shipped. The Varelas were masters at transport.

I was in the belly of a FastFlex plane, marked with a bar code, another crate to be processed.

I stopped screaming myself hoarse. I gulped more water and then suddenly panicked that I'd drunk it all. I started to wonder if the water was drugged when I fell asleep again, and that was a mercy. It could have been ten minutes or ten hours. I awoke when the crate, coffin, cage, whatever it was, fell over. I was conscious of movement but not impact.

"Help me!" I screamed. "I'm inside, I'm inside!"

The crate was righted—I hadn't been lying flat for all this time, but rather I was in an upright position. I could hear nothing outside, nothing.

They had done this to other people. How many? Terror flooded me in a fresh wave.

"I can pay more than they can!" I yelled. I nearly screamed I was CIA, then remembered Kent might still be listening to me.

I sensed movement. I was lifted and then roughly settled again on another surface. I stayed upright. I was suddenly scared as to what would happen if they loaded me upside down, all the blood surging to my brain. Didn't people die from that after too long? But there were people outside, right now, probably looking at a label that told them how to arrange my coffin. I screamed. I fought with every ounce of strength I had against the restraints. I might have sobbed at one point. I hope not. My calm broke.

Then I realized my box had been still for a long time. I couldn't scream anymore.

"Sam," Kent's voice whispered in my ear. "This breakdown is unbecoming of you. Truly."

He could hear me. He was listening to me scream and beg and bargain. The rotten bastard. It's worse to be afraid and to know your enemy is laughing at you.

I wouldn't give him the satisfaction. I said nothing more. I said nothing back. But I decided then and there the last thing he would ever hear would be my voice, telling him good-bye.

53

<hr/>

I MIGHT HAVE slept again. The steady hiss of air kept me company. I would doze, my brain fighting against the horror of imprisonment, awaken, then my mouth would grope for the water valve. A drink. I wished I could smear the water on my face, but I couldn't. Then I felt the crate—I won't call it a coffin, I won't, *I won't*—being jostled again, moved, thudding. I couldn't hear the thud, I could feel it. I shivered against my bonds.

Kent's voice had been replaced by another voice. A woman's voice, calm yet stern.

I will obey. I will do as I am told. I will obey. I will do as I am told. I will tell all that I know. Information is freedom.

"Who are you?" I screamed. "Let me out of here!"

I will obey. I will do as I am told. I will obey. I will do as I am told. I will tell all that I know. Information is freedom. The chant, seductive as the summer sun, inescapable, like a fly buzzing in your ear on a warm summer's day. It droned and droned and droned and the words tried to become brain cells in my head. I realized it was a recording, playing for me inside the soundproof container.

I stopped screaming. I thought of Daniel. I cried. I couldn't help myself, the shame ran so deep. Then I fell back into the darkness.

The droning voice in my ear stopped.

After another eternity, light.

The box was opened.

The suit's helmet cut the glare of the light but I blinked, the light like a razor in my brain. I could see three people, a woman and two men, standing in front of me.

One of the men, in medical whites, removed the helmet. Light lanced my eyes.

"You've had such a long trip," the woman said. She spoke in English, but with an accent that suggested to me she was from South America. She wore a very nice business suit with an odd chain of whitish rectangles threaded on a golden necklace.

"Let's establish a few ground rules before we let you out into your exciting new life." Her voice was fake-sweet, horrible, like Mary Poppins on acid. "Who you used to be doesn't matter. Except in what you can tell me. Information is your best hope for happiness. I do not care about your titles or your money or your background or your family. That's all gone—poof!" She mimed blowing dust from her hands. She studied me. She was fiftyish, perhaps, with dark hair streaked with gray. A plain face, but for her eyes, which were a remarkable green, the color of a snake's scales. "Let's be clear, sweetheart. I cannot be bribed. Neither can my guards. Offer a bribe, or attempt to escape, and the punishments will be most dire. You are number 47. Repeat after me: I am number 47."

"My name is Sam…"

"That was your old name. You don't have a name anymore. You are 47. Isn't that a nice number? Such a pleasing shape. And it's a prime number."

"My name is Sam Chevalier and if you call…"

"Goodness, someone's not using his listening skills. You know, the suit only has so much oxygen. I wonder how much is left!" And then, smiling, Nanny—it could only be her—reconnected the helmet and they closed the box. They sealed it again. I started to scream again.

After an hour…or two or ten, they opened the box again. I shuddered against the light. She wore a different suit. *How long?*...I tried to steady myself. Her persona had to be calculated, a performance to produce a specific reaction, designed by psychiatrists and professionals. It had to create confusion, surrender, an effect of powerlessness. *So don't give into it but don't show that you're resisting.* I closed my eyes.

Daniel, I want to come home to you.

"Let's try this again, 47." Nanny explained the rules again. I stayed still and quiet. "I won't ask you if you understand. I assume you do because I know you're ever so clever." Her voice was like sugar soaked in honey. It was cloying; it rubbed against every nerve. How could she stand to listen to herself? "I know you'll be a very good boy now, won't you?"

I nodded.

She gestured at the guard. He undid the cords binding me to the inside of the crate. I sagged and he lowered me, still in the suit, to the ground. He pulled off the helmet and I tasted the fresh air.

Nanny aimed a gun at my head, a regretful smile on her face. The guard and the man in medical whites eased me out of the spacesuit-like contraption. Beneath I was in a mesh white suit, skintight, a sort of heavy fabric wrapped around my groin. They kept the gun leveled on me while they let me drink a bottle of cold water and I gulped the first few swallows so fast I thought I would retch.

"We were told you were very dangerous," Nanny said, waving a disapproving finger at me. "I don't like dangerous little boys. I want you to remember that. Be good."

I nodded and finished drinking the water and the guard and the doctor pulled me up to my feet and stripped the mesh off of me, pulled off tubing and a bag to catch my waste, and removed sensors and tape and wires that were webbed across me. I shivered, I stood naked. I could smell my own rankness.

Nanny eyed me. "Such a strong boy! So many guests here could benefit from more exercise."

I covered myself, tried to curl up into a ball. The room was cold.

"Cleanliness is very important here," Nanny said. The doctor hosed me off with a jet of water and foamy soaps. Filth and grime sluiced off me, and blood, too. I'd been bandaged on my arm where Kent's bullet had nicked me, and my hands were scraped from the rope.

They toweled me off. The doctor examined me, smeared antibiotic ointments on my wounds and scrapes. He injected me with three different syringes, whispering, "Just some immunizations you will need here, have no fear, 47." Then they put me into clean underwear, an orange jumpsuit, and flip-flop shoes. "47" had been written on the front and the back of the suit in thick black. Then Nanny uncapped a heavy marker and wrote "47" on my right cheek, then my forehead, like I was undergoing a fraternity hazing.

"That way all your new friends can learn your number!" Nanny said. "Of course—who can you really trust? Some of your new friends might be my special friends too."

I thought of the different ways I could silence that diabetes-inducing voice of hers.

"You must be hungry," Nanny said. "You haven't eaten in a long while. Tomorrow is a busy day, what with the surgery, and travel is *so* tiring. Even when you don't hassle with boarding passes and airport parking."

The surgery? I tried to speak, but only mumblings came out of my mouth.

"Now. We don't want any problems here with you, 47, or we'll take extreme measures. It's hard, for instance, to fight without thumbs. Did you know that? It really does affect one's ability to grasp weapons or to make an effective fist."

I nodded, as you would in this insane conversation. Then I saw again the necklace she wore, an accessory to her impeccable suit. No. Not whitish rectangles. Thumb bones, linked on a chain of gold. Couldn't be. But was. Four of them. Covered in some clear compound to keep them from yellowing. She toyed with the bottommost one like it was her favorite bead.

Panic thrummed in my chest. I wanted to hide my hands from her. Her gaze was fixed on mine. "You're a bit young. We don't have many guests your age, 47. Learn from your elders here. Your life will be much easier."

I said nothing. It was struggle enough to keep standing. "Shall we dine? I could do with a snack."

She turned. The guard and the doctor each took one of my arms to keep me from falling, but I steadied myself to walk. We went out of the concrete room and out into a hallway. Also concrete. Steel doors along the hallway. All shut. The building was silent. Nanny opened a door and the escorts led me in. A cot, bolted to the floor, a toilet, a table, two chairs. They sat me down in one of the chairs. A woman, dressed in a gray smock, wheeled a cart of food into the room.

"47," Nanny said, "this can be a place of comfort, or a place of unhappiness. I believe people decide to be unhappy. It's the number-one problem in our world."

The drugs warring inside me made me shiver.

The smock lady brought me a bowl. Tomato soup, with chunky vegetables in it. There was a plastic spoon. And a glass of water.

"Go ahead," Nanny said, although I hadn't waited for permission. I was just suspicious. It made me rebellious that she thought I was kowtowing to her until I thought about what she'd said about thumbs. I needed thumbs to hold the spoon. Or the knife I'd hold at her throat one day. So I said, "Thank you," and I drank down the water. The soup was cold, but it was supposed to be. It was gazpacho.

"Why is the soup cold, 47?" Nanny said.

I ate half of it before I answered because I was afraid it would be taken away. "Because if it was hot I might throw it on the guards."

"That's a very perceptive and revealing answer—my favorite kind." I thought she might stick a gold star to my face, to adorn my number.

She let me eat the rest of the soup. "Thank you," I said when I put down the spoon, since we were playing at a charade of civility. The smock lady cleared the bowl and brought a dish with a sandwich on it. The bread was a French baguette, slices of ham, smeared with mustard and crisp lettuce and onions. I ate half of it, trying not to choke the food down. They all watched me in silence.

"And why is the sandwich cold, 47?" Nanny asked when I was halfway through eating.

"You're not smart enough to operate a toaster?"

"Take the food away," she said, and the smock lady did. I didn't fight it. The guard and the doctor watched in silence. "You won't get to eat again for a while, so I hope your jokes were worth it."

"I don't know what answer you want me to give. It's not a question with an obvious answer." I thought of killing her with the sandwich: shove the ham or bread far up both nostrils, clamp a hand over the mouth, watch Nanny struggle.

"The correct answer is—because I said so. That is reason enough. Most people have not been in an environment of absolute control since they were infants. It's an adjustment."

She didn't smile again. "We have many guests who are, and I don't mean to be unkind, soft. You are not soft, 47. Guests like you sadly, often, do not thrive. It's a shame. Now. Tonight you rest. Tomorrow you have your surgery. And then you can eat again, and you can—what is it the Americans say—find your place here."

"What surgery?" I tried to keep my voice calm. This is *bad*, I thought. Of all the situations you've been in, this is the worst. A chill ran its finger along my bones.

Then she did smile, an awful cruel mask. "Dreadful, not knowing, isn't it? We could castrate you. Or blind you. Or cut out your tongue. Maybe we harvest all your organs and so it's really not a surgery you ever wake up from. I guess that depends on how the day goes." She leaned back from me. "I confess, and it's awful, that I sometimes think that would be the best use for some of our guests."

If she wanted to scare me, it was working. I was scared. I had not been this scared since my office in London was bombed and

Lucy, pregnant with Daniel, was kidnapped before my eyes while the street burned.

"What surgery?" I asked again. My voice was barely a whisper.

Nanny got up to leave. She gestured for me to stand. I did, groggily. The guard picked up the table. The smock lady took one chair and the doctor took the other—apparently I was to be left without a chair. So their hands were busy. And I was scared. But I also thought I might not get another chance.

I thought of Marianne, and the corridor in the hotel, and what had worked in that moment.

I grabbed the doctor, yanked him toward me, seized a used immunization syringe in his pocket. The guard started to drop the table and I grabbed the doctor around the neck. With my thumb I yanked back the plunger and jabbed the needle into his throat.

54

Everyone froze. Except Nanny. She smiled and folded her hands serenely in front of her. "But you were off to such a good start. You didn't even cry. Most of them cry. It's so tiresome."

"Here's what's going to happen," I said.

"Yes, tell us," Nanny said.

I hoped I wouldn't collapse. "If you don't do what I say, Doc here gets a giant air bubble in his carotid." He wriggled against me and I made a little shushing sound.

The guard leveled a weapon at me—a pistol—and Nanny said, "Let's be mindful of the doctor's well-being. Let him go."

"We are going back to the delivery bay where you uncrated me," I said. "And you are going to open the doors and we are getting out of here."

"Please," the doctor said. "Please."

"Now. Or he dies," I said.

"Well, I abhor cliché, but if he dies, you die," Nanny said.

"I think you want me alive," I said. "I just have a suspicion. You have to report to Kent on me. He wants me alive."

"If you love something," Nanny said, "set it free." I couldn't decide if her capitulation was a shade too fast. She put a hand on the chest of the guard. "Let them go. Perhaps a touch of exercise will be good for him."

It was not at all reassuring.

The doctor and I backed past the food tray, the smock lady looked pale and frightened. Back into the hallway. Past the doors. A few were now open and as we backtracked I saw a single person sitting on their bed in each one. Wearing an orange jumpsuit like mine. A number written on their chest. Men and woman, old and young. They looked at me with haunted, gaunt faces, eyes bled of energy, flaring slightly in surprise as a prisoner went by holding a syringe in the doctor's neck.

Guests, she'd called them.

This is a prison.

I was practically running backward by the time we went down the hallway. I was afraid of breaking the needle, losing my leverage, so I slowed down. We got to the delivery bay, where the crate I'd come in lay open—and yes, marked with customs clearance stamps and labeled BIOLOGICAL PRODUCTS and DO NOT OPEN WITHOUT PROPER PROTOCOLS and THIS SIDE UP MANDATORY, in Spanish, Portuguese, and English, all with the FastFlex logo—and beyond that was a garage door.

"Open it," I ordered. The doctor hit a button and the door cranked loudly upward.

The door opened into bright sunlight. We were atop a hill and before me lay an expanse of...green. Jungle. Dense. Overgrown. And nothing else. Not another sign of habitation or another person. A dirt road cut into the green and promptly vanished into the wall of growth.

"There is nowhere for you to go. Nowhere," the doctor said.

"Where are we?" I whispered.

"We're not even on a map," the doctor said. I yanked him toward the door and then the guards were pouring in, one of them coming in from outside, and one fired right into my back. The impact against my spine felt like a fist.

Not a bullet. A dart. More drugs. I let go of the doctor, my fingers numb. He yanked the syringe out of his neck.

"Congratulations. I'm the one doing your surgery tomorrow," he said as the blackness crowded out the light.

55

I woke up on a bed. The drugs still snaked through my blood; my body and brain rebelled against them. At least my spirit did. I wasn't bound to the bed. The doctor walked in and looked down at me.

"Good morning, 47." He didn't look the worse for wear, but there was a bandage on his neck. "Running blood work on you, since we shared a needle, and if you've created a problem for me there will hell to pay."

"I'm healthy."

"You were. What you will be in the days ahead remains to be seen. You'll be glad to know the surgery went well." He cracked a smile.

I realized I was looking at him with just one eye. The other was bandaged. My hands flew to the bandage over my right eye. There was no pain. Just a numbness.

No, no, I thought.

He laughed, he *laughed* at me, and then he tore the bandage off. I blinked. His smile came into full focus. My eye was fine.

"The person who shipped you to us doesn't want you maimed. Yet. That's the only reason your thumb isn't on Nanny's necklace."

"What did you do to me?"

"We implanted a tracking chip in you. We always know where you are. You can't cut it out. We own you now, 47."

"I have a name."

"You had a name. Now you have a number and a chip."

"Where are we?"

"Where no one will find you."

"So, do you have a name? Or do you have a number?"

"They call me Mengele. Obviously not my real name. But symbols carry much weight here."

The numbers written on the face. The necklace of bones. A doctor named Mengele, the name designed to unsettle the nerves. All calculated to strip you of identity, to grow the seeds of fear.

"Mengele and Nanny. Charming. Do the guards have pet names?" I sat up slowly and I could feel the bandage on the back of my neck. That must be where Mengele placed the chip. The infirmary looked like a normal hospital room, larger than usual, five beds, well equipped. All the beds were empty except for a woman in her seventies, pale and fragile, sleeping on the other side of the room. One of her wrists was heavily bound.

Two of the guards stood in the doorway, watching me. I waved.

"Nanny will tell you this," Mengele said, "but perhaps you'll believe it from me, since we bonded during your escape attempt. You're not going anywhere. You can fight the system here or you can adapt to it. Those who adapt have a comfortable life. Those who don't, don't. It's common sense, but I am continually amazed at how many people lack common sense."

"I'll take what you said to heart, Doctor," I said. No way I was playing the game and calling this jerk Mengele.

"Come with us," the guard said.

I stood, unsteadily, and got dressed in the numbered jumpsuit they'd provided me.

The guards sat me in a wheelchair and steered me out of the infirmary. "I'll check on you later, 47," Mengele said. His tone was almost kindly.

The guards wheeled me out into the hallway. We went through two locked doors the guards opened with electronic passkeys they kept tethered on their belts, and then we right-turned into a large open area.

And I saw the other prisoners. Men and women both, a range of ages but most of them older than forty, most wearing white jumpsuits, a few in blue or orange, each with their identifying number on it. They sat at tables, talking in small groups, reading books, staring out into space. They all looked at me like the new kid in school coming into the cafeteria. Silence, awkward, fell. There was only the sound of the squeak of the wheelchair.

And then a man in an orange jumpsuit got up and approached me—younger than the rest, heavy-shouldered, blond, eyes like blue ice—and he kicked my wheelchair over. My guards did nothing to stop him; one laughed. I landed on the cold concrete and the pain in my neck flared like a sudden flame.

"You tried to escape," the man said in Hungarian-accented English. "You try, we all suffer. All of us. No food today. Because you tried."

"I didn't know…"

"Not knowing is no excuse. You don't try to escape, idiot!" He kicked at me again, missed, hit my shoulder. The one I'd wounded before, foolishly saving Rey Varela. I didn't feel it through the haze of painkillers.

"Okay, 32, that's enough." The guard produced a baton and pushed the Hungarian back.

"I'm sorry," I said to the room. "Sorry!" Then I repeated it in Spanish, French, German, Arabic, Japanese, trying to cover my bases. A slight murmur arose from the crowd. Then I looked at the Hungarian. "And sorry to you, too," I said in his native tongue. The crowd stayed silent and they watched the guards haul me back into the chair. The Hungarian just stared at me.

Just standard bullying, I thought, but then I looked up and there were four skulls mounted on the wall.

Human skulls.

With numbers underneath them: 2, 5, 15, 19. In what otherwise would look like a simple cafeteria. Watching over us all.

It made me think of the three Varela wives, their portraits on the wall, mournful queens over that house of tragedy and death.

"Lucky you're not fresh up there," the guard said. "'Course, they put the fresh head up on a pole in the yard. Let nature do its work before they put it where everyone has to eat. Then we boil and scrape off the flesh, what's not taken by the birds; I don't think they use a kitchen pot for that, but who knows." He smiled at my involuntary shudder. "We're not animals here."

He wheeled me to Nanny's office. It could have belonged to any chief executive at a major company. A fine desk, a laptop, fresh tropical flowers on the credenza. A narrow window offered a spectacular view of the endless jungle landscape and the empty sky. The glass was thick. Bulletproof.

Nanny sat at the desk. Her dark suit was immaculate. She was reading a file, or at least pretending to study it.

"47! Good morning. I hope your mood has improved. The surgery seems to have gone well."

"Better than I hoped," I said dryly.

"So. What do you think of your new home?"

"32 attacked him in the commons," one of the guards said. "Sort of a group hug from the other guests."

Guests. Please, let me wake up from this nightmare. I shook the thought away. That was the start of surrender, and that was what Nanny wanted.

"Ah. We don't allow violence here. It's unseemly, considering the excellence of the guest list. I'm afraid you'll both have to be punished."

"He attacked me. I did nothing." My voice rose.

"But he attacked you because of what you'd done," the guard said. "So you're responsible as well."

"Logic is so flexible here," I said.

"Sarcasm is a prison we make for ourselves," Nanny answered.

"This is a real prison," I said.

Nanny seemed to ponder the word. "It used to be a prison. Now I prefer to think of it as an information farm."

"And what, we're the seeds? Growing ripe until harvest?"

"Ah. That's clever. You just seem smarter than your file would indicate. Are you who you say you are?" She smiled again.

"Sam Cheval—" The guard slammed the baton between my shoulders. Below the bandage, below the incision. I nearly collapsed from the pain.

"Your number."

"47," I said through gritted teeth.

"You will not find common criminals here, 47. No. This is the cream of the crop. These are minds worth saving, worth delving into, for their secrets. These are people who both their loved ones and their enemies wish to preserve. For a time, at least. They tell me what they want to know and I make it happen." She touched the necklace.

A prison, in the middle of a jungle. With no rules imposed by law or a governmental authority. No outside observers. No rights. No way to communicate with the outside world. A hidden hell.

"The Varelas' clients are...this prison. Who runs it?"

"That's an excellent question. But not one for which you need an answer. In fact, I'm the one who gets to ask questions. Shall we start?" She got up and poured me a paper cup of water. "I always prefer to give a new guest a chance to start out in a civilized manner. Although I must say, I nearly made an exception of you. You understand now how pointless escape is." She touched the necklace again. A psychopath with her little own bureaucracy.

"I see that now." I was done with defiance, at least to their faces. They could track me. There was nowhere to run. I would have to find my own way out, and the only way to do that was to play along for the moment. Otherwise I'd be constantly drugged, or worse, thumbless, and I thought of the empty gazes of some of the guests in the cafeteria. Was that because they were drugged or because hope had died in their hearts? "I'm sorry for the trouble I caused."

"I don't believe you, but I appreciate the sentiment."

"I'm a survivor, Nanny. I always have been. I get along."

"Except with the Varelas." She laughed, amused at her own joke. "Perhaps you shouldn't brag on yourself at the moment."

I said nothing.

"I am very good at sifting," Nanny said. "I am very good at discerning lies from truth. Because I find ways to encourage others to be their best. To share. To not put themselves first anymore. I made my living at it, during a difficult time in my homeland's history. People lived or died depending on whether or not I believed them."

She was so smug. I fought the anger down. I needed to stay cool.

"They want to know what you know about their operations. What Cordelia told you, or what you learned on your own. They want to know who sent you to Cordelia, who you work for. They want to know what your plan was once you tore down Galo and Zhanna. Simple."

"And when I answer all your questions?"

"Then apparently Cordelia wants you back. Functioning in all the important ways. That's why she's cooperated."

She well might, but I didn't think Kent would let that happen. It wasn't the Varelas running the show now, he was. I wouldn't leave here. They would never risk it. This was a permanent exile.

"Shall we begin?" she asked.

"My answers are simple. I am Cordelia's boyfriend. She asked me to come to a family gathering. I used to work in smuggling and I know how to handle myself in a fight. I was never conspiring against Galo and Zhanna or any of the Varelas; I only wanted to protect Cordelia. I was grabbed by the clients—the owners of this prison, I assume—and asked to deliver a message to the Varelas. I did. I didn't kill Zhanna, someone else did, and now I'm here. So, having done what the very owners of this fine establishment wanted, I find myself punished."

"You spied on Kent and Galo and Zhanna."

"I was trying to protect Cordelia."

"She must be something else in the bedroom, to inspire such effort and loyalty. Is it lined with gold?" Her voice was merry for a moment. "None of that here. Unless you take it by force. Or get taken."

I said nothing.

"Who sent you? Who hired you to attack the Varelas? Clearly you're for hire, a clever boy like you. Tell me."

I was in the position of answering an unanswerable question. In a prison. It wasn't a good feeling.

"No one. I met Cordelia, we started dating."

"Dating," she said with a laugh. "Ah, the Varelas are like a *telenovela* some days. Some men who were following Cordelia ended up dead. I think you had a hand in that."

"I don't know anything about that."

"How did you meet her?"

"I worked security at one of her events."

"Yet in her charity's financial records we cannot find a payment to you for security services rendered."

"I worked for a company owned by someone else. He paid me, not Cori."

"What company?"

"Robles Security."

"Owned by Steve Robles, who is now dead. What do you know about his death?"

"I know nothing. It was a tragedy."

"One of the men who killed him met death himself." One? I wondered where Tellez was now. "I could see you being involved."

"I wasn't."

She folded her hands on the desk. "Who sent you?"

"I told you, no one."

"People always try to stand up for themselves, when they first get here," she said. "They take it as their last bit of defiance." She shrugged. "It passes. It's better for you if this passes quickly, not slowly. Answer me."

"It's not like you're going to let me go home." She thought I meant Cordelia. I meant Daniel, and New Orleans. I couldn't let myself think of my baby. It would break me. I couldn't help it. I shivered, I shook, tears came hot to my eyes. *Daniel. I'll get back to you. I promise.*

Nanny misread the wave of emotion. "If you love Cordelia, cooperate with me, and you will go home eventually," she said. "That is a promise from the Varelas, to you. Now. Just one tiny detail. There's a real possibility Sam Chevalier is not your real name."

I stared at her.

Nanny continued: "Now, I was waiting for you to tell me who you truly are. Really, you could have earned some extras by confessing."

"Why would you think it's not my real name?"

She tapped a pen on her folder. She'd tapped a finger earlier, a nervous habit. In this situation you notice and file away everything because you don't know when it will be useful. And anything could be useful. She was a tapper of pens and pencils, I'd remember that. "Sam Chevalier, former Canadian soldier and onetime smuggler specializing in eastern European routes to London and Paris, has normal levels of financial activity for the past two years. But you don't send any e-mails. We can find no history of e-mails used by your identity."

"E-mail isn't secure. I don't use it often."

"But you have the social media accounts. Yet we noticed that all updates done to those, even though they were marked as being posted across a range of dates over the past two years—if you dig into the account's activity log, like we can, you see they were all uploaded in the course of a single hour. And several of your 'friends'' accounts don't seem to be real accounts."

August—or one of his people—had made a mistake.

She leaned forward. "So you are interesting to us. Coming at the Varelas. Becoming Cordelia's friend. Being friends with a man Cori hired to look into her family, a man we tried to pay off and then had to kill." I said nothing and she smiled. "Cordelia has been talking quite a bit in an effort to save you. Yet these blank bits of your history even she can't fill in. Very unusual. Who do you work for? I don't think you are a police officer. The cover would be better."

"I am who I say I am," I said.

"Your friend in Prague. Mr. František Lada. I know that Mr. Varela's people in Europe questioned him. Well, our people will be talking to him as well."

I betrayed no emotion. If Lada vanished because these people took him, and I hadn't been heard from, then August would know my cover had gone bad.

And there would be nothing he could do about it.

"I don't know what to tell you," I said. "I deactivated my social media accounts for quite a while and then reactivated them. That might be how all my postings were reset to the same time. I don't know." I lowered my voice. "Mr. Lada's an innocent man who just tried to help me. He has powerful friends. If you hurt him, they'll come after you."

They were worried I was a spy sent after the Varelas. Simply being Cori's boyfriend meant I was useless, except for keeping Cori in line.

So make them think I was here for another reason. Make Nanny uncertain.

This could be a fast way to lose a thumb. I couldn't be afraid.

I had to be inside here, the way I'd tried to be inside the Varelas.

"You must be scared," I said quietly. "I mean, you think I'm a spy. And yet you've brought me into the heart of your operation. You must be incredibly afraid of what I represent. But you're afraid of the Varelas, too, that they're the weak link in the chain. It would be difficult to move prisoners here secretly without them—far more people involved if each guest is moved by those who want them here. The Varelas are very good at it and it's hard to penetrate a transportation company, especially a long-established one. You really need the Varelas."

"You're delightfully naïve," she said. "You think that the Varelas have a choice? They've never had a choice. They've been owned from day one."

Owned. Someone owned them? Someone who could protect Rey from his past crimes? The government? More like governments, several, around the world. I kept my poker face in place. "Don't underestimate the Varelas," I said. "I did."

"Take him back to his cell," Nanny ordered the guard. "We'll talk more tomorrow. I know your brain must feel clogged by all the chemicals, and perhaps you'll be more forthcoming then."

They took me out of her office. I stayed in the wheelchair. I asked for a glass of water. They took me back to the cafeteria. It was nearly empty, only a few people. I saw the angry Hungarian and he glared at me. His hands were bound in front of him. The guards were eating but the guests weren't, except for cups of water, and the guests looked miserable. I could smell the guards' food—eggs, potatoes, fried meat—and my stomach rumbled loudly.

People stared at me. There were maybe fifteen of them total and I scanned their faces, trying not to alight on any of them, just trying to see who might be angriest with me, who might, other than the Hungarian, be likely to wreak revenge on me for the day's empty stomach. I had to assume everyone was an enemy.

Then I saw, huddled and alone at a table, with that empty, broken gaze, a face I'd seen before.

Only in photos, in the information package that Paige had sent me on the Varela family, in the den of the house in Puerto Rico.

The empty hole in the family. The ghost boy.

Edwin Varela.

56

I DIDN'T WANT to sleep, but it was the smartest move I could have made. My body needed to get out all the chemical filth in it. I needed to think, to put together everything I knew, the whirl of information I'd gotten, the truth that lay behind Nanny's questions and threats. And I had to get healthy and fit if I was going to get out of there.

And I was.

It wasn't my first time being a captive. I'd been held by the CIA when they thought I was a traitor (wrong), and by a major criminal syndicate (underestimating me). In neither case could you say I'd staged an actual escape.

But I was going to get out. No prison was escape-proof. It had a weak point, somewhere. I just needed to find it. And stay alive while I did so.

But there were challenges. This was a big prison but a small population. So it was harder to go unnoticed by both prisoners and guards and, as the new guy who'd tried to escape, I was under heavy scrutiny from both sides. Also, the guards might well kill me as surely as the prisoners. There was no (sane) warden, no prison board, no oversight to keep you alive.

And I needed to find Edwin Varela and talk to him. He'd gotten up and left when the guards were still escorting me. He was here; it wasn't my drug-addled brain. Did Galo or Rey know?

Did Kent—he must, he was the one who'd sent me here. I felt sure Cordelia didn't know.

Edwin might be able to give me the answers I needed, or confirm my coalescing theories.

The prison was a place of routine. Our doors opened at seven a.m. We were to stand in the doorway and wait. When we were all in our doorways, all accounted for, then we were marched to the cafeteria. We stood in line and the workers served us a simple breakfast. Where did the staff live, I wondered, and what did they think this place was? Most of them never spoke except to point at a dish and wait for you to say yes or no. I got my scrambled eggs and a slice of cheese and an orange—no coffee, no hot drinks—and a cup of water. I saw Edwin Varela sitting at a table, with three other men. There was an empty space across from him and I took it.

He glanced up at me for the barest moment as I put down my tray.

No one seemed too happy that I joined them.

What do you say? "Hi. I'm 47," I tried. Socially awkward.

They said nothing. Next to Edwin was a fiftyish man with arms adorned with Yakuza tattoos; another man, in his sixties, who was bald and gaunt and murmured something in French after I'd greeted everyone; and my buddy the Hungarian.

"What do you think we chat about here? Current events?" the Hungarian said.

"I don't know. What do we talk about?"

The Hungarian—32 written on his jumpsuit—shrugged. "What we miss from real life. When they'll let us go."

"They've let people go?" I couldn't keep the surprise out of my voice.

"Yes. There was one prisoner they let go. So the guards said."

So maybe release wasn't an automatic death sentence. They must have some power over people to ensure their silence. The released prisoner was probably dead. But the idea that people could be released to go back home—it gave hope, no matter how thin the sliver. And hope is a cruel promise.

"An American," the Hungarian said, looking at me. "We don't have so many of those."

"Canadian, actually." With the guests I would stay true to Sam Chevalier's identity. Anyone might be an informant for Nanny.

"Even rarer," the Hungarian said.

I glanced at Edwin as I ate. He did not look up from his plate. He looked like Cordelia, for sure you would have known they were brother and sister. But Cori was healthy and vibrant and Edwin looked beaten down.

The Frenchman finished his plate and he and the Japanese man left. Just three of us left. I willed the Hungarian to get up and leave. But he seemed content to wait Edwin out. I didn't dare speak about the Varelas in front of the Hungarian. Edwin finished sipping at his apple juice and got up and wandered away with his tray.

The Hungarian moved down three seats next to me. "No one can decide if you're legit or if you are a plant by Nanny."

"I'm not a plant."

"You showed spine. No one here likes that. No one but me." He laughed. Coldly.

"What do you mean?"

"Look at these nothings. They've been broken into sheep, or they were sheep from the moment they woke up here," he said. "There are no wolves here but me. And maybe you." And to prove his point, he gave me a wolfish smile.

I didn't smile back.

"You are not like the others, 47. I can tell. Lots of rich people here."

"Rich people routinely go missing?"

"No one thinks they are gone. They moved overseas. They are in a sanitarium. They are on a long trip. All sorts of ways to make a person not be missed."

"Why are you here?"

"Last survivor of a gang that pissed off a powerful man in Budapest," he said.

"Why would he keep you alive?"

"I'm his cousin." He shrugged. "He couldn't look my mother in the eye if he murdered me. This is easier. She thinks I live in Australia. I talk to her on phone now and then."

"And you don't ask for help?"

"There is a knife at my throat the entire time. And I had a girl-friend back home. They will kill her, her family, if I don't play along on the phone."

"And your mother buys this?"

"I am a good actor. Motivated. Maybe my cousin will relent soon. I know a lot about the criminal rings in eastern Europe."

Powerful families. Criminal families. This was a place for them to keep their problems. You didn't have to be Michael Corleone and kill your brother in a rowboat. You could ship him to Nanny.

"But he won't let me back until Mama is gone, I think," the Hungarian said. "I've thought about it. He might think I will tell her what he did."

"Would you?"

"No."

"Is your story typical of everyone here?"

"Many of them. Some are related to terrorists or known crim-inals and are used as leverage. Others, I don't know."

"By whom? Who runs this place?"

"I don't know. Sometimes I think it must be US government, you know, like in a movie, a secret back corner or group. Then I think, no, it is criminal gangs, maybe working together. I can't decide." He jerked his head toward a table where a trio of older men sat. "Like those guys, they handled money or websites for terrorists or syndicates and it's easier to break a service provider than an ideologue—maybe they knew who they were working for, maybe they didn't. Some wanted to be terrorists and told the wrong person. Some have ties, personal or professional, to crim-inal rings and need to be kept alive for a while because they're useful. Some here are bad and some are innocent. But here we all are together."

Betrayed family members. Edwin.

I felt cold. I felt angry, too.

The Hungarian said, "See you around," and got up and left. I was the last person at the table.

I closed my eyes. I thought of the burnt man, all his advice he'd given me. I could hear his voice in my head: *You still have to be an inside man. Just here. You have to sell a story that will help you escape. Think, Sam.*

And I realized hearing his voice in my head meant I was losing my grip.

57

I FELL INTO a pattern. The days were structured. Three meals a day. Exercise-yard time. A channel that showed classic old television shows and movies but no current events or news. There was a library stocked with books in a dozen languages. Presumably there was time for interrogations if scheduled. The walls were high. Guards in the turrets. This must have been a real prison once, built for legitimate reasons, and then bought by Nanny or whoever her masters were.

I waited for Nanny to come to me with more questions. She didn't. Somehow that made me more nervous. If I knew what information she wanted, I'd have an idea of what she knew and what she didn't know. Maybe Lada had gone on the run. Maybe they were hunting him. Maybe the CIA was hiding him. Maybe, maybe, maybe.

Each morning I had an exercise period and today was sunny and bright after a few days of rain. An older couple kicked a soccer ball between them. Two younger guys shot baskets.

Edwin Varela sat in the sunshine. He was reading a battered paperback, thick. It was a collection of Shakespeare's plays.

I walked over to him and my shadow fell across his page. "Leave me alone," he said without looking up.

"Edwin?"

He still didn't look up at me, but his finger froze in its tracks along the small print. The finger next to it was missing. The one that had been mailed to Rey. I could see the scar where his ear had been. "25. I'm number 25."

"You're Edwin Varela. I'm Sam Chevalier. I'm a friend of Cordelia's. I know your family. I've been to your house in Puerto Rico."

His maimed hand didn't move along the paper. "I'm 25," he repeated.

"Eddie." I used the family nickname.

"Twenty. Five," he said with emphasis. Now he looked at me.

"I'm going to get out of here, Edwin," I said quietly. "Do you want to come with me?"

Five heartbeats passed. "I'll tell on you."

"If you're strong like your twin sister, you won't."

He looked back at his book. I couldn't see which play he was reading.

"I don't think your father sent you here, Edwin. Did he?"

He didn't answer.

"Was it Kent? He sent me. He talked to me, in the crate."

He didn't answer, but his finger wavered on the page. He closed the worn book and looked past my legs, at the wall.

"Your stepsister Zhanna is dead. Poisoned. She was pregnant."

Now he looked up at me again.

"I'm blamed for her death, but I didn't kill her," I said.

"Who did?"

"Kent. She might have cheated on him."

"With Galo," he said, as if he knew. "Cori and I caught them once. Years ago. They've been off and on for years. Let me guess, my brother's still not married."

"Nope."

"Zhanna's in his blood. He can't commit to her and he can't be without her. They've been stuck for years."

I knelt by him. "Your father is descending into dementia. And he's disowned Cori, because she's tried to get him to stop the smuggling. The family's at war with the group that has them ship people here." I didn't add that I had contributed to the hostilities. "Why are you here, Edwin?"

"Go away. There's nothing to be done." He got up and walked away from me. I let him. He had to be ready to talk to me.

At dinner he sat alone after everyone else had finished eating, his book open. I sat across from him, drinking cold tea.

I was about to speak but he started, as though we were still in the yard, under the bright sunshine. He'd had time to decide he would talk to me. "I was working for Papa and Galo. I thought I found a hole in our security at FastFlex. What I found was their system to ship people. I took it to Kent because I thought I could trust him—and I was too afraid to confront my own father. And now I'm here." He stood up. "But you know that. You're just a spy sent here by Kent. There, I've done what you wanted, I've talked. Now go away and tell him whatever you have to tell him. Does he think he can hurt me any more than he has? All he can do is kill me."

"You've been here four years. Has Kent ever sent a spy before?"

He worked his hands nervously. "Maybe he has and I don't know."

"I'm not a spy, but I am going to get you out of here and back to Cordelia. Would you like that?"

His face contorted. It was as though hope was trying to break free, after being buried in his heart for too long. "Leave me alone." He staggered away from me. I let him go. It was too much at once for him.

One of the guards, an older man, came over to me. "Nanny wants to see you."

As we walked I could feel the weight of his gaze on me. "You look familiar," he said after a moment. "You sure you're not a repeat offender?" His accent sounded Italian. I started to realize that the guards, the staff, weren't local to where we were. Maybe they were loaned out by whichever dark corners took part in filling this prison.

"No. I have one of those faces you think you've seen before."
I glanced at the Italian, studying his features, seeing if the reverse
was true. He didn't look familiar to me.

He walked me to the office and Nanny was locking her file
cabinets. They didn't use a key but rather an electronic combination. *An information farm.* The secrets she must hold, from
these organizations, the information she drew out...it was clearly
worth a lot to whomever she worked for, pulling out tidbits of
knowledge. Money kept people loyal, and so it would be hard to
break that loyalty. I would have to find the weakest link among
the guards.

Maybe it was this Italian who thought I looked familiar. He
was young, a bit thick-looking. Maybe not the smartest guy in the
room. He'd bothered to speak to me, for no good reason, when
none of the other guards had. It was a breach of protocol. You
have to look for the little mistakes. A dumb guard was my inroad
to Nanny on a more regular basis.

Nanny gestured me to a chair. "Do you miss Miami?"

"Yes. I'll be missed when I'm not there. Am I on the news in
Miami?"

"Hardly. We have cleanup crews to make sure our guests'...
absence...from everyday life is explained. No one really seems
to be missing you. Your address—your neighbors don't seem to
know you."

"I'm not neighborly."

"Have you thought some more about telling me who you
really are?" she said.

"I told you my name, which I don't use anymore." I pointed
at my written-on face. "Now I'm number 47."

"Mengele might get a second chance at you." She took off her
glasses, and the smile she offered was so empty, so fake. I kept
thinking she would have shone at any place of intense human suffering. She liked it here. I thought it would be a shame if I didn't
kill her before I escaped. But getting out was all that mattered.
This might be a way. "You have strong hands," she continued,
"and I have space on my necklace."

I said nothing.

"So," she said, "why not cooperate?"

"I have, Nanny. My name is who I am." And I played my first card against her, the one designed to rattle her. "Let's say my name is a fake. Who do you think sent me? If I worked for the police—any police organization—they'd simply pair up with the locals and raid this place."

"Not if they don't know about it," she said. "You've vanished."

"I found a lot in Miami," I said. "I had a long conversation with Zhanna Pozharskaya. She told me quite a bit before she died."

One simple lie is all you need sometimes. Nanny's mouth worked.

"Sort of poetic justice. She forced her mother to take poison…and then someone might have forced her. I admit nothing. But she talked first."

She stood in anger. "Stop these games. Who sent you after the Varelas?" She slapped her hand on the desk, on my file.

"I am frankly more afraid of them than you," I said.

For a moment she was so angry I thought her English was going to desert her. The thumb bones rattled as she leaned forward. "You are not in their power. You are in mine."

"If I told you, you wouldn't believe me," I said. "And I want to tell you, but I can't. Not yet."

"Yet? What are you waiting for? Mengele will get you talking."

I lowered my gaze.

"Take him back to his cell," Nanny ordered the guard. "No food. No water. Tell Mengele to sharpen his scalpels." She looked at me. "I give you tonight to reconsider, and I give Mengele tonight to decide what he does to you. Tomorrow, the scalpel. Think about it."

The Italian guard pulled me to my feet and hustled me back to my cell.

"That wasn't smart," he said. Some people just can't help themselves; they have to be conversationalists. "You should just give her what she asks for. It's always easier."

"I can't. I have to find out what I came here to learn." I knew he'd run straight back to Nanny and repeat this. "She cannot imagine the war she's brought on herself with this." This was the only way to play it, I thought.

An hour later I was marched back to her office.

Nanny shook her head at me. Marching me back before the appointed time was an admission I'd gotten under her skin, and she hated me for it. "Have you reconsidered your situation?"

"I was thinking about it until you brought me here."

"Cordelia Varela has talked. Her family...persuaded her."

A cold beat of my heart.

"She was told you would be tortured and killed if she did not talk, so she did. She said you own a bar in Coconut Grove. The bar has been closed for a few days. There is a woman in Miami who has been coming by the bar every day and checks on it and then she goes to a coffee shop and reads her book, and then her home."

I scratched the number on my face.

"We know her name is Paige. She was fired from the library system because she used a computer there for hacking. Now, that sounds like someone a clever boy like you might know."

I said nothing.

"Is this Paige your friend, 47? I think if she comes back around your bar one more time she will need a distraction from worrying about you." And she touched the bone necklace again. "I adore imported jewelry."

I said nothing.

"Now. This bar, it is the place where the Colombians who work for us killed a man who was asking questions."

"Yes," I said, "he was my entrée to Cori Varela."

"I don't understand. Are you here because of your friend or because you were sent here by someone?"

If the answer was Steve, then I was worthless to them, just an interfering jerk avenging his friend, and a bullet in my head was the obvious solution. So I had to be more. "I was sent here. I was sent first to Miami to make friends with a Varela. I did so through Steve Robles's connection to Cordelia Varela."

"By whom?"

"I can't tell you yet. Soon. But not yet."

Rage trembled her mouth. "I can have both your thumbs."

"You hire all the guards, all the support staff, right?" I said. She blinked at the sudden change in subject. "So if someone wanted to check on you...on your work...they'd send a prisoner."

Her eyes blazed. "Are you saying *you* were sent here to spy on *me*?"

"I'm not saying anything more."

"Take him back to his cell," she said to the guard. "Tomorrow afternoon, Mengele gets to play with you. I urge you to change your mind."

That night I listened and chartered the rhythms of the night. We were in our rooms by nine. The lights all went out at ten. I went to the doors and I listened. I could hear the guards making their rounds. It was a small prison—a walk-through each hour. At seven the doors unlocked, as if at once, and we stepped out. The Hungarian was four cells down from me. Edwin was not on our hallway. That was going to be a problem.

I didn't sleep well; I wondered if Nanny did. I thought not.

58

THE NEXT MORNING I heard the door to my cell unlock. I opened my door and stood in the doorway until the guard gestured to the guests. I followed the thin throng to the commons. I didn't look up at the four skulls watching over our breakfast. I got a tray of food and I sat alone at a table. I saw Edwin get his tray of oatmeal and an apple and he hesitated. He didn't go to his regular spot with the Hungarian and the older men.

"You understand there is no way out," he said, by way of greeting, as he sat across from me.

"Hasn't anyone ever tried?"

"Yes. Two before I got here. Two more, about a year after I got here. You see the daily reminder up on the wall."

I glanced at the skulls.

"They brought them back," Edwin said.

"And?"

"They made us watch. Nanny cut off their thumbs, with a hatchet. And then the guards put ropes around their necks and hung them in the exercise yard, by the basketball court. I guess whoever sent them here decided they didn't want to keep them here, given the attempt."

"And that broke everyone."

"Most of them were kind of broken already if you ask me.

The two guys who ran, they were ex-soldiers. Most of us have no training in fighting."

"No chance of a rebellion? There are more of us than them."

"Most wouldn't try." He couldn't keep the bitterness out of his voice. "They think they'll get to go home at some point if they cooperate." Amazing, the human capacity for self-delusion and misplaced hope, I thought.

"Home has a strong pull."

Edwin went silent, jabbing his oatmeal with his spoon as a guard wandered by us.

"What?" I asked.

"Did my father send me here?"

"I don't think so. Everyone seems to believe you're dead. Cori misses you terribly. Kent must know. Would Zhanna have cared?"

"Zhanna is—was—a monster. She and Kent both." Edwin put down his spoon. "My father knows he's involved with this prison and I go missing and he doesn't ask if I'm here? That makes no sense."

"I know. Maybe they assured Rey you weren't. He seems to believe you were kidnapped strictly for ransom. He paid it twice. Ten million total."

Edwin breathed the words "ten million" back to me. "But… who would he have paid that to? He works for whoever runs this prison. Why would they have extorted money from him, why?…" His mutilated hand moved to his mutilated ear. "You mean maybe just to convince him normal kidnappers took me?"

"It's possible," I said. "This place. Who do you think runs it?"

"You mean, other than Nanny?" He shook his head. "I don't know. It's a very weird mix of guests."

"Ties with terrorism and crime," I said. "Who would dare to own a prison like this?" I considered my own question. "The guards. One is Italian, at least one is Spanish, two speak Portuguese with Brazilian accents."

"In the past we've had Russians. Brits. American guards," he whispered.

"Why import guards? Maybe they're not hired. Maybe they're sent here. On a duty rotation."

Edwin bit his lip in thought.

"She collects information. If this is a private business, she sells it. But I don't think she sells it. I think she gives it." I looked hard at Edwin. "Your father moved a lot of weapons. He broke the law a lot, but the US government, and some other governments, protected him. Because, sometimes, war is in their interests. And they gave him legitimate work, a lot of it."

"You think the government runs this place? Like another Guantánamo?" He shifted in his seat. "When I found the security holes at FastFlex, Kent said it was secret government work we were doing…since we'd shipped so much equipment and cargo to Iraq and Afghanistan, I believed him. And then he shot me—with a tranquilizer dart. Who expects Kent to shoot them?"

"I encountered that same problem," I said.

"But I can hardly see Kent as a government agent. He's always worked for us…"

"There are skulls up on the walls, Edwin. This isn't a normal government prison. Think of who your dad's clients were, back when he was starting out. I think maybe this is a back dark corner of a government," I said. "After all, your father worked for anyone who would pay him. Back corners of governments and warlords and smugglers. Maybe the dark corners all got together. Pooled resources. Built this to be shared." I stared at him. "Your father said something to me about the CIA and south Florida. All the money the agency poured into the area, funding companies that could be used in operations against Castro. I had a bunch of guys who wanted to sound like Russians grab me and take me to a restaurant off Calle Ocho. One Ricky went to."

"His grandfather owns a restaurant there," Edwin said. "He's owned it for years."

"They grabbed me and one spoke Russian to me, but with a bad accent," I said. "Who does that? Who pretends to be Russian in Miami?"

Edwin shrugged.

"Who has a non-native Russian speaker at hand? The CIA. Maybe the FBI." I knew that well enough. "But why bother? Why try to trick me?"

"I don't know."

"Because this...isn't run by a Russian gang. But they wanted me to think it. There's a reason."

Edwin fell silent.

"Surely the prisoners here have theories," I said.

"Everyone just thinks their enemy has paid to keep them here. And it doesn't matter if their enemy is a politician or official or gangster." Steel came back into his gaze. Maybe for the first time in a long while, having to talk about Kent and his father and Ricky and what had been done to him. "So. How do we get out?"

"You've been here four years, I was hoping you would know." I ate some of my own oatmeal. "Nanny's patience with me is wearing thin. Is there a way out?"

"Supposedly this was a prison built by the Brazilian government, deep in the Amazon," he said. "The drug rings started killing whoever was in charge of finishing it as an act of defiance. So the government stopped building it, and a private investor bought it."

Brazil. It was oddly reassuring to know at least which country I was in.

"How do you know?"

"One of the guards told me."

"The baby-faced one with the Italian accent?"

"Yes. He likes to talk. He's easily bored."

"He's our key."

Edwin shook his head. "You can't bribe your way out. You can't burrow out. You can't climb your way out. Or swim your way out, we're in the middle of a jungle."

Swim. Water's the key to life, in more ways than one. An idea hovered at the edge of my mind. But I didn't want to share my thoughts with him on how to get out quite yet.

"I saw when I tried to get out that one side is solid jungle. What's the other side?"

"It's *all* solid jungle. But we have to get out first. And there's no way to get blueprints of this place," he added.

"They have to exist. Probably in Nanny's office. They would need it for repair work. You have to know where wiring, junctures, plumbing are to fix them."

"Getting into her office is about as easy as breaking out of here."

"Let me think," I said. "Let me think." I only had a couple of hours before Nanny put me under Mengele's scalpel.

And then I saw the answer.

59

I DID THE math.

Forty-seven prisoners, minus the four heads on the wall.

Nine guards among the prisoners. Double and round up to ten more outside on the perimeter. I'd counted a kitchen staff of four to prepare the simple meals we ate. Mengele. Nanny.

Sixty-eight souls, assuming Nanny had a soul. I remained unconvinced.

And sixty-eight souls needed water. A lot of it.

Where did the water come from and where did it go?

No one watched you. I mean, there were cameras, and the doors were locked. But we were free to wander. I went to the library. I browsed. I figured as the newest guest I would be watched. But the guards did not seem that interested in me.

Edwin followed me to the library and sat alone at a table while I walked among the shelves. I got the sense reading was his lifeline. He was reading his Shakespeare again. I had to agree that here Shakespeare might be a comfort, a way of knowing there was still beauty and thoughtfulness in the world.

"I have a way out," I said, very quietly.

He stared at me as though I were crazy.

"Will the Hungarian help us? Can we trust him?"

Edwin nodded, surprised that I sounded so confident. "He's tough and he'll fight. Those are his only virtues."

"What about yours?"

"I don't get rattled and I was a Boy Scout."

"We could end up mounted on the cafeteria wall," I said.

"They'll probably put my four-fingered hand above my skull," he said, and I decided right then that I was going to save Edwin Varela. Not just for Cori. But because I couldn't help but like and respect him. And I wanted him to have his life back.

"Tell him I have a way out."

Edwin laughed for the first time I'd seen. "He won't believe you."

"Convince him. But we have to go, now, Edwin. I think your sister is in extreme danger from these people. Stay close to the cafeteria. Be ready to run."

"How can you…"

"I'm CIA, Edwin." I forgot to mention *former*. But I needed to have him believe in me. "And I am going to get you out of here."

He gave me a look of disbelief. "In the prison escape movies, they plan for weeks."

"We don't have weeks. We have now."

60

I FOUND THE biggest, heaviest book in the library. It was a history of England. I picked it up and I told Edwin to get me a pencil from the desk. I stood at the end of a row of books. I'd studied the surveillance cameras earlier, and this was my best guess for a blind spot in the camera coverage. Pencils weren't allowed, apparently, but there was a felt-tipped pen. Edwin handed me the pen and I told him to get a book and sit and read at his usual spot.

I turned to the middle of the book and I began to underline random letters. Edwin watched, confused. I marked the pages for a couple of minutes and then I gestured him over.

I whispered, "Find the Hungarian and wait for me in the cafeteria. I may not be in these clothes when you see me next, so be prepared."

I left the library, and in the courtyard I found the Italian guard watching two middle-aged men listlessly shooting baskets.

"I've considered Nanny's offer and I've decided to take your good advice, as I don't want Mengele cutting on me. Will you please tell her that I'd like to make an appointment to see her?"

He smiled. "Yes."

"But," I said, "I'll only tell her and you what I've learned. Because it affects the staff here. I know something about who is being sent here to staff the place. Something Nanny doesn't know. There's a spy here."

His face paled. He frowned. He grabbed my arm and he took me straight to her office. I was still carrying the big, heavy history of England.

It was a strange feeling to know I'd either be free or dead in a matter of minutes.

61

I NEED TO speak to the two of you alone," I said to Nanny.

She glanced at the other guard. The Italian nodded.

"Why?" she asked.

I gestured at the big book. Now, when you do something that seems completely illogical, people either start to question you endlessly or they let you talk. "You don't need to bother František Lada about me. I work for the CIA. For a special division inside the CIA. Sam Chevalier is an identity from that division—if you have a CIA contact, they may be able to confirm that. I couldn't say until I could prove what I came here to prove. Which I can only say to you and my friend here."

She digested this news over ten seconds of silence. "Leave us," she said to the other guard, who was still standing in her office. In the reflection of the thick glass overlooking the jungle I could see the guard step out, muttering to the Italian, who patted him on the shoulder. And I saw the Italian put his hand close to his gun's holster. Not a complete fool. Then he closed the door, and it was only the three of us in the office.

"You like the dramatic," Nanny said.

"I'm here because someone has been passing sensitive information from the prison to outside interests. It's not coming from you, Nanny. Someone on your staff is conducting unauthorized interviews with the...guests. They're passing information they should be giving to you to another source."

"Impossible," she said. "I'd know if someone were interrogating the guests."

"The guests are passing information through marking in a code in this book. The staff member is then gathering the information and passing it out of the prison. Selling it. Information that frankly belongs to us," and I made my voice imperial, "and that we, and you, are being cheated out of."

Her gaze narrowed at me, suspicion clouding her face. "Why didn't you just come to me, then?"

"Because I needed to make sure you yourself weren't the problem. That you weren't circumventing your own system. For your own profit."

Her lips thinned. "Show me what you mean," she said. "Prove what you're saying."

I tossed the heavy book on her desk. It made a big, satisfying thud. "The most recent message is on page 456. The pages with consecutive numbers, such as that one, seem to be favored: you know, 123, 234, 345."

She stared at me and the Italian took a step forward, curious. Nanny flipped open the old, heavy book, with its small print and lavish illustrations, and bent over the pages.

"You'll note," I said, using the voice I'd used when standing in front of a PowerPoint presentation to CIA bigwigs on how we were infiltrating the worst criminal and terrorist groups, "that certain letters are underlined. When you put them together, it makes an encoded message."

She looked up at me, then put her finger on the first underlined letter and began to search for the second one. I waited until, with her other hand, she pulled a pad of paper and that sharpened pencil she always liked to tap on her desk.

She held the pencil upright.

You have to be fast and ruthless. It was me or them, and no negotiation.

With all my strength, I slammed my hand into the back of her head and her face smashed into the heavy weight of the book. Before she slid off the desk I had her pencil in my hand and I spun. With the same hand I'd hit her with I slammed a palm over the Italian guard's mouth and I drove the pencil into his eye.

He was dead before he hit the floor. I checked Nanny. Broken nasal bone driven backward toward her brain but she was gurgling, not dead yet. I tightened the necklace of thumbs around her throat and the bones of her victims pressed deep into the flesh. She stopped gurgling.

I dropped her, dead, to the floor.

I pulled an electronic passkey free from her stylish belt. I took the Italian's gun out of its holster, checked the clip, clicked off the safety. Nanny's computer was open and I could see camera feeds from around the prison on her screen. The yard, an empty interrogation room, the main desk at the library, hallways. And the cafeteria, where Edwin and the Hungarian stood, waiting for me. There was an icon marked "Security Status" and I clicked on it and it gave me a map of the complex, with green lights indicating all was well. The prison was ringed with four towers and there were guards in those towers. Ready to shoot anyone who tried to scale the wall.

We would not be going that route.

I took Nanny's phone. It had cell coverage, out here in the vast nowhere, so it had to be a satellite phone. The Italian had one as well, and I stuck one phone in each of my pockets.

I went back to studying the map of the facility. The bottommost level had power lines and plumbing, presumably carrying waste away to a river or a treatment facility. I searched for wastewater on the computer and found a document, in English and Portuguese, that outlined the system the prison used. It fed into a remote treatment tank and then into a river. The lines were tagged for repair people to be able to find them.

And that was my plan, in short: Follow the pipes to the broad stripe of a river. A river will eventually lead you to civilization.

But how to get out? There were outside access doors on the bottom floor, double-locked and reinforced, forbidden to prisoners, where the repair people could go. The map showed a security station down the hall from Nanny's office. Nine guards, but who knew how many were sleeping elsewhere in the facility? There wasn't a camera in the staff quarters; they had privacy.

But first I had to get past the guards.

I put on the Italian's uniform. Sometimes a second's delay or indecision is all you need. Plus, he had better shoes than I did and I faced a jungle trek. I put on his cap, pulled it snug on my head.

Deep breath. Thinking in terms of space, movement, and aim, I made my heart cold.

I opened the door.

The guard Nanny told to wait outside turned toward me and I shot him in the eye. The gun was loud in the concrete confines of the hallway and as he fell another guard raced around the corner from the security office and I shot him, catching him in the throat. He fell and lay gurgling and I couldn't listen or think about that as I ran past him toward the security office.

Behind bars and a thick green layer of bulletproof glass were two guards. Both stared at me in surprise as I used Nanny's passkey to open the door's electronic lock. I raised the gun and shot the first one, and the second one dove behind the desks. Two seconds later he hit a button, I presumed, because an alarm sounded—a deafening, shrill clarion. He aimed a shotgun at me from behind his desk and I ducked as he fired. Then I vaulted over the desk, feet first, my feet slamming into his rifle as he raised it again, and I shot him in the head.

I could see the facility on his map, but along with the alarm the phones were ringing and I knew other guards would be racing here. Four guards dead on this floor; I might have a minute or two. On his computer screen there was a block of text reading LOCKED on each of the main doors and I pointed and clicked with the mouse and the word changed to UNLOCKED.

I clicked them all to UNLOCKED. All of them.

On another computer monitor, a screen showed the tracking devices that violated our bodies. All of them, each prisoner's position a tiny green number. It showed who you got close enough to talk to, how long you spoke to them, where you were at any given second. It was in a window titled "Dermascan"; that must be the software's name. I found the Dermascan icon in the server's applications folder and dragged it to the screen's trash icon and emptied it. The numbers on the scanners all vanished—and presumably vanished from every computer in the network.

I fired into the computer's hard drive. I couldn't think of what else to do, and that twenty seconds might buy us several minutes.

I scooped up the shotgun along with the headset the security guard was wearing, slipped the headset into my ear. I saw a sign on a back-room door: ARMORY. I ducked inside and found another gun, which I stuck in my holster, and grabbed two concussive charges. There was a satchel, and I dumped four more guns and shotgun ammo into it. I moved quickly but I was careful. On the dead guard's earpiece I heard a babble of men reporting in, asking for Nanny to report, for the security desk to report. At the desk there was an intercom control and I spoke into it, in English, because that seemed the lingua franca of the prison. My voice boomed over the loudspeakers.

"The doors are open. Nanny and several guards are already dead. If you want to risk a run, run for it. Fight and run. The doors are open, but the guards are armed. But there are fewer of them now."

Later I would think this was unfair, but you can't prepare everyone. Those who wanted to run and hide under their beds and not take the risk, they could. Those who wanted to take the risk and fight, even though it might mean death, they could. And I wasn't sure who I was unleashing on the world. Good, innocent guys like Edwin, or maybe bad guys. But this secret prison, with no charges filed and no trials, with too many innocent people kept as leverage, mangled with tracking implants, and funded with hidden money, was not and never could be a good place. I could sleep at night, assuming I survived.

A guard hesitated as I hurried down the stairs, coming out of the medical lab, seeing my uniform more than my face. I blasted him with the shotgun and he flew back into the infirmary. Mengele looked stunned, holding up his hands. He held a scalpel, presumably for self-defense.

"Drop it," I said. "Grab a medical kit, and come with me."

He stared at the dead guard, splayed out in his own blood.

"You have three seconds to start moving or I will kill you."

He obeyed me, the scalpel clattering to the floor, and grabbed a white kit. I hurried him to the cafeteria, and there we ran into chaos.

What happens when people are wrongly kept for weeks, months, years? Either their spirit wilts and they cannot fight when the chance comes, or the tiniest spark of soul remains and the human spirit's longing for freedom roars from ember to flame. And I wondered if there was a resentment about seeing daily the skulls of those who had dared defiance, of Nanny wearing human remains as her obscene jewelry. Inside the hallway two of the older women were fighting a guard, their hands pulling at his revolver, clawing at his eyes, him fending them off. The women looked up at me and saw me, a "guard" walking with Mengele, and screamed and raised their hands in surrender. The guard they'd been attacking glanced up at us and I shot him.

"Run," I told the women. They stripped the guard of his gun and baton and fled. I reloaded.

In the cafeteria there was chaos. Guards and staff fighting, two prisoners dead on the floor, and I opened fire with the shotgun, ripping off the cap so the prisoners could see it was the new guy, the bandage from my tracker still on the back of my neck, the 47 mark still blackly written on my face. Four more guards went down, their weapons looted from them, their batons turned against them. I unlocked the kitchen using Nanny's passkey. Prisoners swarmed into the kitchen, arming themselves with the forbidden knives and skillets and whatever they could get to hand.

"Run," I yelled. "Run!"

I hurried Mengele toward Edwin and the Hungarian. They had taken a baton from a guard and whipped him unconscious. I gave them each a gun from the satchel. The Hungarian handled his with ease, Edwin with determination.

"All right," I said. "Lowest level. Where's the passageway?"

"There's not one," Mengele interrupted. "You're an idiot; you'll get us all killed."

"This way," the Hungarian said. I hurried them down to the lower-level doorway, and it was still unlocked from my computer command. A few other prisoners followed us, others ran amok, others hid. To each their own.

In the dark of the basement I hunted and finally found the plumbing array that would lead out of the facility. It'd taken longer than I thought, and panic rose in my chest. I could hear gunfire on the floor above.

We found the service door I'd seen on Nanny's computer display, but it was now locked. I slid in the passkey. Red light. Someone must have locked out the codes in the past few minutes.

I fired the shotgun into the lock. It shattered. We pried open the door. There was another barred door over the exit. I shot out that lock too, but it didn't give. I moved everyone back toward a far wall, near a second door marked ARCHIVES. I wondered how many secrets were there. It didn't matter.

I activated the concussive charge and ran back toward the Hungarian, Edwin, and the others. The charge rolled against the door and it exploded. My ears rang with the echo of the blast. The bars held, but the hinges were damaged enough for the Hungarian to push the door open.

Sunlight. We stumbled onto a grassy area kept free of jungle growth. I remembered the map. The trail of the pipes was marked with little bright-orange flags. I could see patches of orange wavering in the distance at the edge of the jungle. That was our path.

"The guards in the tower may shoot, or they may be busy containing the riot," I said, talking in what I hoped wasn't a yell, my ears ringing from the blast. "We run for the jungle. They may shoot at us from the towers. Don't stop. If they shoot me, follow the orange tags at the beginning of the jungle; they mark the water pipe, so follow them to the river."

We ran. Halfway across, a Chinese woman who had bolted toward the front disintegrated in a blast, an explosion erupting from the soft green lawn, consuming her.

The field was mined.

Smoke and dirt and blood clouded the air. The others screamed. A couple stopped, frozen. The rest kept running.

What else can you do? "Keep running!" Edwin yelled at the others. A shot rang out and I saw an older man go down, but the cloud from the blast seemed to obscure the air, making it harder for the guards in the towers to shoot.

We ran, the Hungarian manhandling Mengele along. To my right there was another explosion, anguished screams. I saw part of an arm land in front of us.

"This is insane!" Mengele yelled.

Before we reached the wall of jungle the Hungarian and Mengele had pulled ahead of me and then they stopped, caught. Strings of barbed wire, colored green, nearly impossible to see. Then I spotted the thin posts holding them in place, fifteen feet away.

Mengele screamed.

"Wire, wire!" the Hungarian yelled, trying to warn the others, trying to pull himself free. I skidded to a stop, went on the ground, crawling. Shots rang out. I found the thin post and I put the last concussive charge against it, set it, and ran back toward the Hungarian.

"What are you doing?" Mengele screamed. "Wait!"

The post shattered. The wire sagged and its barbs tore at both Edwin's hands and mine as we freed our friend and the doctor. Fragments and dust filled the air, giving us a few moments' cover. Mengele was bleeding; the Hungarian was hurt, lacerated by a bit of the post. But the fence was down and we ordered the others to come this way, follow our voices through the cloud of heaved dirt and smoke.

We reached the wall of jungle. We'd lost four. Ten of us left.

"You'll never make it," Mengele said, panting. "Snakes, quicksand, predators, disease-carrying insects. We have no food or water. And maybe they've mined the jungle for the next kilometer or so. You're days from civilization. There's no road. They helicopter everything in and there's not a copter here today." He pointed at an empty landing spot, close to the wall of the jungle. "There's a reason they built it here, idiots."

"What happens to us happens to you. Unless I shoot you first," I said.

"Which way?" Edwin said.

"We follow the subterranean pipe to the river. Then downstream to a village. It may take us a few days. But we're free."

"They'll come after us," the Hungarian said.

"I don't think so," I said. "Where do they get backup in time? They'll try to hold the fort, so to speak, and call for reinforcements." I touched my bandage. "These locators, if they're GPS chips, they won't penetrate the triple canopy of the jungle. It'll hide us until we reach a village."

"And then what, then they'll know where we're at," Edwin said.

"I have an idea."

"How will we get home?" a woman asked.

"First things first. River, village."

From behind us we heard gunfire, and I didn't know who was shooting. I told the Hungarian to get everyone moving forward.

"What are you doing?"

"The same jungle canopy that blocks the GPS in the trackers will keep the satellite phone from working. Get everyone under cover and wait for me; I'll catch up with you. Follow the orange flags. Don't go too far. I'm going to make a phone call." He moved the group forward and the green closed around them. And then I opened up Nanny's satellite phone, before anyone back at the prison thought to cancel or track it, and I made a phone call to Mila.

62

My new suit felt good, with a crisp, fresh white shirt. Good clothes can make all the difference in your attitude. I felt ready, despite the cuts and the sunburn flush across my nose; the nearly scrubbed-clean ghost of the number 47 on my cheek; the stick of the fresh bandage and stitching on the back of my neck. It had been ten days since our escape from Nanny's prison in the wild.

I smiled at the flight attendant as he collected our empty glasses. We were in first class.

"You look like you're happy to be back in Miami," he said.

"Oh, we are," I said. Next to me, Edwin stared out at the skyline, the one he probably thought he'd never see again.

The morning flight landed and we didn't have luggage, only backpacks bought in São Paulo. Mila waited outside in a Mercedes and we climbed into the backseat together.

"Hi. Mila, this is Edwin Varela," I said.

"Lovely to meet you, Edwin. And you're welcome, Sam," she said as she drove into the exit lanes.

"I think I've said thank you multiple times," I said. "But thank you again." Mila had flown in a team to help extract our little band once we reached a village three days after the escape (including two doctors, who relieved us of our subcutaneous trackers). Her people had gotten me and Edwin passports, wired money, arranged travel. The team also dispatched Mengele, whose real

name was Menendez, along with the other survivors, to a Round
Table location for debriefing and assistance. I was fairly sure said
location was my bar in Rio de Janeiro, which sat inside a high-rise
hotel owned by the Round Table, where they all could be hidden
until we figured out what to do with them. I'm sure the Hungarian was having a great time. No one could go home yet. Except
Edwin and me.

The Round Table, the CIA no one knows about. Mila and
Jimmy didn't want to tell me its secrets. Did I really want to
know? Not now. Not while they were useful to me. "What is the
situation this morning?" I asked.

"Ricky is presumed guilty in Zhanna's poisoning. There was
evidence he'd been in the apartment. A combination of poisons
found in his house. Financial records indicating she'd been em-
bezzling from the company and feeding him money. And notes
left between them. A relationship—she ended it; he took it badly.
The police are looking for him. I suspect he's at the bottom of
the bay, put there by the Varelas to prevent too many police eyes
looking too closely at their business. Already the story has begun
to fade a bit from the papers."

"All neatly manufactured. And the police bought this?" I
asked.

"They've looked very hard at Kent, obviously. The wronged
boyfriend. But Ricky's rather nasty past is making for a good alibi
for the family in regards to Zhanna's death."

"Was there a DNA test on her baby?" I asked.

"Yes," Mila said. "The baby was Kent's."

I felt punched. I was sure it was Galo's, just because Zhanna
was sure.

"What about Coma Thug?" Carlos Tellez had been the other
ticking time bomb in my life, if he talked about being chased from
my bar.

Mila glanced at me. "We monitored police communications.
According to an e-mail sent by the detective assigned to the case,
he finally asked to make a phone call to a lawyer but instead of
calling an attorney here in Miami, he called an unlisted number

in Virginia from a hospital phone. Two days later he was dead. Aneurysm. He never gave any statement to the police or answered questions."

"Silenced," I said. Or maybe his injuries really had caught up with him. Maybe the number he called was whatever back corner of the government had contributed to Nanny's prison. I remembered they'd found a matchbook from a Washington bar in his pocket. "Did you get that number?"

"We haven't hacked into the hospital phone records yet. By the way, Paige is a gem and I think you should hire her as a manager. She's working on getting that number."

"Has Cori come by looking for me?"

"She did the first day. Not since."

Because after that first day she knew I was in Kent's power, at his mercy. "I'm sure she's being watched. And I don't want Kent knowing we've returned. No doubt he knows that the prison escape happened."

"Does he?" Mila asked. "The Varelas are just a transport arm, used only when needed. They may not be privy to more information."

"Surely they'd warn him. Ricky is dead; Kent has lost his 'eyes' here in the family, because I think that's what Ricky was to him. Together they would be able to keep the Varelas in line for the clients. Trusted, and close to being family, and above suspicion. Just like how Zhanna's mother was their spy."

"So where do we go, Sam?" Mila asked. "I am not fond of being your chauffeur. Also, you have a nice suit but your face, ugh, the jungle didn't agree with you."

"I want to see my family," Edwin said. "Well, my sister at least."

"I know, but we have to be careful. You can't just reappear and announce you're back. The news media will want to know where you've been for four years."

"So what do we do?" he asked. He wanted the people behind the prison burned to the ground, and I didn't blame him, but he was furious and impatient and I'd spent days convincing him not to go straight to the press in Rio, to play it my way. I thought I had him convinced. But Edwin could ruin everything with a single phone call to the Miami newspaper or a cable television channel. So I had to give him what he wanted, even at a risk.

"You want to see Cori. Okay." I dialed Cori's number. She answered on the third ring.

"Cordelia. It's Sam."

Her voice was a whisper. "Oh my God, where are you?"

"Close. I'd like to see you."

"What…I don't know if that's possible. They watch me now. All the time."

"That's okay. How many follow you?"

"Two guys. They look like FBI agents. Dark glasses, suit."

"Okay, so they follow you. Let's flush them out. Come to The Barnacle park in Coconut Grove; it's right by the bar. Walk down past the old house, down to the mangroves and the woodworking shop. I'll see you then."

"But if they follow me…"

"I'll deal with them."

"Sam, Papa—he's gotten much worse. He's raving most of the time. Zhanna and Ricky dying, it's unhinged him. The clients threatened me. And Galo. We have to stay quiet…"

"We'll get your father some help." Beside me I felt Edwin get tense. "How is Sergei?"

"Not well. Zhanna's death has undone him. Even with all the bitterness—she was still his daughter." And wasn't that the awful truth? Death made a family division complete. I just wondered if he'd made his move yet to take over the business.

"Meet me at the park. Twenty minutes." I hung up.

Edwin gripped my arm. "You didn't tell her I'm with you."

"Let's see how she reacts," I said.

"I can't believe this. I'm home." Edwin stared out at the passing sights of Miami like it was Wonderland.

63

The Barnacle State Park was a strip of land used as a dock by Coconut Grove's original families—both Anglo settlers and Bahamian immigrants—to bring in supplies. A building original to the settlers stood in the middle and you walked down a tree-lined path to reach it (being asked to abide by an honor-system donation of a couple of dollars—I dropped in a ten, in case of damage in the next few minutes). It led down to a boatwright's workshop and an old dock, edged with mangroves, that had been there long before man and would be there long after. Edwin waited in the shadow of the woodworking shack, watching a man plane the wood of a boat. I wondered if the boatwright only worked when a tourist stood close by.

"I'm shaking," Edwin said. He blinked at me.

"She loves you."

I went and stood on the other side of the house, out of sight, cell-phone ear bud in place so I could hear Mila. From my spot I could see Edwin, and I could see the one path Cori could take down toward the boatwright's studio.

Edwin waited, fidgeting. He wasn't used to life without rigor, without guidance.

I saw Cori. And I saw Galo, walking with her. They hurried past the house and then I heard Cori give a shocked, brief little cry. I watched from the corner. Edwin had raised his hand in a slight, shaky wave.

Cordelia and Galo froze for three long seconds and then she screamed and ran for Edwin. He ran toward her. The twins threw themselves into each other's arms, Cori sobbing. Galo hurried up behind them, disbelief and joy fighting on his face, and the twins made room for him to join the hug.

The three children of Rey Varela brought back together, happy for a moment, siblings not dealing with their opposite three: an amoral father, a monstrous stepsister, a scheming, backstabbing adviser.

I blinked. Something in my eye.

Then Mila's voice in my ear: "Trackers at six o'clock relative to you." She was positioned near the park's entrance.

I turned. Two men, in jeans and short-sleeved shirts, ear buds in, watching the reunion. One turned immediately and walked away.

"One heading back to you," I said.

"I see him. He's so darling. I'll stop him for a little chat."

I saw the other one watching and he began to move forward, toward the Varelas, and I ran out of the shadows and punched him. There weren't any tourists around and the park employees were inside the old settler house. It was a good punch, devastating, and he lifted up off the ground and smashed into the path. I picked him up and dragged him by his collar past the house, around some bushes, and into the restroom building. I kicked the door shut and propped him on the toilet. He was starting to come around, spitting blood. My hand was bloodied where it had caught a tooth.

"I'd like to know who you work for," I said. "Kent? Did he send you?"

The guy's gaze wasn't quite focused. I pulled his cell phone out of his pocket. "Did Kent send you?"

Dazed, he nodded.

"CIA?"

He wouldn't answer. I yanked his phone, checked the call log.

Last call to a northern Virginia area code. The dark shadow, coming to life. I pressed the number.

"Grantham Pet Store."

I thought this was right up there with New Horizons Dental Care. "You tell Kent Severin to withdraw from Miami. You tell him to pack up his crew and leave the Varelas alone."

"Sir, you have the wrong number. This is a pet store."

"I'm the guy that shut down the prison in Brazil," I said. "Don't mess with me. You connect me to whoever's in charge."

"This is a pet store, sir."

"I took this phone from your man following the Varelas. I am going to shoot him if you don't connect me to your boss."

"One moment, sir." Ten seconds later a woman's voice came on the line. "Yes?"

"I bet your hired Colombian in the Miami hospital called this number, as did the guy following the Varela family. It stops now. It's over. Over. You pull out Kent Severin and whatever leftovers were backing Ricky."

"You certainly are full of demands," the woman said.

"You are certainly full of problems. Prison's emptied, survivors ready to tell the press about you, and you've lost your transport arm. Life is tough at Omega Investments, isn't it?" Just a stab, just a guess.

It hit home. I heard the woman's angry intake of breath. "And if I give in to your demands, then what?"

"Then you leave the Varelas alone. Forever. No more underside business with them. Or I will go to the press with what I know."

"That would destroy them too."

"Maybe. Or maybe they cut a deal with the federal prosecutors here in Miami. Rey Varela's given a lot to this town. He bought his respectability. He's mentally slipping. They'd probably make him one more deal."

"Maybe him. But one of his kids would have to take the blame. Life's unfair that way."

"You're about to find out how unfair life is. I have the resources to come after you. I really want to come after you. But I think you're going to find yourself shut down soon enough, because you've gone from being an information feed to an information leak. A scandal. A career-ender. You're going to get shut down and your dirty little crowd will scatter to the winds, and I think that's all I can hope for. But if you aren't, I will find out. And I'll come for you."

"I'll find out who you are. Who you really are. It won't be so hard."

"I killed Nanny with just a book," I said. "I killed her guard with just a pencil. And now I have people willing to spill their guts about you," I took a deep breath. "I offer you a truce. We'll stay quiet. I expect Kent Severin to leave and to never contact the Varelas again. I expect Sergei to leave the company alone."

She made me wait ten seconds. Then she said, "It'll be done." And then she hung up. Good. I wanted Kent running. Because I thought I knew where he would run. And there I could trap him.

I took the guy's phone and left him sitting, still dazed. I went back outside and the Varelas were still standing together, blind to the world. Except for Galo, who broke away from his sister and his brother and hurried toward me. He stopped short of me. I'd killed his best friend. But I'd also brought his brother back to him.

I waited to see what his reaction would be.

"You brought us Eddie. You found him."

"Yes." I kept my voice cool.

"Thank you, thank you." Tears welled in his eyes. "Sam, I tried to stop Kent, I swear I did..."

"I don't believe you, Galo." But I remembered him pleading for Kent to not hurt me on the boat. A final memory from that day.

"He said...what they were doing, it was for the government. A secret contract that broke international law but we had to do it. Because of Papa's past." His voice broke. "You were my friend. He said you were a hostile agent, sent to infiltrate us." He laughed, a shattered sound. "He said they were sending you to be questioned...Kent and Ricky aren't who I thought they were. And Zhanna..." He glanced back at his brother. "Where...where was he?"

"I think you know."

He shook his head. "I don't, I don't know. I didn't know!"

And what had Zhanna and Rey kept saying in Puerto Rico? Galo had to be the face of the company. He had to be kept clean. Maybe he truly didn't know.

"Your company has been shipping people from all over the world to a secret prison deep in the Brazilian jungles. Your brother was shipped there, by Kent, four years ago, because he found out the truth."

It was like a physical blow. "Oh my God."

"I think Ricky's family had long, deep ties to the CIA. So does Kent, but to something off the books, not legitimate. It may not be what you think of as a government agency. It's a dark corner, somewhere, maybe a cancer inside, obviously unencumbered by the rule of law. I'm taking care of Kent. Just stay out of my way."

"I have to make this right. Papa, the company, my brother...Kent must have been the one to kill Zhanna..."

"Stay out of it."

His face crumpled. "I want to kill him. I want to make him pay."

"You have Edwin back," I said gently.

"Because of you. Kent took him from us."

"I will deal with Kent. But if you kill him, you could lose everything, Galo. Your company. Your family. Just let it go."

"What do we tell people? We can't tell them the truth...Eddie can't tell them the truth. The company..." His voice trailed off.

"Was built on a lot of lies, and now it's done," I said. "You're not the guilty party. Your father and Kent and Zhanna are. You and the twins are going to have to decide how to move forward. Go to the FBI. Tell all and make a deal."

"But I'm the face of the company now," Galo said. "It's mine. I can't..."

I can't lose it, he was going to say. He couldn't lose the comfortable, enviable life he had. I glanced over at Cori and Edwin. They were survivors. They could restart. Galo had been shaped too much by his father, his family, to be anything except what he'd been told to be.

"Kent's at home." He glanced toward Edwin. "I'm going to call Papa and I'm going to get him here to see Eddie."

"He may have known Edwin was in the prison."

"No way. No way."

"And what will you do if he knew?"

I went to the twins and for the first time Cori let her brother go and put her head against my shoulder and said, "Thank you, thank you."

Life is weird. I'd been determined to bring down the Varelas and instead I'd saved them.

So I thought.

64

MILA AND THE second guard had concluded their "chat"—and he'd surrendered both his weapon and his car keys to her. I don't ask. He'd gone to retrieve his semiconscious partner in the bathroom. We left, quickly. Mila threw the car keys over a stone wall into heavy greenery.

"To the apartment?" Mila asked.

"No," I said. "The bar. It's closer. Let's end this."

The bar was locked, the Closed sign hung on it. I opened it and hurried them all inside. The siblings kept looking at each other, stunned, like the truth was too bright a light to bear. Cori kept holding on to Edwin's arm like he might vanish in a wisp of smoke.

"I'm going to deal with Kent," I said. "But the three of you have to decide what the future is going to be. These people who run the prison are either going to go underground and not try to restart it, or they will. The escapees will be talking. My hope is they'll want nothing to do with you now."

"I'm telling the police everything I know," Edwin said.

"You can't. It'll destroy us," Galo said. "FastFlex will be ruined."

"I don't care," Edwin said.

"We'll lose everything," Galo said.

"I don't care," Edwin repeated.

"Your brother has been through hell," I said to Galo. "Perhaps you should listen to him."

"I'm grateful to you for your help," Galo said, "but this is a family matter."

Edwin showed him his mutilated hand. His ear.

"Oh God," Galo said.

"I'll give you three days to get your affairs cleaned up," Edwin said. "Then I'm talking to the police. I'm telling them everything."

"We can think of a different way...a way that doesn't ruin the company," Galo said.

"Eddie," Cori said. "That could be very dangerous. These are dangerous people." She looked at me. "My charity...it was a setup, Sam. I think it was a way to cycle money out and money back into this organization, cleaning it. I checked every financial trail I could. I think my dad set it up to help clean money for these people."

"You see? We're from a criminal family, Galo, we can't pretend we're not," Edwin said.

"Wait," Galo pleaded. "Papa is so sick, he can't go on trial. He can't bear the shame of all this. We can clean up FastFlex. Give me a chance to do it right. We can close down Cori's charity, let her start a new one, a real one."

"Make it all go away?" Cori said, her voice jagged.

Galo tried to nod.

"Stop worrying about Papa and worry about me," Edwin said. "I can't forgive him, or you. I can't, Galo, I can't." And for the first time I saw Edwin cry. He hadn't wept in the jungle, when we were rescued, when we got decent food and new clothes and a warm bed to sleep in, when we came home to Miami, when he saw Galo and Cori. Not a tear. He cried now because his brother stood before him, unwilling to accept the family's responsibility.

"I'm trying to do what's right for you, Eddie..." Galo stumbled toward his brother and Edwin let Galo embrace him, but he didn't hug him back, not at first.

"Then prove it. Bring me Kent," Edwin said. "Kent is the author of all this, I want him."

"I will handle Kent," I said.

"And do what with him?" Edwin asked.

"Make him talk. Force him to expose every player in this," I said.

"Offer him a deal?" Edwin asked, his voice dripping with anger.

"If that's what it takes," Mila said coolly.

"No. He goes down," Edwin said. "I want him dead for what he's done."

"Edwin," Galo said. "I'll fix this for you."

"You can't fix it, big brother," Cori said. She turned to me. "Sam. It's not like you're safe either. Do you know who we're up against? People that could do these things—they would think nothing of killing us all. Or your family in Canada. We have to know exactly, and the only person who will tell us is Kent."

"He's still here?" Mila said.

"Maybe Kent didn't run yet because he didn't want to look guilty with Zhanna's death. Maybe he had to find help first, someone he could trust to help him run. Maybe he doesn't know that the prison fell—maybe they didn't warn him. He could be their fall guy. Maybe they've left him out to dry," I said. "Call your father, Galo."

He did. He spoke quietly to someone, then hung up. "That was one of the guards. He said a few hours ago Kent left with Papa. He drove them to the office."

"Call the office."

He did. He asked for them, listened, hung up. "They've not been there," he said.

"The office is at the airport," I said. "He's taken your father."

"Why?" Cori said.

"Bargaining chip," I said. "I know where he's gone. Call your office. Get me on a plane, right now, to San Juan."

"I'm coming with you," Edwin, Cori, and Galo said at once.

"No," I said. "Cori, keep Edwin hidden, keep him out of sight. The two of you can stay here."

"I'm going with you," Galo said.

"You're not. Too dangerous." *And I'm not sure you're thinking straight about all of this*, I thought, but didn't say.

"You don't get on a plane without me, Sam," Galo said. "I'm going."

I nodded.

Galo's phone beeped. He looked at the screen then wordlessly handed it to me.

G: Your father's with me. Don't worry about him. I'll let you know where he's at soon enough. He'll be fine.

"Insurance," I said. "Rey's his insurance."

65

GALO CHECKED AS we drove to the airport; Kent had flown out, with Rey, on a FastFlex jet three hours ago. Even before the family reunion. He must have known Edwin was back. Did he have someone watching the airport? Was the dark corner he worked for monitoring us? It was done. Mila used Round Table connections to make a more subtle check: Kent hadn't looted any Varela or FastFlex bank accounts before he took off. He had touched nothing.

He would need money.

And I already knew how he was moving money. The casino chips. He'd paid Ricky that way. He'd paid the unidentified man Cori's friend Magali said looked a bit like me that way. And he'd tried to bribe Steve Robles that way, sending him a casino chip to stop his digging into the company on Cori's behalf.

So for money, he might need to go redeem a casino chip. He didn't know we knew about his system. I'd assumed Ricky had gone to Steve's at Galo's command. I'd been wrong. He'd gone looking for the chip, but at Kent's command.

So the chip money would pass to Kent, either in cash or in a form he could divert to a new account or name. I was thinking the Varelas' ownership of the casino was simply a way to pass them funds for services rendered for shipping drugged, unconscious prisoners to Nanny's warm embrace. Someone with their cash could come into the casino and promptly lose a bundle, and the money was instantly clean. But it was also used to pay whoever Kent needed to pay.

We had to wait an hour for Galo to explain he absolutely had to have a plane, for it to be partially unloaded from its cargo, readied, and flight plan filed, and then two hours later we landed in San Juan and hurried to the Gran Fortuna. Galo was a wreck, antsy, sweating, his mouth set.

"Why the casino?" he asked.

I told him about the chip payment system.

"You didn't send Ricky to Steve Robles's house," I said, just to confirm what I already knew.

"No. I didn't know who Steve was until Cori told me everything, after you were taken."

I'd made a bad assumption. Ricky had gone to Steve's, then to his uncle's restaurant on Calle Ocho. And only then to the Or nightclub. "He was looking for that chip for Kent. Why did you meet with him and Zhanna at the nightclub?"

"Just hanging out; Kent was working late, she was bored."

"It looked like you and Zhanna were fighting."

"She said Kent told her Cori hired someone to dig into our business. I didn't believe her. She wanted to come down hard on Cori and I said no. I told her I was done with her and she slapped me. That happened a lot." He paused. "You were spying on us?"

"Yes."

"Be honest with me," he said. "Are you who you said you are? A guy from Canada who used to be a smuggler?"

"No."

"I didn't think you were. Is your name really Sam?"

"Yes."

"Did you come to tear us down?"

"I came to make my friend Steve's killer pay."

"That wasn't me. That was Kent."

"So you think Kent killed Zhanna, pregnant with his own child, because the clients wanted her dead."

"Yes."

I glanced at him. "I think you want to save this family, and I think you knew exactly what she was. She poisoned her own mother. And you knew about it."

He said nothing, staring out the window.

"I mean, you couldn't prove it. How could you? You were both teenagers when it happened. And then the clients didn't want her to be the person they had to rely on for the smuggling. She'd killed her own mother—who wants to work with someone like that, not to mention her mom worked for the clients."

"She told me once that if I ever married, she'd poison my wife. She...I tried to tell Papa. I think he knew. But he thought she'd freed him from a wife who would spy on him." He lowered the window and let the cool breeze wash over his face.

"She was pregnant, Galo..."

"I didn't know that, Sam." He sounded miserable. "I didn't know." Then he cleared his throat. "What are you saying I did, Sam? Say it. Say it out loud."

"Nothing," I said after a moment. It's somehow worse when you realize a person who is decent at heart has done a terrible thing. "I'm not accusing you of anything."

"I killed a man to save you and my dad. I killed..." His voice faded. "People said Ricky had done away with people. I never believed them. You don't want to believe it." He looked at me. "But I'll kill Kent if I have to."

"You let me handle Kent and any of his buddies," I said.

"I've given everything to this family and I didn't have anything else left to give..." He put his head against the window. "I just wanted her...gone. I wanted all the trouble gone. She's as bad as Kent. Worse, because we tried to love her, we tried..."

I needed him focused, so I told him to be quiet as we pulled into the Gran Fortuna.

The casino was busy.

"He might have already come here," Galo said. "Or had someone else cash in a chip. He must have a contact here who would help him. So, we wait for the blind man to come to the casino?"

"He won't be alone. He's had Ricky to protect him and be his eyes when he needed him and now Ricky's gone. So either he'll have hired help or the dark corners will protect him until he's paid off." I turned to face him. "Galo, you got me here, thank you. But you're not trained for this."

"It's not your family he gutted, it's mine. I'm going, Sam. Sam Whatever-Your-Name-Is."

I spotted Magali at the casino cashiers' cage. I went to the desk, Galo following me. "Magali. Hi. Sam. Remember me?"

She didn't look too pleased to see me. "A blind man with one of those special casino chips? You see him today?" I asked.

She glanced at Galo. "I don't know..."

"Magali, please," Galo said. "It's important. He's a bad man. He hurt my brother Edwin, he's hurt our whole family." He took her hand. "Please."

"He was here maybe an hour ago." She checked the computer. "He checked into the hotel."

"Did he redeem one of those chips we showed you?"

She lowered her voice. "There's a note here for the supervisors...He tried to, but there wasn't an amount attached yet to the number. I'm supposed to call him when the account is...filled."

"And who can fill that? Omega Investments?" It was a payoff from his bosses, I thought. Money to go vanish.

She nodded.

"Can you see if the account tied to his chip has been funded yet?"

She did. "It has. Five minutes ago. I can lose my job for this, Galo..."

"You don't want to keep working here. My family's going to sell our shares, very soon. We'll get you another job, Magali, a better one."

She didn't look convinced.

"Call him and tell him the number's funded. How much is it?"

"Ten million," she said, tense. I suspected if it was the same ten million ransomed for Eddie, put into trust for such a rainy day as this one.

"Call him."

Kent didn't come to the casino cage and flash the chip. Five minutes later another man did. We stood behind a column on the other side of the casino, where we could see the cage. Magali glanced our way, stifled a cough. The man was thin and lanky and I thought of the tall man in big sunglasses at Ricky's grandfather's restaurant who had questioned me in his mediocre Russian.

I ran to the valet stand and waited.

The tall man left the casino cage and walked out into the lobby, heading for the valet's. My car arrived and I got in, hat and sunglasses on. I drove out onto the street and told Galo on my cell phone to come out the back and get in the car.

He did, and two minutes later the tall man, driving a convertible, left the hotel. I followed.

"Where's he going?" Galo said.

"Hopefully to Kent," I said. "So we follow."

66

THE TALL MAN drove into the countryside, along Highway 22, and at first I thought he was headed toward the Varela house. But he stayed farther south, down Highway 2, heading past the surf mecca of Rincón and into the city of Mayagüez.

I remembered I'd seen an address on Lavrenti Nesterov's GPS in the rented Yukon he was going to use to move Rey. An address on the southwest side of the island. Maybe this was where the man was headed.

He stopped at a restaurant. It was a pretty day and he left the convertible's top down.

"Give me your smartphone," I told Galo as we parked the car. I downloaded an app onto it, a tracker, then muted the phone. Then I put Galo's number on the same app on my phone. Then I got out of the car and strolled past the convertible, where I tucked the phone underneath its front seat and ambled back to our car.

"Now we don't have to follow so close," I told Galo.

The man returned to his car with a bag of to-go food for himself, munching on fries. He carried a bigger bag, which he put in the backseat. We followed, Galo driving, heading south along the coast, me watching the phone's screen. Finally he stopped, a few miles ahead of us.

We drove along a private road toward what looked like a ruined lighthouse. A steel fence had been chained shut, but we parked the rental car and climbed over the fence.

"I'm leaving the keys under the mat," I said. "In case we have to run back and leave fast."

"This is a dangerous stretch of coast here, lots of old lighthouses," Galo said. "Abandoned property. Kent could hide here for a while, not be noticed. Especially with this guy helping him."

Mila had given me two guns to bring. I handed one to Galo. He nodded solemnly.

"Do not just start shooting," I said. "You follow my lead. I will shoot anyone that needs shooting. And the idea is to not shoot anyone at all. You have that for defense, do you understand me?"

He nodded. I also had a pair of handcuffs, courtesy of Mila. I held them up before I put them in my pocket. "This is really what we need Kent in, not a body bag. All right?"

"Yes, Sam, I understand."

We walked up an unpaved road to a small lighthouse. The convertible was parked next to another car, presumably the one that had brought Rey and Kent here. They hadn't driven themselves. Which would mean at least one more person to confront.

Other than the cars out front, the lighthouse looked abandoned. It sat close to tall limestone cliffs and below us—far below us—I could hear the pounding of waves against the cliff.

I gestured Galo back from the door.

I kicked it in. The tall man and Kent Severin were in the room, at a long old wooden table, bent over a laptop. Kent's laptop was speaking, announcing that the transfer of files was forty percent complete. Rey Varela sat, head bent, staring down at the table. He looked terrible. Another man stood on the opposite side of the room, short and stocky, and he went for his gun.

I shot him in the hand, and he fell, screaming, bloodied.

"Hands up," I said. "Slowly, gently."

"Sam," Kent said. "You never disappoint." He wore an immaculate suit and he had his hand across the lapel, as if posing for an old picture.

"Don't make me repeat myself," I said.

They raised their hands, except for Rey, who didn't look at us.

"I'm not armed," Kent said calmly. "Neither is my colleague."

I wanted to confirm that, but I wanted Rey and Galo out of there. "Get your dad," I told Galo.

"Papa, come here," Galo said quietly. Rey ignored him, lost in his own world, humming.

"Move away from him," I told the wounded man, who kicked himself along the floor back into a corner.

"You've won, Sam," Kent said.

I'd promised myself in the shipment crate that I'd make him pay, that the last sound on earth he'd hear was my voice. But I needed him alive. I needed him talking. "Galo. Get your dad."

"Kent," Galo said, "I have something to tell you."

Kent said, "I hope it's a confession."

"We have Edwin back, you piece of—"

"Galo," I said. "Remember why we're here. Get your dad."

Galo shut his mouth. He stepped forward and he took his father's arm. Rey lifted his head but stayed seated.

"Eddie's alive, Papa," Galo said. "I'm going to take you to see him."

"They're lying, Rey. Galo and Sam killed Eddie. Just like they killed Zhanna," Kent said, his voice sounding like a snake slithering through grass. Rey stood, pulled away from Galo, stumbling backward, and Rey was between us and Kent and his man.

"You don't touch me," Rey said.

"Here's the deal," Kent said "Leave. I'll let Rey go in a while. And I don't tell the world that Galo killed Zhanna."

He knew it. Galo's face crimsoned.

"Here's the deal. Tell me who you work for and I don't shoot you right this second," I said.

Kent smiled. "For so long I worked for my dear old dad here. And then I worked for the people who owned dear old dad. And currently, I'm self-employed. Do you want a résumé?"

Dear old dad. A little shockwave moved through the room.

"That's a lie!" Galo screamed.

"Don't you think all the times he spent flying in distant ports of call he might have gotten bored?" Kent said, his voice like a knife. "Maybe Lord Caliber left more behind than weapons and contraband."

"He would have told us…it's a lie," Galo said.

"How do you know he knew?" Kent said.

"He's playing you," I said to Galo. "Ignore him."

Galo's hand, holding the gun, trembled.

"Who do you work for?" I repeated. I looked at the tall man and the wounded man. "CIA? Black ops? Private firm? What?"

Neither man answered; both glanced at Kent.

"Professional discipline," I said.

"Obviously, Sam, we're not going to answer your questions," Kent said. "You're going to leave, and we'll let you know soon enough where Rey can be found." And then he grabbed Rey as a shield and pulled a gun from his back and put the gun to the old man's head.

Foolish me. I didn't have a straight shot; I didn't dare fire.

But Galo lost it. He shrieked and fired the gun I'd given him. The tall man toppled back, writhing, and Galo fired a second time and the writhing stopped. Then he shot dead the wounded man who was cowering in the corner.

We all stared at Galo, Kent's gun still on Rey's head. Kent could have shot Rey, and he hadn't.

"Galo…" I said, seconds too late. "I need Kent, don't shoot him." I needed him to give to August and to Jimmy. He was the intelligence I had promised; he had the answers.

"Well, I need a private conversation with Kent here," Galo said. His voice was ragged, torn. "Let Papa go, now." Rey seemed half the man I'd seen before. His eyes blinked, unsure, possibly drugged.

"I could protect you, Kent," I said. "Hide you, give you safety in exchange for information." I was trying to be the adult in the room.

"I'm not interested in being hidden by a bureaucracy," Kent said.

I glanced at Galo. "I'm not talking CIA. I'm not with them."

"Well, clearly not, since you have a murderer as your sidekick. Not that they're always so picky."

"I can hide you, Kent. I can take care of you."

"No, Sam, none of that. He doesn't walk away into a happy life. Not after what he did to us," Galo said.

"What exactly did I do to you, Galo?" Kent said. "I mean, to you specifically? You were always afraid Edwin would be the better businessman. Replace you in your father's eyes." The words were like a hot brand against skin. "Hey, Sam, here's a good one: you know who told me Edwin was suspicious of our operations?"

This is the death of a family, I thought. I could feel the hate and the confusion and resentment storming, like it was a force in the air.

"Shut up!" Galo yelled. "That's a lie, you're a liar!"

"Him. Mr. Perfect Son over there. He's sold his brother out, he's killed his own stepsister." Kent's voice grew cold. "And yet—I'm the family bad guy? I did everything for this family. I was just recruited to do a job, including one that made your family much wealthier, Galo. I didn't even ask to be a son."

"Shut up." Galo's voice went lower.

I decided to state the obvious. "You can't do this alone, Kent, you can't drive away."

He knew it, and I could see how anger at his need for help made him grit his teeth. But he spoke, trying to ensure I knew he was valuable for his information. "I'll talk to you, Sam. Tell Galo to put the gun down. I feel certain he's aiming it at me right now."

"No," Galo said.

Kent ignored him. "I was recruited to be a spy inside the family. To bring the proposal to Rey about the smuggling of prisoners. Rey made sure that the shipments went smoothly; I made sure that his resolve never wavered. That Rey and Sergei, and the wives, and then Galo kept their mouths shut."

"But Zhanna's mom—"

"Was my backup informant," Kent said. "In case I was caught. In case Rey kept secrets from me." He cleared his throat. "I've given my life to this, because we will do what the law is afraid to do. We will protect the world, no matter what it takes."

"And payback against your father, that was just a bonus."

He shrugged. "I like him fine. My siblings? Screw them."

"And who protects us from the protectors?" I asked.

"You're so naïve," he said. Then he made his mistake. "Sam. I have a counterproposal. I have quite a bit of money here. Come work with me."

"He'll kill you, too," Galo said.

Heat was in Kent's voice now: "You're a murderer, Galo. Say what you will about Zhanna, you committed the same sins she had. I've never killed anyone. You get to live with this forever."

I watched the cruel smile on Kent's face.

Galo swung at me. The punch caught me by surprise. Hard, on my jaw. It lifted me up and I was knocked over onto the chair and he was on top of me, seizing my gun and trying to press it into my back.

"Don't," I said. "I'm not going to take his offer."

"Stop this, why did you hurt Eddie?" Rey said, moaning.

"I didn't hurt Eddie. He did, Kent did!" Galo screamed, and then Rey tried to lurch toward his son, and Kent fired in the direction of the sound of Galo's voice, still using the old man as cover. He missed. Galo fired back and the bullet caught Rey Varela in the forehead as he stumbled forward into its path. The old man fell.

Galo screamed and fired again and Kent went down, his sunglasses shattering. A bloody hole where his eye had been.

"Papa!" Galo screamed. He hurried to his father. I went to his side. I checked Rey's pulse. Gone. His expression was oddly peaceful.

"I'm sorry, Galo…"

"I killed him…" Galo said. "Oh God, I killed him…"

I put a hand on Galo's shoulder. "No. This isn't your fault. It's not."

"It is…my dad…Zhanna…even the men I shot…" His hands

shook. "What... what am I? How do I tell this to Cori and Eddie?" His fingertips touched the blood on his father's face.

I tried to soothe him. "Galo. Listen to me. We'll get rid of Kent and these other guys, and then we'll figure out—"

"Figure out what? How? How do we figure out this, Sam?" His gaze locked on me. "You were going to give Kent a way out of this."

"Only to get your dad back."

"That's a lie."

"No, it's not." I moved away from him to check Kent's pulse. Gone as well. I needed him alive. Maybe his laptop had valuable information.

And then the world hammered in on me, hard. Stunned. Blood running into my eyes. I felt the handcuffs I'd brought snap on my wrist, felt Galo drag me to the room's center. The other cuff clicked, attached to a crossbeam of the heavy table.

"Galo..."

"Shut up, I'm thinking. I have to fix this."

Through the blood—he'd struck me with his gun—I saw him pull the bodies of Kent and his associates out of the lighthouse. He grabbed their laptops and fired a bullet through each hard drive. Then he took them outside.

He knelt by Rey, folding his arms peacefully, stroking his father's hair, crying and then wiping away tears. Then he carried his father's frail body outside as well.

"Galo, what are you doing?" I called.

"We have to fix this," he said. "The family. The company. The company doesn't have to be destroyed." He gave me a weak little smile. "I was supposed to have everything, Sam, and now I've got nothing."

He shot off my handcuffs, not bothering with the key. Then he put the warm gun back against my head. "You are going to do as I tell you."

"All right."

"Get up," he said. He kept the gun on my skull like it was screwed on.

I slowly got up. I could barely see. I could feel what felt like a loose flap of skin against my temple; dark circles danced before my eyes.

"I don't want to hurt you, Galo," I said thickly. "You know I can."

He slammed the gun hard into the back of my head, and I collapsed. I was still stunned and he pulled me to my feet, put the gun on the back of my head again.

"Outside."

I obeyed him. The trunk of the convertible sedan was open, two bodies of Kent's men jammed inside. The destroyed laptops and the bodies of Kent and Rey lay in the back seat.

"What are we doing?" I asked, my voice still thick with pain.

"We have to fix it." His voice steadied. "We'll drop them in the ocean."

"Okay. You can take the gun off me now."

"Not yet," he said. "Not yet, Sam."

"What are you doing?"

"Eddie was in a prison. Papa was in a prison, of sorts. I'm in a prison now of my own making. There's only one key to get out."

"Galo...this isn't your fault."

"I killed my father," he said, and his voice didn't sound human. It sounded like every bit of grief and pain in his life dwelled in his throat. "I didn't know Z was going to have a baby, and I killed it. I watched my mama walk into the ocean and I didn't call out to anyone. If I had, and she lived...no Zhanna in our lives. No Kent, maybe. I could have made it all different."

"You didn't understand."

"Maybe I did," he said. "I've always wondered. Get in the car, Sam." His voice was cold. He led me to the convertible and he kept the gun firmly on me. "Drive. Toward the cliffs. We'll dump the bodies in the ocean. Even Papa." His voice trembled, for just a moment. "And then we'll talk, okay?"

The oceanside cliffs. Okay. My every muscle was singing. I drove toward them.

He will jump and I won't be able to stop him, I thought.

"Galo. You just got your brother back. Your sister is safe now. You're free of Zhanna and Kent. Don't do this."

The cliffs lay ahead. Two hundred feet away. Beyond them, a long horizon of blue water. "Please don't hurt yourself."

The blows to my head had me not thinking clearly. He could have just left me handcuffed. He hadn't.

"I'll fix it," he said. He jammed his foot atop of mine, on the accelerator. The convertible exploded forward.

I couldn't talk about what I knew. No one could ever know he'd killed his father.

The perfect solution.

I am strong. I tried to tear my foot out from under his, trapped on the accelerator. I couldn't.

A hundred feet. The speedometer climbing, the sea wind a strong, awakening gust in my face. I tried to rip the key out of the ignition.

He jammed the gun against my head. "I'll shoot!" he screamed.

67

Put the gun down!" I screamed. "Down. Now. You don't want this."

I slammed a fist into Galo's face. He fired the gun, past my shoulder, deafening me.

So it was all silent as the car roared off the cliff, hurtling toward the distant blue shimmer of the water.

The first, instinctive reaction is to brace yourself, to try to cope with the impact. Cope with, never mind *survive*, the impact.

He let up off my foot, the job done, instinctively drawing his leg and arms back to brace himself for the crash.

Next reaction was mine, the peculiar itch in my daredevil's rattled brain, figuring gravity's pull at 9.8 meters per second squared, thinking, We have five seconds before we hit.

In the second of those seconds I felt the gun's cool barrel go back against my temple and realized Galo was aiming right at my head in case the crash or the water didn't end me.

That is attention to detail. That is commitment. He sure loves his family.

Three: The water rushed toward us. I moved forward, reaching, the cool steel barrel staying on me, my fingers along the floorboard groping for my one chance.

I pulled the hood release.

The sky, the water, my last breath, everything blue.

The car's hood popped back, slamming toward us, shattering the windshield as the car cartwheeled, and he gasped, his arms going up to protect himself.

I pushed myself out.

Four: The gun fired.

68

———※《◎》※———

THE BULLET MISSED me, tearing through my wind-billowing shirt, but the water did not. I slammed into it, thrown free of the car, and for one awful moment I thought, It'll be too shallow, it'll break my back. But it was deep—the blue was a sign—and the car bobbed once, upside down, and then sank.

I surfaced, grabbed a lungful of air, then dove downward, trying to reach Galo. I saw the car, drifting off the shallow cut, dropping into deeper water. I saw him, caught in the car, arms and hands spread in a final surrender, his head lolling at a wrong angle, and then the car tumbled again, off the shelf, into the deeper blue. The same blue that had once claimed his mother.

I shot back to the surface.

The tide yanked at me, like an insistent child, me spinning in its grasp. I saw a wave break on a rock very close to shore and aimed myself at it, letting the water carry me closer. I hit the rock, it hurt, the water receded, and I grabbed at wet stone. Water washed over me again. My head pounded in agony.

I studied the incoming tide. The rocks at the base of the cliff were large, flat, glistening. But where the old lighthouse stood like a neglectful soldier, steps had been cut out of the stone, going down to a platform of rock halfway down, with an old weathered, rusted railing. I was a good climber; if I could survive the swim I could scale the rocks up to the platform. I watched the tide to avoid being dashed against the rocks.

I swam. I climbed. And then I walked up the stairs.

At the lighthouse I lay there for a moment, spent, shocked to be alive. I got up and walked back to the gate. I climbed over the fence and went back to the rental car and found the keys under the mat and drove to the closest town, imagining a story for how I could explain my head injury to an ER doctor—I fell by the cliffs, easy enough, shivering, shaking, but the wind and the sun dried my clothes, a heartbreakingly beautiful day, and I wondered how I would tell Cori.

69

I KNOW YOU could have saved him," Cori said. Stormy's wasn't open, but we sat in the cool at the bar, the checkers game between us. Maybe the same one from the night of Steve's murder; maybe no one had ever bothered to finish it. *A game should be played until there's a winner,* I'd told Cori.

But no winners here.

"I could save him only if he let me," I said. "He wouldn't listen. He thought he was doing the right thing."

She didn't touch her wine. It had been five days since I returned from San Juan. I had gone first to give Cori the awful news, then to New Orleans to see my son for a blissful two days and then returned to Miami. I'd decided Stormy's would be sold. I didn't want anyone looking for Sam Chevalier to find me through it. In a few months I'd buy another Miami bar, elsewhere in the city, under another front company, and Paige had agreed to come to work for me as the new bar's manager. I figured she already knew enough of my dirty secrets. She had the Mila stamp of approval.

"I'm sorry," I said.

"This is all my fault. If I'd left well enough alone…"

"Then Edwin would still be in a prison."

She rubbed at her temples. "I know. But Papa…and Galo…"

"They knew what they were getting into, and it was never going to end well." I had not told her about Kent's vicious hints about being Rey's son. There was no proof; there was no point.

"Sam, please don't judge them."

Sometimes when we lose our loved ones they take on a gloss they didn't always have in life. She was trapped in a Shakespearean tragedy and it was over and she was one of the blinking, stunned survivors.

And I was nothing but a reminder of her family's losses and mistakes. I'd been cautious of an entanglement with Cordelia, but now...her turning away from me, I did that typical male thing where all her virtues were magnified. I wanted to see her. I liked her. But I was the guy from the worst time in her life. No one wants to be that guy.

She saw it in my face, the touch of my fingers against hers. "If things were different..." she said. "I brought this on us. I kissed you and said I was saving your life...and I was setting my family's ruin in motion."

"No. This isn't your fault."

The good deed of saving Edwin didn't seem to count for much. It would, I thought, in time, as Edwin came back to being himself. Mila had helped him, in return for telling her everything about his time at the prison, crafting a believable story that he'd been held, moved from remote location to location, by drug dealers who used him to ensure FastFlex helped them with their smuggling. Rey, Galo, and Kent were missing, presumed victims of the same drug dealers, silenced after Edwin escaped his captors. In light of Zhanna's recent death and Ricky's disappearance, the press was having a field day about the once-lauded and respected Varelas. FastFlex would probably have to shut down, sell off its assets. That would have been a horror for Galo, but Edwin and Cori just seemed relieved.

"You made your choices," I said. "But so did they. Every one of them." It wasn't a comfort she was ready to hear.

She drank her wine and I drank mine and then she kissed me good-bye, on the cheek, and went to mend her brother and her world.

I had to go write a report for August. I was standing firm in my commitment to share information with him, although Jimmy didn't like it. But all I had, really, were some names and bank accounts and locations, and it would be up to August to figure out if he wanted to chase a dark corner. It might be beyond his job description, or his bosses might not want him to shine a light there. But I'd passed along one bit of information no one else could share: the bank account numbers that I'd gotten from Magali. If there were still funds in them, and August went after them, I'd ask him to give some of the money to the burnt man, if he was still alive. His advice had saved me.

Mila came downstairs, her eyes measuring me, not wanting to ask if I was okay.

"You care about her."

"I do. But that's that. Let's shut this place up and go see my boy," I said. "I'm ready for New Orleans again."

"No, Sam," she said. "Something Edwin told me. We have someplace to go first."

70

I REALLY DID not want to be here.

The prison's interior had burned and the walls tumbled into rubble, far more than the riot could have done, and I figured its owners had come out of their dark corners and razed it to the ground. Mila and I walked through the wreckage. A pile of bodies lay in the exercise yard, burnt in a heap. It was hard to tell how many there were. Guards, prisoners, both. I felt sick.

All the computers were gone. Nanny's office looked like a flamethrower had doused it. The four skulls remained on the cafeteria wall and Mila saw them and she turned to me. She was not a person given to strong emotion, but I saw tears in her eyes and she took my hand and said, "Oh, Sam. I will not sleep tonight, thinking of you in this place."

"You will not sleep tonight because we're in the middle of the jungle and there's no hotel." We did have a helicopter, so I would have an easier departure than last time. "Okay, you've seen it." I loosened my hand from hers and walked away, running the flashlight toward the exit.

"Edwin said there was a room called 'Archives,'" she said.

"Yes. Near where we followed the water pipe out." I took her down the stairs. The flashlight showed me old bloodstains where I'd shot a guard. I tried not to think of those who'd died as I'd gotten Edwin and the others out to freedom. I still slept at night, but my recent dreams were tattered and bloody and I knew my brain was processing it, like a soldier home from battle. I wanted to turn off that part of me. But what would I be then, what kind of father would I be to Daniel? I had to be a man, not a monster.

The door to the archives had been blown off its hinges. "They threw in explosives," she said. "Small ones. A hurried job."

"I wonder why not the flamethrowers if they wanted to burn all the records," I said.

"Because they weren't allowed in here. Whoever was sent here didn't have the clearance for the information. They didn't want to risk it being seen. Or read. Or they took most of it before they left. We can't know." She sounded disappointed.

There were file cabinets, shattered from the blasts, the former files now cinders. Mila studied the room. Letters on the file cabinets, with an s–z closest to the door. And then she went to the file cabinet farthest from the door, farthest from the blast. The cabinet had toppled over, blackened, one drawer ajar and filled with ashes.

"We might be lucky," she said. She took a crowbar and opened the top drawer, and inside were partially burned papers.

"What are you hoping to find? You said you'd explain once we got here, Mila." Only the fact that I trusted her more than anyone else in the world had persuaded me to come back to this hellhole.

"You said the Italian guard here claimed you reminded him of someone, joked that you were a repeat offender. You said Cori's friend at the casino, Magali, said a man who redeemed a casino chip looked like you. I am wondering." From the cabinet she pulled out a sheaf of crisped papers. Most were burned, but the edges of an inch-thick wad were yellowed but intact. She paged through them, gently.

I looked at the label on the cabinet: A–D. "Are you looking for someone?"

She answered me by holding up a page and I saw the name at the top left, sliced and burned, the letters read CAPR. Below was a thumbnail-sized photo of my brother, looking scared and gaunt.

A side-profile photo of him, Doc's bandage visible on the back of his neck, the rest of the photo burned away.

Below the photo was a date stamp.

Three weeks after he'd been killed in Afghanistan, his throat cut on a grainy video by jihadists.

"I...that can't be." I felt the world around me begin to swim, to shake.

He was here. Danny was *here*, at some point. Danny was...alive. But he hadn't been here when I was.

There was one prisoner they let go...I remembered the Hungarian's words.

So where was he?

"Sam?" Mila asked. "Sam? Are you okay?"

"Yes," I said. "I want to tear this place apart. I want to find my brother."

ACKNOWLEDGMENTS

Special thanks to Mitch Hoffman, Lindsey Rose, Jade Chandler, Jamie Raab, David Shelley, Ursula Mackenzie, Sonya Cheuse, Andrew Duncan, Deb Futter, Emi Battaglia, Beth deGuzman, Anthony Goff, Thalia Proctor, David Palmer, Marissa Sangiacomo, Jane Lee, and all the amazing teams at Grand Central Publishing and Little, Brown UK.

As always, thanks to Peter Ginsberg, Shirley Stewart, Jonathan Lyons, Holly Frederick, Eliane Benisti, Kerry D'Agostino, and Sarah Perillo for their brilliance.

For special help and amazing generosity in Miami I am very grateful to Paige Pennekamp McClendon, Marianne Fernandez, Michael Pennekamp (who can talk his way past any guardpost), Mitchell Kaplan of the wonderful Books & Books bookstores in south Florida, James and Evelyn Hall, and the ever-patient Bella Pennekamp.

My wife, Leslie, is a huge help to me in researching the books (especially during travel to Miami and Puerto Rico) and in keeping me steady during the difficult parts of the process. She and my sons, Charles and William, are the best family a writer could ask for. Thank you.

Any bending of geography, governmental entities, or facts for the sake of the story, or errors, are my responsibility.

ABOUT THE AUTHOR

Jeff Abbott is the *New York Times* bestselling, award-winning author of fourteen novels. His books include the Sam Capra thrillers *Adrenaline*, *The Last Minute*, and *Downfall*, as well as the standalone novels *Panic*, *Fear*, and *Collision*. *The Last Minute* won an International Thriller Writers Award, and Jeff is also a three-time nominee for the Edgar Award. He lives in Austin with his family. You can visit his website at www.jeffabbott.com.